Prologue

Lenox, Massachusetts
July 1872

"Hold there!" Jonathan Smarte's deep voice boomed down the alley, drowning out the ruckus of Boston's streets at midnight. But the thief didn't pause. Perhaps he was the solitary person in the city who didn't know of Jonathan Smarte and his legendary accomplishments.

Smarte darted after the man. His French-made boot heels clicked on rain-slicked cobblestones. His English greatcoat flapped behind him. But the thief was young and quick. Perhaps too quick, thought Smarte as he passed beneath a hissing spray of gold light thrown from a gas lamp. And the slippery thief had a fortune in English crown jewels weighing his pockets. What would Scotland Yard say if he got away again? What would the queen say this time?

Smarte shot forward with a burst of speed when the thief rounded a building and disappeared from sight. Smarte followed, then skidded to a stop.

She was holding the thief by his coat front and looking up at Smarte from beneath the brim of a man's hat as if she'd been waiting on him for hours. Her tweeds were as English as his, her boots just as French, but her accent was

American and her sass palpable. In her palm she cradled the jewels. She'd beaten him again.

"My dear, Miss Maggie Swifte," Smarte said.

"You remember me."

"You're impossible to forget."

"It's been months, Smarte."

"Six to be exact—and three weeks and four days." Smarte took a step nearer.

"What should I do with him, Smarte?"

"Let him go."

Maggie's lips parted with surprise. "Like last time? The queen almost fired you, remember?"

"I don't care, Maggie. Let him go."

"But—" He moved and caught her in his strong arms. She barely heard the thief's escape up the alley. The jewels slipped from her hand and fell between the tips of their boots.

Smarte cupped her face in his hands. "There's no getting away from me this time. I love you, Maggie. My career as the world's greatest lawyer and detective means nothing to me if I don't have you by my side. Kiss me, Maggie."

"I—I don't know how to kiss. I'm only sixteen and you're twenty-four. I've never kissed a man."

"I know. I'll show you. You trust me."

"Yes, I trust you. I've loved you my whole life, Charles—oh, Charles—"

Charles?

Kate Remington stared at the word and cursed her traitorous quill. Much as she loved Jonathan Smarte she'd betrayed herself again. But then again, Jonathan Smarte was Charles's creation, born one summer ten years ago over stolen gooseberry tarts eaten on a branch high up in the biggest maple in the grove behind the Remington's house. Kate had been there at Jonathan's conception and as far as she knew she was the only other person who even knew of

"COULD WE, CHARLES, JUST FOR A NIGHT? COULD WE PRETEND THAT WE'RE SIMPLY A MAN AND A WOMAN?" KATE WHISPERED. "CAN WE PRETEND THERE'S NO TOMORROW?"

"That's never wise." His voice sounded hoarse and husky.

"I don't want to talk any more, Charles. Do you?"

His chest heaved, blood pounded in his veins, conscience screamed, and he deafened himself to it. "What do you want, Kate? You want to explore the world with me because I make you feel safe, is that it?"

"Yes."

"What—you think you want this—?" Charles pressed his mouth to the side of her neck, and tasted the sweetness of her skin.

"Yes—" Her hands were fumbling with the buttons of his shirt. Her lips were trembling. Her eyes were shining.

"Sweet Kate," he groaned and crushed his mouth over hers.

HIGH PRAISE FOR KIT GARLAND AND HER PREVIOUS NOVELS

The Perfect Scandal

"*The Perfect Scandal* is just that: perfectly irresistible and highly entertaining. Kit Garland wonderfully captures turn-of-the-century New York . . . while twisting readers around her finger with a titillating mystery and a delightfully sensual romance." —*Romantic Times*

"*The Perfect Scandal* brings some long awaited diversity to romance publishing: Miss Savannah Merriweather, the heroine, is . . . pleasingly independent, bright, and funny. There's a nice mystery here as well as a romance."
—*Detroit Free Press*

Capture the Wind

"FANTASTIC! You will not find a better book about daring adventures, excitement on the high seas."
—*Bell, Book and Candle*

"Kit Garland has created an old-fashioned, rip-roaring romance . . . reminiscent of the best of Rosemary Rogers." —*Affaire de Coeur*

Embrace the Night

"*EMBRACE THE NIGHT* HAS IT ALL—unforgettable characters and a heartstopping story . . . a must-have!" —*Romantic Times*

"EXCITING, FAST-PACED—a charming historical romance that showcases a talent that's growing by leaps and bounds." —*Affaire de Coeur*

Dell Books by Kit Garland

DANCE WITH A STRANGER
EMBRACE THE NIGHT
CAPTURE THE WIND
THE PERFECT SCANDAL
SWEETER THAN SIN

SWEETER THAN SIN

Kit Garland

A DELL BOOK

Published by
DELL PUBLISHING
a division of
Random House, Inc.
1540 Broadway
New York, New York 10036

ISBN: 0-440-22365-2

Printed in the United States of America

Published simultaneously in Canada

April 1999

2 4 6 8 10 9 7 5 3 1

OPM

This book is dedicated first to Meghan, Caitlyn, Sarah, Max, Ben, and Nicholas: for all the times you sat in the "pink" chair and watched me work, for the times you peeked over my shoulder and asked "Did you write *all* those words?" and no, you can't read any of it yet, but most of all for giving me every reason to get up and be a mom for another day. . . .

And to Danny: for proving to me that living romance could be even better than writing it.

Smarte's existence. She believed it within her rights to borrow him whenever the whim struck. Besides, Charles seemed to have little time for fictional characters while he sweated over law books at Harvard. School kept him so busy he rarely even wrote home. The letters that did come were cryptic, their tone severe and formal, not at all the type of letters Kate yearned to receive from him. Not at all the sort of letters that might be written by a deeply creative young man who loved to steal gooseberry tarts from the kitchen and hide out in the grove spinning tales of mystery and adventure.

Poor Charles. He'd no doubt long forgotten Jonathan Smarte and big maples and gooseberry tarts in favor of torts and motions and long-winded briefs.

But Kate hadn't. Jonathan Smarte deserved a story, a whole series of them, and Kate was determined to give them to him, if only to preserve that long ago lost feeling of lazy warm summer days and the taste of gooseberry juice dribbling down her chin. And she and Charles alone together in a world of their own making, far from the responsibilities that came with school and growing up.

If only she could keep Maggie Swifte from popping up at the most inconvenient times and wanting Smarte to kiss her. Maybe then her stories would not only sound suitably "male," they might stand a chance at getting published in a Boston newspaper. Or for that matter any newspaper, for those long afternoons spent spinning tales of Jonathan Smarte had instilled in Kate a love of writing and the inevitable determination that comes with it to get her work published. As a woman, she knew how difficult this would be.

There was, of course, the other, more immediate, and far more delicate problem. When she wrote her stories, Smarte inevitably became Charles, and she, just as inevitably, became Maggie Swifte.

A sound from outside the window brought her from her

desk. A carriage with the Remington crest on its door drew up on the drive below. The four horses were slick with sweat, and winded. The carriage door opened and a young man alighted, russet-haired and garbed in tailored burgundy broadcloth. He hefted his walking stick, doffed his top hat, and swept into a bow before a footman and a steward. As he straightened, he plucked the white flower from his own lapel and tucked it neatly into the footman's. Kate's lips twitched into a smile as she watched him turn and saunter into the house.

How odd that Jude should return from his new job in Boston so soon. He'd left Lenox just a month before, she'd thought for good. Somehow she knew, but wasn't quite sure why, that his appearance tonight would make things tense in the household. And when things were tense Mother Remington always stitched furiously beside the fireplace and Grandmother said strange things at unexpected times.

Kate pressed closer to the window and had to rub the pane fogged by her breath. A dark silhouette stepped from the carriage. His manner and dress were as reserved as his brother, Jude's, were flamboyant. Kate swallowed. The pane fogged clear up to her eyes but she didn't bother to wipe at it.

Charles. Gone exactly six months, three weeks, four days . . .

The last time he'd visited from school she'd been a girl of fifteen, wearing flannel and pincurls, yet another face among family in a whirl of Christmas holiday festivities. To her memory, they'd barely spoken, barely exchanged a glance, which wasn't so odd given that Charles spent much of his time at home bent in grim conversation with his father. But she could still remember the smell of him when he'd bent and kissed her cheek before he'd disappeared into a night swirling with snow to return to Harvard.

In the months since, Father Remington had tragically

died and Kate had grown up. She's shed some baby fat, banished her flannels deep inside her wardrobe, and, with Mother Remington's help and Grandmother's insistence, had discovered ladies' gowns, silk corsets, her waist, and quite unexpectedly her bosom. Perhaps most significantly, she'd found one day a pile of romantic novels left on the bedside table in Grandmother Remington's bedroom. While poring over every tempestuous word, Kate had suddenly realized that she was quite probably in love with Charles Remington. She had been, she now suspected, for years. Perhaps ever since the day ten years ago when she'd first arrived and met him standing so severe and tall on the Remington porch beside his father. She remembered how cold and snowy the day had been, how thin and insufficient her coat felt against the chill, how huge the Remington house looked compared to the orphanage, and how Charles had looked down at his new "sister" with eyes brilliantly blue and unfathomable. He'd been a wondrous mystery to her then. In many ways, he still was now, so unlike his brother, Jude.

How bothersome that none of Grandmother Remington's books addressed the problem of a girl knowing exactly what true love was, or for that matter what to do if she found herself in love with her own foster brother, a man she'd lived with as a sister for more than half her lifetime. Of course, just because Grandmother Remington's books didn't address the situation didn't necessarily mean it couldn't happen.

Kate strongly suspected it had. What else could explain the butterflies dancing in her belly whenever she saw him or even thought of him, and she did a great deal of that when she wrote, which she did nearly all the time.

The first thing to do about it all, of course, was to find out if Charles felt the same about her. She had to know. If he did, Charles would certainly know what to do about it, how to tell the family, plan a wedding, and live happily ever after. Like Jonathan Smarte, Charles had always known how to handle situations. Yes, he would take care of it. Maybe then Mother Remington would stop the constant embarrassing talk about suitable gentlemen callers and potential husbands for Kate and getting her aligned with the sort of man who would take good and proper care of her for the rest of her life.

Kate dressed in her newest embroidered white silk gown, the "grown up" dress Mother Remington had bought for her just last week when she'd turned sixteen. It had crisp pleated neck frills, a tight bodice that required a corset, and a bustle. Her fingers shook as she worked the tiny white silk-covered buttons through their loops and smoothed the bodice down over the thrust of her breasts. She still wasn't quite used to dressing herself. One day, not long after Father Remington's death, the upstairs servants had all just disappeared. Of course, Mother Remington still had her lady servant, and the cook was still with them. But the others were gone now.

Kate sat on the edge of her bed, wondering if her corset stays were going to split when she breathed. Strange that her palms were sweating. She rubbed them on the coverlet. The family would begin to wonder where she was. When they looked at her would they be able to see into her heart? Would Charles know her thoughts simply by the way she looked at him?

The family had gathered as usual before dinner in the front parlor. When Kate entered she immediately saw Mother Remington, furiously working a needle through linen in her chair beside the fire. Mary Elizabeth sat beside her, her eyes vacant, her face abnormally pale and serenely set, like a child asleep, only she was awake but no more astute in her twenty-three years than a child of four could ever be. "Mentally impaired at birth" was the term most often used to describe Mary Elizabeth. She kept one hand on her mother's person at all times, even at home, a situation Mother Remington seemed to accept with little outward distress.

Charles sat at the corner secretary, bent over something. In one hand his quill scribbled madly. She felt herself grow an inch in her new heeled shoes. The world seemed to stop, as if waiting for him to notice her.

"Good God, it's Kate." Jude swept out of nowhere toward her, his eyes dancing like a young boy's over a new toy. His broad shoulders blocked Kate's view of Charles as he paused and waved a hand that held a crystal goblet. "Lordy, lordy, would you look at my little sister in her new dress? When is she going to stop growing up, will someone tell me?" Jude met her eyes, winked, and gulped from his glass.

"I've not much changed in the month you've been gone, Jude," Kate replied, playfully sidestepping him to move to the piano in the corner. She touched her fingertips to the keys and let her eyes stray to the opposite corner.

Charles was staring at his letter, consumed in concentration, as if he were composing something of the highest secrecy. For an instant Kate allowed herself to drink in the sight of him. Sitting there with the firelight dancing over him, he was a long, lean line of elegance, everything about him graceful yet compellingly strong. No one would have ever suspected he was in any way handicapped.

He was Jonathan Smarte, and so much more.

Her chest seemed to quiver with her breaths.

"William Frye called again for our Kate just yesterday," Mother Remington said from her chair without looking up.

"He's her first beau." Grandmother Remington smiled from her settee where she spent the better part of every afternoon before retiring to her bed. This she did with Kate's help, and often requested that Kate stay and read to her before she fell asleep. As usual, she cocked her head one way, her lips the other, and looked at Kate with a winsome affection that made Kate's heart twist around itself with gratitude. She'd been blessed to have found such a family to call her own, and doubly blessed to have found a man like Charles.

"Zounds, not William Frye!" Jude looked deeply put out. Chest puffing, he strode to the piano and thumped a white-gloved fist on the mahogany finish. "He's a rogue and a wastrel, Kate. He's made a career out of breaking hearts. And when he's not doing that he's drinking and gambling away his allowance."

"Odd that you would know about such things," Grandmother murmured.

Jude rolled his eyes and leaned nearer. "For some it's a pastime, for others, a vice. He will use you ill, Kate, mark my words. I don't care how damned shabby the curtains are becoming around here. It's just not enough that he comes from money."

"Shipping," Mother Remington put in without looking up from her needle. "Descends from a half dozen or so Revolutionary heroes. The family owns three homes. She could do far worse. And so could we. He looked so handsome, didn't he, Mother? He brought Kate flowers. Lilacs, and so fresh for this time of year. He's going abroad tomorrow for three months. We shall miss him, I think. Perhaps Kate most of all. Won't you, Kate?"

Jude drank and stared at Kate. His shoulders were again blocking her view of Charles. She shifted slightly right. Jude leaned toward her and again thwarted her. "Don't listen to her. Pining is for fools. You could do much better and you *will.* Lilacs, pah! You should have roses, heaps of them. Let me be the judge, sweet. I will take care of you."

Grandmother made a strange snorting sound into her handkerchief.

Kate gave Jude a teasing half-smile, lowered her eyes, and played a Bach prelude with her right hand. It was one of the pieces she knew Charles liked best.

"Why should I trust myself to you, Jude?" She quirked a playful eyebrow at him. "A new job of some sort is keeping you so far away from home. I daresay I've missed you terribly. But I thought you were off to Boston for good."

"Yes, he is off for good," Grandmother put in, in slightly elevated tones. "Aren't you, Jude? He should be there now, shouldn't he? If your father were alive you'd still be there, wouldn't you, Jude?" Grandmother twisted slightly and threw over her shoulder, "Wouldn't he, Charles?"

Kate took a full step right and lifted her eyes. Her fingers hit a discordant chord. The room seemed to quiet instantly as if to fully capture the sound and magnify it so that everyone would know she wasn't thinking one bit about Bach or William Frye or why naughty Jude had returned so quickly.

Charles lifted his head and looked straight at Kate. A thunderclap wouldn't have ricocheted through her with the same velocity.

"Jude will be returning to Boston with me tomorrow."

Tomorrow. So soon!

A moment passed, perhaps two. Their eyes connected. Her heart raced. A buzzing filled her ears.

"Hullo, Kate," he said. For one breathless moment he looked at her, then he turned his attention back to his letter.

"Cold bastard," Jude muttered into his glass. "Made of the stuff he's got in that lame thigh of his. All lifeless lead."

"Do play for us, Kate," Grandmother said. "Something lyrical. Doesn't she play lyrically, Charles?"

Kate stood as if poised on the edge of the earth.

Charles again lifted his head, reached for a glass beside

the pages, and brought it to his lips. The narrowing of his eyes on her above the glass made Kate feel suddenly very warm all over. "Yes, Kate," he said. "Chopin."

"I'll turn the pages for you," Jude murmured close to her ear as she turned to sit on the bench. His breath was hot and smelled like Father Remington's had in those months before he'd died.

She smiled and felt herself tremble. Charles was still watching her. "I don't need the music. I know it well enough."

"Then I'll stand here beside you. You smell of lilacs, little sister. Did you bathe in them?"

Kate glanced at him and made a face. Ridiculous, playful Jude. Always poking fun at her, pretending to be her knight even while he played the family court jester. Jude had always been a master at pranks, even from the very start, almost torturous in his teasing of his older, far more serious brother. It seemed only natural to indulge his antics, just as it seemed natural to rely on Charles to ignore pranks and take care of them all.

"Don't let Charles intimidate you," Jude said softly, as if for her ears alone. He squeezed her shoulder, comforting her. "He thinks he can be a tyrant with all of us, just like he was with his men in the army—before the leg accident, of course. Never decorated because of it, of course. Sent home to fester all grim-spirited with the family, and of course frustrated all of Father's big expectations of wartime greatness for him. Now he has to behave like a right proper grand patriarch, filling dear old Father's shoes, keeping up the family's good name like a good ol' boy. But it eats at him because we're all slowly starving to death and you want to know why? Because of him. You see, if he couldn't come home the decorated hero, then Father made damned sure Charles went to Harvard, even if it put us all into debt for the rest of our lives. We'll never dig ourselves out, he'll never make enough to earn us a way out, and he knows it.''

Above the edge of the music holder Kate watched Charles stand up and start to move toward them in his halting gait. The bullet was still embedded in his right thigh, deep in the bone, driven there by a Confederate soldier's gun nearly eight years before. Had he grown even taller and broader in six months? It was hard to tell from so low on the piano bench. Her fingers froze above the keys.

''See how he stalks us?'' Jude slipped behind her. His hands touched lightly on her shoulders, then moved to cup her upper arms. His voice purred low in her ear but she was quite certain he said his words loud enough for Charles to hear. ''How you quiver, sweet Kate? You fear him, and well you should for he plans to marry you off to the highest bidder or the least despicable, most interested of the lot, whichever comes first, as quickly as possible for you are but one of the heavy balls on the chains draped around him.''

Kate felt a strange prickle along her spine and for a moment didn't recognize it for what it was—fear—cold, cruel, sudden, and so horribly out of place here. She shook it off. ''Really, Jude, must you joke so?''

''Joke? My sweet sister, look at him standing before us so stern and severe, shackled by all his responsibilities. Does the man have blood or ice in his veins? Indeed, does he deny what I have just suggested?''

Kate felt her spine arch with a shiver. Yes, why didn't he deny what Jude said as utterly ridiculous?

Charles's eyes lifted from Kate to Jude. He moved beside the piano. Had she not known him she would have thought him the most imposing man on earth.

He was dark as the devil himself. There was a thread of warning in his voice. ''Let her play.''

''Egads, you think it's me she fears? Iceman, it's you. I have taken it as my oath to protect her.'' Jude's hands squeezed her shoulders. "And I intend to, for you are not long with us, if I am to understand the Boston society columns. They've taken keen note of your recent interests. They predict an engagement within the month. Did you hear that, Mother?"

"Oh, yes," Mother Remington said, looking up and blinking as if her eyes required focusing. "Tell me, Charles, have you seen the Curtin girl lately?"

Charles looked at his mother. "Eleanor and I have had dinner several times this month."

Kate blinked and desperately tried to remember who Eleanor Curtin was—a relative, surely, a dour-faced, rheumatism-plagued maiden aunt.

"Very good," Mother Remington said, looking almost pointedly at Kate. "Eleanor Curtin has been touted as the most beautiful and eligible woman in all of Boston. So elegant and blond. So very rich. So very much in love, hmmm, Charles?"

"Yes, I've seen the papers." Charles's voice sounded as if he were in a well, down very deep, as if he were forever just beyond Kate's reach. Why wasn't he denying it all?

Mother Remington's hands relaxed in her lap and she looked at Charles with an expression of unfettered pride. "Oh, Charles, your father would have been so very proud of you. Edgar Curtin's Boston law practice is preeminent. Once you marry Miss Curtin your future there is secure, your success all but assured. You'll be the envy of your classmates. And sweet Eleanor won't mind a visit here now and again. I will need to see my grandchildren, you know. Oh, but we'll miss you so terribly. But of course you've done your family a tremendous service and just when we needed it most—what with all the debts and Jude and his—" She broke off, glanced at Jude as if he'd magically appeared in the room, then looked rather startled back at Charles.

''Don't worry yourself,'' Charles said. ''I've taken care of it.''

Kate felt an even deeper chill creep through her at the callousness of his tone. What had he—? Why didn't she understand all of this? How could any of it be happening? A misunderstanding, that's what it was. . . .

Mother Remington sighed. ''Indeed, with you watching over us all, Charles, nothing will tarnish the Remington legacy. Dear God, but I will miss you as I always do when you're gone. Mary Elizabeth is growing so tiresome for me, and Grandmother Remington is weaker by the day.''

''The devil I am,'' Grandmother snapped, looking as if someone had just poked her awake from her nice, late afternoon snooze. She adjusted herself in her chair and shot her daughter-in-law a curious look. ''Maybe you're just wishing it so you can see what's in my will.''

Mother Remington resumed her furious stitching but one eyebrow inched up. ''I have every faith Grandfather Remington knew what he was doing when he entrusted you with his fortune. I'm quite certain you'll make sure we're all taken care of, though why you would wait to do that until after you die is rather beyond me—''

''Enough,'' Charles said, his voice deep and commanding. ''Grandfather obviously trusted her implicitly. There's nothing further to say.''

For a moment the room fell eerily silent.

Kate stared at Charles. He watched her, with eyes slightly lidded. Jonathan Smarte. What would Maggie Swifte do?

Jude squeezed her shoulders, harder this time. ''Kate? What is it?''

''Play on, Kate,'' Charles said softly and retired again to the corner.

The note made a whisper of sound as it slipped under the door and caught Kate's eye. She left her desk, opened the bedroom door, and glanced up and down the deserted hall. All was quiet, dark, and as it should be at midnight. She'd thought she was the only one awake, desperate and miserable, with her candle burning and her quill scratching. Only seconds ago she'd fallen asleep with her words trailing cockeyed over the paper and tears smeared over her cheeks and splashed on the page.

Tonight Jonathan Smarte had kissed Maggie Swifte. They'd shared deep soulful kisses that Kate had practiced against her own open palm, again and again, until she was fairly certain she knew how a man's lips would feel on her own. At least certain enough to write about it. She'd started crying as she'd practiced, imagining Charles kissing Eleanor Curtin, marrying Eleanor Curtin, bringing Eleanor Curtin's babies home to Lenox.

The letter was folded and sealed with the Remington crest. Kate broke the seal, unfolded the page, and read.

Meet me at the big maple.

It was unsigned but the script was bold, masculine, commanding. She closed her eyes, drew the letter to her chest, and felt hope sputter to life. She tried to deny it but couldn't. It was far easier to believe that she'd misunderstood all she'd heard in the parlor, all the talk of Charles's engagement, and that awful feeling that she was nothing more than a pawn to attract the highest bidder. Yes, she clung to the letter and hoped far more than she wanted to believe that Charles would marry another. Tears sprang to her eyes and she shoved them aside. Moments later she doused her candle and left her room.

She passed closed doors, finding only one slightly opened—Mother Remington's. Light spilled into the hall but all was quiet. No doubt Mother Remington was reading as she always did.

The night was moonless, the air was warm and heavy with the scents of summer. Anticipation quivered in her chest. With one hand holding her robe up to her knees, Kate made her way into the grove, bare feet swishing through dewy grass.

The maple was in a far corner of the grove, some distance from the house. It stood proud, a deeper shadow against the dark skies. She turned once to look back at the house and get her bearings. Only one window shone with dim light. Mother Remington's. She felt drawn to that warm, soft beacon and for a moment considered running back to it and the comfort she had always found with the woman.

She moved deeper into the grove, glanced back again, but the house was hidden now by the trees. She turned back and someone's strong arms were around her, pressing her head to his shoulder and her body up against the hard length of his.

"Shh—" came his husky whisper.

Kate clutched his shoulders and smelled the starch of his white linen shirt. "Yes, but why—?"

"Shh—" He was a formless silhouette above her and then he was kissing her, just as she'd dreamed he would. But in her dreams, he'd spoken to her first of love, of longing, of the torment of the months they'd been apart. In her dreams, he'd spent hours with his mouth pressed to the top of her white-gloved hand and his knees in the wet grass, begging her to love him as he did her, before he attempted to kiss her. In her dreams, his kisses gently coaxed her to lay her trust in him.

In her dreams he was Jonathan Smarte, the gentleman.

In her dreams he didn't have dinners with beautiful blond Boston socialites who were in love with him, and society columns didn't predict his engagement within the month.

Her heart wrenched anew at the thought. The lump of tears clogged in her throat again but all thoughts scattered when he pushed her robe off one shoulder then tugged it to her waist, revealing her nightgown.

He made a sound, something throaty and almost inhuman sounding. She realized it sounded nothing like Charles. Or Jonathan Smarte. It sounded like—

Confusing . . . yes, everything was so confusing in the dark when hurt and despair were consuming her and her dreams were dying all around her. Nothing seemed as it should have been. Her eyes searched for his in the darkness. "Please—" She swallowed and the hurt was an ache now, filling her belly and making her throat feel raw. "I want, that is, not so—" Fast. That was it. Everything was happening much too quickly for her to think clearly.

Hands moved over the cotton covering her breasts and she jerked, startled by them, and even more startled by the responsiveness of her body. She gasped as her nipple tightened and pushed against the fabric. His fingers felt hot through the thin cotton of her nightgown, hot and coaxing and tempting. Yes, tempting away her fears, tempting away the hurt, and . . . tempting her with sudden, unexpected pleasure. . . .

Her voice was husky, her attempt to push his hands away ineffectual. Her eyes began to burn with fresh tears. "No, please—"

"Shh—" he whispered. "Ah, God, you're so beautiful—"

Beautiful. There was a reverence in his voice that tugged at something deep inside Kate. Was this what love sounded like coming from a man? Love and longing and need—

Something pressed into her back—the bark of the tree—and his hands moved with such possessive surety,

Kate felt a sudden need to feel and know something more than girlhood illusion and despair.

She closed her eyes and felt his hands cupping her bosom, squeezing, tenderly at first, then suddenly harder.

She sucked in a breath and opened her eyes. He tugged at the tender nipples but before she could protest his mouth came down hard over hers, his hands came between them, and her nightgown was split to her waist.

"No—" It was out before she could take it back. And yet the first rush of air on her bare breasts seemed to wipe all thought from her mind. The feeling was unexpectedly delicious, and most certainly forbidden.

"Beautiful," he murmured again and she knew he was looking at her breasts. She trembled, shivering suddenly, and gasped when he touched her nipples again. She squirmed and her hips gently pushed against him.

"That's it—" he whispered. He drew her wrists low and pinned her hands to her thighs. He put his mouth on her breasts and hot breath touched her skin. She closed her eyes, swallowed—and confusion, uncertainty, the strangeness of her thoughts all melted away. She wanted to start squirming again when his mouth began to move. Tingles pulsed through her breasts, pooling in the peaks where he suckled, and it was a wondrous, unimaginable feeling. A moan came from the back of her throat.

"That's my girl—" He released one of her hands to fumble between them. "Now—don't talk now—just let me—" Again, he bent his head to her breasts. "Yes, I know you like this—easy now—don't fight me—Christ, but you're a wanton—"

Kate felt a fleeting stab of indecision but the feel of his mouth and his tongue, the puckering of her skin under his lips, the liquid heat that seemed to be filling up inside her—it was all too unexpected, and too much for her.

Her knees buckled and her fears flew like startled

doves. His hand was between her thighs, fingers parting, stroking, tender yet insistent, so knowing of what they were doing, and she was weak and wanting more of it. . . .

She sagged down against the tree. "Please, do you—?" She dragged in a breath and closed her eyes. Her face was smashed against his throat. He smelled of leather. "Do you love me?"

"Yes, yes—shh, now—don't make a noise now—"

"Nothing's going to happen to me, is it? I don't have to leave here if I don't want to—"

"No, shh—" Hands pushed her legs apart and they moved so willingly at his touch, as if she were beyond herself.

Hot breath fanned her face, lips pressed hard over hers, words came in a mad torrent. "Love you . . . love you, sweet . . . that's it . . . tremble for me. . . ."

An enormous surge came against her accompanied by a blinding flash of pain, like a knife embedding into her womb.

Her sob broke against his palm. "Jude."

She froze, afraid to move. Yes, she'd known, perhaps all along.

He thrust once, painfully, against her, made a shuddering sound, and went slack. An instant later he rolled off of her and tossed the edge of her robe onto her belly.

Kate stared at the sky and felt raw and needful in a way she didn't understand. She groped to reassemble her robe over her torn gown and groped harder to make sense of what had just happened . . . and the part she'd inevitably played in it.

He reached for her hand, got to his feet. "Quiet now. Come." He tugged on her hand. She was almost afraid to get up, afraid her legs wouldn't hold her. He tugged harder, drew her up then briefly into his arms. "That's my girl, Kate."

His voice. It was unmistakably Jude's voice. It had been Jude's hands on her special places . . . the places she'd wanted to save for Charles.

He kissed the top of her head. "Go now."

A lump wedged in Kate's throat. Her fingers dug into his arms and warm liquid trickled down her inner thighs. Part of her didn't want to go. Part of her needed to stay here with him, to understand how this had happened.

She'd known.

"Go." With both hands on her shoulders he turned her to face the house. A gentle push. She took a step, felt the rawness seeping up from her wet feet, up her legs, up deep inside her where it curled like cold smoke. She looked back at him. "Go—" She turned, took two more steps, looked back again. His white shirt, the only thing visible about him, billowed in a sudden waft of warm wind. He said nothing.

And she suddenly wanted to run away from him, to reach her bed. She started to shake. Cold . . . suddenly, so very cold, her feet felt like frozen blocks attached to wooden legs. She entered the back of the house and took the rear stairs, like a servant would have, or an intruder.

Or a girl ashamed of what she'd done, of who she was, of the passionate, seductive, unholy yearnings of her body. . . .

She stumbled down the hall and found the door to her room through the haze covering all but a slender tunnel of vision. She shoved the door open and realized instantly that it was not her room.

"What?" Grandmother Remington's head snapped up. She was seated in a chair beside the windows where she slept against a stack of pillows. "Oh, Kate."

Kate battled an incredible urge to throw herself at the woman's feet and weep. She felt Grandmother's eyes on her and ducked half behind the door to shield the shambles of her nightdress and robe. She tried to find a level voice. "I was writing and I heard a noise. Are you—are you well, Grandmother?''

Grandmother frowned. ''A noise? Can't say that I heard any and I hear them all. Yes, I'm well enough with my back as it is. Dear Kate, is something wrong? You look distressed.''

''No, no, I'm just—'' A lump squeezed her throat. Tears burned. She'd even betrayed this dear woman with her foolishness. ''It's late. Sleep now, Grandmother.''

''Come kiss me good night, dear Kate.''

''I—good night.'' Kate gently closed the door. She'd always kissed Grandmother good night, every night, or whenever the older woman asked. It felt very wrong to deny her.

Back in the haven of her room, she moved stiffly, almost afraid to move too much, bending one way or another as she removed her soiled clothes and washed herself from a cold basin of water. She dumped the bloodied water from her window and hid the rag under her bed.

Too numb to think, too cold to feel, she dressed in a traveling gown and packed a small valise with the first things she touched until she couldn't fill it further.

However surreal she felt, the situation was clear. She'd been sullied, and willingly so. The family would consider only one resolution: she would have to marry Jude. And for the rest of her life she would face Charles, his elegant, blond bride, and their elegant children, over the Remington table. Whenever she looked at Jude she would be forever reminded that she'd been all too eager a partner in the grove, all too willing a lover, all too mindless a slave to her body's wanton, willful desires. . . .

Or had she secretly wanted it? There was no denying that she felt affection for Jude, that his antics and naughtiness intrigued her, that she had always enjoyed his company—

So opposite Charles, the man she believed she loved and respected more than any other man she'd ever known.

Confusion flooded over her. In the dark, her mind could have played tricks on her. In despair, she could have very willingly sought comfort and love in Jude's arms. A broken heart seeking revenge against Charles for his betrayal of her. . . .

For years she'd known there was no love lost between the brothers. Charles was always righting Jude's wrongs. More often than not these wrongs had to do with women Jude had disgraced.

Had they been as willing as she to barter their precious virtue in exchange for revenge?

The tears spilled from her eyes and she swiped at them in disgust. She was a humiliation to Grandmother Remington, Mother Remington, perhaps most of all to Charles and to herself.

She reached for the pages on her desk, missed, and they scattered to the floor. Dropping to her knees, she scooped them together and stuffed them into her bag. She stared at her pale hands and remembered the moments when tree bark had bitten into her back and desire had flooded through her body and Jude had kissed her breasts. A croaked sob came from her lips. She could almost hear her dreams washing away.

In a small jewelry box on her dressing table she found the gold wedding band and diamond brooch given to her by the orphanage nuns the day her mother had died. All the woman's worldly possessions given to her six-year-old child before the nuns had taken her away to Our Lady of Divine Humility Orphanage. The pieces were even more like buried treasure to Kate now. She slid the gold band onto her left ring finger and stuffed the brooch into her pocket.

She scribbled a farewell note on a last remaining sheet

of paper, left it on her desk, took up her valise and the first hat she found in her armoire, and eased open the door.

As she stepped into the hall and tugged the door behind her, her foot passed over something on the floor. A stray page from her story, no doubt. She hesitated. Footsteps sounded from the back stairs.

No time to retrieve stray pages. *Run* . . .

By the time she reached the street, she'd come up with a plan. By noon, she'd peddled her diamond brooch and was on a train bound for New York City.

Chapter 1

Boston, Massachusetts
January 1878

The door opened at his knock. "Where is he?" Charles asked.

Ruby rolled her eyes to the stairs behind her. "Upstairs. Second door on your right. Been here since last Thursday. Ye might be interruptin' sumpthin' again."

"Nothing I haven't seen before." Charles pressed several bills into her outstretched hand and pushed past her. He moved to the steps without glancing at the women watching him from nearby chairs and settees. Snow fell from his coat onto the risers with each hindered step. He welcomed the cold. It numbed the ache in his thigh. Heat worsened it. Damp heat made it excruciating to walk.

His brother was throwing up on the soiled red carpet when Charles entered the room.

"Ain't no use t'any woman." A worn-out blonde wearing a shabby corset and torn stockings shouldered past Charles. "Diseased bastard—" she said, slamming the door behind her.

"Ah, God—" Jude gasped, lifted his head, and saw Charles. "Christ."

"Not hardly." Charles scooped a tangle of clothes from

the floor, tossed them at Jude, and moved to the window. Throwing open the drape, he cranked the casement and drew in clean air, as clean as could be found in this part of town where everything seemed soaked in vomit and liquor, his brother perhaps most of all. The window opened to the brick side of another building. Snowflakes dribbled from an orange-black sky. "Grandmother Remington died yesterday."

Jude grunted. "Didn't think this was a social call, Brother."

Though appalled at Jude's lack of emotion, Charles was not at all surprised. What was surprising was how completely Jude had allowed himself to sink into a life of utter squalor. "The will was read this morning. We couldn't locate you. I understand you've been here for nearly a week."

"Goddamn that Ruby. Traitorous bitch. Suppose the bill collectors were following you up the stairs." Another grunt and Jude collapsed back on the bed, clothes clutched to his chest, snow white naked legs spread, eyes closed. "So tell me what I missed. Ah—but of course you're here to gloat. Did you get it all, oh-reverent Brother? All couple hundred thousand and change, just as you planned?"

Charles rubbed the pearl handle of his walking stick with his thumb. "Grandmother had a peculiar sense of humor—much like Grandfather."

A moment passed. Jude thrashed up to his elbows. "Egad, you mean to say she left it all to me?"

"You would never own Our Lady of Divine Humility."

"No, I can't say I've ever wanted to own an orphanage and the name—egad." An awkward moment of silence passed. A liquor-soaked brain needed to take its time. "You mean to say Grandmother left it all to—to—those goddamned *nuns*?"

"Every penny."

Jude made a choking sound. "I think I'm going to puke again. Or maybe I should laugh. The joke's on you, Brother.

You do realize that. You're the only one who stood even a remote chance at getting it all. Even after the scandal broke about you, she was the only member of the family who stayed in your corner. Even our very own mother kept to her chaise lounge for a month despairing over the news.'' Jude shrugged. ''I suspect Grandmother finally got some sense and decided to write you out of the whole fortune.''

''I might agree were it not for the small stipulation in the will.''

''Ah. The humorous part. Wondered when you were going to get to that. Then again, you never laugh, do you, old man? You might try wearing your trousers a little less close to the flank, eh?'' Jude again collapsed.

Charles turned from the window. ''It seems Grandmother was most concerned with Remington bloodlines.''

''That's all been up to you, Brother. You've known that for four years now.'' Jude's voice came muffled from behind the arm he'd thrown over his eyes. ''Can't understand why you haven't stepped up to the responsibility yet. You don't usually ignore all your goddamned duty. Always doing the godawful right thing. It can be so boring, especially when you always make me look bad. No, I suppose it's too much to ask that you might have left a few by-blows along the way, eh?''

''Interesting word. By-blows. Grandmother used it specifically in the stipulation. It was almost as if she suspected that there might be one out there somewhere.''

Jude snorted, hiccuped, and the clothes on his chest slid to the bed. He looked pale and slender and weak, a shadow of the man he'd been only four years before, before his headlong dive into gambling and liquor and women had taken its toll. Charles felt the stirrings of his own vomit in his throat and averted his eyes. He found himself staring at his own reflection in a fuzzy wall mirror. He looked so much like his father he was startled and had to again turn away.

Jude said, ''So the fortune goes to the orphanage if no by-blows are produced. And if they are?''

''The fortune goes to the child. We've a year to produce one.''

''Christ almighty.'' It was a mild explosion of emotion. ''Almost makes a man wish—'' Another hiccup. ''But hell, when a man takes a bullet in the balls, what's he good for? I've always hated Robert Ericson for what he did to me for a rather mild seduction, in all truth—damn his aim—and now, God, more than ever.''

''It was pitiful recompense for what you did to his wife. And to him. He never recovered from the scandal.''

''Let's not talk about ruined reputations, eh, Big Brother?'' The venom in Jude's voice was palpable. ''You've your own skeletons, remember? All of Boston remembers. Every now and then the society pages will burp something about the Curtin-Remington wedding that never was. But I believe they've stopped wondering what happened to you since that bit of career suicide. It's been, after all, over five years and sweet Eleanor has since married. Tell me, why *did* you break it off with her?''

Charles again turned to the windows, dismissing his brother's question as easily as he'd dismissed all the others'.

But his brother persisted. ''All the papers said it was another woman you were in love with, and yet to this day, you live like a monk, no other woman anywhere to be found. To my eye you look like a brokenhearted man, carrying one hell of a torch. Though I suppose now you'll find it very easy to set aside your lost love and marry some woman, the more fertile the better, eh? After all, you've sunk into relative obscurity and almost certain poverty with your career here in Lenox helping the common man, haven't you? Not much money in that, and never will be. There's much more to be found in producing an heir."

Charles started toward the door. He winced once. The room was hot and stuffy, an airless, tasteless hell that made his thigh throb. His brother deserved to be wasting his life here. Charles felt no sympathy for him. He wasn't worth a moment of Charles's time or thoughts.

"By-blows—" Jude's voice was slurred, as if he'd half sunk into sleep. "No chance of that for me—always been careful—no, there was one—just one—but she's gone now. Left right after. Don't know what the hell happened to her that night. Ah, Kate—"

Charles froze. He looked sharply at Jude. Heat suddenly radiated from his throat in pulses. "What about Kate?" he rasped, profoundly aware that he hadn't spoken her name aloud in months.

"Gone—but once, just once—"

Charles watched Jude's chest rise and fall. His vision throbbed. He gripped his walking stick so hard his fingers numbed. He didn't want to ask it but couldn't seem to help himself. "Once—once what?"

Jude sighed, drifting. Several moments passed. "I bedded her—" A soft droning snore parted Jude's lips.

Charles gripped the door handle. A red haze filtered over his vision. Oxygen trapped in his chest. The mother-of-pearl buttons on his shirtfront pushed into his chest. He couldn't breathe. He had to get out.

Then suddenly he was bent over Jude, his white-gloved hands wrapped around his brother's neck, squeezing. "You bastard—you raped her—"

Jude's eyes bulged and he thrashed against Charles's hold. "No—no—never that—"

"Lying bastard, I could kill you—"

Jude squeaked, clawing at Charles's hand. "I swear it—*she wanted it. . . .*"

"As if I would ever believe you—" It was a numbing thought, watching himself squeeze the life out of his brother.

Worthless . . . not even worth the effort. . . .

Charles released him, gulped several deep breaths, then turned away in disgust. Brushing a trickle of sweat from his brow, he left the room, managed the stairs with one stumble, and burst into the night air.

"Now—" he snarled at his footman as he lurched into his waiting carriage. "Downtown. Quickly."

"Sir?"

"Pinkerton's Agency."

"Sir?"

"Dammit, man, I'll find it. Just get me downtown. We've already wasted too much time. Go—hurry."

"Anything?" Charles asked even before the door to his study closed. He pushed back from his cluttered desk and got to his feet as the detective pulled his bowler from his head and swung a bulging valise onto a chair seat.

"I'm afraid not. I'm sorry, Mr. Remington. But as we discussed, matters like this take time."

"Yes, yes, I know; but, Christ, it's been over four months since I hired you."

"Playboy types like William Frye aren't easy to find. They don't even want their families to know where they are. And it's been years. I finally tracked him down in Philadelphia. Turns out he didn't even remember her. It's been too long."

Charles looked up sharply and couldn't keep the snap from his tone. "I told you from the start that was a red herring. She wouldn't have gone with that damned Frye on a buggy ride, much less run off with him to Europe."

"But the note she left behind said—"

"I don't give a damn what her note said. I contacted Frye's family the day she disappeared and for several months afterward. They hadn't seen or heard from her."

"But the note—" The detective swallowed. "I—I thought that's why you still had it in your possession, sir, after all these years. Even you believed it for all that time."

Charles felt his face tighten and looked out the window to keep himself from punching the detective in the face. Yes, he'd wanted to believe it, even if it made little sense. But only because he hadn't wanted to believe that *he* was responsible for her running away—that she'd been pushed out the door with the words he'd written that night in the letter he'd slipped under her door.

At the time it had seemed all too logical an explanation: innocent girl, terrified by the passionate depths of her foster brother's sudden expression of feelings for her, knows she can never return his feelings and runs away. He'd cursed himself a thousand times since for choosing the letter as his forum. At the time he'd thought it the obvious course, given their mutual love of writing and the romantic nature of a love letter. But perhaps it would have been far better to face her with it, to have gently swayed her with spoken words and affection.

Perhaps he would have believed differently all this time had he found the letter somewhere in her room. But he hadn't and had assumed she'd taken it with her.

He'd come up with no other explanation for her disappearance until Jude had spilled his secrets and the truth of it all was slammed into his face, like a heavy door.

Maybe the fault lay with Jude.

Perhaps it was Jude she truly loved and she'd fled to avoid the inevitable confrontation between the two brothers.

She loved Jude. . . .

"I—er—I found more of these, as you requested, sir. Don't know what good they'll do you. Like I've told you, if someone wants to disappear, their best bet is to head west. Trouble is they rarely advertise where they've gone. Most change their names. Hell, it's like they've fallen off the edge of the planet." The detective drew a stack of newspapers from his valise and handed them over the top of the desk. "Might as well have died."

"Don't ever say that again." Charles realized his fists were clenched against his thighs. He sat down and began flipping through the papers. Most were from towns he'd never heard of. Their single pages were smeared with blurred type and screaming headlines.

"Get me more," he said, without looking up. "I want a copy of every paper printed in any town from here to San Francisco."

A moment passed in silence. "What exactly are you looking for, sir? Perhaps I could help—"

"I don't know what I'm looking for."

"I see. Fair enough. Er—Mr. Remington, as we discussed the fee for this will be—"

"Yes, I know. Whatever it takes." Charles looked up and pinned the man with his stare. "Do you understand? Do whatever it takes and find her."

Several hours later Charles was still hunched over the stack of newspapers when a knock came on his door. He slouched back in his chair and watched the servant enter. His eyes hurt from focusing on bad type. His head felt heavy. In his chest there was a strange twisting kind of ache gripping him. It hadn't abated in four months.

He jerked his cravat loose and worked several buttons at the top of his shirt free. "How is my mother?" he asked.

"Resting as comfortably as can be expected. I gave her warm milk with honey tonight with her laudanum." She paused at a crystal decanter on a nearby table and filled a glass with brandy.

"And Mary Margaret?"

"Asleep." She walked toward him. Her face was a porcelain pale landscape beneath a sweep of dark chestnut. For a breathless instant her coloring reminded him of Kate's dusky beauty. It wasn't the first time.

"Everyone's asleep," she reminded him. She set the glass in front of him and waited, the dutiful servant. He'd chosen her well, this warmhearted caregiver who sat at his ailing mother's bedside day after day and also bathed poor Mary Margaret and put her to sleep. Three days after the servant had come to Remington Manor, he'd found her waiting for him in his bed.

He reached for the glass. She touched his sleeve. He drank until the glass was empty then set the glass down and focused on the paper in front of him. "Thank you," he said, dismissing her as he always had and knew he always would.

Less than a week later, when the detective returned with a new stack of papers, Charles found what he was looking for. He almost missed it and nearly discarded the paper simply because the type was so badly set and blurred it made his eyes ache to decipher it.

It was on the second page of the *Crooked Nickel Sentinel,* in a column titled, "Editorial Opinion," beneath which was printed the standard editor's disclaimer.

"Sheepherders Unfairly Strong-Armed by Greedy Cattlemen: Range Wars Unnecessary Evil" the headline said. And beneath that, in fuzzy, crooked type was the editor's name: Jonathan Smarte.

Crooked Nickel, Wyoming
June 1878

"I say we round up all the cattle fellas an' we all go on down to the *Sentinel* an' start by coatin' him with sorghum molasses an' sand burs then ridin' him around town on a wooden rail. That's what the folks up in Dancing Waters did to their editor when they didn't like what he had to say. Sheepherders unfairly strong-armed, my ass. I'm so sick of hearin' this kind of crap. We gotta make it stop. Everyone knows we cattlemen hold exclusive claim to the open range. Sheepherders is just a buncha ignorant immigrants with dumb animals trespassin' on property—"

"Now hold on, Elmer. Did ya read this part on page one?"

"Cain't read, Virg." A clang registered from the cuspidor set in the corner of the general store.

"Ain't you a lucky bastard. Listen to this—hell, if I can read it, damned type's too fuzzy—here—" Virg cleared his throat, rattled the paper and read haltingly, "*There's no better or more dee-zirable place to be found in Wyoming than Crooked Nickel.* Did ya hear that, Elmer?"

"I heard it. So how's Mr. Smarte know that? I heard he lives in a big house up in Laramie."

"I heard Denver. Leastways that's what Bessie Mae Elliot told my ma. She said he was an old friend of Harry McGoldrick's, from back in the days when Harry was runnin' the *Denver Chronicle*. Musta been twenty years ago."

Elmer snorted. "Friend a Harry's oughta know better'n to go spoutin' off about sheepherders' rights. What happened to Harry could happen ta him."

A moment passed. "You said that was an accident, Elmer."

Elmer laughed dismissively. "'Course it was, Virg. Couple words exchanged over drinks, things heat up, and guns go off. Happens by accident all the time. You heard Sheriff Gage say so, didn'ya? Took my gun, looked at it real close, and said it was an accident, just like I said it was."

"But Harry didn't have no gun, Elmer. I saw it fer myself."

"Whiskey bottle can look like a gun in certain light,

Virg. Funny, ain't it, that ol' Harry didn' leave the *Sentinel* to me in his will.''

''Maybe 'cuz you cain't read, Elmer.''

''An' who says Smarte can? Bastard cain't write to save his dandy ass an' now he owns the damned paper. Probably owns a dozen other papers, too. What good is he livin' in Laramie? Bet he ain't never seen the railroad depot here. What's he look like?''

''Ain't never seen him. Nobody has. Not even the clerk what runs the *Sentinel* for him. Here, Elmer, listen to this: *Situated on one of the most beee-utiful and romantic streams imaginable, Crooked Nickel is as pretty a site as could be well selected, built up with neat, substantial, and elegant buildings. Composed of a class of people who for energy and enterprise are not excelled.*'' A moment of silence passed as both men contemplated the window and the dust-bitten stretch of deserted road that passed through the center of Crooked Nickel. ''Hell, he might bring some new folk into town. Ya gotta be happy 'bout that, Elmer.''

''So long as they ain't no more sheepherders.''

''Hell, they're good for business. I been waterin' the whiskey as much as I can to get me by lately.''

''I say we rally the boys an' try to run another one out. Whatdya say, Virg? Feel like slittin' a few sheep's throats tonight like we did last month?''

''The paper's not makin' the war, Elmer. You are.''

''The hell I am.'' Another clang registered from the cuspidor. ''Railroad's payin' Smarte to say that crap and make all this land they own worth somethin'. Hell, Virg, river's been dry goin' on three years now. Railroad must be payin' him real good. No wonder he don't have the guts to show his face in town. Harry shoulda left his paper to his kid.''

''Walter's only five.''

Elmer snorted. ''Like I said, we'd a been better off. One

of these days I'm gonna find Mr. Jonathan Smarte an' me an' the rest of the boys, we're gonna make him pay. An' I'm gonna start by carvin' out whatever innards he's got. An' if that don't work, maybe take him over ta the saloon—''

The can of beans teetered on the top shelf and banged to the floor. Chairs scraped on the floor. Kate closed her eyes, whispered a curse, then turned to face Elmer and Virg as they poked their heads around the end of the aisle of shelves. Kate pasted on a smile and hoped she didn't look like the blatant eavesdropper she'd become.

Virg rushed forward, dragging his hat from his head. ''Mrs. McGoldrick, you all right? Good God almighty, you coulda been kilt. Here, ma'am, let me.''

Kate murmured her thanks as Virg retrieved the fallen can of beans and a fresh can from the top shelf and handed it to her. She glanced at Elmer Pruitt, only because he was looking at her. She even clasped her black, lace-gloved hands demurely over her waist and smiled again, a truly Herculean feat given her near hatred for Pruitt. But, then again, since she'd come to Crooked Nickel she'd become a master at putting on a suitably benign face, even more so since Harry's death.

It had been Elmer Pruitt's gun that had killed Harry that night in Virg's saloon in front of a dozen witnesses. And it hadn't been an accident, no matter what Sheriff Gage and the witnesses had said. Harry's unbending support of the sheepherders had earned him the cattlemen's hatred. It had ultimately killed him. She knew it. Pruitt knew it. She suspected Virg and the others knew it. But no one had yet had the guts to prove it.

Kate masked her sorrow and her suspicions well. She'd learned how to keep emotion to herself since coming to Crooked Nickel. Living two lives. That's how Harry had rationalized it, his dark eyes all atwinkle as if this were a truly enviable and entertaining circumstance. In many ways it had been, especially when Harry had been alive to share it with her.

He'd pulled his ultimate fast one in this town, achieving a success he'd never dreamed of after his publisher in Denver had sent him packing. Too many empty whiskey bottles hidden in his desk. And then there'd been the scathing editorial about the adulterous candidate for Congress, a piece of workmanship that had gotten Harry's house burned to the ground. At least that's how Harry had dismissed it all.

Denver, he used to say, was a rough town for newsmen.

Shortly after, in the Denver train depot, he'd met Kate, as hell-bent as he was on escaping to a no-name town and making a living as a writer. Their shared desperation and love of writing forged a quick bond and together they'd hit on the idea of inventing Jonathan Smarte, an editor with no bad history in places like Denver or otherwise. They'd ended up in Crooked Nickel, Wyoming, a dying, dust-bitten town on a forgotten spur of the Union Pacific. Shortly thereafter, they'd founded the *Crooked Nickel Sentinel.* There, while Harry had run the business and splashed the sheepherders' plight on every front page, Kate, ghostwriting editorials as Jonathan Smarte, had honed her writing skills.

By virtue of Smarte's editorials and Harry's headlines, the paper had come to the attention of the Union Pacific. They began to pay the paper to spread good pioneer cheer and propaganda to its readership, the better to lure buyers to their properties. Sheepherders had flocked to the town, their families with them. Jonathan Smarte had been both Harry's and Kate's pride and joy and, ultimately, their bankroll.

Only now, with Harry gone, the press going bad, and the bill collectors growing more and more impatient, keeping up the pretense as Jonathan Smarte was more difficult than it had ever been. But then again, without her ongoing masquerade as Jonathan Smarte, Kate never would have been able to keep control of the paper, keep the railroad men back in Boston happy, and keep food on the table for her son. Without Jonathan Smarte, she never would have been able to tweak cattlemen like Elmer Pruitt and get away with it. Through Jonathan Smarte and her support of the sheepherders, she was determined she would have her revenge on Pruitt for the death of her husband. She owed it to Harry for what he'd done for her. She owed it to Harry for the kind of proud and noble man he was.

Pruitt sank his head down between his mammoth shoulders and hooded his eyes with his typical pompous attitude. He looked like a bulldog. "Ma'am."

Virg gave her a look of sympathy that Kate assumed all widows became accustomed to after a while, only she wasn't accustomed to it yet and doubted she ever would be. She refused to think of herself as an object of pity. She'd refused since the day she'd set out from Lenox on her own with no place to go. She'd known little of the world then and she'd survived. She could survive Harry's death. She could survive looking at his killer every day, and smiling.

Not that Kate hadn't mourned Harry. She had and still did, much as she would have the loss of a dear and closest friend. But loneliness wasn't something she'd ever get used to—not the loneliness of body, but the loneliness of spirit. It had been especially difficult after she'd found out at the funeral that Harry had whiskeyed away all their savings down at Virg's saloon. Little wonder Virg always looked so sympathetic. With the money he'd collected from Kate right after they set Harry in the ground in his pine box, Virg had built himself a new house.

At the moment, Virg's face was bright red. Kate supposed any man would feel guilty speaking about the dead, knowing he'd been overheard. "I didn't see ya come in, ma'am." Obviously. "How's your boy, Walter?"

Kate's face felt like it would crack from smiling so fake. "Fine, just fine."

"Doin' well at school?"

"Very well, thank you. He's reading and writing like—" The bell over the door tinkled, the door slammed open with enough force to send it thudding against the opposite wall. Footsteps thundered on the wooden floor as if a herd of buffalo had suddenly detoured off the street for a chat around the cracker-barrel.

"Hey, Mr. Logan. You got them peppermint sticks again!"

"No." Kate spun around, darted to the front counter and grabbed the lid of the candy jar just as a grubby hand tried to yank it off. She kept the lid secure with a good deal of pressure. Enormous blue eyes jerked up at her through a fringe of poker-straight blond bangs. Brows slanted downward over a nose dotted with pale freckles.

"Aw, c'mon, Mama."

"I said no."

"You always say no."

"That's right, Walter McGoldrick, so you'd best learn to stop asking. Thank you, Mr. Logan, but this will be all." She laid the can of beans and a sack of flour on the counter. "If you could—add it to my bill, I would be grateful, sir."

Logan's lips thinned then jerked in a faint smile.

Walter poked out his jaw and stared longingly at the peppermint sticks. Kate ran a finger up the back of his neck, a spot she kissed most often when he slept. He arched away from her but gave a little giggle. She scooped up her brown paper package. "Let's go, Walt."

They headed west along the boardwalk, Walt scuffing one foot into the dirt street, dragging his school satchel in the dust behind him, then loping along to catch up. Kate kept up a steady, fast clip. She passed by the newspaper office, noting that the clerk, Mr. Gould, was at his post, then continued on to the milliners. There, she paused in front of the windows to wave at her friend Victoria Valentine, the shop's owner. Victoria was always easy to spot in her crimson satin. Kate caught a glimpse of her own reflection in the glass. She wondered what she would look like in something other than black. For seven straight months she'd worn it.

Another half block farther along she pushed open the door to a building whose sign out front read "Douglas Murphy, Attorney at Law."

"Sit there and don't move," she said to Walt, pointing at a ladder-back chair against the wall and handing him his satchel.

Walt poked out his jaw. "I don't want to read."

"Reading is good."

"You always say that."

"Because I believe it. When I was a little girl—"

"I know. You used to climb up in the biggest maple tree in the grove and eat blueberry tarts—"

"Gooseberry tarts."

"Yeah, I know, and you would eat them and read all day."

"I also wrote stories."

"I don't want to write stories. I don't like gooseberries."

"Fine. Then sit there and be quiet for just a minute." She cupped her hand around his head until he looked up at her and his lips quirked ever so faintly upward.

Douglas's door was open. He was alone at his desk, staring at a page in his hand, and idly stroking his handlebar mustache. Kate often wondered how working in Crooked Nickel Douglas managed to put food on the table for his wife and three children. He'd been one of the many who'd dragged his family from a cozy midwestern town to find the streets of gold and acres of fertile soil awaiting him out on the Wyoming prairie. Like most families, he'd spent his life's savings getting out here and setting up a home. It was easier to stay than to think about packing up and heading back east to nothing. Besides, most folks found it hard to give up the dream that prosperity wasn't just a day or two away, particularly in cattle country.

When Douglas saw her, he stood up and jerked his chin at the newspaper in his hand, simultaneously peering at her over the tops of his glasses. "No self-respecting cattleman even wants to be mentioned in the same sentence as the sheepherders. You're going to start an out-and-out war with this, Kate."

"Oh, I don't think so, Douglas. I'm not the one threatening to slit sheep's throats. The cattlemen are. I'm just reporting it."

"They're dangerous men, Kate. I'm worried for you."

"Don't be. They're angry at Jonathan Smarte. And we both know where he is—er—rather *who* he is. You can't have a war with an invisible man. You can't kill him either." Douglas motioned her to a chair and they sat down facing each other. "Harry would have approved."

"Well, hell, Kate, Harry willed his newspaper to an imaginary person named Jonathan Smarte, so who can judge what our Harry might have done. I still think I could be disbarred for being party to that."

"Sole party, Douglas. You do remember that?"

"My wife doesn't even know. You know I'm a damned nice fellow, Kate."

"I know, Douglas. You've always been such a good friend. Harry thought so highly of you—" She heard her voice catch the slightest bit and sat up so straight her spine felt as rigid as whalebone.

"Doesn't take much between men, Kate. Share a few war stories over a couple of whiskeys, and hell, we'd lay down our lives for each other. Besides, Harry and I were both writers. Lovers of words. What's a phony will between friends?" Douglas drew such a deep breath his vest pulled taut at the buttons. ''Nothing in the whole scheme of things, especially if it helps you out.''

''Yes, it has. It's been the only thing since Harry died—'' Her throat swelled closed for a second. She glanced over her shoulder at Walt. He was slumped over sideways, sound asleep. The way his hair fell over his brow and the proud thrust of his jaw brought to mind another's face, from a lifetime ago. She'd thought she'd buried those memories deep. The tears were in her eyes before she could even think to swallow them back. ''I—'' She lowered her head, wrested open her reticule, and placed the gold wedding band on the desk top.

''Jesus, Kate—''

''I need to put food on the table for my son, Douglas.''

''For God's sake, listen, Kate—'' Douglas started reaching in his pocket.

Kate almost leapt out of her chair. ''No! Please, don't do that. God—I didn't come here for a loan.'' She jerked a hand over the stray lock that fell over her eyes. ''At least not from you. Just hear me out, Douglas. The only skill I have is writing. But as a female I can't find anyone to publish me—except Harry, of course. The Union Pacific will pay Jonathan Smarte enough to get by . . . so long as I say what they want me to say. And without support, the sheepherders might just decide to knuckle under to the intimidation coming from cattlemen like Elmer Pruitt and that would be such a tragedy. I need to keep the paper and the sheepherders' cause alive, Douglas. I have to. Harry died for it.''

''You're worrying me, Kate. This has become a personal vendetta for you.''

''It would be for you, too.''

Douglas was silent for several moments then leaned his forearms on his desk and spoke softly, ''So why are you hocking your wedding ring if you're getting by?''

Kate stared at her fingers twisting in the cords of her

reticule. She could hear the toot of the Union Pacific locomotive pulling into town. Today the whistle sounded lonely. "I need a new press, Douglas, or my type will be hopelessly illegible by the next issue. My rent is two months past due. My clerk, Mr. Gould, hasn't been paid in over three weeks—my ink supplier in a month. Poor Mr. Gould has to avoid him whenever he comes into town asking to speak to Jonathan Smarte. People are going to start getting suspicious. The money I've received from the Union Pacific has all gone to pay off Harry's debts—and there are still more. I've never been good with numbers, Douglas—"

"Put that ring back in your purse."

"Douglas, if the Union Pacific finds out that a woman not only *owns* the *Crooked Nickel Sentinel* but has been running it out of her kitchen and masquerading as Jonathan Smarte, they'll—they'll—" She bit her lip and frowned. "Well, I'd imagine they'll fire me."

"At the very least. They might throw you in jail for violation of their contract—and me right along with you. Railroad barons hate being made to look like fools. They'd much prefer we all wear that hat."

"That wasn't either Harry's or my intent at the outset. I simply wanted to write. And he wanted to help me. I never imagined it would come to this. And now the sheepherders are involved and a murderer is walking free out there, Douglas, itching to cause more trouble for the sheepherders. I feel responsible for them, Douglas."

"You've a generous heart, Kate. I know Harry loved that about you."

Kate worked the ring between two fingers. The words seemed to stick in her throat. "I think I need you to get me a financier."

"Now, wait a minute, Kate—"

"You have connections back east, in Denver—even Laramie—men you shared war stories with over whiskeys?'' She hesitated before looking up at Douglas.

Douglas peered at her over the top of his glasses. ''The old boys at the U.P. wouldn't want to get wind of that. Investors tend to want a finger in the pie.''

''That's why you need to find me one who won't care about being anonymous.''

''You overestimate my talents, Kate, and my connections. I'm a prairie lawyer now.''

''Please, Douglas—I can't think of any other way. I can't run away from this any longer. I just can't.''

''Yes, I imagine this is your last resort. You're a proud woman.''

''Pride suffers a swift and painless death sometimes.''

''The interest rate on any money could be astronomical.''

''I've considered that. And right now, I don't care. Please, Douglas—''

He hesitated then reached out and gently patted her hand. ''I'll give it my best, Kate.''

Chapter 2

The pinched-faced clerk looked up at Charles for the fourth time. His mouth jerked but his words were inaudible through the storefront window. Charles glanced up at the "Crooked Nickel Sentinel" painted on the sign dangling by one hinge over the door. The sign needed fresh paint. So did the building.

He'd stood there for fifteen minutes and had seen no sign of Kate. He glanced east up the two-block length of street. Crooked Nickel looked as if it had no reason to be sitting in the middle of the Wyoming prairie. Still, more than a handful of people had alighted from the train with him, the majority of them women. He'd overheard several of them breathlessly remark about a fine millinery in Crooked Nickel owned by a woman named Victoria Valentine, who was supposedly known even as far as Denver as carrying the latest in Paris fashions. They'd all swished off with great excitement.

A wagon rumbled past. The driver looked at Charles but didn't tip his hat or soften his expression. People dotted the boardwalks, some walking, others lingering outside the storefronts. Those who passed stared boldly at Charles for long moments, making him think that not many strangers passed through this town.

He scanned the faces of each of the women he saw,

mentally adding six years to the memory of Kate, but none registered even the vaguest familiarity. At the end of the farthest block, a dozen horses stood tethered at a hitching rail in front of a squat building with "Saloon" painted on its windows. Opposite that was a shack with "Jail" painted over its door. A man sat on a tipped-back chair in front, boots propped on the hitching rail, hat pulled down over his nose. Sunlight flashed off the star pinned to his vest.

Charles squinted west, directly into a blast of sun slamming down the street. Sweat carved a path through the grime caking his throat and trickled into the top of his collar. His nose and mouth were coated with the same film. Over it all he wore a dusting of the oily black stuff the locomotive had spewed on the journey from Laramie. He focused on a sign over a two-story building farther up the street: "Hotel." Written beneath that was "Bedbugs scaled thrice each week."

The door to the newspaper office slammed open.

"I ain't the owner," the clerk bleated at Charles in a twangy voice. He jerked the door closed behind him, locked it, then marched down the steps. He paused beside Charles and squinted up at him. "An' I don't carry no gun. Just a clerk, tryin' to do my job, best as I can, since I ain't been paid in three weeks." He scrunched up his nose and gave Charles a once-over. "S'pose you're from the government or the railroad, come to shut the place down. I say, took ya long enough. Press's been bad fer months. On its last leg. Without it there won't be no paper come this time next week. Yep, you look like a railroad gent. You Union Pacific, or Denver and Rio Grande?"

"Neither."

"Shoulda known. You look East Coast. You a cattleman?"

"From out east?"

"You'd be surprised the folks what's got a stake in

cattle out here. Ain't here for cattle? Then you got no reason to be in this town. Best buffalo huntin's in Nebraska, if that's what yer after. Grand dukes all the way from Russia come to Nebraska to hunt buffalo. Came in January. Folks is still talkin' about it."

"Is that right. Is—uh—Kate here?"

"Who?"

A moment passed. Charles felt a lonely hot wind in his face and knew such overwhelming disappointment his chest ached.

The clerk's brows suddenly shot up. "Oh, you mean Mrs. McGoldrick."

"Mrs. McGoldrick."

"Ain't seen her around lately. She stops in occasionally, helps out from time to time. I think she comes to the office because she misses her husband."

"Her husband."

"'Course she can't do nothin' about my pay. She's scrapin' the bottom of her barrel, I 'spect. It's the fancy fella what owns the place you wanna talk to. Smarte's his name. I heard he lives over in Laramie but I ain't never met him. You been there?"

"Laramie? Just came from there."

"Hrmph. You'd best go back. Trouble's brewin' 'round here you don't wanna witness." The clerk muttered something, then turned and ambled eastward down the street.

Charles tugged his hat lower over his eyes against the glare, bent for his valise and started west up the boardwalk. He'd taken maybe five steps then suddenly froze.

A woman had just stepped from a building a half block farther along. She was chestnut-haired and young, it struck him then, almost too young to be wearing such rigidly tailored black. During the war, he'd grown immune to the faces of the eighteen-year-olds in black bombazine, widowed far too early in life by Confederate bullets and cannon balls. But in the years since the war had ended, the shell that had hardened him to premature grief had eroded, bit by bit, so slowly he was almost always taken aback when he realized it.

The dress made her skin look translucent as porcelain. When she moved, he sensed strength and agility in her that no amount of black bombazine could suppress. Youth. Perhaps he was becoming so attuned to it because his own was fast fading. But thirty wasn't old. So why the hell did it feel that he'd lived three lifetimes?

She was looking back into the building. Her hair was dark, darker than he remembered, or maybe it was the way she was wearing it that seemed different—pulled low and severe at the back of her head. She said something and a lock fell over her eyes. With a sweep of her fingers, a movement that was jarringly familiar, she slid it back in place and held out one arm in a gentle curve. A child stepped from the building into her embrace and thunked his forehead on her hip.

A boy—five, could easily be six, rangy-limbed and blond. This woman was his mother.

She said something to him and started up the boardwalk with him trudging wearily along beside her, his satchel dragging on the boardwalk.

They were headed straight toward Charles.

He stood with legs braced, heart slamming around in his chest, unable to breathe for several moments. All he could see was this woman and child, silhouetted against a blinding afternoon sun.

There was aching familiarity in her silhouette. He would have known her no matter what the distance.

Sweat popped from every pore on his body. Some dripped in his eyes. She looked up, her face a blur, then looked back down at her son.

They were getting closer.

He made an instantaneous decision, lunged for the nearest door, and shoved it open. A bell tinkled loudly, heralding his entrance for all as if someone had screamed, "Coward!" He slammed the door closed behind him, turned, and pressed close to the glass. He was breathing so hard he fogged the pane. He swiped at it just as they passed by. They didn't see him.

"Kate."

"I'm sorry, sir, what did you say?"

Charles spun around and blinked at the gorgeous redhead looking at him. "What?" He swallowed. "Nothing." His head jerked around. He still couldn't seem to catch his breath. "Hats," he said. He spotted the gaggle of women from the train in a far corner. A plump, apple-cheeked one met his eyes, smiled, and waved excitedly. Another glanced at him and giggled. They looked as if they had a patch of squashed cabbages on their heads.

"I'm Victoria Valentine."

"Yes—I know." He glanced at her, frowned, and worked a finger in the top of his collar. This town was too damned hot. The store smelled as if it was steeped in women's perfume. His thigh was throbbing. He couldn't seem to clear his head.

"So you know me, eh? I believe I would have remembered you." She was a stunner, even in that outrageous red dress with her hair all piled up on her head. She was nearly as tall as he, but slender as a reed, with ample bosom and hips and full lips painted the same color as her dress. She was smiling. Her eyes were green and glittering as if she found him mildly amusing.

"What?" he said again.

Her eyes narrowed, swept over him, his valise, then back up, and he felt at once as keenly sized up as he'd ever been by a client or another lawyer. "Are you looking for something special? Or are you lost? All you East Coast tenderfoots look the same.''

He shook his head. ''Yes—yes, that's it, thank you.'' Swiftly he left the shop.

He stood on the boardwalk looking east for several minutes. Kate had disappeared. He felt compelled to follow her but instead walked in the opposite direction. Curious, he paused outside the door of the building she'd come from. He touched the door handle. Was it still warm from her—or was it simply the heat of the day?

He hesitated a second, read the name over the door, and pushed it open. The place was sparsely furnished and hot. He'd stepped into a small vestibule. A door leading to another office was open.

He set his valise on a chair and drew his hat from his head. ''Douglas Murphy?''

''In here.''

Charles moved to the door. A man was coming around his desk toward him. He was almost as tall as Charles but a good forty pounds lighter, with graying hair and mustache and a tiredness around his eyes that reminded Charles of the overworked lawyers he'd known back in Boston. He had to wonder what kept Douglas Murphy so busy in a prairie town that looked as if it had no more than fifty residents.

Charles spotted the framed diploma on the wall. ''You're a Harvard law man,'' he said, meeting Murphy's gaze with a quirk of his lips.

Murphy froze, his hand outstretched toward Charles. His eyes did a quick summation of Charles's broadclothed torso, squeezed closed, then opened. ''Oh, Christ, not another one. This town's not big enough. Not enough people here to despise both me and you. The first lesson you learn out here is that no lawyer west of the Mississippi will ever be remembered as beloved.''

Charles clasped his hand, not surprised at the strength

in Murphy's handshake. ''We'll have to see about that, Murphy. I tend to recognize the rascalities of the profession. I do my best to avoid them.''

''I should have known. You have a look about you that screams jurisprudence. The East Coast variety. What the hell is a fella like you doing in my office?''

''I just got off the train from Laramie.''

''You should have kept on going. The only people who get off the train here are cattlemen and women looking for new hats. You don't much look like either.'' Murphy had drawn himself up, head slightly tilted back, eyes watchful. Curious or suspicious, it was impossible to tell, and it really didn't matter. ''No business in Laramie, eh?''

''Not interested.''

''What about back in Boston?''

''Tired of it. I'm considering relocating. Do you mind?'' Before Murphy answered, Charles slid into the chair set before the desk. It was then he noticed the scent in the air—a woman's—like an invisible hand was dribbling lilac petals throughout the room and the sun slanting through the side window was heating the scent.

Kate.

Murphy's chair scraped as he scooted behind his desk. He was looking at Charles very closely, as if trying to decide whether he could be trusted. ''You can't be thinking about hanging out a shingle.''

''Considering it.''

Murphy snorted. ''Here?''

''Don't you read your paper, Murphy? This town's full of enterprising people.''

''Right. I forgot.''

''That's according to the railroad prospectuses I saw in all the depots from Chicago to Omaha.''

''Haven't read one lately.''

"Something brought you out here. I'd say it was opportunity."

"Something like that. Everyone came west after the war ended."

"And why not? Out here it's all waiting to happen to a man, if he plays his cards right and buys land. Of course, he can get into some legal trouble along the way, the kind that ruins all his dreams and sends his wife and kids back east without him. The kind that would even keep a Harvard lawyer busy."

"I tend to spend more time catching horse thieves, to be honest with you." Murphy looked straight at him. "What's your angle?"

Charles shrugged. "Back east, it's all corporate finance. The focus is making money on top of money and deciding what the hell to do with it all when the company owner kills himself from all the pressure. After a while a man starts to wonder what he's doing with his life—if he matters any more. Out here, the rules don't apply. The stakes are much higher, morally. A man can make a difference."

"No philanthropies in Boston anymore?"

"Let's talk about the war that's being waged between the cattlemen and the sheepherders. Sounds like there's going to be enough work to keep at least two lawyers busy."

Murphy sat forward quickly. "There's not going to be a range war."

"The editor of the *Sentinel* might not agree with you. Or is all that just to sell more papers?"

"Hell is full of newspapermen who killed themselves blowing lies for some little one-horse town. 'Course it's no different in Boston—or Topeka—or even Virginia City. Folks are used to newspaper drama. Print's pretty powerful on the frontier. A good paper is mother's milk to an infant town. Keeps it thriving, particularly if the railroad comes through. You travel much?"

"Some."

"What are you looking for, gent?"

Charles steeled his gaze. "The right business venture."

Murphy seemed to go still. "A what?"

Charles's smile cut across his face like a pickax over a landscape of ice. "Something to sink some capital into. A dying enterprise, worth saving. You know of any?"

Murphy blinked. "I—well, I'll be goddamned."

"Is there a problem, Murphy?"

"No. No problem. Just wondering about life. It's strange sometimes."

"How so?"

"Oh, when opportunity falls out of the sky at just the right time, most people go to church and thank the good Lord for answering their prayers. I tend to get a little uneasy. For instance, here's this dandy East Coast attorney, looks mildly successful and must be if he's got capital to spare. A Harvard man, probably from some highbrow Boston law firm—"

"Lenox, Massachusetts, actually."

"Just closed up shop to come out here?"

"I have an associate who can manage things while I'm gone."

"Indefinitely."

"Perhaps."

Murphy looked even more dubious. "You're sitting here, covered in dust, and you want me to believe you're looking for something way the hell out in Crooked Nickel?" Murphy laughed under his breath. "You know most of the people in this town came out here to hide from something back east. You can disappear in a place like this."

Charles looked straight at Murphy. "I can understand that."

Murphy seemed to gnaw on this. "What happened to your leg?"

"Confederate ball at Bull Run."

"I was at Bull Run. The second battle. Under John Pope."

"I was with Porter. Your reinforcements."

A moment passed. The men stared at each other. "It was a hell of a loss," Murphy said finally.

Charles nodded slowly. "A ball in the leg isn't much, Murphy, considering."

"I know." Another moment passed. A clock in the vestibule seemed to tick louder. "Listen, gent—I'm having a hell of a time trying not to trust you."

"Quit trying so hard."

Murphy smiled fast then seemed to catch himself. "You want to make a difference? I've got a venture for you. There's one catch."

Charles waited.

"You're strictly the financing end of it. You stay out of the day-to-day operations. I'll be the man in the middle."

"For ten percent."

"Fifteen."

"What's the risk?"

Murphy shrugged. "Minimal. Fella who owns the paper needs help getting a new press."

"Mother's milk is going dry?"

"He's having a temporary financial setback. Union Pacific's backing him."

"So why not go to them?"

Murphy shook his head fast. "Uh-uh. The boys at the U.P. in Boston would fire an editor for breathing wrong. I like the fella. He's a good editor—actually a damned fine person. Doesn't deserve to lose it all over a bit of—you know—mismanagement."

"Gambling?"

"Something like that."

"Smarte, isn't it?"

Murphy seemed to hesitate a moment then nodded. "Right, Jonathan Smarte."

"He lives here in Crooked Nickel?"

"Uh, no—over near Laramie."

"But he writes the editorials."

"That's correct. Always has."

"Who runs the shop?"

"Fella named Gould runs the press, does the books, and tends to daily operations. Oh, Mrs. McGoldrick helps out with things occasionally."

"Mrs. McGoldrick. A woman meddles in a newspaper office?"

"She's Harry McGoldrick's widow. He founded the paper. Guess most folks tend to understand why she stays involved and they don't ask questions. Harry was killed about six months ago."

"Killed."

"Shot in the saloon down the street. Sheriff says it was an accident."

Charles studied Murphy, saw the glimmer in his eyes. There was some mystery here surrounding Harry's death. "So Harry McGoldrick found Jonathan Smarte."

"He left the paper to him."

"Lucky fellow, Smarte."

"Today he got even luckier, I'd say."

Charles leaned slightly over the desk. "One thing I would have to insist upon, Murphy, if I invest in the venture."

"What's that?"

"Anonymity."

Murphy cocked a brow. "That's easy, gent. I don't know your name."

"Charles Remington." He reached into his topcoat inside pocket and withdrew a leather billfold. "Smarte's—um, gambling problem—is that taken care of?"

"Just about. He's—uh—broken himself of the habit."

"And his debts?"

"Almost all paid off."

"Very good. Let's hope he keeps it that way. I wouldn't want Crooked Nickel to lose its paper—or its fine editor." He flipped open the leather and withdrew a bank draft. Reaching for the quill in its holder, he glanced at Murphy. "How much?"

"I—" Murphy swallowed. "But we haven't discussed terms, interest rate—"

"Whatever you think is fair, Murphy. You know the man. I trust you." Charles looked up and smiled uncompromisingly. "But you're still only getting ten percent."

Kate swiped her hands on the dishrag and blinked at Douglas Murphy standing on her doorstep. "What did you say?"

He smiled and lifted his brows. "I'll tell you again if I can come in out of the rain."

"Oh—God, of course—so sorry—please—sit—" She jerked back from the open door and offered Douglas a seat at the kitchen table. "Walt's sleeping but I'll make coffee—"

"Sit down, Kate. You want to hear this more than you've ever wanted to make coffee."

She turned and looked at Douglas. "Say it again, Douglas. You found an investor."

"I found an investor."

"I can't believe it happened so soon. Who is it—? No. I don't want to know."

"I know you don't. Sit down, Kate. You're making me nervous."

She slid into a chair opposite his at the table, clasped her hands, unclasped them, then fiddled with the lace doily in the center of the table as he withdrew a bundle of papers from his briefcase. ''How did you do it so quickly, Douglas?''

''You wouldn't believe me if I told you.''

''Whatever I can do to repay—''

''No, Kate. I won't listen to any of that. Here—'' He laid a page in front of her that read ''Contract'' at the top. ''Read this.''

Her eyes briefly scanned the print, then lifted to his. ''I don't have to. You wrote it. And you signed it.''

''Read it, Kate. Otherwise one day you might say I strong-armed you into signing it.''

''I would never say such a thing about you. Oh, fine. I—oh, Douglas.'' Her breath came out slowly, drying her mouth in an instant. ''It's for five thousand dollars. They're loaning me five thousand.''

Douglas leaned back in his chair, folded his arms over his chest, and shrugged. ''A nice, fat, round number. Think of it as a new press, past due debts, and two years' worth of working capital. Keep reading. The best part is coming.''

Her eyes flew, lips moving. ''Interest rate—''

''Yes, that's the part. Keep reading.''

''One percent, per annum.'' She frowned. ''That's fifty dollars a year. What sort of return on an investment is that to a person?''

''Not a very good one, you can be sure. But you know those philanthropists.''

Kate looked at him. ''I don't know any philanthropists. Someone from Denver, maybe?''

''I thought we agreed that their identity is to be a well-guarded secret, Kate. I intend to keep it that way.''

''Yes, of course. So do I—I think. Well, whoever it is, they must have good reason to want the paper to stay very much alive. They're giving me—'' She frowned at the page. ''Douglas, you made an error here. It says the loan is to be repaid monthly, in an amount up to the borrower's discretion but no less than fifteen dollars a month."

"It's no error. That's what it should say."

"At that rate I could be in this thing for a lifetime."

"Or longer. Upwards of fifty years, figuring roughly."

"Who is this person?"

"I told you, Kate—"

"Yes, you did. But the terms of the loan seem so—so—lenient."

"A gift."

"Yes, my thoughts exactly." Kate chewed at her lip and thought for a moment. Then she slid the contract toward Douglas. "I can't sign it."

Douglas stared at her. "For Chrissake, Kate—"

"Don't swear at me, Douglas. And lower your voice. Walt is sleeping. I told you, I can't sign it."

"And why not?"

"It's too good."

"All the more reason to pounce on it."

"This from a man who turns a cynic's eye on life? I don't think so."

"Kate, trust me, the world's worst cynic would sign this."

"It makes me uncomfortable . . . like I'm missing something."

"Like? The terms are all there, simple and straight forward. I composed the thing myself."

"It's what's not there that worries me."

"There's nothing to miss, nothing to hide. Trust me. This investor is purely motivated as far as I can tell, moral highbrow kind of thing. The paper is yours to run. So run it. This fella isn't going to interfere with that. Make the Union Pacific happy as all hell so they pay Jonathan Smarte what he deserves for his editorials. And then pay off the damned loan in a few years if the terms bother you so much."

"Yes, I could do that." Her fingers toyed with the edge of the page. Again, she chewed her lip. "Something about this doesn't feel right, Douglas. It feels like a trap."

His hand reached out and curved over hers. "Maybe things have been bad for you for so long you've forgotten what something good feels like. You're long overdue on opportunity. Don't let it pass you by. You deserve it. And so does Walt."

Instinctively, she glanced over her shoulder at the closed door to Walt's bedroom. The rain started to hammer on the roof. In another few minutes she would have to empty the bucket under the ceiling leak in her bedroom. She could tell by the deeper plopping sounds coming faster now from that back room. Yes, Walt deserved more than this, surely more than a mother torn by angst and despair over where her next meal would come from.

When she again glanced at the table a bank draft for five thousand dollars was sitting on top of the contract. The draft was made out to Katherine McGoldrick.

"Show me where to sign, Douglas."

Chapter 3

"Good morning, Mr. Gould." Kate laid a bank draft on top of the open ledger the clerk huddled over at his desk. She watched his ink-stained fingers lift the draft and his mouth gape open.

"Three weeks' back pay plus a week in advance," she said proudly. He was blinking at her from a narrow space between the bottom of his visor and the tops of his spectacles. She couldn't help the surge of satisfaction that brought a smile to her lips. "For your patience," she added.

Never one to overplay his hand at gallantry or gratitude, Gould nodded stiffly and with a slightly befuddled look, stuffed the draft into his shirt pocket. "Ma'am."

Kate reached for the stack of new mail in a basket on the corner of Gould's desk and began to leaf through it. "Anything of interest for Mr. Smarte?"

Gould again huddled over his ledger. "The usual. Past due bills and the half dozen threats to burn us down, run us out, horsewhip and lynch us if Mr. Smarte doesn't stop mentioning sheepherders in the same sentence as cattlemen."

"Elmer Pruitt's boys?"

"Judging by the misspellings, Mrs. McGoldrick, yes."

Kate studied one of the notes printed on the back of an old handbill. Its telltale scribble of almost indecipherable script had been written in what looked to be dark purplish-black ink. Or blood.

She stared at it and remembered the blood staining Harry's blue worsted-wool topcoat and pooling around his body as he lay on the floor of the saloon. By the time she'd gotten there the blood had turned this shade of dark purple-black. She'd never gotten the stains out of the front of the dress she'd been wearing when she'd thrown herself onto his lifeless body.

"That was nailed to the front door this morning," Gould said. After a moment, he added, "S'pose it's time we might wanna tell the Sheriff 'bout this, eh? If Harry were here he would."

Kate gave a brisk shake of her head. "Harry knew Gage was in Elmer Pruitt's back pocket. He still is. The only reason Gage is Sheriff is because Elmer Pruitt and the cattlemen made him one. Gage may patronize us but he won't help us."

"It's a dangerous game Smarte's playin', ma'am, printin' such inflammatory tripe."

"It's not tripe, Mr. Gould," Kate said sharply.

"Well, ma'am, I for one think Mr. Jonathan Smarte's stirrin' up trouble with the cattlemen for his own reasons."

"And I believe Mr. Smarte cares very deeply for the rights of those not given their due, Mr. Gould. We're just reporting the news. It's our duty."

"You don't know the man, ma'am. Nobody does."

"I know that he believes in the power of print, and in the unbending power of the truth. Harry knew that or he wouldn't have left the paper to him. Jonathan Smarte is upholding Harry's legacy." Her chest trembled as she drew a deep breath. "Harry didn't found the *Sentinel* to print lies and exaggerated tall tales that wouldn't make his paper worth the price of printing it. He left that to every other fool west of the Mississippi who dared to call himself a newspaperman. There's one in every town from Dodge City to San Francisco, Mr. Gould. Those kind of men bow to the threats. Those kind of men have long ago forsaken their ideals. Those kind of men will never make a difference beyond being propaganda machines.''

Gould looked up at her and they both knew what she didn't want to say. *Those kind of men don't get murdered in saloons for printing the exact truth.*

Gould cleared his throat and shrugged. ''Far as I can tell the U.P. brass in Boston is darned happy 'bout what we used to be printing, ma'am. Some would call that its own kind of propaganda.''

''It's always wise to keep one's boss happy, Mr. Gould. Jonathan Smarte believes he can without forsaking his ideals.''

''An easy enough thing to do, ma'am, when he's all safe and cozy in some big house in Laramie or wherever he lives an' we're here duckin' bullets.''

''No bullets have yet flown at this office. There's a reason Pruitt and his men are reacting to Smarte's editorials. We're doing what Harry would have wanted us to do. We're getting the truthful message out, Mr. Gould. It's only a matter of time before someone with enough influence will read it.''

''Influence?''

''Of the political sort, Mr. Gould. And not the hanging judge variety. I'm talking about legislation, the sort enacted by congressmen and governors with strong political agendas. That's what Harry's goal was. Not to fuel a war but to effect that kind of positive change for the sheepherders.''

''And in the meantime?''

Kate's back drew up stiff. ''We go to press with every editorial and every letter to the editor—the decipherable ones, that is.''

''And I learn to shoot a gun.''

"If need be, Mr. Gould. But I believe men who make threats like this are cowards."

"I hope you're right, ma'am. Because once they make good on even one of their threats, this paper will be without a clerk. It's my loyalty to Harry McGoldrick's memory that keeps me here, ma'am. He gave me a job when I needed it most—when I was struggling he believed in me—"

"Yes," Kate murmured thoughtfully. "He had a way of saving people and making them feel worthy when they needed it most. It was a rare gift—" After a moment, Kate went back to shuffling through the mail. The bills accumulating in a neat stack would be paid today. Every last one of them. And so would her balance due at the general store. She smiled when she envisioned the stunned look on the grocer's smug face. "Come now, Mr. Gould. I thought you were a man of the highest ideals. Cincinnati-born-and bred ideals if I remember correctly. Something about a crooked editor there who taught you the value of the moral high ground."

"Ideals suffer quick deaths in the face of a six-shooter."

Yes, they had once. She couldn't argue that. But if Harry had been tough enough to face his enemies, she was strong enough to vanquish them for him. "It's not going to come to that ever again, Mr. Gould—" Kate paused in her shuffling and studied one particular envelope. "What's this?"

Gould glanced up. "Came this morning. It was tucked inside the door. I didn't open it."

"It's addressed to the editor, Mr. Jonathan Smarte." She studied the handwriting, a bold but elegant script. They'd never received such a fine-looking piece of mail.

Gould peered at it. "Looks like it was written by an educated and influential sort—you know, some lawyer or politician type—"

Gould paused. His mouth stayed open. They looked at each other for a moment in complete silence.

Kate tore into the envelope. "Mr. Gould, do you think—do you possibly believe we might have finally reached the ear of someone who could help us? You said it. It could be from some politician."

"I—I—it could be, ma'am. Anything's possible."

"But probable. Is it likely? It's not altogether unlikely. Do you think? Harry always said luck happens to those who work the hardest. Harry believed in jumping at every opportunity. He told me opportunity is like a pear dangling in front of you, but you have to be smart enough to see it, then smart enough to grab at it and not be blind—hmmm."

"Ma'am?" Gould peered up over his glasses. "What does it say?"

"It says, 'Meet me at the Hotel St. Excelsior. Two o'clock today.' That's in less than an hour."

Gould snorted. "Tough to find Mr. Jonathan Smarte in Laramie in less than an hour."

"Smarte's not going. I am."

"Now hold on, ma'am. You're not going alone to meet some strange—"

Kate plunked the stack of bills in front of Gould. "Mr. Smarte would like you to pay these today, Mr. Gould."

"What?"

"In full." She steadied the black straw hat on her head, removed the pin and jabbed it in again. "Do close your mouth, Mr. Gould. You did hear me correctly?"

Gould's jaw snapped shut. "Yes, ma'am, but, ma'am, we're—that is, you're not—" Gould surged out of his chair, his chest puffing up enormously out of its typical sunken state. Kate almost expected him to thump on it with his fist for good measure. "Ma'am, I cannot allow you—a woman—to meet a perfect stranger in that louse-infected, flea-bitten excuse for lodgings."

"There are no other lodgings in town, Mr. Gould—well, there's Louella Lawless's boarding house—er—rather—house of ill—well, you know. No self-respecting man would choose Louella's place over lice."

"A sorry enough excuse. Ma'am, if Mr. Jonathan Smarte can't be here, I believe I should be the one to represent the paper . . . for your—your protection."

Kate beamed at him. "Why, Mr. Gould, look at you. You *are* a gentleman, aren't you?"

"Why—why—" Gould flushed clear to his receding hairline. "Why, of course, ma'am, I am."

"Good. Then as a gentleman you should heed a lady's wishes."

"Yes, a gentleman should."

"Very good. I'll be at the Hotel St. Excelsior. I shouldn't be long. I have to be home when Walter comes after school." She turned to the door.

"But, ma'am. There's the matter of money, or rather our lack of it."

"Mr. Winters at the bank will reassure you about that. I made a deposit with him on behalf of Mr. Smarte this morning. Five thousand to be exact."

"F-f-five—"

"Thousand. Yes."

"Ma'am. I'm beginning to get concerned."

Kate laughed and opened the door. "Good heavens, Mr. Gould, whatever for? We finally have enough money in the bank and possibly an influential ear interested in what we're saying. Why the devil should we worry? Have a good day."

The common room at the Hotel St. Excelsior resembled a saloon much more than it did justice to the hotel's grand and inspiring name. The floor was rough, unpolished wood, the walls faded crimson, the lighting insufficient, and the tables, to the very last, deserted. Behind a desk in one corner an oily-looking man sat studying a ledger and alternately scratching his head then picking at his teeth with the same grimy hand. He didn't glance up when Kate entered.

The clock ticking over his head read two o'clock.

"Excuse me," Kate said. "I'm to meet—that is—a gentleman arranged for a meeting here at two. But I don't see—"

The man's head jerked in a vague direction but he still didn't glance up. "Split Rail Creek."

"What?"

"He's over by the bridge at Split Rail Creek."

"The gentleman?"

"Yep. Looked like one, leastways. Guess the place didn't suit him well enough fer what he had in mind." With a deeply affronted-sounding grunt, the man let fly with a stream of brown goo that fell several inches short of the cuspidor set in the corner. "One gussied up and re-fined lookin' bastard, he was."

Kate's gloved fingers gripped around the edge of the desk and she leaned slightly nearer despite the foul odor that hung in the air around the man. "Did he say who he was?"

"Hell, no. Strolled in here yesterday, took one look at my rooms upstairs an' left. He arrived on the U.P. from Denver."

"Denver." Kate tried to ignore the sudden leap in her chest. She'd seen enough hard times and injustice in the last five years to doubt very much that luck had chosen this moment to shine on her, particularly given her luck with the investor just yesterday. This gentleman could be anyone. A visitor from back east. A railroad official.

A Denver politician . . . She could almost hear Harry whispering it to her, his face alight with buoyant, unflagging optimism. That optimism had helped him find tremendous success. That optimism had also made him blind to the threats. He hadn't believed that newspapermen could get killed for the words they wrote.

Kate did. And she was more of a cynic and a pessimist now than she'd ever been with Harry.

She thanked the man and quickly left, heading directly east along the boardwalk. She could feel the spirit in her step. She couldn't deny it. But hell and be damned, if by some small chance the man was a politician, it would feel glorious to know that the editorials she composed late into the evenings had reached someone. Harry's death would not have been for nothing.

She rounded the corner at the bank and picked up her pace. The bridge at Split Rail Creek, situated a good half mile from the center of town, was actually a rather unusual spot to choose for a business meeting given that it had long been a favorite hideaway for Crooked Nickel's lovers and young boys bent on mischief. The creek itself had nearly dried out, but the wooden bridge over it was nestled on a tree-lined lane that wound from the edge of town and disappeared into a sea of gold wheat that stretched as far as the eye could see to the south.

Obviously the gentleman wanted privacy, and a clean breath of air far away from the Hotel St. Excelsior. She could hardly blame him. That he'd arrived in town yesterday and hadn't stayed at the Hotel St. Excelsior gave her a few moment's pause. Louella Lawless's place provided the only other accommodations in town, unless one chanced his luck one stop farther up the line in Turkeyfoot Run, a far-flung chance at best in these parts.

Then again, Harry had often remarked that the more influential Denver politicians often found Louella Lawless types a bit hard to resist.

So the man had a few vices. She didn't need a saint. She needed a champion.

But her champion was expecting Jonathan Smarte. A

small problem, but one she felt confident enough to manage. She'd carried off the masquerade for six years. No one but Douglas Murphy knew the truth of it. No one, not even Mr. Gould, suspected that the infamous Jonathan Smarte was indeed Mrs. Kate McGoldrick.

And no one would ever suspect. More so now than ever before, Kate was bound and determined to protect this.

By the time she reached the bridge she was carrying her bonnet, her side was aching, her face flushed and hot, and a blister was smarting on her right little toe. Perspiration trickled down her chest. The bombazine had never felt so cumbersome and restricting.

She stepped onto the bridge and sighed through her teeth. Where was he? She scanned the thicket growing on either side of the creek. Sun blasted down on her head, pressing like a hot oven mitt. The scent of lilac water emanated from her skin with each hammer of her pulse.

Dammit if she'd been tricked. . . .

The cattlemen. Elmer Pruitt's threats echoed in her mind.

She knew an instant of panic and then—

"Hullo, Kate."

Chapter 4

She didn't turn around. It seemed forever that she stood there and to Charles the sound of the wind stirring the trees became almost deafening. He stared at her, strangely disbelieving that he had finally found her after six long years. There had been months of searching, hours of agonizing, sleepless nights tormented by thoughts that she might not have survived. There had been heaping self-doubts and anger—years of it, first directed at himself, then at her, then at Jude, then again at himself for not suspecting the truth of it. The sacrifices he'd made because of her loomed in his mind. It all stretched like an unbreachable chasm between them and yet, seeing her, he felt a joy and relief so profound he couldn't think of a thing to say.

And then she turned. He froze, one hand coming slightly up in a supplicating gesture as if even now he was afraid that she would again flee from him. He heard his breath come out in a soft burst as their eyes met and held for the first time in six years.

"Charles." It was a murmur of sound, a womanly voice spoken with a tremble of a smile, a disbelieving narrowing of soft green eyes, and the sight of her made his knees go liquid. She wasn't the Kate he remembered, the woman-child version of Kate he'd fostered in his mind for the last six years. Perhaps he'd never truly known her.

"Kate." He moved toward her, or was she moving toward him?—the space between them closing up and then they met in a hard jolt of an embrace and it was all he could do to keep his arms from crushing her. Her head brushed under his chin, her arms pressed close and warm around him, she made a soft noise against his chest, and he wondered if she could feel the frenzied pounding of his heart or could imagine the lump lodged between his chest and his throat. He closed his eyes and felt as he imagined a person would if he'd suddenly been released from a prison.

The questions that had tormented him remained mercifully at the edges of his mind. He didn't want to ask them, didn't want to know the answers, didn't need to know her reasons. For now it was enough that she was safely in his arms, close against his heart.

Memory flooded over him, images of holding her like this over the years, of her looking up at him with tears in her eyes and a bloodied knee. He'd always been there to comfort her. But she wasn't a child anymore. The Kate in his arms was a woman, full grown. There was a band of gold encircling her left ring finger.

Mrs. McGoldrick.

His Kate, all dressed up in a widow's clothes and a woman's too-ripe body. His heart seemed to twist in his chest. Six long years had passed. Six years of a life unshared.

His hands moved, cupped her shoulders, felt the womanly fragility of her and he realized that in all the times he'd touched, held, and comforted her, he'd never done so as a man does with a woman.

His body registered this with a mild implosion of disbelief and yearning.

"No—I—please—" She pushed and turned and was

out of his arms, just beyond his reach, swiping and sniffing and keeping her head down and half turned away. "I can't believe—I—" She shook her head, swiped again at her cheeks, and looked up at him. "I can't believe you're here—you're standing right here."

"I am." His chest was expanding so far, so deeply, it ached. His arms were aching too, aching to feel her again. He kept swallowing over that lump in his throat, swallowing and blinking and staring at her. She was at once the most dear and familiar friend to him as she was a perfectly wondrous new stranger. How could he keep the questions from crowding into his mind, forcing rational thought, forcing the truth of it all into the open? There was a horrible inevitability to it all. At some point they would stop staring and the talking would have to start.

"You—" Her lips parted with a rush of breath then tweaked into a fleeting smile. "You look so well, so—" Her eyes moved over his face, his hair, the width of his chest and shoulders as if registering all the changes in him with an almost childlike wonder. "Older," she murmured with that heart-twisting curve of her full lips. As a child her mouth had made her impish. As a woman, it made a man think of things better left until much, much later.

"We've all changed, Kate." He could feel his body tensing up, could almost feel the questions flooding back into his brain. The words were out before he could think to take them back or even think if they were the proper words to start it all. "You should have written."

She looked down at her hands, at the ring of gold. Her voice was small, half whispered, half tossed out over the yellow prairie. "I know. I think about it and I know I should have let someone know but—" She shook her head again, then lifted her chin, and he saw a determination in her gaze that he'd never seen there before. He wondered for the hundredth time about the hardships she must have faced in the last six years—and the inevitable scars they'd left behind. "I couldn't, Charles. It was wrong but it was—it was all I could do."

"Kate—" His own voice sounded strangely husky and felt thick, like the words couldn't come out. "Have you any idea? We searched—I—" *Agonized. Prayed.*

"Yes—" Her eyes strayed over his shoulder, clouded. "I think about Grandmother Remington every day—I think of all of you. Tell me, is she—is she well?"

"She died six months ago."

She looked down again. Her shoulders moved, slightly hunching, and he wondered if she too felt the painful constriction of her insides like he did just looking at her. Another swipe of her fingers over her cheek. Another sniff, a delicate shrug that perhaps was meant to stave off the grief. He took a step toward her but she turned and gripped the rail of the bridge so hard her knuckles whitened. She was looking down with a wistfulness that made him ache to know all her secrets, every last detail of the years she'd spent away from him.

"Somehow I suspected she was gone," she said quietly. "I never got to say good-bye—even when she asked me to—but, Charles, it seemed at the time—I don't suppose you can imagine but sometimes certain choices seem like the only paths open to us and then looking back—"

"Do you look back, Kate? Do you think maybe you should have stayed?"

"No." She looked up quickly and her voice rang deep and low with passion and determination. "No. I did the best given the circumstances. I know that now."

The questions were pouring into his mind. "The best you could was not to leave the home and family who loved and cared for you, Kate." The tone in his voice was challenging. His own passion was seeping through the outer shell of restraint he'd forced himself to erect. The betrayal he'd suffered was rearing its head and he didn't want it to.

Her eyes never strayed from his. Her chin didn't waver. Neither did her conviction. "I explained that in my letter."

"Ah. You ran off to Europe with that—what was his name again?"

She blinked, had the good sense to flush, clear up to her hairline, but didn't turn away. "I—I believe I've forgotten."

He was standing close enough to smell her every time the wind blew. Lilacs. She'd smelled of lilacs the night she'd left them all in Lenox. The vision of her seated at the piano that night had haunted him ever since. The sight of her now seemed to feed, fill, and sustain him, even as it tortured him. "You never went to Europe with William Frye, Kate?"

"No, I didn't." Their eyes met, held, and the air between them was suddenly charged with a tension that seemed completely out of place between them. Her eyes narrowed slightly, softened, and his chest ached with the injustice of it. They'd been so close for ten years. But in six years they'd become virtual strangers. So much still unsaid—

"Tell me—how is the rest of the family, Charles? Mother Remington, Mary Elizabeth—"

Jude.

He felt the tension work over his features. His eyes followed the flight of a hawk for several moments. "Mother and Mary Elizabeth are still at the house in Lenox. They're both well but I have someone caring for them. It's impossible for Mother to see to Mary Elizabeth by herself anymore, though she insists she could."

"Yes, of course. Does Mother Remington still sit by the fire?"

"She refuses to replace the chair even though it's badly worn."

"And Mary Elizabeth sits at her side?"

''Yes. Just as she always has. And no matter the weather, Mother always requires a fire, and tea in her best porcelain.'' He watched her closely, the twitch of her lips, the far-off warming look in her eyes, the underlying sadness in her. She seemed to hunger for tales of the home she'd left and the people she'd loved and felt she had to betray. The loss she'd allowed herself to suffer was enormous. Only a cataclysmic event would have made her run away in the middle of the night. A betrayal so complete . . .

''Mother Remington never tired of Mary Elizabeth,'' she said. ''Isn't it strange what a mother can endure for the sake of her child?''

Charles watched her and remembered the stories he'd read in all the frontier newspapers as he'd searched for some clue about her. There had been tall tales, tales of hardship, tales of woe, tales of joy and sadness, new life and meaningless death. Kate had the face of an innocent angel but her eyes held the wistfulness of a person who'd seen far more than she ever would have in the cozy confines of Lenox.

''And Jude? How is he?''

The question startled him. ''Jude.'' He looked at her and felt a new pain in his chest, an anguish and regret so profound he could taste the bitterness on his tongue. Jude. There were questions that begged to be asked.

''Jude is in Boston,'' he said.

''Did he marry?''

''I don't believe he will.''

''I see. And you? How is your wife—your family?'' Her smile was slight, her eyes huge and shining and curious and utterly unfathomable.

''I—that never came off.''

She said nothing, just looked at him.

He cleared his throat, shifted his shoulders, and looked her square. ''I realized that that would have been a mistake.''

She looked away again, her face a beautiful unreadable mask.

''Who was the man you married?''

Her lips softened and something twisted in his gut. ''Harry. Harry McGoldrick. He was a newspaperman from Denver. He died six months ago—suddenly.'' Again she looked down at the ring on her finger and seemed a hundred miles away from him. She must have loved Harry McGoldrick very much to have forgiven a mountain's worth of gambling debts.

The collar felt suddenly tight at his neck.

''He founded the paper and let me write as Jonathan Smarte. Do you remember Jonathan Smarte, Charles?''

He took a step nearer. His voice came deep from his chest. ''Do you think I would forget?''

She looked up at him. ''No, I don't suppose either of us will forget him. That's how you found me, isn't it?''

''I searched every paper from every town from Boston to San Francisco. I actually couldn't believe it when I saw the name. I knew it had to be you.''

''You were always very smart, Charles.''

''I know you're a writer. Like me.''

''Yes. Just like you. That won't ever change, will it?''

No, it wouldn't. But they had.

''It was a blind man's guess, Kate. I tried everything to find you.''

''You didn't tell anyone—?'' Something flickered across her face, an expression so fleeting, yet so intense it took him a moment to name it. Fear.

''No,'' he said quickly. ''No one knows why I came. I told my assistant I was coming west to Crooked Nickel for business in case he needed to contact me. I also told the woman seeing after Mother and Mary Elizabeth. I doubt any of them would suspect.''

''Why now, Charles, after all this time?''

"I don't give up easily, Kate."

"I can't go back to Boston with you, Charles. Please don't ask me. I have a new life now."

"I can see that."

"When are you returning?"

"Returning?"

"Yes, to Boston. Soon?"

"I wasn't planning on it, soon or otherwise."

"What?" Her lips parted then quickly compressed as if she gave great thought to masking her emotions. "I see."

"I might stay on awhile in Crooked Nickel," he said.

She blinked quickly. "I—" She swallowed and seemed to get a shade paler. "I'm pleased that you'll be here and we can get reacquainted. It seems strange somehow—"

"Very strange."

"To know you and yet know so little about you now—"

"Almost like strangers."

Her smile was brief. "Familiar strangers." Her hand slid over the bridge rail toward him. "Did I tell you how good it is to see you, Charles?"

His fingers reached, touched hers, intertwined. "Tell me again, Kate."

She laughed low, husky, withdrew her hand and yet there was a flirtatious undertone to her that stoked Charles's basest passions, perhaps because she seemed almost unaware of it. "What would you want to stay in Crooked Nickel for, Charles?"

"Business."

"In Crooked Nickel?"

"There's a range war brewing, Kate. At least that's what your paper leads me to believe. It is your paper to own, run, and write for?"

"Harry was very generous with me."

"And you were obviously quite capable."

"He gave me opportunity when there were no others.

He—'' She paused, for a moment lost in thought. ''No one in the town knows—well, except my friend Douglas Murphy.''

''We've met.''

She looked sharply at him.

''It seems we were both at Bull Run. And at Harvard. I thought it best to stop in and see the local attorney, let him know he might have a bit of competition.''

''I see.'' She seemed to ruminate on this a moment. ''Everyone else in town believes Jonathan Smarte owns the paper, runs it, writes the editorials.''

''Your secret is safe with me, Kate. You know that.''

''I—'' She stared at him a moment with almost grim concentration. ''Yes, I suppose I should know that.''

''You've done well for yourself, Kate. Little wonder you don't want to come home.''

''I've made a new home here.''

''It's as good a place as any. Certain accommodations in town are as good as any I could find between here and Denver.''

Her expression flattened. ''Where are you staying?''

''A boarding house in town. Clean beds. Decent food. No bugs and a friendly enough staff.''

''Louella Lawless's place?''

''Yes, that's the one.''

Lips pinched, parted, blossomed full again. ''I see.'' She blinked several times. ''I think you should know that rumor has it Louella Lawless—''

''I already know.''

Her jaw clicked shut. ''I see.''

''Are you pleased that I'm here, Kate?''

She frowned slightly then laughed. ''Why do you say that? I'm perfectly pleased that—'' She froze. ''Oh, no, what time is it? No, oh, God, I'm late.''

He caught her arm when she would have stomped right past him. "What is it?"

"Walter. He'll be home from school and I promised I'd be there. My—" She looked right up at him, her eyes deep green pools of uninhibited emotion. It was the first display of anything from her that wasn't guarded. "He's my son, Walter McGoldrick."

"Then I should meet him."

She stared at him and he thought he saw regret in her eyes. "Yes. Perhaps you should."

"Lead on, Kate." He set off after her.

Walter was sitting on the front stoop of her white clapboard house at the edge of town when Kate arrived, winded, hot, sweaty, and very eager to be home with her son. Even if it meant that Charles would be putting his well-heeled feet up on Louella Lawless's velvet-tufted ottomans. She needed time to think, time to compose herself, time to reconcile her joy at seeing him again with the fears hovering around her like ghosts. Yes, like ghosts from the past she'd never intended to confront again.

What was he doing in Crooked Nickel?

"You're late," Walter announced, shoving a forearm over his eyes, sniffing in deeply, and getting to his feet. His jaw gave a belligerent thrust and he blinked up at her. "You promised."

"I know." Kate pulled him close against her hip and felt him wipe his face back and forth against her skirt. "But I had to meet someone and—"

"You're always late." Walter was craning his head and peering around her.

Kate frowned. "Not always." Something prickled at the back of her neck. Instinct. Charles was listening and watching very closely.

"Let's go inside," she said.

Walter resisted her nudge. "Who's that man?"

"Charles Remington. He's the man I had to meet. Walter, say hullo."

Walter said nothing and buried his face deeper against her.

"Hullo, Walter." Charles's voice seemed to vibrate through Kate. She felt him behind her. Or maybe it was just the sun's heat blasting off the dusty street, pulsing into her back, through sweat-dampened bombazine, and into her skin.

Charles was here. And she felt it and felt him as if she'd suddenly been roused from a six-year slumber.

She hadn't thought about him in a long time. Maybe she'd forced herself not to. She'd married Harry and immersed herself in raising Walter, keeping a home and her editorials. Yes, it had been a relatively easy thing to do—forgetting his face, the sound of his voice, the startling blue of his eyes, the love she'd felt for him—by burying her gold-spun dreams of youth and fairy-tale love in a marriage that was responsible, mature, comfortable, and easy. She'd never questioned how much gratitude had played a hand in her love for Harry. She'd loved him as best she could and was a good wife to him. They'd shared dreams and ambitions, occasionally shared a bed, and they'd shared Walter. Harry had given her direction and a home and a father for her unborn child. Surely that was enough. Surely she would have betrayed him if she'd allowed herself thoughts of another man.

She'd thought the wanton in her had died that night in the Remington's orchard. She'd been certain when she'd lain content beside Harry. And she'd been almost pleased about it.

Charles grasped Walter's hand. "Pleased to meet you, Walter."

Kate watched her son's grubby fingers get swallowed by Charles's broad hand. There was something inherently intimidating about his presence, something that made keeping any secrets from him rather foolish and pointless. Charles Remington always knew or suspected far more than he ever revealed.

Walter turned his face full into the sun and looked straight up at Charles. He was the image of his father, Jude.

The gold cufflink at Charles's wrist winked up at her in the sunlight. It was an elegantly attired wrist, as elegantly attired as the man, from his suit and shirt, down to the polished boots. An influential-looking man, indeed. Influential. Powerful. Clever. And in that instant she knew a fear so consuming she felt her stomach turn itself over.

Afraid—of the man she'd once thought she loved.

"Please—" Her voice sounded strangled. "In, Walter. Let's go. Get your satchel." She took his arm and felt him go limp as a sack of flour.

"But, Mama—"

"In. Now." She nudged him along to the door, fumbled with the key in the lock and finally shoved the door open. She pushed Walter in ahead of her, took one step inside, turned abruptly around, and bumped her nose on Charles's chest.

He'd followed her into the house.

His hands were on her upper arms. When she moved to step back he kept her there. "This is where you live," he said.

"Yes, it's—" Hot. Too damned stuffy and hot especially since all she could smell was him and his starchy shirt. She didn't want to look up at him. She felt his chin brush the top of her head and the tips of her breasts touch his chest.

She closed her eyes and lifted her fists to push against him. Dammit, he was not Jonathan Smarte. She was not

Maggie Swifte. Nor was she the naive young girl who'd imagined that torrid, tempestuous love existed between them. She was a woman now. She was responsible. She had a son to protect, a new life to lead, sheepherders to champion, and Harry's death to avenge. *She would not fall victim to her own romantic delusions ever again.*

His finger touched her chin, tilting it up, forcing her eyes up to his. "It's so good to see you, Kate," he said.

"Yes," she managed in a voice that sounded like a breathless plea. *Yes?* When every instinct was shouting that he'd come for reasons as yet unknown? When instinct was telling her that he was in some way a threat?

He gently released her and watched her with blue eyes hooded and brows severely set.

Like a predator. No. He'd always had that look about him. Six years ago she'd have labeled it determination and noble responsibility. Now—now she had secrets to keep and protect.

"We'll be seeing each other, Kate." He gave the briefest nod, a quirk of his lips, turned, and left the house.

"What's wrong with his leg? He walks funny."

Kate didn't realize she stood in the open doorway watching Charles walk away until Walter tugged on her hand.

"He was shot," she said.

"With a bullet?" Walter asked, sounding as obviously impressed by this as the average man would be.

"Yes. It's still in his thigh. It always will be. That's why he walks funny."

"Where's he staying, Mama? At the hotel?"

"No." She felt her teeth press together and reached out and slammed the door. The small house seemed to shake on its foundation.

"He's big," Walter said. "Bigger than my pa was."

"Yes, much bigger."

"And kind of mean looking."

"He's always looked like that."

"Have you known him a long time?"

"Yes. From years ago."

"I want him to stay with us."

"God, no. He can't."

"Why not?"

"Because I said so."

"Why?" He followed her through the kitchen and into her room at the rear of the house.

The shades were drawn against the sun but the air was stuffy, thick, and unmoving. Her fingers moved on the top buttons at her neck. "Please, Walter, out. Mama needs to change."

"I don't want to. I want to talk about Mr. Renton."

"Remington."

"I can't say that."

"Yes, you can." It was his name. Walter Remington McGoldrick. It was his blood. It made him half *theirs,* and only half hers. A trembling kind of scared feeling gathered in the pit of her stomach. "Out please, Walter, just for a minute."

"I don't want to." He set his jaw, stared her down, and looked so much like Jude she felt tears of helpless confusion burning in her eyes.

"Now—please—don't make Mama yell."

"You always yell." He thumped the door closed behind him.

Always yell. Always late. What sort of mother . . .

The buttons seemed to resist her tugs. Her fingers grew slippery. Sweat trickled down her brow. A droplet fell from her lashes. Her room felt confining, like a prison. She saw the bed with its white coverlet, the bed that she and Harry had shared, the bed in which she now slept alone. On the night table beside it sat a stack of pages, the editorials she was determined to print. This was how she spent her evenings.

She tugged at the last of the buttons. The fabric clung to her damp skin. The narrow sleeves bit into her flesh as she struggled to peel her arms free.

She twisted, groaned, and stepped free of the dress. She turned, braced her hands on her dresser, and found herself staring into her mirror. She was breathing as if she'd just run the distance from the bridge as fast as she could. She met her eyes and saw in them the look of a wild animal caged for far too long.

She stood straight up and drew in a steadying breath. The knot of hair on top of her head had slid halfway over to one side. Some hung in wisps down her back, wet and plastered to her skin. Her white cotton shift was damp, her skin shiny, pink, and pulsing. She stared at the nipples clearly outlined by the wet fabric. She touched one and it sprang up taut against the cotton. She touched the other then pulled the ribbon loose at the top of the undergarment and worked the tiny buttons open. Straps slid from her shoulders. One shrug and the chemise fell to her waist.

She pressed her fingertips to the base of her throat and felt her hammering pulse. Her fingers traced down from her throat, over her breastbone, into the valley of her bosom, and beneath one breast. Her eyes closed. Lips parted, she brushed her thumb over one nipple.

''Mama.'' A thunk came on the door. ''Hurry, Mama. I'm hungry.''

''I'm coming.'' She turned from the mirror, opened her armoire, and reached for another dress among a row of black bombazine.

Chapter 5

"You wanna swipe up the rest of that grease with some bread or you done?"

Charles nudged his plate away with his thumb and folded his napkin next to it. He glanced up at the young barmaid and nodded. "You can take it. Good meal."

The girl leaned over the table to reach for his plate. She kept her eyes on his, not on the plate, and he presumed this had to do with her wanting him to notice that her breasts were jumping out of the top of her dress.

She was blond, mildly attractive, astonishingly built, and couldn't have been more than thirteen. He gave a regretful smile. Obviously misinterpreting, she grinned and showed a mouthful of half-rotten teeth. He felt a stab of pity and reached for his drink. It was the first whiskey he'd tasted since he'd left Boston that wasn't half watered-down.

She glanced quickly toward the bar where a bald, mustached barkeep with massive forearms dried glasses. Above his head hung an oil painting of a naked woman reclining on a scarlet divan. She was white-skinned and chestnut-haired. One small hand touched a spot between her breasts. The other touched the shadows between her plump thighs. Charles looked into those painted eyes and thought of Kate.

"I can show my titties to ya fer a dollar," the girl offered as she moved around the table. "You can touch 'em fer two dollars. Anythin' more an' we'll have to go out back.''

Charles caught her wrist just as her hand dove between his spread thighs. ''I'm not interested.''

She gave a girlish giggle. ''That's what all the politicians say when they first come in. An' they don' mean a word of it.''

''I'm not a politician.''

''Ya look like one. Or a gambler. Them gamblin' men wear all black, jest like you do. So do the preachers. But you don' look like no preacher fella to me.''

''How old are you?''

Her chin inched up. ''I'll be fourteen in four months.''

''Where's your mother?''

Her face went hard. ''My pa came home from the war without his legs and kilt her when she got herself another man. Then he kilt himself. I come here an' Miss Louella found me.'' She wriggled her hand. ''Whatcha got hidin' down there in yer pants, mister—?''

''Excuse me, Goldie?''

The girl froze and lifted wide eyes up over Charles's head. Her face paled instantly. It was then that Charles noticed the purple-green bruise circling her left eye. The make-up had been more liberally applied to the area but the bruise was still slightly visible.

''Yes, ma'am?'' the girl said.

''Zeke needs help in the kitchen.''

Goldie eased away from Charles. ''Yes, ma'am. All right, ma'am.''

''You have trouble remembering what we talked about.''

''I know I sometimes do, ma'am. Please let me stay out here, ma'am.''

''Go now. We'll talk again later.''

''Yes, ma'am.'' She turned.

"Take the gentleman's plate, Goldie."

"Oh—yes, ma'am." Goldie reached for the plate, knocked it to the edge of the table and almost into Charles's lap. Looking horrified, she blubbered an apology, grabbed it in two shaking hands, and scurried away, disappearing through swinging double doors behind the bar.

"She's a bit too anxious," the woman said. "But she can be trained."

She moved around him and into the chair opposite. She smiled and when Louella Lawless smiled she was something just this side of beautiful. But she was quite obviously a business woman. Experience and seeing too much of the seamy underside of life had left a telltale mark on her. Charles sensed that beneath the painted and powdered mien, and the sophisticated facade, she was bone tired.

She wore her jet black hair on top of her head in a severe and elegant style. Her dress was ivory silk and brocade, its neckline demure and tasteful, yet the gown had obviously been cut to accentuate her ample charms and whippet-narrow waist. Diamonds bobbed at her ears and around her neck and wrists. She wouldn't have looked out of place at any highbrow Boston soiree, her cultured voice included.

The common room and bar area of her boarding house were as sumptuously appointed as any top-drawer, East Coast hotel. It was still early evening. Louella's place was relatively deserted. From another room came the sound of a piano tinkling.

Charles glanced at several of the women who were watching them from nearby settees. He wondered how many of them were thirteen like Goldie. Again, he gulped from his glass.

Louella glanced at the barkeep, and nodded. In moments, a stunning redhead in emerald silk delivered another whiskey to Charles and a glass of what looked to be the same for Louella. The redhead gave Charles a lingering glance, a demure smile, and moved away.

Charles watched her bustle swish across the floor then looked at Louella. She was watching him steadily.

"Fifty dollars and she can be yours for the evening. She's the very best."

"She's serving whiskey."

"She's wanted to meet you since you came in here looking for a room the other night. Her name is Isabelle. I promise, Mr. Remington, you would like her so much you would want to buy her."

The whiskey left a fiery trail deep into Charles's stomach. "I'm afraid not tonight."

"You want her younger? She's only seventeen." Her laugh was husky, all-knowing. "All you politicians like the young ones. I have a virgin, if you want. I found her just last week. She ran away from an orphanage in Denver. She's the blonde in the corner."

Charles glanced at the girl. She looked like a child painted up and dressed in her mother's gown, no more than ten years old. He made no attempt to hide his scowl. "I'm not a politician, dammit. And I'm not interested."

Louella smiled. "That's what all the lawyers out here used to say. But I got them to change their minds. Now, I couldn't stay in business without their patronage. They come from as far as Abilene and Virginia City and all points in between, married and otherwise. Judges, congressmen, greenhorn lawyers, even U.S. Cabinet members. Indeed, Mr. Remington, because of my relationship with influential politicians, a Union Pacific spur was put out this way."

"Yes, it would be difficult for the U.P. to buy up government land for nothing without connections in Congress."

"I believe it's men doing one another a favor. This politician needed a quick way to get from Laramie up here to see me in Crooked Nickel. So he wrote to several of his Union Pacific friends and the spur was added from the main line. The cattlemen will tell you otherwise. They think it's their business that keeps the railroad alive out here. They also think it's their business that makes the world go around. I won't try to change their minds. But I know better."

"A wise course, madam."

"I try to be a wise woman, Mr. Remington. It's never good business to cross one's best customers."

Charles's brows lifted. "The cattlemen?"

Louella's nostrils flared slightly. "Even I need regulars, Mr. Remington. Everyone's welcome so long as they obey my rules. Several have difficulty with that sometimes. They think this is a run-of-the-mill bordello. They act like it at times. That's why I have Ace over there behind the bar. And Zeke in the back. They take care of the things a woman can't on her own."

She didn't seem the sort of woman who needed any taking care of.

"Besides, their money's the same color as yours." She seemed to melt into her smile and he realized she could be quite charming. "They just like to spend their's a bit more than you."

"It depends what I'm buying," Charles said.

Louella sipped her whiskey. "You're not married."

"That's not the reason I'm not buying."

Louella gave that husky laugh. "A man who looks like you? She must be quite something. Ah—" Her eyes narrowed on him. "You came to find her. No one comes to this town who isn't looking for something . . . or running from something."

"Just thinking I might hang out a shingle."

This time her laugh was big and genuine. "Mr. Remington, the prerequisites of a fine frontier attorney are flowery language, knowledge of a few Latin phrases, and a God-given gift to act. Law degrees matter very little. He must be capable of leading an entire jury into sobbing over the fate of a stolen horse or cow. He must be able to paint innocents as villainous liars and cheats and do it with such flamboyant oratory that guilt or innocence no longer matters. He does not suffer over the fates of virgin orphans. Now—'' Louella inclined her head and gave him a piercing look. ''I don't think you've come here for business.''

Charles gulped the last of his drink. ''Good night, Louella.'' He gave a brief nod of his head, stood, and met the eyes of the redheaded Isabelle. She was standing against the wall, arms down and pressed flat to the wall, head slightly turned, watching him with sloe eyes. She was tall, slender, bosomy, gorgeous, and interested.

He turned and was halfway to the stairs and the solitary peace of his room when the front door opened and several men entered, followed shortly by another. Charles wouldn't have paused to notice the men had it not been for the sudden crash that came from behind the bar, a crash that coincided with the arrival of these men. He saw Goldie standing over a tray of broken glass at her feet. Ace, the barkeep, said something to her. She shook her head, gave him a terrified look, then spun around and darted through the swinging double doors.

''Gentlemen, welcome.'' Louella's greeting seemed to encompass all of them but her focus was plainly on the taller of the three, a well-dressed gentleman with a close-cropped graying beard, elegant clothes, and a tall, white, broad-brimmed hat. She murmured something to him, touched his sleeve, smiled, and followed his gaze as it swept about the room full of women. He bent his head to Louella and they exchanged a few words. Louella nodded and their attention at once settled on Isabelle. The girl seemed to hesitate.

Louella escorted the man just into the room, where Isabelle met him.

The smile Louella then turned on the other two men was distinctly less warm. They'd obviously come together, and the distinguished gentleman alone. The two wore the broad-brimmed hats and prosperous paunches that marked them as successful cattlemen.

One gave Charles a suspicious but dismissing sweep of his eyes, shoved his hat back on his head, hooked his thumbs in his belt loops, and jerked his chin at Louella. "'Evenin', Miz Lawless."

"Mr. Pruitt." She looked at the other man. "Virg. Your preference this evening, Mr. Pruitt?"

Pruitt stuck out his jaw and jerked it at the bar. "I don' see her."

"She's not available tonight."

Pruitt shoved his hand into his pocket. "I'll pay extra."

"Indeed, Mr. Pruitt. You're one of my best customers."

Pruitt gave a greasy smile. "You know how I like 'em, Miz Lawless. The younger, the greener, the better."

"Then I have someone special for you tonight." Louella touched his sleeve, murmured something to him, and he dug deeper into his pocket. He quickly peeled off five bills and flicked at his lips with his tongue. Louella turned and looked straight at the young virgin in the corner.

Something inside Charles went cold. The words were out before he could stop them. "No."

Pruitt glared daggers at him. "Huh?"

"Put your money away, Mr. Pruitt," Charles said, looking straight at Louella. "I believe the girl is mine."

"Yours?" Virg squawked. "Ain't none of these wimmin belongs to nobody. Not even to Dan Goodknight over there an' he's got more money'n head a cattle than even Elmer here does." Virg jerked his chin at the bearded gentleman sitting at a table with Isabelle.

"The hell he does," Pruitt snarled. "I've got more head than any other cattleman in the state."

"I ain't countin' the ones what you stole."

"Shut up," Pruitt spat.

Charles caught the arm of the young girl as she approached, keeping her at his side. Beneath his hand he felt her trembling. She barely came up to his waist. He looked deep into Louella's worn and world-weary eyes and prayed he'd correctly gauged her dislike for Pruitt. "You can name your price."

Louella's eyes shifted from the girl to Charles. "Make it the usual, Mr. Remington."

"The usual?" Pruitt snarled in elevating tones. "Goddammit, I wanna buy myself a virgin whore."

Louella paled. "Mr. Pruitt, lower your voice."

"The hell I will. I want that virgin whore standin' right there."

"Mr. Pruitt." Louella's voice was a hiss. "I will ask you to leave."

"Leave?" Pruitt's eyes bulged from his head. "Goddammit, no fancy slut's gonna throw my ass outta her place. No gussied-up bastard's gonna steal my—hey! Hey, wait just a goddamed minute. Who the hell are you?"

Ace, the bartender with the bulging forearms, appeared, lifted Elmer Pruitt out of his boots with one arm and dragged him toward the front door.

"You can't do this!" Pruitt barked, boot tips dragging. "You know who I am! Nobody does this to me an' gits away with it! I'll bet you got them bastard sheepherders in here with ya. I can smell their slimy sheep shit boots from here ta—"

Ace threw open the door and tossed Elmer Pruitt out into the street like a sack of garbage. Virg scurried after him like an obedient puppy. Gently, Ace closed the door, nodded at Louella, and went back into the bar.

Louella swung bared teeth on Charles. "I don't like to make enemies."

"He's mine to worry about. Not yours."

"Elmer Pruitt can make trouble. I'm not talking about mischief. I mean bad trouble."

"You sound scared, Louella."

Louella seemed to draw herself up. "If I am it's with good reason. You think I'm nice to assholes because I like them? It's business. It's called protecting myself. Only a fool courts trouble. Look at the mess brewing over at the *Sentinel.* Mr. Jonathan Smarte's going to get his place burned down or worse."

"Worse?"

"Someone else is going to get killed over those editorials. And it's just words. You'd think they'd have learned."

Charles stared hard at her. "What do you mean someone else?"

"Harry McGoldrick didn't die by accident"—she dropped her voice, looked quickly at Dan Goodknight—"though that's just rumor. But I'm a smart woman and I know what Harry was printing about the cattlemen in his paper. Two days later he's dead in the saloon. An accident, of course. Or self-defense. It always is, you know."

"No, I don't know."

"Harry didn't carry a gun, Mr. Remington. A whiskey bottle, yes. But never a gun. He made enemies out of the wrong people for telling the truth about what they were doing, and he paid a price. I don't want that to happen to me. I'm certain you understand."

"Yes, Louella, I do." Charles inclined his head at the girl. "Get her cleaned up and put to bed. I'll take care of her tomorrow, along with the particulars."

Louella quirked a brow. "As you wish. But you can't clean up this place, Mr. Remington. Out here there's always more bad than good. It's no place for fancy East Coast idealism. Mine died the day I got here. Yours will too, if you stay long enough."

Charles bid her good night and made his way up the stairs.

Sleep was a long time in coming.

Chapter 6

"What the devil are you doing in there?"

Kate blew at a tangle of hair that had fallen past her eyes, and then she pushed herself up and out of the upside-down pits of her press. Swiping ink-stained hands on the apron tied at her waist, she glanced at her friend Victoria Valentine. In her pale yellow sheath dress with matching feathered hat and fringed parasol Victoria looked like a tall glass of French lemonade.

"This press is old enough to be preserved as a curiosity," Kate said. "I'm almost positive that mice have burrowed in the balls. There are no rules left, no leads, and the types are all nearly rusted."

Victoria scrunched up her nose. "It sounds messy."

Kate swiped a forearm over her brow. "It is."

"Man's work."

"I don't have a man."

"You have Mr. Gould."

Kate frowned at her press. "He's at the bank. Besides, he's not a man. He's an accountant." She sighed. "The new press is being delivered sometime today. I'm just wondering if I should keep this old thing. You know, for posterity."

"For Harry?"

"I don't know. Yes, I suppose it reminds me of Harry."

"Mmm. When are you going to start wearing real clothes again?"

"I told you. I'm in mourning."

"Yes. So you said. But a mourning widow doesn't look at an ancient, beaten up old press and think of her dead husband. She lies in bed and cries because she's so God almighty lonely, and I haven't heard a word about that from you in six months."

"And you won't in the next six, either."

"Didn't hear much about that bedroom when he was alive either—"

Kate faced her friend and felt her voice crack. "I think about Harry every day. I miss him all the time. And I have laid in my bed and cried because I was so God almighty lonely and mad that he left me and Walt much too soon, but I'm not going to talk about it because talking about it and crying about it don't help me, Victoria. Somehow being here, in this office, does help. The paper was his. I mourn him in my own way."

Victoria's cheeks flushed profusely. She reached out and grasped Kate's hand and the words tumbled from her lips. "I know—I—God help me, I always say too much but we're best friends—"

"Of course, we are. We've been since the day we met."

"Yes—I remember that day you first came to town and you didn't seem to judge me at all, like the rest of the folks here did. I could be myself and you didn't seem to mind about anything in my past. I can't help but want the very best for you—"

"Shh." Kate squeezed her fingers. "You don't ever have to apologize for caring."

"I've felt so awful that you've been alone. A woman isn't meant to be alone, Kate, for seven months or otherwise."

"I'm not alone. I have Walt. Perhaps I should get a dog."

Victoria's look grew very fierce. "You need to start thinking about certain things."

"We're not going to start this again, are we?"

"You need a man."

Kate scowled. "God, I knew it. Don't you have a shop to open? Heads to hat? Backsides to bustle?"

"I'm headed in that direction. I thought I'd stop in first thing and see if you'd met *him* yet."

Kate pushed a strand of hair from her cheek. "The last *him* was a sheepherder old enough to be my grandfather."

"You're not being fair." Victoria gave her a look of mild reproach. "He could have taken very good care of you and you wouldn't even allow him to court you. This one could take care of you just as well, perhaps even better."

"I'm not interested. I'm mourning."

"Yes, you told me that. He's the new lawyer in town. The one staying at Louella's. You have ink on your cheek now. Have you met him?"

Frowning, Kate swiped at her cheek. "Yes, I mean, no, not—I mean, yes, I've met him."

Victoria's eyes flashed with interest. "You did? You smeared it now. Not at Louella's?"

Kate blanched and reached for a rag on the wall of bookshelves. "God, no. I don't like—I mean, I don't know her exactly but I don't like what she does." She rubbed her cheek with the rag. "Did I get it now?"

"No, you just smeared it more. And now there's some on your chin. Ace told me that he was causing trouble at Louella's last night. I think he stopped into the shop the other day."

"Ace?" She was rubbing hard at her chin now.

"You're still smearing. No, Ace didn't stop at the shop. He doesn't visit me there. We like my front porch swing best.'' Victoria's full lips curved whimsically. ''God, what a man. The strength in those arms . . . I tell you, Kate, when that man holds me against him and whispers love words I swear I stop thinking about what a rat my first husband was.''

Kate stared at her. ''The new lawyer did this?''

Victoria laughed. ''He sure looks like he could but I don't think Ace would much like it.''

''What kind of trouble was he causing at Louella's?''

Victoria shrugged. ''Something about a girl there.''

For some unexplained reason Kate felt her whole body tighten up. ''A girl.'' She turned to Gould's desk and snatched up the morning mail. Resting one hip on the desk, she started shuffling through the mail so fast she saw none of it. ''So, who's the girl?''

''A new one. Ace didn't know too much about what happened other than Elmer Pruitt got thrown out of the place because of it.''

''Because of this girl.''

''And the new lawyer.''

Kate's lips pinched. ''I see.''

''So—?''

Kate glanced up. ''What?''

Victoria gave a sidling smile. ''You met him. Isn't he godawful handsome?''

Kate scowled. ''That's no measure of a man. I'd think you'd know that by now. Any mature woman knows that. Handsome. I suppose I—uh—never even thought about it.''

''It's a good place to start.''

''I'm in mourning.'' Kate returned to her shuffling and Victoria strolled to the windows overlooking the street.

''You don't know how glad I am that Wilson just up and left me. If he'd died and I'd had to wear that awful black stuff for a whole year for a man I didn't truly love I would have—well, all I can say is a woman shouldn't have to put up the pretense when a man's good and dead, should she? It was enough I was married to him in the first place and—why, would you look at that? There he is and—here he comes.''

Kate didn't look up. ''Who?''

''The new lawyer. And he's got the girl with him.''

Kate jerked up off the edge of the desk. ''What?''

''God, she looks young. Don't you wonder where Louella finds them?''

''What?'' Before she could stop herself, Kate pressed her face up to the window to get a good look. She had to swipe once at the glass to clear the fog from her breath.

It was Charles Remington, all right, looking tall, godawful handsome, and enigmatic as hell in topcoat and black silk hat. The sight of him left her momentarily breathless. Until now she hadn't realized how desperately she'd been waiting to see him today. Next to him was a little darling of a child with wind-tossed golden ringlets. *This* was one of Louella's girls? The thought made her suddenly queasy and just a bit chagrined that she'd thought the worst.

They were walking across the street, heading straight toward the *Sentinel.*

''What is he doing?'' Kate murmured half to herself.

''He's walking across the street with his new doxie.''

Kate's breath came out of her nose. ''That's not his doxie.''

''The devil if it isn't.''

''Charles doesn't have doxies.''

''Charles? Good God, you know him.''

''I told you I did.''

''No, I mean you don't just know him, you *know* him.''

''That was years ago. In Boston. We were—we lived in the same house.''

Victoria folded her arms over her breasts. ''Oh, this is going to require tea. A whole afternoon of tea. I won't leave until you promise me you'll have tea with me and talk until I know everything I want to know."

"I think the whole story might bore you." Kate shoved away from the window and absently reached a hand to her hair. "Don't leave. I'd rather not be alone with them."

"Oh, really? You know him from long ago, enough to suspect that girl isn't his doxie, and yet you don't want to be left alone with him? I'll make lemon tarts to go with the afternoon tea. Maybe even lunch. I think it's going to take a long time for me to get all of this out of you. Bye, now."

Kate spun around. "Don't—please—"

She caught her friend's breezy wave as Victoria tugged open the door and swept out. An instant later footsteps sounded on the boardwalk.

Kate turned her back to the door and reached for the first thing that made her look busy, which turned out to be the mail.

The bell above the door tinkled open. Kate blew at the hair falling in front of her eyes and felt the warmth of the day for the first time. And the confining tightness of her bodice. She suddenly couldn't seem to get enough air.

"Hullo, Kate."

A simple greeting. Why did it pack such a walloping punch of conflicting emotion? How could she be overjoyed to see him and yet afraid of his true motives? It made no sense. And Kate considered herself, if anything, sensible.

She lifted her eyes to meet his. The effect was like a thunderclap jolting through her. "Good morning."

He smiled at her and for a moment seemed content merely to do that. It made Kate conscious of the ink that she'd smeared all over her cheeks.

"I've come to ask you a favor," he finally said.

Kate blinked. "A favor."

"I need a job."

"You need a what?"

"No, not for me. For my—" He inclined his head. "This is Nan."

"Hullo, Nan," Kate said, smiling at the girl.

"Ma'am." The girl bobbed her head. God, she couldn't have been more than ten, an age when she should have been scrambling up big maples in orchards and inventing tales of adventure—an age when she shouldn't have known what women did in places like Louella's.

Charles's look was direct. "She had to leave Louella's before she could begin her—uh—occupation. I knew you would help."

Yes, he knew she'd have compassion for a desperate runaway girl looking for any means of survival. She'd been that desperate when she'd gotten off the train in Denver. She knew what that kind of desperation felt like—alone, trapped by circumstance, terrified of the world, wondering if she'd done the right thing, missing the people she loved most. It was only when she'd met Harry that she'd realized her writing skills had saved her from a much more dire fate. Harry could easily have been someone who would have exploited the more obvious. The West teemed full of such people. And the obvious were perhaps the only assets Nan would ever possess. Unless she was taken under wing, trained . . .

Before she could begin her occupation . . .

Charles had rescued this girl. Kate looked at him and felt warm from the inside out. This was the Charles she knew, the Charles she'd dreamed of, the Charles she loved.

No. She'd left schoolgirl fantasies out in the Remington orchard six years before. Since then she'd seen enough heartache, death, and desperation to know that fairy tales don't come true.

And that she had to live with the choices she'd made.

She quickly averted her face, her chin came down, and her hands fiddled with the mail. "She needs clothes. Something more suitable to her age. Victoria Valentine's shop is just up the block.''

''Very good. We'll go there.''

''Victoria might also be able to help her with work. You know—the needle and thread sort of thing. She could find a job in any city as a seamstress.''

''Ah. Yes, of course. Don't know why I hadn't thought of that. Thank you, Kate.''

Kate shrugged, lifted careless brows, and flipped through the mail for the tenth time without seeing any of it. She felt him watching her. ''I—if she needs a place to stay, Charles—'' Their eyes met. Kate felt her lips tremble slightly. ''I would be happy to have her with me. I'm sure I could find the room.''

Nan bobbed her head. ''Thank you, ma'am.''

Charles's eyes narrowed, his face grew thoughtful, then he touched his fingertips to his hat brim. The bell over the door tinkled. Kate listened to their footsteps fading on the boardwalk and contemplated the emptiness that suddenly touched her. How strange. It was as if she missed something she hadn't known was missing in her life until now.

An envelope caught her eye. Printed in the upper left corner was the name and address of the Union Pacific Railroad corporate offices in Boston. Correspondence from the corporate offices arrived occasionally with the monthly stipend the railroad paid to Jonathan Smarte. This correspondence typically addressed whether the higher powers at the U.P. offices believed Smarte was doing his job properly.

It was clearly understood that the job of an editor at the town paper with a U.P line running through it was not to necessarily report true and actual facts as they happened. His concern was first and foremost to promote the settlement of lands along the railroad's right of way in the town, thereby affording the railroad the opportunity to profit by the sale of these lands given to them by an overly generous government. This, Jonathan Smarte and Harry had done exceptionally well when they'd first founded the paper. In promoting Crooked Nickel and its prime grazing lands, they'd lured cattlemen as well as sheepherders from the troubles they were having with land-grubbing cattlemen farther south and with them had lured their wives, families, and friends to settle in Crooked Nickel.

But there was the crux of Kate's current dilemma. Having had a hand in bringing the sheepherders here, how could she now ignore their troubles with Elmer Pruitt and his boys and abandon the cause that Harry had died for, even if it meant truthfully reporting a range war? The big Union Pacific boys in their comfortable offices would blanch at such a thing. After all, how much would Crooked Nickel resemble a "paradise awaiting development" if its townsfolk were shooting at each other in the streets? Any good editor would squelch such talk and do everything to keep it from the pages of his paper, the better to be paid by his railroad.

Any good, obedient editor would look the other way when innocent sheepherders were denied their lawful right to land, particularly when that denial was perpetuated by the one business that kept the town on the map: cattle.

Kate fingered the unopened envelope. Would the railroad threaten to close the paper if the editorials didn't stop? Kate slid her thumbnail into the top of the envelope and realized her mouth was dry. What would Harry have done? He wouldn't have run scared. He would have fought for what he believed in until he couldn't fight anymore.

She remembered him laying on the floor of the saloon. She remembered Elmer Pruitt looking at her with a cold, lifeless look in his eyes and a gun in his hand.

She hadn't had a chance to say good-bye.

She stared at the floor and felt very much alone.

The bell above the door tinkled. Kate didn't glance up.

"Oh, good. You're back. Mr. Gould, we need to get this press moved to the back room."

"I believe I saw Mr. Gould at the bank. He looked busy."

Kate looked up sharply. Charles stood just inside the door, Nan nowhere to be seen. He tossed his hat on a table, then shrugged out of his coat and tossed it over the back of a chair. Something about the gesture and the way he moved toward her as he did it brought Kate up off the desk and back around the side of it, away from him.

"I can move the press," he said, starting to roll his shirtsleeves.

"No—that's not necessary—"

"You need it moved."

"Yes, but Mr. Gould can—"

"He looks awfully busy. It may take him all day at the bank. I hope you pay him well."

Kate felt her chin poke up. "Exceedingly well."

"Business is good, then?" His look was direct, unreadable, and yet the air between them seemed to have changed.

"Never better."

"Ah."

Kate's brows quivered. Something about his response made her think that he knew otherwise. But how could he know that just two days before she'd wanted to pawn her wedding band to pay for supplies . . . ?

A sudden, unthinkable notion wriggled into her mind. It left her so shaken she refused to even consider it. "What do you mean, 'ah'?"

He frowned at the press and flicked at a loose hammer with his thumb. "This looks like something I'd find with the trash out in back of Miller's Mart in Boston. Antiquated thing. Where'd you get it?"

"Harry found it—somewhere—when we first set up shop here."

"He was a writer. Just like you and me." He was looking at her with those brilliant blue eyes and it was so very hard not to notice that he was as godawfully handsome as Victoria had suggested.

Why had he come to Crooked Nickel? She found herself suddenly looking at him as if he were more stranger than friend. In some ways the fact that she'd known him once made it all the more difficult to read him now. And she'd become adept at reading strangers ever since she'd fled Lenox. Who to trust, who to be wary of. Her survival had depended upon instinct. But instinct told her that Charles Remington had not come all the way to Crooked Nickel merely to visit. Or to set up shop. He had responsibilities in Lenox—a business, Mother Remington, Mary Elizabeth. He'd never shirked his duties before and she doubted he intended to now. He planned to return there. But when?

She wanted him to stay. She also wanted him to go.

She shook herself from her thoughts. "Yes, yes. Of course, Harry was a writer. Well, actually, he liked editing better."

"You did the writing. He edited and handled the business end of things."

"Precisely."

"It sounds like a good business partnership. You had everything you wanted."

"Yes, I did."

"And the marriage?"

Kate felt her chest heave slightly, saw his eyes flicker over the prim little tucks of black that hugged her breasts, and felt scalded. She opened her mouth. "I—it—" She swallowed. "Harry was a good husband. I"—she had to look down and away for some reason—"I miss him."

"I'm sorry for you, Kate." His voice had changed. It was deeper, darker. Was this brotherly concern? Curiosity?

It didn't sound like that in his voice. No, it certainly didn't feel like brotherly concern in a room that suddenly seemed far too little and airless to accommodate both him and her. She realized that they were alone . . . and that there were questions that he was going to start asking, things he was certain to figure out, and she knew it.

She'd spent six years leaving her past behind. Charles was here to push it all back in her face. If only he would move from her path. . . .

How strange that she would consider running from him. He wasn't holding her captive and yet she felt pinned to the spot.

She sucked in a breath. "He was a good father to Walt."

"And that was better than raising him alone?"

She looked up at him. Lying to him was impossible. Surely she hadn't considered it? "Yes," she said. "He was generous-hearted."

"You were damned lucky you didn't end up like Nan."

Her cheeks went hot. "I know—"

"Do you?" His expression had darkened.

"I know that if it hadn't been for Harry—" She paused. He was watching her so intensely. "Looking back, I honestly don't know what I would have done—where I would have gone, but then—" Her voice caught. She caught her lower lip with her teeth.

"Then?" He'd turned from the press and faced her square, hands on his lean hips, shoulders blocking out the front windows.

She lifted her chin slightly. "Then I convinced myself I knew what I was doing—that everything was going to be just fine. I had this"—her fist pressed to her breastbone—"this feeling right here that made me almost fearless. I didn't allow myself to think about anything. I had money in my pocket and I wasn't too hungry yet. Looking back, I suppose I was really rather foolish."

"Young—only sixteen—little more than a child—"His expression hardened, lips compressed. "Christ, Kate—you knew nothing of the world beyond Lenox. You'd only just begun to grow up. Hell, you were still giggling over dresses."

That brought her back up stiff. "They were grown up dresses, Charles. With bustles. And corsets."

"Yes. I remember one with a row of white, silk-covered buttons running from your throat past your waist." His voice dropped off to a rumble. He was staring at her.

Her mind skittered. Yes, the night she'd left she'd worn a new white silk gown. He remembered.

She looked quickly away.

"Did you cry, Kate?"

She rubbed a finger in the dust on the edge of a nearby desk. "I—I suppose I cried. I was crying when Harry found me at the railroad depot in Denver. He was—running away like I was." She waved her hand slightly. "Something about his making enemies with local congressmen in Denver. We were both looking for a place to start over."

"And hide." He arched a dark brow when she looked up at him sharply. "You and Harry picked a hell of a spot to disappear. After all, it's taken me six years to find you."

"You weren't looking that long."

"If you're asking me if I lost hope, yes, Kate, after the first several months with detectives searching and finding nothing, we all lost hope. To this day Mother believes you were kidnapped and forced to write your note at knife point." His brow darkened even more. "But I knew the note you left behind was a ruse. You weren't the kind of girl to go running off *to* something—like an illicit lover. You were running *from* something. And I knew it had to be something utterly devastating for you to give up your home, your family, your entire life. I suspected what it was."

Kate's heart slammed in her chest. "You did?"

"I was wrong." A moment passed. Beyond the windows a wagon clattered past on the street. "In some ways I wish Harry McGoldrick was alive so I could thank him. He saved your life."

Kate had a sudden, disturbing vision of introducing Harry, her husband, to Charles. "Yes," she said. "I was very grateful."

"So grateful you married him."

"He wanted to be a father to my child."

"And in return?"

"I was a wife to him." She felt a lump forming in her throat. "I grew to love him—not as—not as I'd thought I would but—" Her voice caught. Again, she looked away.

"You would have done whatever it took to survive. And you did. Anyone who gets on a train and crosses the Mississippi to find a new life already understands the survival trick. You knew what you found in Harry McGoldrick the instant you met him. And you did everything you could to make the best of that opportunity, for you and your boy. What makes you any different from the Louella Lawlesses out here who go chasing their own kind of dream?"

Kate's mouth tightened and she felt her voice rise. "Are you saying that I'm no different from a—a—woman who runs a—a—" She blinked, flushed very hot, and stuck out her chin. "Well, I believe I am."

He stepped nearer. "You're right about that. For starters, you had the good fortune to have opportunity land in your lap. For another, Louella does everything she can to keep her nose out of trouble, even if it means forsaking whatever she used to call principle. Survival is one hell of a priority. But you—hell, you're courting disaster like you've got a rack of Winchester rifles in that back room that you know how to use and nine lives in which to use them all.''

She blinked again. ''So I don't know how to use a gun.''

His look was fierce. ''Don't bother learning. You won't stand a chance against the cattlemen if they decide to cause you any more trouble. You'd better hope to God they don't find out who Jonathan Smarte really is.''

She felt the blood drain from her face. Her trump card. And Charles Remington held it in his broad, capable hands.

She backed up and right into a stack of bookshelves. A paper fluttered from a top shelf and landed on the floor. Several books slid sideways along a shelf and fell over. Charles reached for her. She stiffened, brought up both her hands, and the envelope from the Union Pacific fell to the floor. ''Don't.''

''The hell I won't. You look like you're going to faint.''

''I've never fainted.''

''My point exactly. How do you know that you won't?''

She shook her head. His voice was so soothing now. It had been so full of anger and concern not moments ago. Concern.

Tears suddenly filled her eyes. God, a little tenderness and compassion from a man and she was going to crumble. She hadn't cried in months.

She turned her face away and felt a storm of conflicting emotion twist in her belly. ''Please leave, Charles.''

''The hell I will.''

She felt his hands on her upper arms, big, broad, and male. His touch seemed to suck all the strength out of her. Her hands touched his forearms, her fingertips touched the bare skin there, and held. She suddenly felt like a sixteen-year-old again, in the Remington parlor, struck giddy at the sight of him.

His breath was warm and seemed to come from very

deep inside his chest. "I know how Harry died, Kate. I know what you think you're doing. It feels right"—his fingers brushed the spot high on her chest and seemed to burn through the fabric—"right here and you feel fearless because you've got all that vengeance twisting around inside of you, making you strong but also making you foolish."

She couldn't look up. Instead, she stared at the page that had fallen on the floor and realized it was a bill four months past due. "I know what I'm doing. I know the difference between right and wrong. How can I live with the injustice of my husband being murdered? His killer walks free, unpunished, and brazenly attacks other innocent men. It has to be done."

"Not by one woman, it doesn't."

"I have the power to do it, Charles. Nobody else does. I have the voice of the paper and an alias in Jonathan Smarte. The paper reaches people who have the kind of influence it would take to change things."

"Kate." He cupped her chin, forced it up, and at the same time brought her closer against him. It was at once the most comforting and disconcerting feeling she'd ever known. His eyes looked as deep as the ocean. "You can't fix the world all by yourself, Kate."

Why were her lips trembling? She swallowed and it sounded like a strangled gulp. "I can try to fix my little corner of it. Harry tried. What else am I to do when I see injustice going unchecked and I possess the power to do something about it? If I don't even try, Charles, how would I get up every morning and face myself in the mirror?"

She glimpsed a softening in his eyes, a certain resignation of his features. She felt his fingers on her jaw. It was a caress, the kind of caress a man gives a woman he cares for.

Instinct told her this was not brotherly concern.

His thumb touched the center of her lower lip. "Dear, earnest Kate . . ."

She closed her eyes. Her heart was hammering in her chest. Her mind was telling her this was not good. She opened her eyes and his face came closer. She decided to close her eyes again.

"Oh, Kate," he murmured. "How did all this happen?" And then his mouth touched hers briefly. He groaned something, then his mouth touched hers again, this time lingering until the only thing she could do was part her lips, grip his strong arms, and give herself over to the rush of feeling that swallowed her whole.

His hands tight on her arms, his chest pressing hard into hers, pressing her deep against that bookcase, pressing her like Jude had pressed her into the bark of a tree in the Remington orchard so many years before . . .

But then she'd been scared and confused. And now . . .

Now she was scared and confused but she didn't want him to stop. And that made her no better than a silly, romantically deluded sixteen-year-old whose only course had been to run away.

And she'd vowed never to have to run away again.

Even if it was Charles she was running from.

She twisted her head away, grabbed his arms. "No—" It came out like a last gasp for air. She was breathing as if she'd run the length of town and back. So was he, but he wasn't moving away.

"Kate. We need to have a talk."

She pressed the back of her hand to her mouth. "No—I know why you've come and I—"

The bell over the door tinkled.

Chapter 7

"Mrs. McGoldrick!"

Charles spun around and offered a weak smile. "Mr. Gould. I'm so glad that you're here."

Gould shut the door and frowned up at Charles. "You are? I don't even know you."

Charles stepped forward and shoved out his hand. "Remington. Charles Remington. We met the other day."

Gould scrunched up his nose and regarded him dubiously even as he pumped Charles's hand. "Oh, yes. You're the railroad man."

Charles kept his smile in place. "Not exactly. I'm a lawyer."

"Lawyer, eh? S'pose you look more like a politician. They all dress fancy like you. So whatcha doing here? Someone send you? I tell you we're paid up on all our past due bills. Did that just yesterday. Isn't that right, Mrs. McGoldrick?" Gould peered around Charles then again regarded him warily.

"That's why I'm glad you're here," Charles said. "She's not well."

An exasperated sound came from behind him.

"A brief fainting spell, I believe," Charles said, hearing Kate huff. "It was the heat. I do believe that—er—dress may have had something to do with it."

"Mrs. McGoldrick's in mourning," Gould saw fit to point out.

"I can see that," Charles said, still tasting her lips under his and hell if she'd tasted like she was in mourning. She'd tasted warm. She'd felt God almighty womanly. The way her hands had gripped his arms had hinted at an eagerness that begged to be tapped.

And he was all kinds of a fool to be thinking such things no matter how much she appealed to the basic man in him. He had a fortune to think about. And the boy Walter. He had explanations to get out of her. Tangling himself up with thoughts of touching and kissing her was the quickest course to disaster.

If he needed a woman to ease his lusts on he had his pick at Louella's place. He knew that. The trouble was it didn't seem to much matter now.

He needed to coax Kate to trust in him the way it used to be between them. He didn't need to give her any more reason to look at him with suspicion. When she'd backed up into that bookshelf, all white-faced with eyes huge, hair falling down, and ink smeared on her cheek, she'd reminded him of that little girl in Boston who'd looked at him as if he were a knight who'd just ridden out of a fairy tale. He'd always wanted to be that hero for her, to hold her close and comfort her and protect her from all the trouble she found herself in.

Not to crush her in his arms and take what should have been his to take from the very start.

He felt his face clench. Gould was staring at him oddly.

"I'm quite fine now, Mr. Gould," Kate said, swishing past Charles and adding a pat to her hair for good measure. Despite her fluttering, moments before, she obviously understood that being found as they had by Gould was a compromising situation at best. "Mr. Remington was just going."

"I believe I still have a press to move," Charles said.

Kate waved a dismissing hand. ''Mr. Gould can do that.''

''Oh no, please,'' Gould hastily piped up, even going so far as to smile at Charles as he shuffled behind his desk and made a great show of moving papers busily around on it. ''I wouldn't mind in the least if you moved that old thing, Mr. Remington. New press is arriving today. Long overdue, if you ask me, but times have been so darned hard, that is, until yesterday and Mrs. McGoldrick—''

''That will be fine, Mr. Gould.'' Kate's smile was tight. She glanced at Charles, then looked quickly away, but not before he was certain that she'd blushed when their eyes met.

''The press, Mr. Remington?'' she said quickly.

''Yes, of course. The press.'' By the time he'd lugged the thing into a back room and returned to the front office, Kate had disappeared.

''Mrs. McGoldrick told me to thank you,'' Gould said without looking up from his scratching quill.

Where did the woman think she would run in a town the size of Crooked Nickel? Charles reached for his coat and swiped at a smudge of dirt on his shirtfront. ''You must be anxious for the new press to arrive, Mr. Gould.''

''Legible type would be a luxury around here, Mr. Remington. No excuses then not to print all the letters to the editor.''

Charles paused as he shrugged into his topcoat. ''You print them all, then?''

''Indeed. That's how we preserve the power of print. We make it accessible to the common man.''

''I see. And who replies?''

''Mr. Jonathan Smarte. He lives in a big house over in Laramie.''

''Yes. You told me that.''

''Mrs. McGoldrick handles all the correspondence with

him, just like her husband, Harry, did. I've never met Smarte. No one has, except Harry, of course. But I don't like him, leastways that's what I say. After what happened to Harry McGoldrick, most folks is smart enough to agree with me—'course I don't say that either. All I say is that poor Harry had too much whiskey one night and got himself killed. Yep. That's all I say."

"But you believe otherwise."

Gould's voice dropped very low. "I *know* otherwise, Mr. Remington. Harry McGoldrick didn't own a gun and didn't know how to shoot one. Everyone in town knew that."

"And how did they know that?"

"'Cause of what happened the night the cattlemen all rode into town and dumped the dead sheep on our front steps right out there." Gould's chin jerked at the door. "You look close enough you can still see the blood stains on the wood. The cattlemen were out there shooting at the sky and shouting for Harry to come out and fight like a man. And ol' Harry goes out there and he's got his hands out in the open and he just told them he didn't have any guns and he didn't know how to shoot one either so they'd best stop asking. He told them the only way to stop him and the paper was for them to stop harassing the sheepherders." Gould shook his head. "Couple nights later some fellas broke into Harry's house and tied him and Mrs. McGoldrick and Walt up and stole all the money and all the whiskey. They looked for guns but they didn't find any. Leastways that's the way we reported it in the next day's paper."

Charles suddenly realized his hands were balled into tight fists, pressed against his thighs. The vision of Kate helplessly tied up, at the mercy of hoodlums, burned into his mind. "He couldn't even protect his family."

Gould's head jerked in a nod. "Yep. I think he thought nobody would hurt him if they all knew he didn't have a gun. I think he thought that gave him a free pass to say whatever he wanted to in the paper. But he was wrong. And there's nothin' nobody can do about it now''—Gould settled back into scribbling in his ledger—''if they want to stay alive, that is.''

''I'm coming to understand that.'' Charles spotted an unopened envelope on the floor, flipped it over, and placed it on the corner of Gould's desk.

Gould glanced at it and snorted. ''Another stipend for Mr. Jonathan Smarte from the big Union Pacific office in Boston. He needs to keep the bosses happy or he gets fired.''

''Fired?''

''And they bring in someone who can do the job they want done. It's easy enough to do even from as far away as Boston. Couple months back some poor editor over in Turkeyfoot Run had no news one day and upset the big cattleman in town by accusing his wife of resembling an ambulatory hay bale. Editor lost his situation the minute the railroad found out about it. Last I heard he couldn't find an editor's job in any town with a railroad running within twenty miles of it.'' Gould looked up and pondered the front windows. ''If you ask me, Mr. Remington, it's not print that's powerful out here. It's cattle.'' Gould shrugged and returned to his work.

Charles bid him good-bye and left the office. He stepped into the blasting heat of the day, the kind that sucked a man's throat dry in an instant. The sunlight reflecting off the dirt street was nearly blinding. A wagon rumbling past churned up enough dust to coat him from head to toe. Only a few people dotted the street and boardwalks.

He turned in the direction of Victoria Valentine's shop and became aware almost immediately that he was being followed; the footsteps sounding close behind him were heavy and steady. A man's footsteps.

He stopped sharply and turned around. The man was tall, ruddy-faced, and potbellied. He had a brown, broad-brimmed hat pulled low against the glare and a tin star pinned to his vest. One hand rested on the gun riding in a low-slung belt at his hips. He'd braced his legs wide when he'd stopped, almost as if he'd expected a fight.

The man worked the chew around in his mouth and spat into the street. "Charles Remington?"

Charles nodded slightly.

"I'm Sheriff Gage, highest ranking lawman in these parts. Thought I might give ya a friendly ree-minder seein' as yer a tenderfoot in town."

Charles narrowed his eyes. "I didn't realize I'd been told anything that needed reminding."

Gage's bushy brows jerked slightly. "I's just tellin' you now, Remington. Folks here don't like it when tenderfoots think they can start trouble. 'Specially folks what's got a stake in the main livelihood in this town."

"Ah. You must be a friend of the notorious Mr. Pruitt."

"I know Elmer. I know Dan Goodknight, too."

"You don't say."

"Pertectin' the townsfolks' interests is my job, Remington."

Charles puckered up his brows. "All the townsfolks, Mr. Gage?"

Gage's eyes narrowed. "It's what I said, weren't it?"

"Just wanted to make sure I understood you correctly. Some would argue what the main livelihood is in this town, depending on the time of day."

Gage's jaw moved in slow circles. "Yeah?"

"Cattle from dawn to dusk. Louella's from dusk to dawn. I rather think there's an argument to be made there."

"Yeah?"

"My point, Mr. Gage, is that one would argue—if one were so inclined to do such a thing with a man like you—

that the interests of cattlemen like Elmer Pruitt and Dan Goodknight are just as important, say, as those of a young girl over at Louella Lawless's boarding house."

"Is that what yer sayin'?"

"No, I suppose I'm asking you, sir."

Again, Gage rolled the chew around his mouth and his eyes flickered to the street. "Yer talkin' importance to the town, ain't ya?"

"There's several politicians in this state, Mr. Gage, who know for a fact that the railroad came through Crooked Nickel on account of one business interest alone. I can tell you it isn't cattle."

Gage's eyes narrowed to slits.

"So I'm asking you, sir, would I be wrong and outside of the law to protect the interests of someone under Louella's roof?"

"I don't know where yer goin' with this, mister. All I know is you upset my friend Elmer."

"And from what I'm gathering, he's guilty of far more."

"What're you accusin'?"

"No accusations, Sheriff. Merely hearsay. But while we're talking about protecting interests, perhaps we should consider those of a slain local newspaperman and his widow and child. Perhaps justice wasn't served there."

"Elmer's gun went off by accident."

"Maybe. Maybe, as you say, Pruitt's guilty of nothing more than upsetting my friend Nan. Ah, that's her right there, Sheriff, coming out of Victoria Valentine's shop."

Gage glanced down the boardwalk as Nan and Victoria stepped from the shop, then he turned to Charles and shrugged. "Yeah? She's a kid."

"Orphaned since she was five. All of ten years old and desperate as a child could be. I found her last night at Louella's. I don't know, Sheriff, but where I come from what your friend Elmer Pruitt wanted to do with that girl is illegal.''

''No laws like that here. A fella can do what he wants.''

''Indeed. He can cheat, steal, murder—especially if the Sheriff's position in town depends on him, eh, Gage?''

Gage met his eyes square and the look on his face was pure meanness. ''Watch yer step, Remington. That's all I'm gonna say. Ya been warned.''

''I appreciate your concern, Sheriff.'' Charles inclined his head and stepped past Gage. The other man shifted slightly so that their shoulders bumped, brushed. Charles paused and looked straight down the boardwalk.

''I'll be watchin' you, tenderfoot,'' Gage snarled half under his breath, then shrugged away and continued on down the boardwalk in the direction opposite Charles.

''Making friends all over town today, Mr. Remington?'' Victoria Valentine asked Charles with a slight smile when he approached. Despite the ever-present look of blithe amusement on her face, her eyes were wary as they flickered over his shoulder in Gage's direction.

''I'm gathering very quickly that this town is divided into two camps,'' Charles said.

''Nobody will ever claim that to be true—at least nobody who values their life and their property. And that includes Sheriff Gage.''

It was statements like these, made with the offhanded ease of someone who faced life and death struggles every day, that made Charles's insides twist up with dread about Kate. She'd grown just as offhanded about her struggle for revenge against Pruitt. He'd yet to face her about what had happened between them, about Walt, about the fortune that hung in the balance, and yet he felt far more urgency to find her and make her listen to reason about her game of vengeance.

''You look wonderful, Nan,'' he said, noting with great

relief that Victoria had dressed the girl appropriately for her age and new occupation.

Nan splayed her hands over the skirt of her pale yellow and cornflower-blue gingham dress. It was long-sleeved, high-necked, and as demure as any dress could be. Her smile beamed up from beneath the rim of a straw bonnet. "I got me some new clothes, Mr. Remington. And I got me a new situation to pay for my dress and a place to stay."

Victoria waved a beautifully manicured hand. "I have a spare room at my place that I've been thinking to rent out. Besides, I can keep a good eye on her there and make sure she practices with her needle."

"I'm gonna be a sewer," Nan said, looking up at Victoria with starry eyes. "Just like Mrs. Valentine."

"Miss," Victoria corrected quickly. "It took me long enough to get that back. I want everyone to know it, okay, honey? Maybe we'll have to call our little shop 'Miss Valentine's Sewing Home for Stray Orphans.' Now go on back in. Mr. Remington's seen quite enough of you for now. I'll be in, in just a minute."

After Nan stepped inside Victoria glanced dubiously at Charles. "There aren't any more there like her, are there, Mr. Remington? If so, I'm afraid you'll try to save them all and then I'll be forced to help you."

"Coercing you was the most effortless thing I've ever had to do, Miss Valentine."

"Oh, I wanted to help, Mr. Remington. I suppose the troubling part of it is that I never thought to do it myself. Then again women in this town are either respectable or they're not. Everyone knows the difference. They also know the two simply don't mix. Our businesses might be on the same street but it's as if we exist in different worlds. I understand that more than most folks here. Back east in New York I was in that other world."

Charles smiled slightly. "I don't believe you."

Victoria laughed quickly. "It's not what you might think. I was first a product of the theater and that brings a woman down several rungs on the respectability ladder. And then I became divorced and none of my friends ever called on me again. All the men thought I was suddenly loose. My only choice was to reinvent myself. So I did what most folks do when they want to start over. They jump on a train, change their name, and head west." Victoria's voice dropped very low. "Don't tell anyone, Mr. Remington, but my last name really isn't Valentine. It's Schwartzky."

Charles copied her whispered tone. "And I doubt very much that Louella's is Lawless."

Victoria's eyes slowly traveled up the street in the direction of Louella's place. "I suppose I never thought she had the conscience to do one honorable thing." Victoria's eyes shifted to Charles and held. There was suddenly a cat in cream kind of look about the woman. "Kate tells me you two knew each other in Boston."

"We haven't seen one another in years."

"Imagine that," Victoria mused. "She's always been such a busy woman, and ever since Harry died it's only gotten worse—you know, her wanting to be at the newspaper office where Harry used to be all the time. Funny but some women hide their loneliness and unhappiness by keeping busy. You know, distraction."

"She must have loved him a great deal."

"Oh, I think she did. She cried at his funeral. She even cried after Virg showed her Harry's bill at the saloon. She loved him but"—Victoria's full lips pursed and her look became thoughtful—"but even when he was alive, it was almost as if she missed something, Mr. Remington. I couldn't quite explain it except that they seemed more like an uncle and his niece. Strange, isn't it, that I would think that what with the boy Walt and all? But Harry didn't seem to mind. Maybe he just understood what I didn't, hmmm?"

He saw the upward tilt to her mouth and the dancing in her eyes. This woman intended to cause mischief. And her little fire didn't need any feeding. Although something she'd said earlier had struck a nerve in him. It was well worth remembering. It had something to do with . . .

Distraction.

The plan sprang into his mind, full-blown. His impatience to be at it astonished him.

"I'm sorry, Miss Valentine, but I have an errand."

She smiled and looked amused again. "Yes, of course."

"No, really," he felt compelled to add. "It's very important."

"I believe you, Mr. Remington. I also believe it has something to do with my friend, Kate."

"She's my friend, too," he said gravely. Then, with a brief incline of his head, he turned and headed down the boardwalk toward Louella's place.

Chapter 8

Kate's step was light on the boardwalk. It was early morning and she'd just walked Walt to the little schoolhouse at the east edge of town. The day promised to be full of dry heat and wind but this morning, before the winds got to blowing, the air was wondrously clear.

This helped her spirits. So did the editorial she had tucked under her arm. She'd been up writing the thing past three in the morning.

Sleep had proven more elusive last night than she'd remembered it ever being. Her thoughts had strayed to places they had no business going. She'd tossed, punched her pillow, and sworn she wasn't going to remember what it felt like to be kissed by Charles. But she'd failed, miserably. However much she felt she should be on her guard with him, in the darkness with the sounds of a summer night all around her and an empty place beside her in the bed, she couldn't seem to remember anything but the comfort of his arms and the warm passion of his kiss.

And that had led to the sort of thoughts she'd had six years ago when she'd lain in her bed in Lenox and kissed her pillow and whispered Charles's name. A child's thoughts, but now they were colored by a woman's experiences, experiences she'd had in this bed, with another man.

She'd never felt this kind of restlessness with Harry. She hadn't been kissed so passionately before. She'd never responded so passionately either.

With these thoughts swirling in her head, she'd kicked off her sheets and pulled them back up at least a half dozen times before she'd decided that what she needed was distraction.

Writing.

And in that solitary world she created in her bedroom, with the bedside lamp burning low and her quill scratching over the page, she'd been emboldened enough to take her firmest stance yet and issue a clarion call to the politicians of the county to stand up and fight for the rights of the sheepherders being unfairly intimidated out of their grazing lands and their livelihood.

"Good morning, Mr. Gould," she announced as she entered the newspaper office. "Oh, would you look at that. Isn't that a sight to behold?"

"It's still shiny," Gould replied, leaning back in his chair and eyeballing the new printing press with all the chest-puffed-up-pride of a new father. "Arrived the other day from Denver. Paid 'em in full, I did, and I don't mind telling you, ma'am, it felt God almighty good to do that."

"Very good. I say we put it to its proper use." Kate unpinned her hat, tossed it on a desk, and waved the editorial pages. "From Mr. Jonathan Smarte himself. It's a barn burner, Mr. Gould."

Gould blanched. "Please, ma'am, if you'd refrain from such talk. You scare me."

Kate took a chair behind a desk opposite from Gould. Morning sunlight slanting through the windows set the pile of pages on her desk aflame with light. She tucked a stray strand of hair behind her ear and picked up an envelope lying on top of the pile. It was addressed to the paper first, then to Jonathan Smarte, editor. "We really must do something about the clutter of paper around here, Mr. Gould. If I misplace something, I'll never find it again.''

''It's all mostly bills and late payment notices, ma'am. We could paper the walls of this office with them, if you don't mind my saying, and still have some left over.''

''We need to get rid of them,'' Kate said, sliding open the envelope. She glanced up at Gould and smiled as she took out the folded page. ''We're all current now. And happily so, I might add. I—'' She scanned the page in her hand. ''Oh, no.''

''Not another threat, is it?''

''No. It's from him.''

''I didn't think Pruitt used clean paper and envelopes. He uses nails on the front door, old handbills, and dead sheep.''

''No, it's not from Pruitt. It's from Mr. Remington.''

''The politician?''

''Yes, that Mr. Remington.''

''The one you fainted with.''

Kate's lips pressed together. ''I don't ever faint.''

''He was holding you up like you were fainting, ma'am.''

''Did it ever occur to you that Mr. Remington might have overreacted—oh, I can't print this. It's inflammatory.''

''Then I want to read it.'' Gould's chair legs scraped hard over the floor as he jerked to his feet.

Kate's eyes skimmed over the letter. ''What the devil is he trying to do?''

''Does he talk about the sheepherders, is that it?''

''No, nothing about sheepherders. It's nothing like that. I believe he intends to get the women of this town entirely up in arms. I can't print it. Listen to this: *In doing her part to chase the dream of streets of gold and prosperity in the new frontier a woman's only duty must be to find, nurture, and support a good man, and to give him the home and comfort he needs to secure his dreams. If she has any dreams of her own she must sacrifice these for the good of creating a family. A woman's work never leaves the bounds of her home.*'' Kate's brows quivered together. ''I do believe he's poking at women with a white-hot branding iron.''

''Ma'am?''

Kate frowned up at Gould. ''You heard him. Suffragism is sweeping the nation, Mr. Gould. Mr. Remington knows that. And yet he's chosen a stance in direct opposition to that held by most women.''

''Even you, ma'am?''

''Yes, of course, even me, Mr. Gould. That you should even ask—it's inflammatory. I won't print it.'' She pushed back from the desk and got heatedly to her feet. Flicking the letter to the desk she muttered, ''Woman's only duty, my arse.''

Gould's eyes popped wide and his Adam's apple jerked in his throat. ''Ma'am?''

''Find a good man. What sort of backward thinking is that?''

''If you don't mind my saying so, ma'am, it's the thinking of most of the women in this town. Save for Miss Lawless, of course.''

''Miss Lawless?'' Kate scowled at Gould. ''I should say it is not. Mr. Gould, I swear Mr. Jonathan Smarte will double your salary if I find out the women in this town think like that.''

''Double, ma'am?''

''You heard me.''

''Then you'll have to print it.''

''I don't have to do any such thing.''

''How else will we find out? Remember the power of print, ma'am.''

''Yes, yes, I know. But fighting about sheepherders' rights to make a living off the land is one thing. Fighting about what a woman's duties are—why, that's as bad as making up tall-tale news when there isn't any news, just to keep the readership reading."

"I thought it was giving voice to the common man, ma'am. Or in this case the common woman. Leastways that's what I told Mr. Remington."

"You did what?"

"I told him we're bound by our oath to print all the letters to the editor. I wonder, ma'am, how Mr. Jonathan Smarte will respond."

"Like any halfway intelligent person would, of course. He'll disagree. Heartily."

"You sound so very certain of that, ma'am."

Kate drew herself up quickly and opted for the affronted stance. "What other course does he have, Mr. Gould? This paper must present opposing viewpoints. Mr. Smarte knows that. And above everything else, he is an intelligent man." She grabbed her hat and plunked it on her head.

"Where are you going, ma'am?"

Kate stepped around the desk and headed for the door. "To visit Douglas Murphy. Set the type for the editorial, Mr. Gould. And fine, set the letter from Mr. Remington. It can go to print this evening. I'd hate to be strung up for going back on our word. A pity we'll have to wait several days for Mr. Smarte's reply." She yanked open the door and marched out into a blast of hot wind.

It suddenly seemed to suit her mood. She headed at a quick pace toward Douglas Murphy's office, so much so she nearly plowed down a man who'd hurried up from the street and planted himself like a big oak in front of her.

"Ma'am—pardon me, ma'am. A moment of your time, Mrs. McGoldrick."

Kate didn't recognize him at first. At first glance, he looked like most other men in town at this time of day, dingy and dust-covered, wearing faded denims and a work-shirt. But this one had tugged his hat from his head when he'd stopped in front of her and was smiling at her. When he did, his dark eyes crinkled and his lips quirked lopsidedly. He was, she realized, mildly handsome under all that dinge. Tall, blond, deeply tanned, rugged. The hand holding his hat was callused.

"Bertrand, ma'am." He wiped his other hand on his pant leg and stuck it out at her. "John Bertrand. We met at Logan's General Store some eight months back when I first came to Crooked Nickel."

Kate blinked and then she smiled and clasped his hand. "Oh, yes, you're one of the sheepherders from Kansas. I remember now—you were restocking supplies for your friend who'd been burned out of his farm by the cattlemen. How is he?"

Bertrand grinned. "Completely rebuilt, ma'am. Five hundred head of sheep and more soon to come. 'Course it's taken him a while and he don't sleep much with one eye open and two rifles in each hand. 'Course a fella can learn to sleep anywhere if it means saving his farm."

"It's not getting much better for you, is it?" Kate asked quietly.

Bertrand's eyes narrowed on her. "Ma'am, I come into town 'bout once a week to get supplies, mostly to get the *Sentinel.* I've looked for you each time—and I—I just have to thank you, ma'am."

"Thank me? Good heavens, whatever for?" Kate flushed and flexed her hand, which he'd almost crushed. "I just do a little paperwork at the office, Mr. Bertrand, and keep Mr. Gould company."

"That may be, ma'am, but you're the one I know suffered the most when your husband was killed. I hear the talk. I know what everyone thinks happened to him. It makes me so angry because your husband died telling the truth of it and the cattlemen make him out to be some kind of drunken fool.''

Bertrand grabbed her hand again when Kate averted her eyes to the street. ''No, please—I'm sorry, ma'am. I don't mean to—every man's allowed to enjoy his whiskey. It's just that—I believe you made the greatest sacrifice, ma'am.''

''No,'' Kate replied quietly. ''Harry made the greatest sacrifice. And he died for nothing—''

''No, ma'am. He didn't. The paper isn't forgetting about us sheepherders. It's still reporting everything those cattlemen do. It's that Smarte fella I want to thank. The one who writes the editorials. I say he's mighty brave considering what happened to your husband.''

''Mmm—brave. Yes. You might say that. Of course he lives in Laramie. There's not much the cattlemen can do to him there.''

John Bertrand nodded and didn't look at all inclined to move on. ''How's your son, ma'am?''

''Very good, thank you.'' She opened her mouth to ask about his family and remembered suddenly that he had none. He wasn't married.

A good man.

The phrase leapt to mind and hung there. Odd, blasted thought. A good man needed a good woman. . . .

''I hope to see you again, ma'am.'' John Bertrand put on his hat and angled it over his eyes. His grin lit up his face. ''Real soon, ma'am.''

''Yes, that would be—yes, fine. Good day.'' Kate moved quickly past, suddenly mortified. A woman in mourning shouldn't encourage young, handsome men hoping to see her very soon. She certainly shouldn't notice that they were young and handsome in the first place. For that matter she shouldn't lie in bed at night like a love-struck sixteen-year-old and dream about kissing a man.

She should be thinking of ways to help good men like John Bertrand keep their grazing rights. She should be thinking about how to avenge Harry's death. She should be figuring out why Charles had come all this way . . . and why he'd kissed her and what it meant after all this time. . . .

She didn't realize she was frowning until she glanced across the street and spied someone watching her from in front of the barber shop.

Charles. Shaven, shorn, and looking at her with that dark and brooding stare that made her insides jiggle. She wondered how long he'd been standing there in the heat and wind, perhaps long enough to witness her exchange with John Bertrand.

Her immediate thought was to cross the street to see him but thinking the better of it she jerked her eyes straight in front of her and marched on. She could feel Charles watching her the entire way to Douglas's office, as if he was poking her right in the back, and the feeling was not a comfortable one. She gripped the office doorknob, turned it, and shoved against the door. It was locked.

"Goddammit," she said.

"*Mrs. McGoldrick!* Did I hear you correctly?"

Kate spun around and faced the shelflike bosom and imperious glare of the town gossip Bessie Mae Elliot. Bessie Mae lived on the edge of town with her mother and had never married. At twenty-eight, she seemed destined to remain that way. She was plump, shaped like a square, and the straw hat plunked on top of her tight blond ringlets looked three sizes too small. Or maybe her cheeks were just several sizes too large. Or maybe she was just too puffed up to speak. Kate had the odd thought that if she pricked Bessie Mae in the side she'd deflate like an overfilled balloon.

Kate raised innocent brows. "Uh—no. I don't suppose you did hear me correctly or you wouldn't be looking at me like that. How are you, Bessie Mae? How's your mother's rheumatism?''

''Worse as ever. Just worse as ever. She can barely move around the house. Who were you talkin' to down the way? I think it was one of them sheepherdin' fellas, weren't it? You better watch yerself 'round them, Mrs. McGoldrick. Trouble followin' them like flies on sheep dung, or so I heard. 'Course you know that after Harry 'n all.''

''Yes, I do know that.''

'' 'Course you bein' in mournin' an' all, you got no business to be talkin' to no men. Harry's only been dead six months, ain't he?''

''Seven.''

Bessie Mae folded her hands over her thick waist. ''See there. You got a good five, six months of mournin' left. You hot in that black dress? You sure look hot. Me? Why, on days like this my mama lets me go without my petticoat and bloomers.'' Bessie Mae suddenly looked as scandalized as if someone else had just said those same words. She blushed a shade of bright, shiny pink, and glanced surreptitiously up and down the street. ''I mean—well, it's the fresh breezes what'll cool you.'' She giggled but it came out as a gurgling sound stifled behind her plump hand. '' 'Course I hope the wind don't blow too hard, if you know what I mean. Best I move on. I need to stop by Mr. Logan's General Store an' see if he's heard any more news about dead sheep anywhere. Oh, and I bet he's heard 'bout that new politician what came to town. Has all the ladies in a state. I heard he's a congressman come to clean up Louella Lawless's place. And I say it's long overdue. Have you heard anything?''

''About the sheep?''

''No, not about the sheep—though I have to say when they hung that poor lamb by its neck right outside the railroad depot last week I just about cried—anyway, no, I mean have you heard anything about the fella?''

"No," Kate said. "I haven't heard a thing."

"That's funny. I thought you might. Bye, now!"

Kate watched Bessie Mae amble back up the boardwalk and studied the swish-swish of her pink checked skirts. It was probably the most difficult thing to imagine that Bessie Mae wore nothing beneath those skirts.

The idea was a curious one. And just a wee bit titillating. Obviously Bessie Mae didn't believe it a woman's only duty to find a good man to be a good wife to.

Kate turned directly into the wind, clamped a hand on the top of her hat to keep it there, and marched on. Charles was still standing in front of the barber shop. He was leaning against one of the posts that seemed to hold up the whole front overhang of the roof. One hand was tucked in the pocket of his black trousers. The other hung at his side. One boot was casually crossed over the other, and wind ruffled through his black hair. He looked like a smooth, slick, and elegant gambler.

Or a gentleman full of dark passions.

And he was watching her.

She tried not to look at him when he shoved away from the post and started across the street with long, halting strides. She quickened her pace. He kept on coming, straight at her, even after a buckboard clattered past and threw up a throatful of dust. He emerged through the thick of it and stepped into pace beside her.

"Good morning, Kate."

"Charles."

"Did you sleep well?"

She grabbed the top of her hat and angled her eyes up at him. "Yes, as a matter of fact, I did. I wasn't up all night composing ridiculous missives to stir up trouble. Really, Charles, I hate to bother Jonathan Smarte for the favor of a reply."

"I'm afraid you must. Your readership will demand it."

"I have no choice. Mr. Gould will demand it." They passed Logan's General Store. Kate caught a glimpse of Bessie Mae Elliot's chubby face pressed up to the glass as they passed. Bessie Mae's mouth jerked with soundless words and she knocked on the glass. Kate ignored her and hurried on.

She might as well set the headline now for tomorrow's paper: *Local mourning widow makes fast and loose with good and handsome sheepherder and would-be politician in same day!*

"You've kept up quite a pretense with Jonathan Smarte, Kate. It has to take a good deal of effort."

"Don't believe for a minute that I enjoy duplicity. It was Harry's idea from the beginning."

"Which you went along with so you could write. I understand. You don't have to explain."

"I'm not explaining. I'm rather proud of the fact that we kept Mr. Smarte and his opinions alive for so long."

"Interesting that you would choose those words. Here—" He took her arm and steered her back across the street and right into the Hotel St. Excelsior's lobby. Kate felt her knees straighten and her back draw up rigid.

"Relax, Kate. It's a public place."

"This is a hotel," she hissed, looking quickly around to see if they were being observed. The lobby was, thankfully, deserted. "I'm a widow in mourning. And you're an unmarried man. You can bet Bessie Mae Elliot saw us come in here. This is a hotel, for God's sake."

"Yes, you just said that." He directed her to the common room filled with round tables. The place was deserted save for a barkeep polishing glasses behind the bar. "Good. I just wanted a little privacy."

"Privacy?"

Charles pulled out a chair and directed her into it with

slight pressure on her arm. ''Sit down, Kate. We need to have a conversation.''

''Yes, I know we do.''

Charles slid into the chair next to hers and motioned to the barkeep. ''Two whiskeys,'' he said when the man approached.

Kate's spine was rigid as old oak. ''I don't—I've never touched whiskey—'' *Ever since Harry . . .*

''Relax, Kate.'' He laid a big hand over hers on the table and kept it there with a good bit of pressure. ''You're acting like you don't want to be here with me.''

''I'm not sure I do.'' She was feeling the heat of his hand over hers. There was a consuming warmth to it, like the consuming presence of him. In a room full of people he would have commanded attention from her. Alone in a room, he nearly overpowered her.

''We grew up together, Kate.''

She didn't look up when the whiskeys were set on the table. ''I know. Why doesn't it feel like it?'' She watched his fingers curl around his glass.

He lifted it, drank, set the glass down. ''Time hasn't erased that. It's still there. We just need to get to know each other again.''

''It seems like so long ago. I've tried to forget—do you know that? I tried to make myself forget everything, Charles, and now you're here and I look at you and it's almost like you're forcing me to remember things I don't want to remember.''

''And I look at you and remember when you first came to live with us—how small and alone and scared you seemed in your little brown coat with the snow falling on your bare head. Father told us about the fire at the orphanage and how the nuns who'd taken care of you had died. Just like your mother had died and left you alone. He told us that we'd have to take care of you and never leave you alone. I still want to, Kate. Nothing will ever change that. It's as much a part of me as my heart and soul. But then you were a sister to me and Jude and Mary Elizabeth. You got in trouble like we did. You did chores and schoolwork like we did. You were the little girl my mother had hoped to have and see into womanhood. And then at some point—I'm not sure when—you became something else—'' He leaned toward her and she reacted without thinking, pulling back and away from him.

''You're afraid of me,'' he said in very soft tones.

She kept staring at the table, focusing on the pattern of the grain of wood, but she couldn't help smelling him, the clean, windswept, freshly shaved smell of him, and it seemed to fill up her head and yes, it scared her, because she didn't trust herself, her feelings, his intentions. . . .

Something else . . .

''I promise I won't kiss you in here,'' he murmured.

''I didn't think you would in a newspaper office either.'' She gently pulled on her hand and he released it. She found hers cupping around her whiskey glass. ''Things are so different now, Charles.''

''Yes, I know.''

''They'll never be the same. I don't need looking after. I'm not that little girl anymore. I've seen more of life—''

''Yes. I want to hear about all of it.''

''—and I've made mistakes.''

''We all have. I live with regret every day.''

She looked up at him and felt an achingly deep loss for what never would be. ''I think about that night six years ago, Charles. . . .''

He looked straight at her. ''I know. It was the night you left. Tell me why, Kate—why you left the family that took you in and loved you as one of their own?''

Tears sprang to her eyes. Anguish twisted in her chest. ''I know—I was so grateful I almost forgot that I wasn't a

Remington. I loved all of you, and that's why I had to''—she shoved a hand over her eyes—''you'll never understand—''

He leaned forward, grasped both her hands, and there was an urgency in his voice. ''Then tell me. Make me understand why you were so desperate that you never came back, why you let us all think the worst—I had nightmares, Kate—''

She stared at him and felt her heart hammering. ''I think you already know.''

He went very still. ''Jude told me something. I've been hoping it's not true.''

''He—he doesn't know all of it.''

''I know. He doesn't know you bore him a son.''

Chapter 9

There he'd said it. What needed to be said, not tiptoed around any longer. Done. Spilled like dark red wine on a fancy white tablecloth.

And yet part of him wished he hadn't said it. Part of him wanted to take it back and let her tell him on her own or never tell him, if that's what she wanted, because there was a deep sorrow in her eyes that made him regretful of even thinking he had a right to intrude on the life she'd made for herself.

Who the hell was he to come and throw her mistakes in front of her when he had his own closet full of them?

He was the man who'd loved her, of course, the man who would have forgiven her anything, even the darkest of mistakes made on a warm summer night.

"Yes," she said so quietly he had to strain to hear her. "I had his son." She looked out of one of the windows and lifted the whiskey to her lips. He watched her drink, watched the moistness cling to her mouth, watched the dusky, mysterious beauty of her and wondered for the thousandth time if she'd ever been his to lose.

To Jude or otherwise.

He had a need to know this more than anything ever before in his life.

He watched her with mouth parched and heart pounding

in his chest. He again reached for her hand, squeezed it between both of his, and stared at the smallness of her fingers, the tidiness of her short nails. "I would have forgiven you anything," he said, his voice coming from the deepest part of his chest. "And yet somehow you doubted me."

"You wouldn't have forgiven me, Charles, no matter how much you believe now you would have. When it all would have come to light"—she looked at him with eyes worldly-wise and weary—"I went to the orchard willingly."

Charles felt his jaw tighten. "He coerced you there—words, nuance, the man has charm enough for ten men."

"Yes, he did. And I went there full of hope—foolish, blind hope—" She paused, looked down at their entwined hands, and lifted a wistful brow. "I was still such a child, you know. I had dreams—gold-spun dreams of love and longing. I was very passionate about them, passionate to experience them, passionate to be in love, passionate to be held and kissed by a man—just like the women in Grandmother Remington's books. Looking back, I think she knew how I felt because those books were always within my reach, as if she put them under my nose on purpose. I think she knew I believed I was very much in love, Charles."

"With Jude."

"Perhaps a little—perhaps more than a little in some ways. But even more so I was in love with you." She looked up at him, and he felt like a man's solid fist had just pounded into his chest. Again, the wistfulness drifted over her features, making her seem entirely out of his reach. "And you were in love with Eleanor Curtin."

"No," he said huskily, "I wasn't. I didn't marry her."

The quiet sorrow seemed to have embedded itself into her features. "Somehow that only makes it that much worse, doesn't it?"

Charles closed his eyes, hung his head for a moment, and rubbed his thumbs back and forth over her fingers.

"Listen to me, Kate. I was bound by duty—hell, I was steel-wrapped in it. Bound by responsibility and a promise to my father to protect and keep my family the best I could—yes, I was all that. I was also living up to everyone's expectations of me, living up to the dreams that had died on that battlefield when my career ended. I was proving myself worthy enough to have plunged the family into a lifetime of debt I'm only now getting us out of." He lifted his head and looked at her. "I was drowning in all of it, Kate. I could feel it sucking the life out of me bit by bit. I could feel the cynicism eroding me. I found myself resentful of everything and everyone. I knew it completely when that situation with Eleanor Curtin came about. And for the sake of honor and duty I sold myself into the law firm and into the marriage idea."

"You did it for the family. You were always utterly committed to them. I knew that."

"But I didn't do it. I couldn't. That night—the night you left—I came home for one purpose."

"I remember you weren't staying long."

"I came to see you, Kate." His breaths were coming deeper now. "I came to see if the thoughts I was having of you while I was away weren't merely idle thoughts. I came to see why the idea of marrying another woman made me think only of you."

She was looking down at the table. "You said nothing. I had no way of knowing—"

He felt his mouth tighten. "I've regretted that every moment since. Because if I had"—he stared at her so hard his eyes burned—"I would have been in the orchard with you, Kate."

"No—" Her lips seemed to quiver. "You would have chosen other methods, I think."

"Don't count on it."

Her eyes shot to his, then she quickly looked away. Two

spots of warm rose shone on her cheeks. She seemed to take a moment to gather her thoughts. "I knew none of this then. I thought you were marrying that woman because you loved her. I couldn't face your disappointment in me—Grandmother Remington's—I had my own shame and could live with that, but yours I couldn't have borne."

"Jude would have likely lived with the secret for years, even if you'd stayed."

"Perhaps. But I would have known, even had there not been a child. I would have known." Her voice became deeply impassioned. Her chest expanded with each breath. "I would have had to face you and your fiancée over Mother Remington's table. I would have had to face Jude and remember every time I looked at him how much I'd humiliated myself—"

"There's no humiliation in being played false, Kate."

"Indeed. And what of allowing one's passions to get the better of good sense? Surely I'm entitled to some humiliation for that." She leaned slightly nearer and her voice dropped to an ominous purr. "Jude didn't force himself on me, Charles. I allowed him. And we both knew it."

He took a long moment to look deep into her eyes. "I still would have forgiven you."

"Because you think so little of Jude."

"Because I cared so deeply for you."

Her lips parted as if her breath had caught. She leaned back and regarded him with a slightly dubious look. He realized then that she'd erected a wall around herself as impenetrable as stone.

"You believed I was marrying someone else," he said softly. "You went to my brother for comfort."

"I'll never blame you."

"Maybe you should. I blame myself."

"It's easy to do, isn't it?"

"It's torture. I'd rather blame Jude."

Her fingers curled against his. "It seems like so long ago. A lifetime ago—like it happened to two different people."

"And in many ways it feels as near as yesterday. The feelings I have for you, Kate—"

Her hand lifted and splayed. "Please, no—I don't want—" There was a look of warning on her face. "Tell me, does Jude know about Walt?"

Her question startled him. "No—no one does. How could they? No one in the family even suspects that I came here looking for you. I told them it was a business matter."

"I don't want anyone to know, Charles. I want it kept private. The life I've made for myself and my son might not be the very best, but it's all he knows and it has to stay as it is. For Walt."

A strange chill gathered in his belly. "And what am I to do? Simply leave you here?"

Her look was direct and unreadable. "You have tremendous responsibilities in Lenox—a business, a mother and sister who need you. Much as I would like you to stay, I'm sure that you can't—"

He felt his teeth come together in a tense click. "You could come back to Boston. I'd like to bring you home."

"This is my home, Charles."

"There would be no scandal, Kate, I could assure you of that. I know you think it would be difficult, and it would be, I know, in some ways. In others—"

She seemed to be sitting very stiffly in her chair. "I have a life here, Charles, dreams and aspirations—"

"Vendettas."

Her face tightened slightly. "Yes, that, too. I'm not leaving. And neither is my son."

She exuded a strength of will and character that astonished him. He met her stare, saw the futility of arguing with her at the moment, and forced a slight shrug. "As you wish.

But if you're not coming back to Boston then I'm staying on a while—as long as I can. I want to know Walter, Kate."

"Yes, I suspected that. But you have to understand he was very close to Harry and he's missed him very much. He's the only father Walt has ever known."

Yes, Charles knew that.

"In my mind he's all yours, Kate. When I look at him I see more of you than I do Jude or anyone else." He paused, narrowed his eyes. "But he's a Remington. At some point he needs to know who his—"

"No." She was up and out of her chair in an instant.

"Wait—" He caught her wrist and tightened his grip on it until she looked down at him. "It's useless to run away from me, Kate. I'm here. Let's be done with this now."

She arched a brow at him. "This isn't some task to accomplish, Charles. This is a child's life, not the ticklish legalities of a business deal from which everyone will go home happy afterward. Harry was the father he knew from birth. He's the only father he'll ever know. I won't slander Harry's memory that way."

"Jude is the boy's father. True, he's in Boston squandering his life away in liquor-soaked whorehouses, and Harry was here for both of you. Harry McGoldrick was not a perfect man, Kate, but I won't argue that he was an infinitely better man for a boy to have known as a father. I certainly don't want to destroy anything more for Walt—at least for now."

"Harry was a good man." Her face looked haunted.

"A good newspaperman and father, yes, I suspect he was. But he wasn't the martyr you've painted him to be. You seemed to easily forgive his debts and his drinking—and I'm not faulting you for that—but this blind devotion to avenging his death in the face of the cattlemen's brutality, I suspect there's a deeper reason behind that as well."

"Such as?"

"Guilt."

She frowned slightly. "I don't agree with you."

"Gratitude begets a certain kind of love, I'd suspect, but not the kind you'd dreamed of. And you knew Harry knew it. And now you're trying to make it up to him."

She tugged slightly on her wrist and her eyes glowed like hot emeralds. "We were discussing Walt, not Harry."

Charles loosened his grip on her wrist. "You're right. Now, sit down."

She looked almost startled then eased back into her chair.

He leaned slightly forward and lowered his tone. "I'm his uncle, Kate."

Her face was pinched. "He won't understand who you are."

"I'm an old family friend." He watched her. "Kate, he needs a man in his life."

Her eyes shot to his. "He has me. That's enough. It's been enough since Harry was—" She stopped in mid-sentence and looked down, lost in thought. Then she took a deep breath and pronounced, "If you want to know Walter, Charles, I suppose I have no difficulty with that."

"I'm not suggesting that you have any deficiencies as a mother raising a boy alone."

Her laugh was short and a bit caustic. "I expect I'll find that out in your next letter to the editor."

"If you need distraction, yes, you just might."

She looked at him with grim contemplation. "You're simply an old family friend."

"Simply that."

"And I don't suppose I have a choice."

That caught him off guard, as did the sudden, pronounced jut of her chin. "Meaning?"

"You've somehow managed to find out my most precious secrets. My identity as Jonathan Smarte. Jude being the father of my boy. No one in this town even suspects that Harry didn't father him, not even Douglas Murphy. You and I both know you can do with those secrets what you want, when you want.''

''Don't accuse me of blackmail, Kate.''

''You're quite good at not stating the obvious.''

That brought him forward, blood suddenly pulsed in his temples. ''I'm even better at protecting my friends,'' he said in a tone that seemed to make her listen very well. ''When you remember that you used to trust me, we'll be much better off.''

She stared at him and her lower lip trembled for an instant. He almost groaned with defeat. She was so goddamned womanly, so fragile on the outside, so strong on the inside, he wanted to thrash her and kiss her all at once and then take her back to Boston where he could keep her well and love her. . . .

Her breaths were coming deeper. He could see the heavier rise and fall of her breasts and it spoke to his desire for her.

''I'm supposed to trust you and yet''—she swallowed—''you have the power to take my boy away from me.''

He looked right at her. ''I could. I have the connections. The law in these matters is almost entirely on my side. You as a mother have far fewer rights than I do as his blood relative, most particularly since he's the sole Remington heir. We both know it. I won't deny it.''

She looked as if she'd taken a blow straight to midchest. He reached for her hand on the table, crushed it in his, and wouldn't let it go even when she yanked on it and tried to get out of her chair.

''Kate, that's not why I'm here. I had to find you—I couldn't ignore it. I knew nothing about Walt when I came out here, dammit, listen to me—''

She was shaking her head, looking away, swiping at her cheeks.

''Christ, Kate—'' He grabbed her upper arms with both hands and pulled both her and her chair between his parted thighs. It wasn't a well-thought-out move on his part, bringing her so close to him, given his total body awareness of her. He realized this, of course, several moments too late when the blood seemed to shoot straight into his loins.

He felt his lips part and his throat go bone dry. She was sniffling and making noise about the barkeep. Charles glanced at the bar.

''He's gone—he's not—nobody's here, Kate. No one will be able to talk about this to anyone. Jesus, stop—''

''I can't,'' she whispered, shaking her head some more and staunchly refusing to meet his eyes. ''I don't know why I'm crying.''

''I can guess. Sometimes it feels good to cry. Remember, Mother used to say that whenever my father became too much of a tyrant and she resorted to one of her spells—''

She nodded. ''She'd take to her chaise lounge for a week.'' She sniffed again and the tears seemed to come a little faster. ''But I don't have a chaise lounge I can take to . . . and I—I don't allow myself to cry very often, really I don't—''

''You should have a chaise lounge,'' he murmured, aching to take her in his arms and make her world a heavenly haven, ''done in emerald velvet with silk pillows and gold tassels—''

''Stop it, Charles. I've never needed any such thing.''

His lips quirked. ''They make them in Boston, you know. All the well-kept women there have them.''

She sniffed again. ''I'm well-kept enough, thank you.''

''I know you think you can hold the world up all by yourself.''

''I should be able to, otherwise I'm—I'm fit only to be

a woman in need of a good man. And I don't want to be . . ." She choked something, sniffed, and then she threw her arms around his neck and smashed her face into his chest. "Oh, Charles—"

He stared over her head, his mouth gone suddenly dry, and felt her pull closer. She was clinging to him, pushing her soft breasts into his chest, rubbing her stiff black skirts against the erection humming in his trousers, as if she didn't know what the hell she was doing.

Like a virgin tease. Or a woman in need of comfort and still unwilling to admit it. He knew the difference. He also knew what she was.

He cupped the back of her head with his hand, rubbed her arm with the other, and closed his eyes. She smelled like a meadow full of wildflowers. He drew the essence of her deep into his lungs and felt it swirl up into his brain like a drug.

His fingers touched the back of her neck, where the hair curled and was swept up. He breathed through parted teeth, eased her head up.

"Charles," she breathed and his lips touched hers, parted.

She drew back, uncertainty and confusion painted over her features. He couldn't bear it. His mouth crushed over hers in an onslaught so powerful he could hear the deafening crash of good intentions all around him. He didn't wait for encouragement. He didn't wait for refusal. He didn't wait before he filled his hand with one breast and touched his thumb to the nipple distended against the fabric.

She sprang away from him as if she'd been scorched.

"No—God—" He reached for her, needing and wanting her with every fevered pulse going through his body. But this time she was quicker getting away from him. Not the most agile, however, and her chair toppled over with a crash.

She stared at it, at him, and at the barkeep who'd appeared behind the bar. She looked horrified, and Charles wasn't certain which of the three was the most horror-inspiring to her.

"Listen to me—" he said, standing up and shoving his chair aside. He started toward her and she backed away.

"No—no more. No more talking. No more hotels. No more—" She touched the back of her hand to her mouth and almost seemed to wince. "No more. I was confused. I needed—"

"I know what you need, Kate." He took another step.

"You might have once. But you don't now. Don't confuse the two, Charles. Now, please—I have a son to tend to." She turned and fled.

Charles listened to the bang of the hotel's front door echoing through the place. He brought his fingers to his mouth and remembered the feel of her through that dress.

Then he tossed several coins on the table, nodded to the barkeep, and left.

"Whatsa matter?" Walter asked.

He was seated at the kitchen table with chalk in one hand and the fingers of the other hand splayed. His lips moved silently as he counted his fingers with the tip of his chalk.

"Nothing's wrong," Kate replied, pushing meat around in a skillet on the stove. "Why?"

Walter kept silently counting, then leaned forward, poked his tongue out the side of his mouth, and wrote something on the slate in front of him. When he finished, he glanced up at her then scowled at the small vase of wildflowers she'd picked that afternoon. She'd put them in her best glass vase and set them on the doily in the middle of the kitchen table. "You've been cleanin' up everything."

"That's because everything's a mess, Walter, and there's always more to be done in a house no matter what a mother does."

Walter tilted his head and pondered his slate. "Yeah, but I like it messy all the time. Just like my pa did. 'Cept he kept papers all over and his shoes—remember his shoes, Mama? He always kept them under the table."

Kate jabbed the meat around then glanced under the table. Walt's boots sat end over end between the table legs. She bit her lip to keep from scolding him to move them. "Yes, he did."

"How come you keep walkin' to the windows and lookin' out like somethin's the matter?"

"Nothing's the matter."

"You've been doin' it every night when you cook dinner."

"I'm just looking."

"At what? Are the cattlemen gonna come and nail a dead sheep to our door like they did at Tommy Bartlett's house?" He was counting again.

"No, they're not going to do that here, Walter. Good heavens, don't think things like that."

"Is that man coming over for dinner?"

"Who?"

"Mr. Renton. Is he coming for dinner?"

"No, Mr. Remington is not coming here for dinner tonight—or any other—no, that might not be quite true. But he's not coming tonight. Why would you think that?"

His tongue slipped out of his mouth again and it seemed to take him a great deal of time to make his numeral on his slate. Kate waited. Again, he shrugged. "I don't know. You're acting like somebody's coming to visit. And you dressed up like you did for Pa's birthday, remember? Remember how you made the cake and it was all gooey in the middle? I remember Pa ate it anyway. I didn't. It was too gooey."

"I'm not dressed up," Kate adamantly replied, her hand skimming down her skirt. "I was just—tired of black."

The skirt was dark blue. The bodice was white cotton, high necked, and shirred. She looked like a trussed-up school matron but when she'd put it on she'd felt like she had when Mother Remington had bought her her first big-girl dress. She'd even fussed with her hair a little this evening, setting the knot looser and lower on her head so that wisps softly framed her face.

But she hadn't done it because she expected a visitor. She'd done it for herself.

"Hmmm," Walter said.

A knock rattled the front door.

Kate's wooden spoon clattered to the floor.

"See?" Walter said without looking up. "It's him."

"Stay right where you are," Kate said, the look in her eyes keeping Walter in his chair. "I'll get it."

She nervously touched one hand to her hair, another to the top button at her throat. The dress was severe in line and appropriately modest. Then why had she felt a delicious tingle of anticipation when she'd put it on and noticed that it made her waist look very small and her breasts look very full?

The silhouette of a man shadowed the curtain over the front door window. She gripped the handle, pasted on a bland, couldn't-care-less-if-you're-here-Charles smile and tugged the door open.

"Mr. Bertrand," she blurted and instantly hoped he didn't detect the disappointment in her voice.

His crinkly-eyed smile faded just a bit. "You were expectin' someone else, ma'am?"

She forced herself to laugh but it came out all wrong.

''No, no—absolutely not. Actually, I wasn't expecting anyone.''

And she hadn't dressed up either.

''I see. If you'd like, ma'am, I can come another time.'' He met her eyes and she saw warmth, compassion, and appreciation in his expression. He was very tall, very broad, and smelled very clean. His shirt was bleached white and his denims were worn and faded almost to white. His blond hair looked damp and freshly combed. The bouquet of flowers he held in one hand was large and white. So was the hat he held against his other thigh. His fingernails were clean.

He looked like a knight and he'd come calling. When she glanced over his shoulder she half expected his horse to be white as well. A chestnut gelding stood at the hitching rail.

She looked back at John Bertrand and he jerked his eyes up from her chest area.

The dress suddenly seemed entirely inappropriate. Why the devil had she put it on?

''You look very fine this evening, ma'am.''

''Thank you. So do you.''

His grin broadened. ''Thank you, ma'am.'' His eyes shifted over her shoulder and she felt a hesitation to invite him in. Again, her eyes strayed over his shoulder and down the street. There were no other tall, broad, silhouettes coming toward her house. Just a relentless evening sun blasting through a day's worth of dust.

The past two nights had passed exactly the same.

''Who is that?'' came Walter's voice behind her. He touched her skirt and poked his head around her. ''It doesn't look like Mr. Reninton.''

''It's not Mr. Remington, Walter. It's Mr. Bertrand. He's a sheepherder. Say hullo, Walter.''

Walter said nothing.

But John Bertrand didn't look very concerned. He was standing tall and still smiling at her.

"Finish your schoolwork," she said to Walter, glancing down at him. When he didn't move, she placed both hands on his narrow shoulders and turned him. "Mr. Bertrand and I will be on the front porch."

"On the swing?" Walter asked, climbing back into his chair.

"I—" Kate lifted her brows and shrugged. "Yes, I suppose on the swing."

"I'm hungry."

"Dinner's going to be a while."

"That's what you always say when I'm hungry."

There it was again, that accusatory tone. And God help her but it made her wish, as it always did, that she'd chosen a better life for her and her son. No matter how much she wanted otherwise, she suspected she alone was not enough for the boy. She alone couldn't get him to say hello and obey and at the same time gently nurture him. All the trying in the world wasn't going to change that.

She let the door swing shut behind her, went out onto the porch, and sat on one end of the swing. John Bertrand sat on the other end and nearly tipped the thing over like a seesaw when he did.

"Whoa there, ma'am," he laughed, scooting closer to the middle. "There, now, that's better."

He was a large man, hard muscled and lean hipped. She glanced at the enormous hand resting on his thigh and knew beyond a doubt that he could crush a sheep's head in it if he wanted to.

The swing idled back and forth at the nudge of her toe. She stared down the street that led back to town, and John Bertrand stared at her.

"Would you like something to drink?" she asked, moving to get up.

"No, ma'am. Please, don't, ma'am. You see, ma'am, I have to tell you—"

She tensed and didn't look at him.

The swing rocked as he shifted closer. "Ma'am"—his voice plunged deep and raspy—"you are the most beautiful woman I've seen in a good long time, ma'am. Yes, ma'am, you are the loveliest—"

"Thank you, Mr. Bertrand. You're very kind."

"No, ma'am. Kindness has nothin' to do with this. I can assure you of that. Oh, here, ma'am. These are for you. Picked them myself on my land."

He handed her the flowers and she laid them in her lap. She rubbed a dusting of yellow pollen against her skirt with her thumb. A vivid image of hulking John Bertrand stooping to pick delicate flowers blossomed in her mind. It was a humbling thought.

"I have a hundred acres of land, now," Bertrand said. "Two thousand head of sheep, a big barn, and a nice farmhouse. Well, it needs a little work. A woman's touch. And a new front porch. But the house is big enough for me and a family."

"It sounds lovely."

He edged close enough that Kate could detect the clean soap smell of him. His voice rumbled very low. "I make a good living, ma'am. I work hard. I don't drink. I don't whore around like most fellas do when they come to town. I'm different from most men an' I guess that makes it easier for some folks not to like me."

"Cattlemen."

"Yep, but it's always been that way. I live a clean life, ma'am. My mama taught me down in Kansas to defend myself and my claims, maybe a bit more than the other sheepherders think I ought to. 'Cept for my friend Jack Barnes. Owns the sheep ranch next to mine. He's the only one I told I was comin' here tonight. 'Course I suspect most folks saw me ride into town lookin' fit for nothin' but romance.'' He looked at her a moment then shrugged. ''I gave up the fight for my land once down in Kansas. I'm not gonna give it up again.''

''I don't blame you. I would do the very same.''

''I also know how to string a line of barbed wire better than most.'' He flashed a grin. ''Know how to move it, too, to reset the bounds of my land when the cattlemen come in and move it on me. One foot here, a couple more there. The cattlemen don't appreciate when you know how to play their game by your rules. But I'm not afraid of them, ma'am. I don't think any of us should be.''

She looked up at him and felt her chest swell with compassion. Charles had been wrong. She wasn't mindlessly avenging Harry's death so much as she was helping honest, hardworking men like John Bertrand.

He looked at her mouth and inhaled very deeply. His face sobered almost instantly. Before she could stop him, he swallowed her hand in one of his. ''I know you're in mournin', ma'am, and I hope you don't think I'm bein' too forward—''

She raised her brows and tugged on her hand. ''I believe I might—''

''No, please, ma'am, I'm not gonna let go. It's not that I don't have respect for you and for the rules and honoring the dead and all, 'specially since your husband died defendin' my rights to make a living. And I swear I wish he was here so I could thank him for doin' that for me. But comes a time when the rules don't make sense anymore. The way I see it—an' I've been thinkin' about this a lot since I met you, ma'am—there ain't no use in two people bein' lonely if they don't have to be.''

''That's quite true,'' Kate said. ''But—''

''You've been keeping to yourself, ma'am.''

''Indeed, I have.''

''People talk in town, ma'am.''

She felt her lips tighten. ''Yes, I know they do.''

''You haven't been called on by any man since your husband died.''

''The townsfolk have that correct, yes.'' The image of the grieving, duty-bound widow in black made her spine go rigid. She'd never wanted to be an object of pity.

John Bertrand exhaled slowly. ''That's a crime, ma'am. Woman who looks like you—'' Again, he stared at her mouth. His big chest heaved several times. ''If you would do me the honor, ma'am—''

''The what? Mr. Bertrand—''

His fist tightened over her fingers. ''Ma'am, I want to court you and then I want to marry you.''

Kate blinked at him. ''You what? Just like that?''

''I think I've waited damned near long enough to tell you how I feel, ma'am. There's a shortage of young, healthy women here that nobody told me about but I promise you that you will love me. And I promise you that I will take care of you and your boy—''

Kate had to look away. The earnestness on his face was almost too much to bear. What the hell was wrong with her? Why did she feel as if she'd left her heart somewhere and that she was never getting it back no matter who came along? It was the same feeling she'd had when Harry was alive. It had made her feel very sad and sorry for Harry . . . and all the more grateful.

Just as Charles had said.

''Please, Mr. Bertrand—''

He was on one knee in front of her.

She closed her eyes. ''Get up, please, Mr. Bertrand, you're embarrassing me.''

The front door thwacked open. ''What's he doin', Mama?''

Kate waved a shooing hand. ''Inside, Walter, please.''

"I don't wanna go inside. I wanna know what he's doing."

"Walter McGoldrick, I swear if you don't get back in that house something very bad is going to happen to you—I'm not quite sure what that is—but it will be the worst thing that's ever happened to you and I promise you will cry."

"I still don't wanna go inside 'cause, see, Mama, I told you he was comin' for dinner. There's Mr. Reninton and he's ridin' a big white horse real fast." Walter jabbed a chalk-stained finger at the street.

Kate craned her neck to peer over John Bertrand's big shoulder. She would have jumped up if he hadn't been on his knees on the floor in front of her. Still, she got a good enough look.

The horse was white like a charger or a knight's destrier, just like the horses in Grandmother Remington's romantic novels. And it had obviously come down the street at a decisive pace. Dust clung in its wake. Its sides were heaving. And its rider wore a look that promised he had serious business to accomplish.

She caught the warning look in his eye as he dismounted, threw his reins over the hitching rail, and started toward the house at a pace that must have tested the lead ball in his thigh. He didn't even wince. But still the look of him made her want to defend to the death why a man she hardly knew was on his knees in front of her.

"Who the hell is that?" John Bertrand asked, eyes very narrow on Charles.

"Um," Kate said, wondering why her heart had suddenly decided to jump to life. It was slamming around in her chest and she was shaking inside as if she'd been caught doing something very naughty.

John Bertrand looked at her and frowned. "You look pale, ma'am. Is he a cattleman, is that it? I'll take care of him."

He surged to his feet but Kate laid a hand on his arm just as Charles's boot thudded on her porch. "No—no, please, he means no harm."

"Hullo, Walt," Charles said, extending one hand to the boy.

Walt tucked his chin under, turned away, and said nothing.

Charles cupped the boy's head, gave it a gentle shake. When he got no response, he turned and looked right at Kate. He was wearing his typical suit of black with cutaway topcoat. But his white shirt was open at the throat, he wore no cravat, and his hair was windtousled. It made him look dastardly and haltingly handsome. Her heart seemed to roll over in her chest.

"Kate," he said, sweeping her with his eyes in such a decisive head-to-toe manner that she felt thoroughly branded in an instant. He looked at Bertrand with a dead calm on his face that betrayed nothing, and stuck out his hand. "Charles Remington."

Bertrand grasped his hand. It was like two forces of nature colliding. "John Bertrand."

Charles looked at Kate.

She lifted her chin. "Mr. Bertrand is a sheep farmer." There that should do it.

"Ah," Charles said, looking very fierce.

"He's here—um—calling."

John Bertrand grabbed her hand. "I asked Mrs. McGoldrick to marry me."

"Ah," Charles said again, still looking at Kate.

John Bertrand looked at Kate as well. "She hasn't answered me yet."

Kate lifted her brows and attempted a shrug. "He just asked me—just as you were riding up. That's why he was on his—his—knees."

"Who is he?" Bertrand asked, still looking at her. "Did you cook him dinner?"

"What? No, heavens, no. He's my—" She looked at Charles, tried waving a dismissive hand, and sighed. "He's just a family friend. We've known one another for years. Actually, he's more Walt's friend."

"No, he's not," Walt grumbled, scowling first at Kate then at Charles. "I don't like him."

"Stop it, Walt. You can go inside and to bed without supper." Her voice held a distinct edge. Her son was sulking and both men were looking at her. She could get them something to drink. She could invite them both for dinner. She could tell them both to leave.

"Are you leaving?" Charles asked John Bertrand.

Bertrand faced him square. "Just about to ask the same of you, gent."

"No," Kate said, moving between the two men. She faced Charles, head tilted back, arms folded beneath her breasts. He was staring at her as if at any second at his choice he would devour her. She felt Bertrand's hands come up on her upper arms and had an uncontrolled urge to squirm away. "Please, Charles, this isn't what you think."

His voice plunged very low. "Convince me otherwise."

"You know very well I can't—"

A shout came from down the street, accompanied by a thunder of hoofbeats. A lone rider approached, dust churning in his wake.

"Bertrand!" he shouted, pulling the horse up in front of the house and clamping his hand on top of his hat. "John Bertrand, come quick! Your barn—"

"What is it, Jack?"

Jack Barnes drew in great lungfuls of air. He must have ridden at a breakneck pace from the farm. "It's burnin', John. Sheep's inside—probably dead—"

"Christ almighty," John Bertrand snarled and effortlessly swung himself up over the front porch rails. He hit the ground and dashed for his horse.

"I'll send help!" Kate shouted after him. "If I can rustle some up," she added, half under her breath.

He nodded at her as he swung up on his horse, and with a furious tug on the reins he and the animal went hurtling down the street.

"It's the cattlemen," Kate cried, realizing too late that she'd turned and was gripping Charles's arms. "Oh, God, Charles, we have to help—"

He looked down at her, his face a mask of no expression. "Let's go." He grabbed her hand and reached for Walt's. The boy hesitated a moment then tentatively gave his hand.

"Wait"—Kate's feet skidded on the porch—"I have food on the stove."

"And flowers on the kitchen table," Walt put in.

"For John Bertrand?" Charles said in ominous tones, then threw the door wide. "Get it off the stove before it burns. Then let's go. You can cook for me another time."

For the sake of the sheepherders and burning barns and good men like John Bertrand, she decided to let that one go.

Chapter 10

Charles knew the barn was gone the instant he spotted the smoke on the horizon. Billowing black puffs of it belched into the sky. The setting sun cast rosy pink, apricot, and violet hues as far as the eye could see. The black column of smoke looked almost evil against such a landscape. But the air was breezy, the wind had been strong all day, and the earth was parched. Conditions couldn't have been better for setting a devastating fire.

Charles dug his heels into his horse's flanks and tightened the arm he had wrapped around Kate's waist. She bobbed in front of him and clung with both hands to his arm, cocooning herself back into him like any woman would if she was as terrified of horses as Kate insisted she was.

Still, with a cause to be championed and burning barns to save, she'd shed all inhibition and had rustled up the townsfolk to come lend John Bertrand a hand, exuding a buoyant energy and convincing forthrightness that any big city politician would have coveted. When they'd paused at Victoria Valentine's shop to drop Walter off for safekeeping, Charles was certain Kate hadn't considered the consequences of charging off on horseback with the stranger in town. Victoria Valentine had looked at Kate as if she needed gentle reminding of that, burning barn or no burning barn.

After all, Victoria had pointed out, if wasn't as if Kate was responsible for the barn burning.

Victoria had even offered her buckboard to get Kate where she wanted to go. Kate declined, and seemed oblivious to Victoria's point. Charles's white horse would be much faster, thank you.

She was a spirited woman, a staunch defender, and as compassionate a champion as anyone could ask for. But Charles hoped that she would now begin to understand that the cause she was avenging was indeed a very dangerous one.

The cattlemen's fight had taken an ominous turn.

Charles and Kate were the first of the swarm of townsfolk to arrive at John Bertrand's ranch. Bertrand and Jack Barnes had given up the fight for the barn and were throwing buckets of water on the nearby farmhouse as the flames licked furiously at the roof. It was an impossibly defeating task for just two men, Charles realized, as he watched them run back to the water pump and frantically fill buckets. If the wind continued they wouldn't stand a chance at saving the house.

He slid from the horse and Kate all but jumped into his arms in her haste, gripping his shoulders as he took her weight against him. ''You get the pump and fill,'' he said into her hair. ''I'll help with buckets.''

They worked furiously for the next three hours. When the last of the flames had diminished and only a thin column of simmering smoke curled into the night skies, Charles put down his bucket and looked around the barnyard for Kate. The area was dark but moonlit. Townspeople were scattered about standing in groups, staring at the charred remains of the barn. Others wandered about, looking to help where they could. Sheepdogs trotted about aimlessly, as if they were searching for something to do.

Beneath Charles's boots the earth was a quagmire. Every muscle in his arms and back screamed. He tasted smoke deep in his throat. And his thigh ached intolerably.

"Tough fight," a man said, clasping Charles on his shoulder. Charles nodded and realized the man beneath the soot was Ace, the barkeep from Louella's place.

"The house is still standing," Charles said.

Ace rubbed a meaty hand over his brow and shook his head. "Wonder how long. Trouble's come home to roost. Bertrand says the pasture behind the house is full of sheep with slit throats. One was hung up by the back door with a noose. Had a note in its mouth to get the hell out of these parts and take the rest of the woollies."

"Bertrand's the leader of the sheepherders. He was the most likely target."

"An' they're givin' him the worst of it. I heard 'bout cattlemen puttin' poison like saltpeter in the sheep's' grain ta kill a few head. Read that in the *Turkeyfoot Chronicle*. But I never seen or heard nothin' like this. Bertrand's best sheepdog was found shot in the head. I never seen a man cry before but they say a sheepherder will sigh to lose his friend, groan if his wife or child dies, but if his dog is dead, part of him dies with it." Ace lifted his brows. "Bertrand's a fighter. He's not goin' anywhere. He's just more mad now. This is a war. Every cattleman in the county better sleep with one eye open."

"It seems a bit rash to blame all of them for the sins of the few."

"What ones did it don't matter. They all know and they keep their mouths shut, whether they like it or not. Hell, Pruitt and his boys been promisin' this for a long time an' no one stopped 'em. An' now it's here. I for one don't know how we can fix it." He looked at Charles. "Maybe you do, bein' a politician an' all."

"Lawyer," Charles said, feeling weariness settle like a

sack of solid rock on his shoulders. "Most folks around here don't like my kind."

"You're right 'bout that. 'Course same folks'll change their mind real quick you do somethin' about this. Fear isn't somethin' I want to live with, Remington. I wanna walk down the street an' say hello to someone an' not wonder if they're a sheepman or a cattleman or for that matter an ass man or a tit man. I don't wanna wake up on fire 'cause I chose the wrong kinda friends. Nobody does. Not even lawyers. As it is we all took one helluva risk comin' out here to help. Damned near puts us on the side of the sheepherders, from a cattleman's point of view."

"From what I've seen it's just neighbors helping neighbors. No one's chosen sides."

"I hope I won't be explainin' that with a gun barrel shoved up my nose." Ace nodded and moved on.

Charles scanned the barnyard and felt an unconscionable need for Kate. Was she tired? Hungry? Was she with John Bertrand, brave leader of the sheepherders, holding his hand, comforting him and saying she would be his good and faithful wife here in the life she'd chosen and made for herself? Was Charles simply to remain a ghost from her past with no chance to carve out a niche in her heart?

His strides were as long and purposeful as he could make them. His feet slid and squished in ankle-deep muck and the pain in his leg was like a knife embedded there. He heard the plaintive bleat of a sheep somewhere out there in the dark. And then he heard Kate's voice.

If she was with Bertrand he'd—

"There now, if I hold it right there—like this—does it feel better?"

He whirled in the dark and spotted her by a dim lantern, kneeling down, bent over a pair of outstretched, denim-clad legs.

"Kate." His voice sounded nothing like it usually did.

It sounded pumped up full of jealousy and rage and ridiculous, childish notions. Blood throbbed in his temples and his fists balled at his sides, almost itching to be used. And he would use them, dammit, even if the man's barn had just burned to the ground, even if he'd never used them on a man before.

She looked up, lips parting with surprise, hair completely atumble all around her, and then she smiled at him and he was instantly bewitched.

"Oh, Charles, look at you. You're a mess."

"I am." He swallowed and watched a young boy sit up behind her, holding a swathe of bandage over his brow. The bandage was edged with lace, like a woman's petticoat. Charles realized then that he hadn't seen a woman's petticoat for quite some time. Too long. He also realized this was quite probably Kate's petticoat, and the effect on him was as if he'd just seen her in it.

"He was running with his bucket, slipped in the mud, and hit his head on the side of a buckboard wagon," Kate explained, securing the knot of the bandage. She moved slightly and Charles noticed that she'd hiked her skirt up past her knees, probably to get at the petticoat. Her leg was covered in a mud-splattered white stocking.

"There," she said to the boy. "No, you lay there for a while. You don't want to fall and hit the other side."

Charles grabbed her elbow as she struggled to get up. "I thought you might be tending to injured sheep," he said, as they moved deeper into the shadows.

"Doc's doing that—oh, Charles, it was a massacre. I don't know what to say to John Bertrand."

"Nothing. There's nothing you or Jonathan Smarte can say or do to fix it."

"I feel so responsible."

"You didn't set the fire or kill the sheep."

"It was my words in that editorial tonight."

"And you were speaking the truth, Kate."

"The truth? And if I came out and called Elmer Pruitt a murderer of an innocent, unarmed man? That's the truth and you know what would happen to me? He'd kill me or burn us all out. No one in this town says anything about the truth because it's too dangerous to do it. And yet I think I can say what I want and hide behind the paper and an alias, and look what happens?" She looked toward the barn rubble and her eyes suddenly glistened. "Why didn't I think it would happen—that they would go this far—when they shot my husband dead like he meant nothing to anybody? They're animals, Charles."

"They're like children daring someone to stop them. They'll go as far as they want until someone does."

She pressed her lips together. "We can't even go to Sheriff Gage and have Pruitt and his henchmen arrested. We can't do anything. We can't even prove it's them even if there was someone who'd listen to us. We're absolutely powerless and I feel like someone's shoving that in my face. I think I'm only now realizing that."

A breeze tossed a strand of hair over her lips. Charles reached up and drew it aside with his finger. "I know you don't want to hear this. Quiet the paper for a while, Kate. Let things cool down."

"That would be giving up and I vowed I wouldn't. That's giving these sheepherders no chance at all in this fight. They can't do it alone, Charles. They need someone with influence to take notice of this and help them, someone above the cattlemen, someone even above the damned railroad. Someone who can give them grazing and watering rights on their own land, legally. How can I help them do that if I don't have the voice of the paper?"

"It's not surrender to be smarter than your enemy, Kate. Sometimes in a war, generals know when it's better not to engage in the battle. They hunker down and wait to see what the enemy does.''

She looked up at him as if she were giving this deep consideration. ''You think so?''

His thumb touched the upper slope of her cheekbone where soot had smudged. ''You have other editorials to write.''

Her brows quivered together and she looked as if she was trying very hard to glare at him. ''Yes, I do. But it seems a bit frivolous to fill the columns of the paper discussing a woman's duty to her husband when barns are being burned and sheep killed and rights trampled.''

''Sometimes it's what's needed after something like this. You can't cook on high flames forever, Kate.''

''I like high flames,'' she said, tilting up her chin. ''It's never boring.''

''No,'' he murmured, looking deep into her liquid eyes. ''No chance of that.'' He let his fingers curl around her upper arms.

''Your hands are dirty,'' she said. Her eyes skimmed over his face, down his throat, past the open neck of his shirt, and his chest heaved as if he suddenly couldn't get enough breath.

''I know,'' he said, keeping his hands where they were. The dim lamplight shadowed the vee of her dress where the top buttons had been left opened to the base of her throat. He let his eyes roam lower down the row of tiny buttons, over the shirred pleats that hugged the fullness of her bosom. The white bodice was soot smudged and blood stained and would probably never be white again. He knew she watched him and silently dared her to stop him. He almost wished she would try so he could prove his point beyond a doubt.

''Did you dress this way for John Bertrand?'' His voice was deep, rasping.

"Really, Charles—"

"You're not going to marry him?"

"I—don't—"

He brought both thumbs to the sides of her breasts and gently rubbed once. He heard her small intake of breath.

"You're not going to marry him." He lowered his head and pressed his mouth to her temple. Her skin tasted smoky and salty. "You're not going to cook him dinner and let him sit on your front porch either."

"Your hands, Charles—" Her voice was breathless.

He closed his eyes. "I want to sit on your front porch," he whispered. "I want to eat dinner with you."

"Charles, please—"

"No one can see us."

She grabbed his hands. "I can."

He lifted his head. "I'm not going anywhere any time soon. I can promise you that."

"That sounds like a threat."

"That depends if you trust me. I thought it sounded comforting and reassuring. Now, let's go, before Bertrand finds you and wants to stake a matrimonial claim. I'm just not in the mood to hit the man tonight."

She resisted the tug on her hand. "No, I'll find a ride back with—"

"You're coming with me. My horse is right over here. I got him at a decent price at the livery. You liked him well enough for the ride out."

"But—"

"Don't argue with me, Kate."

"I'm not arguing."

"If you'd prefer, I could prove my point and carry you." He stooped, curved his arm around her waist, but she made a nervous sound and shied away like a skittish deer.

"You're awful, Charles Remington," he thought he heard her murmur as she passed him.

It sounded more like an endearment than a scolding. His lips quirked into a genuine smile and he set off after her.

Kate jerked awake. "What?"

"Shh." A man's voice rumbled in her ear. A man's hands were around her waist, gently pulling her from the saddle toward him, and it seemed the absolute right thing to do to slip into his arms. After all, she felt as if she had a wooden stake shoved up her back and her bottom felt abused, as if she'd been jarred on a hard chair for a good long time.

A weary, grumbling groan came from the back of her throat when her arms looped around his neck.

She opened her eyes briefly, saw moonlit skies and a man's face silhouetted above her. "Charles," she said, closing her eyes again. Her head fell on his shoulder. "I can walk, you know."

"I know. I've watched you. You do it well." He was carrying her, holding her close against him and she was just too tired to attempt all the squirming and wriggling it would take to make him stop.

Besides, she didn't really want him to put her down. Even if he smelled like smoke and got her dress dirty. What had he said about giving up the fight? It wasn't complete surrender, was it? Just a reprieve. Even the toughest generals needed time to rest and close their eyes and enjoy a moonlit night.

Charles pushed open her door then kicked it closed behind them. His boots thudded on her kitchen floor.

"Where's Walt?" she asked, stifling a yawn.

"With Victoria, remember?"

He moved across the kitchen, heading right for her room. Her head poked up. "Wait just a minute."

"Is this where you sleep?" He stopped in the doorway

to her room. Moonbeams streamed through her window and set the white coverlet on her bed aglow with blue-white light. They both stared at it for several moments. Lace curtains stirred in a warm breeze. A fragrant floral scent drifted through the air, beckoning.

Kate swallowed thickly. "I think you'd better put me dow—"

But he moved right into the room and set her gently on the edge of the bed. "Really, Charles—" She stood straight up, felt her knees wobble and buckle, pain sliced up both her thighs, and she collapsed back down to the bed. She didn't realize she'd grabbed hold of his arm until he hunkered down in front of her.

"You really ought to learn to ride," he said. "I would have thought you would have already if you intended to stay here forever." He looked very stern despite the gentleness of his tone. He also seemed incredibly large. Or maybe the room was just too small for the two of them.

Alone. It seemed suddenly a delicate situation.

Kate licked her parched lips. "Really, Charles, I'm quite capable—" Her voice snagged. His hands had disappeared under her skirt and warm fingers encircled her ankles right above the top edges of her black, button-up ankle boots.

"You're going to be worse off in the morning," he said. "I'm just warning you. Best thing would be to hop right back on the horse. No, let me." Long fingers tugged on the boot laces. His eyes glittered, watching her.

She averted her face and wished she could think of a good reason to stop him. "I should light a candle."

"We have enough light."

Yes. She could see him clearly in the moonlight.

He eased one boot from her foot then the other. She curled her toes against the hooked carpet and closed her eyes. His hands rested on the tops of her feet, his thumbs gently moving back and forth over the arches. She wondered what his touch would feel like without the stockings.

The clock over the kitchen mantel struck once.

With fingers spread, Charles slid his hands up to cup the backs of her calves. She should tell him to stop, tell him she was immune to his charms, that he should go back to Boston and forget about seducing her for whatever it was he wanted.

But it would be a lie, all of it.

She felt the coverlet beneath her fingertips and thought about the endless nights she'd lain there with it drawn up to her chin and had forced herself not to think of being with a man. She thought about the tears she'd cried in six years, how she'd cried every day at first, and how she'd cried less and less over time until Boston and Charles and unrequited dreams of her youth had been all but forgotten.

And now they were back.

There was so much to say and yet it didn't seem the right time to say anything when all she could concentrate on was his touch and the nearness of him after so long. It was as if she'd woken up in a dream.

He touched the backs of her knees. Shivers whispered through her and she felt perched on the edge of a yawning precipice. She knew she was going to fall, no matter how hard she hung on, it was only a matter of minutes. But the realities of her life seemed far less grim from the moonlit depths of a summer night. Surrendering to her passions seemed effortless.

Charles rested his hands on her knees and stretched his fingers up her thighs until they curled into the tops of her stockings. She sat there trembling, needful, tired, and wanting in so many ways her head spun. He leaned forward and laid his head on her lap.

Like a lonely, weary man. And it occurred to her that he was perhaps as lonely and weary as she was.

A ball of emotion wedged in Kate's throat. She licked

her lips and felt her insides tremble, as if she were about to take a first step into uncharted territory. "I've—I've found that loneliness can be like a bottomless pit of despair," she said, her voice sounding thick and hoarse. Charles didn't move, as if he listened to her with such intensity he feared she'd stop talking. The night seemed to have grown unusually quiet around them. Kate released her breath and plunged on. "A person can be in a solitary prison even in a room full of people. I think—no, I know I've been there for years, ever since I left Lenox—maybe even when I was married to Harry—in some ways—I was very much alone. Even with Walt sometimes I feel so—" She paused. "It's only when I write that I find myself. It's as if I belong someplace else. Strange, isn't it?"

Tentatively, she touched Charles's head and slowly traced the curl of one lock. He made a sound, low and husky, lifted his head, and splayed his fingers around her bare thighs, pulling himself up.

"Not strange," he murmured. "I've been lonely for years, and trapped—but even writing didn't help. Nothing did. So I just blotted it all out and stopped dreaming."

"So did I," she whispered. "Only now—somehow I feel like this is all—not real."

"A dream," he murmured, staring at her mouth.

"Yes—"

He leaned toward her and touched his lips to hers. He drew back once, looked into her eyes—and she knew it was her last moment to stop him—and then she was pulled deep against him, his mouth crushed over hers.

The effect was like slamming into a wall. All the breath was driven out of her. Her senses scattered. His scent, the warm taste of his mouth, the touch of him bombarded her. She was drowning in it, but she wouldn't run from it again—not when it seemed, for this moment, so right.

She sensed he was not the refined, gentle Charles she'd

once known. This man was possessed of deep, consuming passions. He was like tinder ignited. And he was setting her aflame along with him.

"Ah, God—Kate—" Their mouths parted with a gasp of air and she realized he'd fallen to his knees with her in his arms. She didn't know how—didn't care why—but her arms were clasped around him and her hands cupped his head closer as he buried his face in her neck, then lower where the buttons of her dress defined the curve of bosom.

"Charles—" It was an explosion of air. He was touching her, pressing his hand against her breast, lifting it, and gripping her bare thigh beneath her dress with an urgency that took her breath away. And then buttons were unfastened, impatient fingers were brushing the white cotton undergarment, and his mouth was pressing hot kisses to her skin there, above the ribboned neckline. His voice came in a rumbling murmur, memory of another time six years ago, another place in an orchard drifted over Kate and she felt the same abandonment, the same pull of wanton surrender, only deeper, stronger, as if her soul were wrenching around itself.

Charles slid his hand up her thigh, cupped her buttock through the thin cotton pantaloon, and pressed her loins deep into his. She groaned with the utter animalistic abandon of it and felt air on her breasts and the brush of cotton falling away from them at the bidding of his hands.

"I have to—" he rumbled and then his mouth was on her breasts, his tongue was laving her nipples, his hands were caressing and delighting in her, and she was lifted into the heavens in a spiral of sensation where memories and pain and responsibilities were forgotten.

And it all settled with an urgent, throbbing, desperate kind of need high between her thighs. She squirmed and his husky murmur of pleasure fired her passions. Her hands fumbled with the buttons of his shirt, pushing it aside. Palms splayed on his chest, on skin that emanated a fiery heat. "Charles—what are we doing—? We have to stop—"

"I know—I'm trying—I promised myself I wouldn't—" One tug of his hands and she was on the floor and he was pressing her deep into the rug and kissing her with a passion that stripped away every last vestige of reason or resistance. His hand was under her skirt, parting her thighs, searching for that slit in her pantaloons where the pulse of her seemed to emanate from, and for a moment the world stopped.

He touched her, groaned from the depths of his chest, then stillness. Suddenly her skirts were pushed up; he poised above her, looked down at her, and froze.

"Jesus Christ almighty," he said.

She blinked up at him, licked her parched lips, and felt a stinging disappointment come over her. "Charles—" She would have placed her hand on his chest but he caught her wrist.

"No—God—Kate—this is—not good." He did something to the front of his trousers in a swift, impatient motion. "This isn't what I came to do—not like this—not like it was when you and—and, Christ, we haven't even talked about—" His breath came out as if through bared teeth. He closed his eyes almost as if he were in pain for a moment and she felt his chest push deep into hers three times. "Kate"—he cupped her head in his hand and rubbed his thumb over her temple—"until now I thought I was a man possessed of good common sense. It seems I was very wrong. I'm—sorry. I know you're in mourning. I know how you felt about Harry—how you still feel. You're vulnerable and I'm—I should have been the one with some sense—" He pressed to his mouth the back of her hand. "Forgive me—please—"

She blinked. "I—" But she didn't want to forgive him. She hadn't wanted him to stop.

She—the mourning widow, risking her life and the lives of others to avenge Harry's murder and here she was, eager to lay beneath another man so soon after his death.

The implication of it left her shaken with humiliation.

He moved off of her, took her hand and tugged. "Come." His voice was gently coaxing.

She got to her feet and tried with little success to hold her chemise and dress together. She felt the sting of tears in her eyes and blurted, "Charles, did I do—?"

"No—Christ—" He pushed her hands aside and took her into his arms. She felt the warmth of him engulf her and wanted to steel herself against the feelings stirring inside of her. "It's as if I was born to do the right thing by you, Kate," he said hoarsely. "And I will. I've promised myself, I promised my father, and I promise you."

"I don't need looking after, Charles."

His hands cupped her upper arms. She could feel him watching her and kept her eyes averted. "Believe me, Kate. I know you're a woman now. And that's why I'm going to leave before I do something even more stupid."

"No," she whispered. "I wouldn't want to do any more stupid things either." Stupid—slanderous. The kinds of things a woman does when she has no control over herself. Hadn't she vowed not to make the mistakes she'd made six years ago?

She glanced down and worked the buttons closed over the valley between her breasts then took each end of the chemise ribbon in her fingers and worked it into a clumsy bow.

He didn't move. She could hear him breathing, feel him watching her, and then she spotted on the floor at her feet a tangle of white. It was soft wool, well worn, and must have fallen off the bed when Charles had pulled her into his arms.

And then she remembered it was Walt's blanket. He'd

come into her bed sometime during the previous night and hadn't taken his blanket back to his room.

She bent and picked up the blanket, held it close against her chest, and lifted her eyes to Charles's. "You're right, Charles. We can't make any mistakes. There's too much at stake. We've both, I think, too much to lose."

He pulled her into his arms and tucked her head under his chin with a hand at her nape. "I know, Kate. Abandoning everything at this point would make all that's passed for both of us seem somehow pointless. I know—" He pressed a kiss to the top of her head, whispered something, and left.

The sound of the door thudding closed behind him was the loneliest sound Kate had ever heard.

Chapter 11

"No more business in Turkeyfoot Run, Mr. Remington?" Louella Lawless asked Charles as he passed the open door to her library. The room was a scarlet velvet testament to Louella's passion for overdone, East Coast, top-drawer parlors. She sat behind an ornately carved, gilt-edged desk, bathed in the light of a three-tiered candelabra, quill in hand, dressed in afternoon black-and-ivory-plaid taffeta. She smiled when he paused in the doorway, and gave him an assessing head-to-toe-and-back-again look. "You stayed the night there."

"My business took longer than I expected."

Her eyes glittered. "I certainly hope my competition there didn't woo you away from me."

Charles crossed his arms over his chest and leaned his shoulder against the doorjamb. "Why, Louella, what makes you think I would go looking for something like that in Turkeyfoot Run?"

Louella gave an elegant shrug. "I would indeed doubt your character and obvious good taste. But then again Turkeyfoot Run is the county seat and offers much more than Crooked Nickel in the way of gambling, fine dining, and good conversation with the locals. Had you stayed long enough I'm sure you could have witnessed a hanging. The judge in town is notoriously forthcoming with death sentences for murderers and the like.''

''Yes. I met him. We had dinner together.''

''Ah.'' She nodded slowly, looking thoughtful. ''You keep very much to yourself here, Mr. Remington. One has to wonder where a man like you takes his pleasures.''

''It wasn't there.''

''Then she's here.'' Louella didn't strike him as a gossip. He'd noticed the way she looked at him when he walked through the common room. Her eyes followed him very keenly. There was nothing of the flirt in her, but his instincts told him her interest was of a romantic nature.

Her dark eyes narrowed slightly. ''I will miss you when you leave, Mr. Remington.''

''That won't be soon.''

Louella smiled. ''Very good. You're a bit of a mystery. I haven't known a man who's intrigued me this much in years. Oh, there was one, several years ago.''

''Dan Goodknight.''

The surprise on her face was genuine. Apparently she thought she hid her feelings well enough every night when Goodknight arrived and asked for the redheaded Isabelle.

Louella glanced quickly at something on her desk. ''When Dan first came to town with all his hundred odd thousand head of cattle, his California fortune, and his army of Mexican servants, there wasn't a woman breathing in this town who didn't notice him. The trouble was he had a very young, very beautiful wife.''

''And no interest in your place.''

''Not until after she died, along with the baby she was carrying for him. And even then he didn't step foot in my place until three years later. I thought he'd found another wife in the meantime. As it turns out he was mourning her death for that long. I don't believe he'll ever recover from the loss. Oh, he wouldn't admit any of it, of course, and there are men who believe Dan Goodknight was born without a heart.''

''No man accumulates wealth and success by being nice, Louella. And no woman, either.''

Her chin came up. ''Yes, I know that. There was a time I had to try very hard not to care about every poor cuss I met out here. After a while, it was much easier not to care. Now—hell, now I can buy and sell orphaned young girls into prostitution. Maybe that's why Dan Goodknight never comes into my place looking for me. I've forgotten how to be human.''

Charles had a sudden, peculiar thought that back in the days when Louella's last name wasn't Lawless she'd been very much like Kate: fiery, smart, independent-minded and full of grand ideologies. A hard life on an unforgiving frontier had a way of sucking all the fire out of a person. It was a chilling thought that in several years Kate could be as roughly seasoned and jaded as Louella Lawless. Hadn't he already seen the wall of defense she'd begun to build around herself?

''I'm keeping you,'' Louella said, and in an instant she drew her parlor-room mien about her. Face elegantly set, chin tilted at the perfect angle, she seemed untouched by the harsh world around her. ''Where are you off to this afternoon? Business?''

''Not today.''

''Not calling, I hope.''

''My intentions today are bent on someone quite young.''

''Ah. Saving another ten-year-old?''

''No. This one's five.''

Louella's eyes snapped wide. ''Five. Good God—''

Charles shoved away from the doorjamb. ''His name is Walt. His mother and I are old family friends.''

''Wait just a minute.'' Louella was out of her chair and

Charles took that cue to head toward the front door. Her heels clicked on the polished oak floorboards behind him. "Are you talking about Walter McGoldrick's mother—that—that—what's her name?—oh, yes, the widow, Kate McGoldrick? You know her? She's in mourning, Mr. Remington."

"Yes, I know." He paused at the front door with his hand resting on the knob. "I'm going to see her boy."

Louella seemed to contemplate this. "We don't much care for one another, she and I."

"I find that odd. You're very much alike."

Louella looked at him strangely. "Oh, I quite disagree. Kate McGoldrick takes great comfort in hiding behind a dead husband and clinging to propriety. And yet her best friend is hardly a step down the rung from me."

"I don't think Kate looks at it that way. And neither should you. Good afternoon, Louella." He gave her a brisk nod, stepped out onto the porch, and turned in the direction of the newspaper office.

His heart rate immediately jumped. A day and a night spent in Turkeyfoot Run, away from Kate, had done nothing to assuage his guilt, anger, and utter disappointment in himself and his behavior on her bedroom floor two nights ago. For a man who'd spent the better part of his life steeped in responsibility, following the meticulous life-plan laid out for him, and doing everything he could to exceed everyone's expectations of him, he'd damned near lost everything in one blazing moment of indulging primal lust. There was, it seemed, one facet of his life where he had very little self-control. And he wasn't the least bit proud of it.

It made no sense. Every part of his being told him that success with Kate lay in his ability to keep his wits about him. His own brother Jude had made it a lifelong quest to succumb to his vices and make his relatives live to regret it. There was no better example for Charles. And yet with Kate two nights ago he'd behaved no better than the rutting, lascivious monster he'd been scorning his entire life.

She didn't know about the enormous inheritance intended for Walt.

She didn't know she owed Charles five thousand dollars and the future of her paper.

More than anything she still didn't trust him. And the longer he kept secrets from her, the less likely was it that she would. But how did he tell her the truth of it, admit his deception, and win her trust all at once? And when he'd won it, what combination of words would convince her to leave the life she'd made for herself and the revenge she intended to have?

There was no escaping that he'd come in part to find Jude's possible heir. In his heart he felt that Kate and Walt should be back in Boston, where sheep weren't slaughtered and barns burned, where schools were of prime quality, where opportunity for great achievement existed. They should be where he could watch over them, Jude be damned. But the longer he stayed in Crooked Nickel, the more time he spent with Kate, the more convinced he was that she would never leave until she'd avenged herself of Harry's death. And he was loath to rob her of that.

There was little doubt that there was a woman inside Kate that was trembling to be released. But he wasn't going to indulge that part of her and himself, however much it seemed the only thing he'd been born to do, when it would threaten every hope of anything beyond immediate physical release.

"Hold on there, Remington." Sheriff Gage stepped onto the boardwalk in front of him, chest puffed up, hands stuffed into his pockets. A toothpick poked out of the corner of his mouth and he worked it as if he had just swallowed a mouthful of stringy beef.

Charles nodded and tried not to look bored. He had a

tremendous desire to see Kate and very little tolerance at the moment for this man's attempts at intimidation. "Sheriff."

"Heard you rustled up the folks to help that sheepherder the other night. Yer a friend of them sheepherders, ain't ya?"

Charles showed his teeth in a fake smile. "I like to think I'm a friend to all, Sheriff. If your house was burning down, I'd feel a great compulsion to be right there in the bucket brigade, helping out. Because if I didn't, why, the house next to it could catch fire, and the one next to that, and probably Louella's place at some point and then where would I sleep? Call it selfishness."

Gage snorted. "Damned stupid of ya, Remington. Ya made it clear what side of the fence yer sittin' on."

"I don't believe I chose any side of a fence. And I'm not alone in that sentiment, Sheriff. We had no trouble rallying the townsfolk to help put out that fire. I'd think you'd be shouting the praises of the people here in Crooked Nickel. The Union Pacific would love to hear about it. Sells acreage, Sheriff. Now that I think about it, there were so many of us at Bertrand's farm, you'd have a hard time singling out just a few to stop and threaten on a boardwalk. I've got to wonder why you've picked me."

The toothpick flicked to the other side of Gage's mouth. "I told you once I'll be watchin' you. Tenderfoot's is easy to spot. Besides, yer a friend of the Widow McGoldrick."

Charles kept his tone deceptively soft. "You have no quarrel with her, Gage."

"I do with tenderfoot's what come to town and stir up old trouble and try to make new trouble."

"Just finding a few things hard to swallow, Gage. Maybe I haven't been here long enough."

"Maybe you ain't scared enough yet."

Charles met his stare. "Indeed. Why don't you ask John Bertrand how scared he is now? He's another who would have been hard for you to miss when he rode into town the other evening, looking like he'd come for a night out. I suspect he rode right past your jailhouse that night. That is your chair out front, isn't it? And that is you I see sitting in it all day?''

Gage's eyes narrowed to beady slits. ''What're you sayin', tenderfoot?''

''Whoever set the fire had to know Bertrand wasn't at his farm. He's a strong man. I'll wager he even owns a shotgun or two. I wouldn't sneak around his place unless I knew he wasn't there to catch me.''

Gage's whiskered nostrils flared. ''Folks in town talk. Anyone coulda seen him.''

Charles smiled. ''Yes, I know. It was just a thought, Sheriff.'' Charles moved to pass him but again, as in their previous meeting, Gage blocked his path. ''Now what is this, Sheriff? Is something else troubling you?''

''Leave it alone, Remington,'' Gage snarled. ''Just stay the hell outta things that don't concern you.''

''Odd that you feel a need to warn me. You don't know me, Sheriff, enough to care one way or the other about me. Then again, maybe you've finally realized that the townsfolk and the sheepherders simply need someone to rally and unite them. And once they do, they will become something far more than a nuisance to men like Elmer Pruitt. Then—why, Sheriff, you'll be out of a job. Good day to you.''

Charles felt Gage's eyes following him the length of the boardwalk.

''Women have had the right to hold office and vote in this state for more than ten years,'' Kate said, looking up at Douglas Murphy as he settled himself on the corner of her desk. ''That's the crux of my argument.''

''And I could argue back that most of the men who

passed the woman's suffrage law assumed that the ladies would simply choose to stay home where they belonged. Doing their duty.''

''And I would argue that a woman's duty can reach well beyond the four walls of her home. Listen to this—'' Kate flapped open the paper in front of her and cleared her throat. '' 'Wyoming's first woman officeholder was fifty-seven-year-old Esther Morris.' '' Kate again glanced up. ''She's one of the territory's most renowned suffragists.'' Again, she looked at the paper. '' 'Despite a lack of legal training, she was appointed justice of the peace for the southern mining town of South Pass City. She ran her court with an iron hand for nearly a year and never had a decision reversed by a higher court.' ''

''What is that?'' Douglas asked, leaning over.

''*The Free Suffragist.* It's a Laramie paper.''

''Odd name for a paper. Every suffragist I can ever remember meeting would tell you rather adamantly that she's free. So would every wife and mother in this town.''

''I'm not so certain about that. And I'm not so certain that those women don't hide copies of magazines like this under their mattresses after they're done beating them in the front yard. Douglas, all-male higher courts never overturned Esther Morris's decisions. They approved.''

''Do you want me to think of something for the sake of argument? No, I won't bother. Rather soon I suspect I'll have more than enough of that in my life. With Charles Remington. He's your friend from Boston.''

''Yes, I—I know him,'' Kate said, shuffling papers around on her desk until she found her half-written rebuttal to Charles's letter. Her heart was doing funny little stutters in her chest. ''I didn't know he was planning to stay that long.''

''Seems to me he's considering it. A little friendly competition in town will keep me honest.''

Kate worried her lower lip and quickly glanced out the windows. There was no sign of Mr. Gould. She'd sent him off to the bank when Douglas arrived so she and Douglas could have a private chat. "I think I should tell you he knows I'm Jonathan Smarte."

"Mmm," Douglas said, frowning at a page in his hand. "He seems like a fine enough fellow. Being an old friend, and all, I wouldn't fret over it, Kate."

"Fret? No—no—I'm not fretting. He's a fine enough friend."

"We fought on the same battlefield," Douglas said, looking important and utterly impressed. "He took a ball in the thigh at Bull Run. He'll live with that for the rest of his life."

A strange feeling rooted in Kate's belly. "You act as if you know him very well. He just came to town."

"We're both Harvard men," he replied as if that spoke for itself. "And besides that, I'm enjoying seeing you all up in a lather over something besides the sheepherders."

Kate's brows quivered. "What lather? I just don't like being bothered with antisuffragist editorials disguised as newsworthy items. Now I have a rebuttal to write by this afternoon, which seems completely foolish since the smoke is still coming from what used to be John Bertrand's barn."

Douglas slid off the desk and shrugged. "Townsfolk rally around curious issues. This might be something they need right now, especially the women, to take their minds off the fear. I think your pal Charles Remington knows that."

"Perhaps." Kate brandished her quill with renewed vigor and dunked the tip into an ink pot. "I hope the womenfolk of this town respond by holding a suffragist rally right in front of the jail. Maybe that will get Gage out of town for good." Kate brightened at the idea. "Bessie Mae will make a wonderful suffragist champion, don't you think?''

The bell above the door tinkled and Charles strode in.

Kate felt her belly do a flip-flop and she focused on the page in front of her. Where had he been for the last day-and-a-half?

''Murphy.''

''Remington. How the hell are you?''

The two exchanged handshakes. ''Spent the day and night yesterday in Turkeyfoot Run,'' Charles said. ''Nice town they have there.''

''Too many lawyers,'' Douglas replied cheerily. ''And I know all of them. But the sitting judge there—Warner's his name—is one hell of a mean cuss. Hails from Denver by way of Washington. Got himself appointed when the previous judge was gunned down in a trial over a stolen cow. I've never met the man but he's supposedly out to strike all the lawlessness from these parts.''

''It would be one hell of a job even for ten judges. Mrs. McGoldrick.''

Kate met his blue eyes. The smile flirting on his lips made her remember the feel of his lips on her breasts, and she blushed from the inside out. She looked quickly at Douglas, who was looking curiously at her, then blushed even more and focused again on the page in front of her. ''Mr. Remington. Stirring up trouble again today?''

''No trouble. Just friendly calling. Where's Gould?''

''I sent him to the bank.''

''I have to say, Mrs. McGoldrick, your paper yesterday looked like something I'd find printed in Boston. I could read every letter.''

Kate felt her chest swell with pride but kept her eyes on her handwriting. ''Yes, the *L*'s didn't look like *I*'s. It's doing a top-drawer job. Just as I suspected it would.''

"A pity Jonathan Smarte didn't invest in it a bit sooner."

Not a question and yet Kate felt compelled to answer him even as she felt her back growing more stiff. Instinct told her Charles suspected the real reason. She didn't temper the sweet little bite in her tone as she lifted her eyes again to his. "Jonathan Smarte has only recently gotten himself around to the financial matters of running the paper. But how could he have the time for such matters, Mr. Remington, when he's busy responding to letters written by people who come into town and think too much."

Charles's eyes narrowed very intently on her mouth.

"Very good then," Douglas said, a bit too energetically. He moved toward the door. "Good seeing you, Kate. Remington. Gosh, I've been gone so long I'll bet a line's forming outside my door."

The bell tinkled and the door thudded closed behind him. The office plunged into an uncomfortable silence.

"He's a good friend to you," Charles finally said.

"Yes. He has been since Harry's death. He was there when I needed an advisor."

"There's no shame in that, Kate."

Her chin inched up a notch. "I know how to ask for help."

"Do you? I think it's become very difficult for you to consider relying on anybody ever again. I think you're afraid nobody is worth your trust. Look at what Jude did to you. Look at what Harry did."

Her head snapped up and her voice came suddenly from very deep in her chest. "That's not fair, Charles."

"Maybe not entirely but they both left you, Kate. Jude in his own, sordid way. And Harry—he was gunned down because he ignored the threats from the cattlemen to stop printing his stories. You warned him, didn't you, Kate?"

She looked quickly away and felt her eyes begin to

burn. Yes, she had, countless times, with tears flowing from her eyes and Walt's tiny hand curled in hers.

Charles leaned closer over the desk, hands braced, shoulders broad and blocking out the light. "A wife would warn her husband, the father to her son. She would beg him to stop whatever he was doing to incite the threats against him. You warned him and he didn't stop, did he?"

She closed her eyes, remembering. "No—" she whispered. "He didn't. He believed in what he was doing so much he thought no one would hurt him."

"A pity he believed in it more than he loved you."

That brought Kate out of her chair and fumbling to gather the pages together on the desk. "I can't listen to this—"

Charles's big hand flattened the pages onto the desk top. "You can trust again, Kate. You can trust me."

She looked up and felt a chill enter her voice. "Really? Just because you tell me to, I should?"

"Absolutely."

"And why is that?"

"Because I'll never leave you."

There was such compassion in his voice she almost believed him. "You're returning to Boston, Charles."

"That's right. And I'm still planning to take you with me."

Her heart jumped. They were all but nose to nose, so close she could smell him. She'd smelled him all night—almost as if her skin had absorbed his scent. She felt tingles in her breasts, felt them tighten, and looked quickly down. "Go away, Charles. I have a rebuttal to finish writing."

"I'm not going to kiss you, if that's what you're asking."

Heat shot clear up to her hairline. "I'm not asking—"

"Good." He moved around the side of her desk with a purposefulness that made her heart slam around in her chest.

His hand touched the edge of her desk where several envelopes looked ready to fall to the floor. He caught them and stuck them between several loose pages. "I came to make amends. I'm embarking on a new path, Kate."

"And what is that? Something to do with judges in Turkeyfoot Run?"

"No. Winning you."

Kate swallowed and stared at his fingers braced on the desk. He had the manicured hands of a gentleman. Her soul seemed to ache in a way she hadn't allowed it to for years. "I'm afraid it's too late, Charles."

"I'll argue that until I'm ninety."

"I have responsibilities I intend to see out—here. You can't force me to leave."

"When you come, Kate, it will be willingly."

The tone of his voice sent a tremor through her. He sounded so certain of himself and she was suddenly reminded that he was a consummate businessman. He was also used to getting what he wanted. Growing up she'd always relished that in him. But now—now she sensed he wanted something from her she wasn't ready to give up.

He leaned toward her and swallowed her hand in his. "Don't think so much, Kate. You've been doing too much of that already." He squeezed her hand very gently, then released it and moved away, back around the desk.

She had the sudden notion that she should shout something before he reached for the door handle, just to keep him there.

"I'd like to pick up Walt from school today."

"I—uh—don't think that would be—he's missing Harry terribly."

"I know. He doesn't seem to like me much. That's why I was thinking I'd take him out on my horse. He seemed much more interested in him. Call it bribery." He smiled, lips twisting a touch, hair ruffled from the wind, and she glimpsed her son's face in his. Almost like the shadow of a ghost. And it wasn't the first time.

"I could use the time to finish the rebuttal. And if you have him home for dinner—that would be fine. I made soup before I left."

"Soup. Very good." Again he smiled, a flash of teeth that made her blood tingle in her veins. He reached for the door handle.

"You could join us," she blurted out.

He looked at her, eyes driving straight into her. "I would like that," he said.

They stood staring at each other for several pulse-pounding moments.

"Fine, then," he said. "We'll be there." He tugged open the door and stepped out.

The bell over it had barely quieted when Kate left the quill in the ink, scooped her pages together, and tucked them under her arm. The rebuttal could wait. She needed to see Victoria and ask about that cornflower blue and yellow gingham dress that she'd had in her window. Maybe she even had a hair ribbon to match, and some nice pale ankle button boots in soft kid leather.

"It doesn't hurt that much," Walt said. He rolled his big blue eyes up at Charles and seemed to drag his right leg in a more pronounced limp in the dirt. He looked at Charles for several moments to make sure he was being watched then rubbed his thigh and formed his mouth into a silent "Ow."

"I thought the horse stepped on your foot," Charles mused, looping the horse's reins around the hitching rail and giving his neck a hearty pat.

"Oh—it did." Walt scrunched up his nose and lifted his left foot.

"Other foot," Charles muttered, giving the child a sideways glance. "Let's go, cowboy. Your mama's waiting on dinner." He grabbed his topcoat from the saddle horn, cupped a hand around Walt's head, and directed him toward Kate's front porch.

The house was small and needed paint. One end of the porch was slightly lower than the other but the window boxes at the front two windows were spilling over with colorful flowers. The porch, in great need of repair, had recently had a good sweeping and scrubbing. A broom leaned against the side of the house just outside the front door as if it had been left there in a great hurry.

A whisper of anger flared through Charles. He had never known Harry McGoldrick, true. But for all that the man had provided for Kate—and Charles believed he'd saved her from a fate far worse—he'd left her to tend to life with nothing but a mountain of debt, a life sentence of pretense, and a quest for avenging his reckless death. Her porch should have been straight. Her house should have been brightly whitewashed and kept that way. She should have a fine and fancy buckboard wagon to take her places and a horse she knew how to ride and handle. She should know how to hold a gun or at least look as if she knew how to use it.

She should have been as well tended as she'd been in Lenox. It was a thought-provoking notion, he realized, as he stepped onto the porch. She'd run from that life once. And now she was making it clear she preferred the life she'd made for herself over anything well tended and provided for by anybody else back in Boston. At least no one could take all this away from her.

She was as proud as any Remington, and twice as stubborn, hell-bent on her causes. He imagined that she'd spent the better part of the last four hours scribbling vengefully with her mighty quill.

The door swung open before he could reach for the

handle. And then she was looking up at him and his heart seemed to do a quick stutter.

"Hullo," she said, lifting a hand to brush a stray tendril from her eyes.

Her dress was a pale blue and yellow confection that made her neck look yards long, her waist look just inches wide, and her breasts look enticingly full. Roses blossomed high on her cheekbones and on her wide mouth. Her hair was piled loosely on top of her head and a streamer of pale blue ribbon trailed from it down her back. She looked freshly sprung from a hothouse and as delectable as anything he'd seen in years. If ever.

"What's wrong with you, Mama?" Walt asked. "You look funny."

Kate frowned at her son. "I do not look funny."

"You've got something in your hair," Walt replied, shoving up a dirty finger.

"It's a ribbon."

"Nuh-uh. It's right there."

Kate swatted at her cheek and hair. "Go wash up. You're filthy."

"Flour," Charles said, picking the clump from her temple.

"I made biscuits," she said, turning from the door. He followed her inside, letting the door thwack closed behind him. Walt shuffled to the sink. Charles watched the bustle of Kate's dress swish.

"I can't, Mama," Walt said when she slid a stool to the sink with her foot. Plastering on a pained expression, Walt gripped his left leg first then quickly changed his mind and gripped the right. "It hurts me, Mama, real bad."

"What hurts?"

"Where the horse stepped on me."

"The horse did *what*?" Angry green eyes swung on Charles. "Do you want to tell me what happened?"

"Hold on a minute, Kate."

"Hold on for what?" Hands found her waist and her brows dove low, the lioness guarding her cub. "I trusted you to take care of him and you let that horse hurt him."

"He's walking just fine, Kate."

"He's limping!"

"He's embellishing it a bit, I think."

"You think." Her eyes were flashing now. "Why is it men allow things to happen to children and then behave as if it's really nothing at all? Why is it that it ends up being the woman's fault for caring too much when a child gets hurt, or the child's fault for demanding attention? Why is it that men always—"

There was only one way that Charles could think of to shut her up when she was becoming irrational. He shoved aside a chair and moved toward her. Her eyes widened and she bumped back against the edge of the sink counter.

"Wait a minute," she said quickly.

"Just one minute?" he asked silkily, laying both hands on either side of her on the counter. "You don't even realize what you're doing."

"What? Of course I know what I'm doing. I've been doing it for five years. I'm concerned for my son. I'm his mother."

"No one's arguing the obvious."

"Go to your room, Walt."

Walt blinked up at her then looked at Charles. "I don't want to go. I'm not being bad."

The irritation was marked on her face and she'd folded her arms over her chest as if to keep him at bay. "Please, Walt. Now. Go to your room like Mama says."

"But, Mama, I want to stay and watch you and Mr. Reninton fight. You fighted like this with my pa when I got my hand stuck in the printing press, remember, Mama? You were screaming and crying then, too. I heard you even when you sent me to my room.''

''Walter,'' she said, her voice cracking.

''Go, Walt,'' Charles said in one of his more deep tones. The look he leveled on the boy brooked no argument, even from a five-year-old. But, even so, the boy seemed to weigh his options for a good ten seconds before slowly turning and shuffling from the room.

Kate swung flashing eyes up at Charles. ''Harry and I made it a point never to exchange words in front of Walt. I thought—I thought he never heard us.''

''He obviously did. Did it happen often?''

Her lips compressed. ''I don't want to discuss Harry with you.''

''Fine. I'd rather not. But I think Harry was trying his best to keep you from coddling your son. And you fought him like you're fighting me.''

Her eyes flashed wide. ''Coddle? You can't tell me how to love my child.''

''Love him, Kate, love him as much as you can but let him grow up to be a man. Not some overgrown boy.''

She blinked furiously at him, then in a flash she ducked under his arm and moved away from him. For a moment she stared out the window above the stove, then spun around with her hands on her hips. A crumb of flour still clung to her temple and her ribbon had worked its way loose and hung down her back.

She looked so God almighty beautiful he almost gave up the fight right then and there. But he couldn't, not when he knew she struggled daily with a child who had her and all her motherly love wrapped around his little finger.

If she'd had a man to love he was certain things would have been different for her.

''No one can raise him better than I can,'' she said. Her voice was deeply impassioned, and her chest expanded as if she could hardly draw enough air. ''No one in Crooked Nickel can. No one in Lenox can. No governess in Boston can—no one can love him as much as I can and I won't let you take him away from me—''

''Whoa—wait a minute, Kate—'' He started toward her.

''No—'' She backed up, one hand outstretched, fear etched into her features. ''No, you listen. You can't take him from me.''

''Christ, Kate, what do you think I'm made of?''

''Then why are you here? Why are you staying when you know I won't leave?''

''I told you why. Because of you.''

She shook her head with mounting frustration. ''I've learned, Charles—I've learned so much since I left Lenox.''

''You've learned not to trust anybody.''

''And rightly so! Life is hard and harsh and everyone thinks only of themselves. Look at Louella. Look at Pruitt. Look at Jude and Harry. And I'm one of them. I think about survival every day. I've had to. I've lived the past six years of my life looking over my shoulder hoping nobody will find me. And now you've come. Now you know all about Walt. You know I won't leave Crooked Nickel. And I won't give you my son. So I believe you want to prove that I'm not a good mother to him. Well, I am. I know he sasses me and he doesn't mind me . . . and I have to ask him to do the same thing again and again . . . and it feels like I'm not doing the right thing sometimes—but all I want''—her voice caught, she looked out the window, and tears suddenly shone in her eyes—''all I want—it's so simple—but I just don't know how to do all of it—''

''Kate—'' He reached her in two strides and took her in his arms even though he knew she would resist, even though he knew *he* should resist even if she didn't. He tightened his arms around her until she stopped pushing to get away from him and then she was burying her face in his chest and sniffling, and her slender shoulders were shaking as if only now she'd realized she had far too much piled on them. "Kate—don't cry. You're breaking my heart."

"I can't help it. You make me cry. Why does this always happen with you? I never cry—"

"I know. My mother swears she never does either."

She sniffed and rubbed her face on his white cotton shirt. "I used to hear her even when I was in my room. Just like Walt heard me. I try very hard not to be weak, Charles. You don't believe me, do you?"

"I know you're trying very hard to do the very best you can, Kate." He pressed his face to the top of her head. "You smell like soup and biscuits and lilacs."

She glanced up at him. "You smell like horse."

He pushed his thumb over her cheek, catching a tear. She looked up at him. He felt the warmth of her waist under his hand and his fingers pressed gently. Warning bells went off in his mind. Soft breasts in cornflower blue pushed into his chest with every fluttering breath she drew. The ache in his loins became almost unbearable.

There was a certain resignation on her face. "Walt looked—he looked happy when he came in just now, even though he was limping. I suppose I should thank you for that."

"Don't thank me, Kate. I wish I could take all his sorrow away. I wish I could make it right for both of you and the damnedest thing of it is that I think I can if you'll give me the chance—"

"It's not for me to give," she murmured.

"Then don't take it away." He lowered his head, praying, hoping, squeezed her waist gently, and their lips touched. Her mouth was warm, her lips soft and so achingly sweet he felt a pain of denial deep into his bones more acute than any agony a bullet could cause him.

To lose her again after all this time would kill him.

He tore his mouth away and brought both hands up to squeeze her upper arms. ''Kate—''

''Mama?''

They turned almost as one and saw Walt standing in the door to his room.

Chapter 12

Kate had never felt guilty or ashamed in front of her son. She'd never even contemplated such a thing, or puzzled over the answers her behavior might require her to give one day. It was a peculiar situation, as if he were suddenly the responsible one standing in the room, and she the irresponsible one.

It was a decidedly uncomfortable feeling. It was also, she realized when she felt Charles's hands fall from her arms and she chose that moment to slip quickly past him, the first time Walter had ever seen her in a man's embrace.

While Kate and Harry were married, they'd never once embraced in Walt's presence, never once kissed, never once touched or fondled each other the way Kate often supposed married people did.

That had been saved for the bedroom, beneath the coverlet, in the darkness, and even then it had happened a handful of times. A groping hand on her breast, another on her thigh, Harry asking her if she wanted to, murmuring his affection, and she acquiescing out of duty, out of guilt, out of gratitude and love, and more than anything out of a consuming desire to make a good home for her son. And that meant being a wife to Harry in every way. She might not have found the love of her life in him but when she'd lain awake afterward and listened to his snores, she'd been content knowing that she'd given herself her best chance at a good life.

Elmer Pruitt had taken that away from her. And Harry had let him.

Walt was looking up at her with a perplexed frown. He was also looking at Charles strangely. Until now Kate hadn't considered what effect a lack of open affection in a household might have had on her son. She also hadn't anticipated what effect it would have on her. She'd thought she'd become immune to a man's touch. She'd been wrong. If anything, she seemed to need it now more than ever. And she intended to fight it.

She hunkered down in front of Walt and searched his freckled face. If only there were books to tell mothers what to say and do at times such as these. She could hardly lie to her son but it seemed cruel to lead him to believe that Charles was anything more than a friend . . . a friend who would soon be returning to Lenox alone. A part of her sensed that Walt wanted very much to replace Harry with another man, and her heart ached that his doing so would only bring him more tears and sorrow. And she would do anything to prevent that. She dug deep for a lighthearted tone. "You look very serious, Walt."

His eyes angled up at Charles, looked back at her, and his tongue poked out of his mouth. "Um—I wanted to tell you that I have a limp in my leg"—his lips quirked sideways in a true Remington grin—"just like Mr. Reninton does."

"And you're quite proud of it, aren't you?"

"It's not a bullet, Mama."

"Thank goodness."

"It's from a horse."

"Yes, I know." She looked very closely at him, eyes slightly narrowed, digging for the truth of it all. "He didn't quite kick you, did he?"

Walt stared at her several moments, then his chin started tipping a wee bit down. ''Noooo—'' he said very slowly.

''Did he step on your foot?''

Walt sucked in his lower lip. ''Nooo—well, not exactly.''

''Not exactly?''

''He almost did.''

''Ah.''

''No, really, Mama. He was this close—'' Two grimy fingers, thumb and index, came up and measured a distance of less than an inch right in front of her nose. ''See? This close. His hoof was this close to my foot.''

''Don't tell Mama tales, Walt.'' She heard the tiredness in her voice.

Walt's face lost every ounce of animation. ''I won't.''

''You did.''

''I know I did. But I want my leg to hurt like Mr. Reninton's. He's very brave, Mama.''

''Yes, well, most soldiers are. And they never tell tales, do they, Mr. Remington?''

''The brave ones don't have to,'' came his deep rumbling voice.

''See there?'' She stood up and gave Walt a stern look. ''No dessert after dinner tonight for telling tales. Now, wash up.''

Walt bounded to the sink, ailments obviously all repaired.

''Mr. Reninton can sit in my chair,'' he said, splashing water everywhere as he washed. He looked over his shoulder at Charles in a way that made Kate's throat get all clogged up and her eyes feel misty. She had to turn to the sink and busy herself.

''I'd be honored to take your chair,'' Charles said.

Kate opened the oven door, grabbed an oven mitt, and pulled out the sheet of biscuits. As she nudged the door closed with her knee, she felt Charles move past behind her. He touched her waist as he did so, one hand lightly at her back as if to tell her he was behind her.

It was a casual touch and yet the tin sheet of biscuits wobbled in her hand, then slammed down on the stove. Every nerve in her body seemed to scream out for something.

Perspiration popped out on her forehead and trickled between her breasts. She knew what the sleeping wanton in her wanted. She wanted more of that touching and kissing. She wanted an entire night of it. She'd been without it for far too long.

And Charles knew it, too.

She turned to the soup pot on the stove and grabbed a ladle. Charles moved past her to the sink. From the corner of her eye, she watched him roll his shirtsleeves to his elbows and make a great show of soaping up his hands. He made it look so appealing, Walt even decided to wash his hands again, clear up to his elbows, imitating Charles. At that moment Kate felt a vulnerability in herself and her son so raw it was like a freshly opened wound. It was then she realized that Harry's death had impacted them on an emotional level she hadn't even comprehended before. They were both like sitting ducks . . . and Charles knew it.

She had an overwhelming urge to tell him to leave—leave and never return—leave her and her son to their life. Her insides started shaking as she moved to the table. She was afraid, for herself and for her son, as she'd never been afraid before.

"Mama never makes soup," Walt announced when Kate placed a bowl on the table in front of Charles.

Kate glared at her son, then without glancing at Charles said, "We had soup just last week. Coffee?"

Walt scowled at her. "Me? Yuk. I don't like coffee."

"No, not you. I mean—" She knew she wasn't a coward and yet she couldn't shake the feeling that she'd invited the enemy to dine at her table. And that by his simply being here, she'd lost a part of herself.

She glanced at him. He was looking at her, focusing on her mouth. And something in her nether reaches did a little quiver. He looked rugged and windblown and he sat very large in his chair.

His eyes lifted to hers and she wondered if he had the ability to read the turmoil of her thoughts. She was suddenly glad Walt was there, otherwise Charles would have dug it all out of her, twisted it up, and made it all seem as simple as a matter of trusting him.

He was watching her very intently. "Coffee—yes, if it's no trouble."

"I—no." She returned to the stove and fumbled with the water and the strainer. She knew he was watching her. She placed his cup on the table and found herself hoping he didn't get grounds in his first sip.

"Strong," he said, looking at her, only she was staring at her food. "That's exactly how I like it." The appreciation in his voice was unmistakable.

She toyed with her spoon, dipped it around in her soup, and remembered quiet dinners at this table with Harry, quiet evenings spent on the porch discussing the paper. A quiet life without any of this mental unrest and physical longing.

From across the table came Walter's slurping sounds. "I don't like this," he muttered.

"Eat," Kate ordered him.

"It's an old recipe," Charles commented to Walt. "My grandmother's cook used to make this soup when your mother and I were growing up." Charles leaned slightly over the table toward Walt and half-whispered, "Your mother didn't like it at first either."

Kate scowled at Charles until he met her eyes, then quickly glanced at Walt who was smirking at her. "I still ate it," she said hotly. "And so should you."

Walt shrugged, dipped his spoon into his soup. "So, you knew my mama a long time ago. Did you climb in the big tree and write stories and read all the time like she did?"

"Yes, but I was the one who stole the gooseberry tarts," Charles replied.

"He doesn't need to know that," Kate muttered, moving soup around in her bowl.

"Tell me more," Walt said eagerly, eyes all atwinkle. "Was my mama ever bad?"

Charles was looking at her. "Never. She was always very good."

Walt looked somewhat disappointed. "I thought everyone was bad sometimes."

"Hmmm—" Charles laid his spoon down and, with chin propped on one hand and eyes very narrow and piercing, contemplated Kate. It made her so uncomfortable she could hardly eat. "Let me think, Walt. There had to be something—"

Kate arched a cool brow. "I'm quite certain there wasn't. Your soup's getting cold, Mr. Remington. And it won't be good then."

But Charles kept his focus on her. "Something—something—ah. The piano."

Walt eagerly leaned over the table. "What about it?"

"She hated practicing," Charles replied, his voice dipping lower, as if memory flooded into his brain. "She would stomp very hard on the steps when she was told to practice, and the louder she stomped the longer she had to practice. Sometimes she would sit on the piano bench with her back all straight and she wouldn't play for quite some time. And Mother would be in the other room, waiting, and the silence was louder than anything you could imagine. I used to sit at the top of the stairs and listen to the ticking of the mantel clock and wait for her to start. She was quite good, even when she pounded on the keys."

"Did she cry?" Walt asked.

"No, she never cried. But I do remember once when she came to me crying—"

"This is ridiculous," Kate said, feeling exasperated. Memory was haunting her, too, reminding her that she and Charles had shared a history and a family and far too many intimacies to be strangers now. He was coaxing her in his brilliantly effective way, charming and nudging and thawing her from the inside out. She had to make him stop.

"When did she cry?" Walt asked.

"Someone had played a mean joke on her," Charles said. "People can be nasty, Walt."

"That's enough," Kate said crisply. She looked straight into Charles's blue eyes. "Please—"

"What, Mama? What did they do to you that was mean? Tell me, Mama. Mr. Reninton will, won't you?"

Kate pinched her lips together and looked at her son. "Mr. Remington's brother—his name"—she felt her throat close up and realized she'd never spoken the name to her son before and yet the man was his father—"his name was Jude—he said something mean to me, but I didn't know it was a joke. Jude was always doing things and I was never certain if he was joking. I never really knew or understood why he did the things he did—" She felt Charles watching her. "Actually, looking back on it, I think he didn't like it that Mr. Remington and I were such good friends. We liked doing the same things. We were very much alike and Jude was different. I think he did things to get our attention. And sometimes he was mean. It explains a great deal, actually."

Walt's face was somber. "What did he call you, Mama?"

"He called me fat."

Walt frowned. "You were fat?"

"Never," Charles said.

"Kind of," Kate put in. "At least I thought I was and I was very hurt when he said that."

"And Mr. Reninton made you feel better."

"Yes, he did." Her eyes drifted slowly to Charles's. Their gazes locked and for the life of her Kate couldn't drag her eyes away.

Several moments passed, then suddenly Charles glanced at Walt and smiled his lopsided smile. "I knew exactly how to make her feel better, Walt. I stole another gooseberry pie and she helped me eat it."

Walt sat back with a big grin. "And that made her forget the bad things."

"Maybe we should try it now," Charles rumbled, looking meaningfully at Kate.

She avoided his stare and waved a hand in a vague direction over her shoulder. "I think I'll get the biscuits—"

"I'll get them," Walter said quickly. Before Kate could tell him to keep his fanny where it was, he lunged from his chair. Elbows flew and one landed in his soup bowl and flipped it toward the middle of the table. Soup splattered and spilled all over her white linen tablecloth.

"Walter!"

Walt froze, big eyes getting huge. "I'm sorry, Mama."

"Sit!"

He didn't move. "Don't you want me to clean it up?"

"I'll get it. Now sit." Kate reached for a rag and lunged over the table just as Charles came up out of his chair. "No—no—" she said, laying a hand on his arm then taking it quickly back. "Please, sit. I'll do it. If I just get most of it up with this, we should be fine."

Charles sat back down but not before lifting her vase of flowers from the middle of the table for her. She pressed the rag over the table, leaning over, dabbing here and there, and feeling Charles watching her.

"I don't want any more soup," Walt said, nudging his empty bowl away.

"Have a biscuit then," Kate said, placing them on the soup-soaked table. She slid into her chair and watched the other two grab at the biscuits.

"I'm done," Walt said through a mouthful of biscuit a few moments later. Half of it dribbled in crumbs from the side of his mouth and fell to his chest. He swatted at it and sprayed crumbs on the floor. "Can I go and pet Mr. Reninton's horse now? Please, Mama, can I? His name is Sundance. I'll be careful, I promise."

"Clean up after yourself first," Kate said and almost winced when Walt swiped a hand over the table and crumbs sprayed. "Your mouth and face, too—not—!" But the warning was a second too late because Walt always found the front of his shirt far more practical and close at hand than a napkin to wipe his smudged face.

He grinned at her. Kate sighed, feeling somewhat exasperated by the meal and somewhat disinclined to let Walt leave them alone.

"Don't walk close behind him," Charles said.

"I won't," Walt replied, before bounding out the door. The slam of it shook the house on its foundation.

"Dessert?" Kate said, scooting her chair back before any sort of intimacy could encroach on them. "I—I have gooseberry tarts."

"You made them?"

Kate turned quickly to the sink and wished in a perverse way that she had. "No—actually—Victoria made them and wanted to share so she wouldn't eat all of them."

"You had a rebuttal to write."

"Actually I—" She hadn't written a word. She'd bought a new dress, a new hair ribbon, and had tidied up her house and fussed with her hair. Oddly enough, she hadn't thought about the rebuttal all afternoon. Looking back on it all, she wished now that she'd busied herself with something other than self-indulgence, because that's what it had been, pure self-indulgence. Making herself and her house look nice had had nothing to do with Charles.

If she had any sense she would realize that.

She turned and placed a tray of tarts on the soggy table. "The rebuttal will be in tomorrow's paper."

"I can hardly wait." He tossed his napkin on the table and looked up at her. "It was a fine meal, Kate. My grandmother would have been proud. Thank you."

"I—" She gave an airy shrug. "It was nothing. I make that soup all the time." She felt the stirrings of a flush and reached for his bowl. She took that to the sink and returned with the coffeepot. He was watching her again as the coffeepot scraped on the edge of his cup. She jerked it up and coffee sprayed back on her hand, making her gasp.

"Easy there—" Charles grabbed the pot from her hand, put it on the table. "Hold on, Kate—here—let me see—you're trembling."

Kate tugged on her hand, then winced when he wouldn't release it. "Ow—I mean—it's just a little burn. Hardly worth any trouble."

"You've never been trouble to me," he murmured.

Her knees felt wobbly. Little shivers were racing up the fingers that he held. She realized she was standing quite close to him—or had he somehow pulled her a bit closer? He looked up at her and that wondrous tingly feeling began in the tips of her breasts and they tightened and pushed against her dress.

She jerked her hand away and turned back to the sink.

"You should put something on it," he said.

Her whole body felt as if it was throbbing. "What?"

"Your hand. You should put something—"

"Oh, yes, of course. Something—"

"Butter."

"Yes, butter. I'll just—" She waved her free hand in a vague direction.

He stood up and come closer.

She tensed.

His hands cupped around her upper arms and she had to close her eyes as sensation washed through her. She had Harry to think about, about avenging his death. She had her son to think about and the life she'd promised herself she'd give him. She loved him more than anything else in the world. Surely all this was more important than the physical stirrings of her body. A mature woman who knew her responsibilities would know that there was no choice to make. She'd made her choice the night Walt was conceived.

Charles's chest pressed against her back. She could feel his breaths pushing into her, coming deep, deeper. They seemed to suddenly match her own.

"It's so quiet here," he murmured, and she felt his chin brush the top of her head. She opened her eyes and wondered if he was looking out the window at the windswept expanse of gold prairie. "It's so beautiful. So different from Boston. A man could find himself getting used to it."

A peculiar tingle worked its way up Kate's spine. She felt as if she were holding her breath.

"I'll send Walt in," he finally said.

She swallowed. "Yes, please, do."

"Good night, Kate." And he left.

A circle of men was gathered around the cracker-barrel in back of Logan's General Store when Charles stepped through the door the following morning. They stopped talking and looked up at him long and hard.

Elmer Pruitt gave him a sneer. "Tenderfoot, woolie-lover ain't left town yet, boys. Maybe he needs some persuadin'. Too bad he ain't got a barn to burn. Just a room over't Louella's."

His buddy Virg muttered something under his breath to the man seated next to him, then jerked his chin at Charles and showed yellow teeth in what Charles supposed was a threatening snarl. Charles counted seven men. They were bold and reckless to be parading their hatred for all to see. They obviously knew they owned the town, owned the Sheriff, and had a good measure of fear at their fingertips to bandy about as they wished.

The man behind the counter, Logan he assumed, looked at Charles as if he had a black mask over his face, a six-shooter in each hand. "I don't want no trouble here, Remington."

Charles moved to the counter and tossed several coins on it. "Morning, Logan. I just stopped in to buy a paper." Charles jerked his head to the *Sentinel*s stacked on the floor behind Logan. "Any news?"

Logan slapped a paper in front of Charles and snorted. "Not 'bout nothin' anyone might be interested in. Not even a word 'bout John Bertrand's barn burnin'. That's why folks is so happy here today." Logan glanced at Pruitt and his boys and dropped his voice. "They's scairt over't the paper, Remington. Scairt like the rest of the smart folks in this town are. Scairt they're gonna find a poor sheep nailed to their front door. An' I for one say it's better to be scairt than dead."

Charles picked up the paper, tucked it under his arm, and nodded. "Good day to you, Logan." He turned, looked straight at Pruitt, and wondered how Kate had managed to look the man in the eye knowing he'd murdered her husband.

"Best mind yer own business," Pruitt warned him in elevated tones. "An' that means keepin' away from the woolies and the widows in town. 'Specially the purty ones.

Everybody in town knows what yer doin' with Mrs. McGoldrick an' I'm here ta tell ya that woman needs a real man, woolie-lover. Not some fancified tenderfoot and not some whiskeyed up ol' newsman too dumb to fight back with nothin' but words—''

Virg grabbed Pruitt's arm and muttered something to him that made the red in Pruitt's face redder.

Pruitt jerked his chin at Charles. ''You think I killed McGoldrick?''

Charles kept his voice level and his stare on Pruitt. ''Everyone in town knows it, Pruitt. And I intend to prove it to a judge smart enough to hang you.''

''That'll never happen,'' Pruitt preened.

''I like my odds.'' He turned and tugged open the door. A stream of foul language followed him out of the store. He paused on the boardwalk in a glare of hot morning sun, wondering if he'd pushed Pruitt a bit too far, then glanced at the front page.

The headline read: ''Ladies to Meet for Monthly Crooked Nickel Ladies Auxiliary Garden Club Hosted by Miss Bessie Mae Elliot; Tea and Sponge Cake Will Be Served.''

Below and to the right of that was an item in much smaller print, but it was indeed there and Charles assumed it was by Kate's hand: ''Annual Sheep-Shearing to be Held Next Week: Shearers Expected to Arrive Later This Week.''

Her rebuttal was on the back page. He skimmed it, smiled, and tucked the paper again under his arm. Reading it was something he intended to savor, over a good cup of coffee on a shady front porch. He thought immediately of Kate.

''Morning, Mr. Remington.'' Victoria Valentine smiled up at him from under the brim of a fuchsia-fringed hat. She was dressed in bright pink from head to toe.

''Sir.'' Nan was standing next to Victoria. The little girl

gave Charles a small curtsy and smiled. She was wearing a simple shirtwaist of white and blue and looked well tended and happy.

Charles touched his brim and nodded. "Ladies."

"Did you dine well last evening?" Victoria asked with a tell-me-everything smile.

"Very well, thank you, madam."

Victoria preened. "How very fine. Very fine, indeed."

"Mrs. McGoldrick looked quite lovely."

"Did she?"

"I believe it was a dress I admired in your window just the other day."

"All my dresses are to be admired, Mr. Remington."

"Particularly when a beautiful woman is wearing one."

Victoria's eyes widened deliciously. "Oh, Mr. Remington, we must have a good chat one of these days. I just have to know—"

"Excuse me—pardon me—" Someone jarred Charles's elbow. It was Mr. Gould, trying to wedge his way past on the boardwalk while juggling an armful of newspapers. He shoved one into Charles's chest without looking up. "Here you are, sir, your free copy of *The Crooked Nickel Sentinel.* Hot off the press and—oh—" Gould squinted up at him. "Good heavens it's you. Mr. Remington, sir, I'm so sorry. I should have recognized you simply by the cut of your coat. How are you, sir?"

"Very well, Gould. And you?"

"Never better, sir. Well, actually, sir, Mrs. McGoldrick sent me out this morning very early with all these papers. I believe she wants to make certain everyone in Crooked Nickel gets a copy. She said to me 'particularly the ladies, Mr. Gould.' Yes, that's what she said and she took a big stack to distribute as well. Oh, my, yes—I almost forgot. The ladies—" He turned and handed a paper to Victoria.

After some small talk the trio headed off down the boardwalk with cheery "good days."

Charles watched them and felt loneliness creeping over him. He looked down the street, his eyes keen for a slender, black-bombazined silhouette marching along with hand clamped to the hat on her head and newspapers fluttering determinedly in her arm.

She'd looked utterly delicious and nothing at all like a suffragist-in-training last evening in her yellow and corn-flower-blue, standing beside him with her hurt hand and her hair coming down. It had taken every ounce of will he possessed not to reach out and touch her. He hadn't mistaken the longing in her eyes. It had haunted him the night through. But longing once sated became suspicion, regret, and betrayal if trust wasn't strong and belief not true.

He'd lain in his bed, stared at his ceiling as dawn crept over darkness, and vowed to suffer a year of meals at her table keeping his hands to himself if at the end of that year she believed in him. But he'd also tossed in his bed, listening to the sounds that inhabited a place like Louella's, and longed for Kate to be there with him in a way that left him panting and shaken and desperate.

He was not a patient man. It would not be a year's worth of meals, to be sure.

He turned and headed down the boardwalk toward Louella's.

Someone pounded very hard on the front door.

"Just a minute—" Kate called out but the sound was muffled since she was bent over on the other side of her bed, tucking in a fresh sheet.

Another round of bangs made the front door hinges squeak. Kate shot up with a scowl and a grumble, swiped the flyaway hair from her eyes, and marched from her room.

The silhouette beyond the door was large and undefinable.

Charles.

That was her first thought before instinct told her Charles would never stoop to door-banging. No, his tactics were more of the touch, fondle, and squeeze variety, the kind that made a woman tingle with desire, not bristle with agitation.

She patted her suddenly hot cheeks and blew her breath out very fast.

Another pounding came, accompanied by a woman's high-pitched, "Mrs. McGoldrick! Are you there?"

Kate threw open the door. "Bessie Mae, for goodness sake, you'll wake poor Harry in his grave."

Bessie Mae didn't seem to care whom she woke. "I have darned good reason for it. Here, let me in. I have to speak to you about something."

"And what would that be?" Kate asked, pulling the door wide enough for Bessie Mae to squeeze through.

"This." Bessie Mae plowed past waving a page over her head. She took three steps into the room, gave it a thorough once-over assessment, then turned and thrust the page at Kate. "Did you read it?"

"Read what?"

"This." Bessie Mae poked a plump pink finger into the paper. "Right here. Your Mr. Jonathan Smarte, that's what."

"Ah." Kate had to bite the insides of her cheeks to keep a triumphant smile from her lips. "The rebuttal. What did you think?"

"What did *I* think? That's why I'm here. I'm holding an emergency meeting of the Crooked Nickel Ladies Auxiliary Garden Club to discuss this."

"You're what?"

"Tonight. And I want every woman in Crooked Nickel to attend."

"Wonderful!"

"Something has to be done," Bessie Mae said sternly.

"Yes, I quite agree."

"To stop him."

"Stop who? Oh, you mean Mr. Remington."

"I should say not. Why the devil would I want to stop Mr. Remington?"

"I—I don't know, I—"

"Why, of course, you don't. You're his friend. That's why I had to come here first. I saw you walking with him right in front of Logan's General Store the other day. Do you really think that's wise, Mrs. McGoldrick, you bein' a widow less than a year an' all?"

"I—we were just talking, Bessie Mae."

"Yes, I saw that. My, but he's a godawful handsome man, isn't he?"

"Just godawful," Kate said, wondering why Bessie Mae was noticing anything about the man besides his heinous letter. She should be blinded by his audacity, not knocked breathlessly silly by his godawful handsomeness.

Bessie Mae poked her face at her. "Very good, then, you'll be there?"

"Yes, of course, I'll be there. But I don't—"

"Oh, I don't have time to chat, Mrs. McGoldrick. I've got word to spread. Seven o'clock. Sharp." Bessie Mae charged toward the door and Kate had to scoot ahead of her to pull it open. Bessie Mae paused, swept her eyes over Kate's simple off-white shirtwaist, and set her chin low. "I have to say, Mrs. McGoldrick, though I suppose there's most who wouldn't agree with me, but you look rather handsome when you're not wearing all that black."

"I"—Kate blinked a moment—"I suppose I'll take

that as a compliment, Bessie Mae. And, please, do call me Kate.''

''Well, if you say so. Kate, it is. Oh, goodness, I must see myself off.'' She started out the door, then again paused and turned to Kate. Her voice dropped to a whisper, which was extraordinary since there was no one else within ear-shot. ''Just a hint, Mrs. McGoldrick. A bowl of quicklime in a pantry or closet removes all the dampness and kills all the mildew odors.'' Bessie Mae smiled, gave a brisk nod, turned, and marched out.

Kate closed the door behind her, faced her kitchen, sniffed, frowned, and set about throwing open all the windows.

Chapter 13

Bessie Mae Elliot lived with her mother at the west end of town in a whitewashed house with matching picket fence and immaculately tended flower beds surrounding it. The inside of the tiny house was as perfectly kept as the outside, with knickknacks and gimcracks adorning every available freshly polished inch on the tops of all their East Coast–acquired furniture. In the front parlor, doilies were spread over the backs of every chair and settee, and adorned every silk screen placed just at the proper angle in every corner. The place would have felt warm with all the windows open and cooling cross breezes sweeping through it.

With all the windows closed and twenty-odd women crammed into it, the parlor was as stifling as an oven.

Kate chose the end of a settee nearest a window in the hopes that Bessie Mae might ask her to open it. The chances of this, however, appeared dismal as Bessie Mae's mother sat in a rocker opposite Kate, swathed in a knit shawl and looking rather chilled despite the heat. She smiled at Kate, the dry folds of her powdered face wrinkling, and Kate smiled back and felt damp from the inside out. She'd worn her black bombazine, preferring not to look ''rather handsome,'' for the sake of propriety. After all, the focus of the evening was not on her. It was on the editorials and amassing a rebellion the likes of which Charles Remington wasn't likely ever to see again.

Still, she couldn't have chosen anything more uncomfortable to wear. As she watched Bessie Mae amble into the room, she had to wonder if perhaps she should have done as Bessie Mae undoubtedly had and gone without her undergarments. The thought made her wriggle uncomfortably in her seat and wish very much that she had something to drink.

And yet she couldn't help feeling quite smug about the entire thing when she looked around at all the expectant and eager faces. She'd issued a rallying cry that had been answered, in droves. She couldn't have planned it better herself. Perhaps this would keep her mind off of her turmoil with Charles.

"Ladies—ladies—" Bessie Mae squeezed her way into the center of the room and clapped her hands. "We'll get started in just a minute. We're waiting on several more guests. Oh, yes, Mrs. Dora Pickins brought her lovely tea cakes for us to enjoy and Miss Harriet Edwards will again share a bit of her special—er—tea with us—"

An appreciative murmur passed through the assemblage.

Bessie Mae glanced about. "Harriet—? Oh, there she is. Yes, serve it in the china teacups, dear. I believe that would be best. If you'll all stay seated, Harriet will find you."

In short order, the tiny, white-haired Harriet passed through the room balancing a dozen or so dainty teacups on a silver tray. Dressed in violet-sprigged white linen, she smiled, nodded, and whispered softly as she delivered each cup along with a lacy napkin. It was done so elegantly that Kate felt as if she were at a fancy East Coast tea party.

"Mrs. McGoldrick," Harriet said, smiling at Kate, which was a bit of a surprise as Kate had seen Harriet only from a distance when Harriet made her weekly trek to church on Sunday in her fancy buggy with the white wheels. She lived with her spinster sister several miles from town and kept very much to herself, save for church and her monthly garden club meetings.

She seemed so very sweet that Kate silently chastised herself for not getting to know the woman better. Her eyes followed Harriet around the room and she lifted the teacup to her lips. She really ought to get to know all of these women better if only she had the time and—

Harriet's special tea was tepid as it touched Kate's lips but the trail it left down her throat was liquid fire. Kate audibly gasped, drawing stares from several of the women around her.

"Sip slowly, dear," the one next to her whispered. "Just a little at a time. Not too much too fast"—the woman's eyes glittered naughtily beneath the prim edge of her bonnet—"if you know what I mean. Harriet makes the wickedest brew in these parts. Much better'n mine—"

"Better'n mine, too," another put in, sipping from her cup, then licking her lips as if to savor every drop. As she did so, the bird in its nest on top of her hat teetered from side to side. "It's somethin' with her still but she won't tell me her secret. An' I can't complain about it at home else my husband'll know why we all come to these meetings, and then he won't let me come no more."

"That's why I came," another chimed in. "Bessie Mae promised Harriet would bring her brew. And I don't ever want to miss that."

"Me neither," the first said. "'Course I made sure I read the paper today so I'd know what we're talkin' 'bout."

Kate set her teeth, lifted her teacup, and sipped very tentatively. This time it tasted sweeter, more like apples, and invited her to sip again. And again. She glanced about and wondered if Harriet was going to pass through for seconds.

"We have a newcomer this evening, ladies," Bessie Mae called out. "Mrs. Kate McGoldrick—stand up if you will, Kate."

"I don't—" Kate shook her head.

Bessie Mae planted her hands on her generous hips. "Oh, for goodness sake, stand your fanny up and let us all see who you are. Come on—very good, so everyone can see you. As you might know, Kate's recently widowed—well, not quite six months ago—"

"Seven," Kate felt compelled to add, then felt a hiccup leap from her chest. She sat quickly down and gulped from her cup.

Bessie Mae continued smoothly on. "Kate's here to lend us her support since she knows—"

A knock sounded on the front door.

Bessie Mae's face lit up. "That must be our special guest. Stay where you are, ladies, if you can—yes, yes—oooh, goody." Bessie Mae rubbed her hands together, then fluttered them in front of herself. "Yes, yes, please come in. We'll find room, won't we, ladies?" She giggled and blushed and fussed, and twitters erupted all over the room, and then Charles's big frame filled the doorway.

He was immaculately dressed. His eyes swept the room and momentarily settled on Kate. She felt a great need to fan her face and she didn't know what to blame: the heat, the drink, the ludicrousness of the entire situation, or him.

She watched Bessie Mae contort herself this way and that to reach Charles. Once she did, Bessie Mae hung onto his arm as if she were suddenly on a ship's deck in stormy seas and he was the only thing that would save her from certain death.

"No, wait right here, Mr. Remington. We have something for you. Cora—Cora, dear, put down your tea. It's your turn, dear."

A chubby little woman dressed in apricot and matching

feathered hat surged to her feet, cleared her throat, and lifted an open, paper-covered book in her hand. Kate tilted her head slightly, squinted, focused, and silently read the title on the cover: "The Old Farmer's Almanac."

Cora, looking grave, adjusted the glasses on her nose and began to read very slowly from the book. " 'When a man of good sense comes to marry, it is a companion whom he wants, and not an artist. It is not merely a creature who can paint, play, dress, and dance, it is a being who can comfort and console him.' " Cora looked up at Charles, pushed her glasses back up on her nose, and beamed.

"Well done. Thank you, Cora," Bessie Mae said. "You can sit down now. Ladies, I believe I can speak for all of us when I say that we have found ourselves a champion to fight the scourge of suffragism that is sweeping our great frontier and poisoning the minds of young women and children everywhere. Mr. Remington, sir, we proudly honor you as that champion. It takes a brave man to stand up to the man-eating women of today, sir. What have you to say for yourself?"

Charles gave his self-effacing, slightly crooked smile and Kate imagined that every heart in the room trembled at the sight of it. She stuck her nose in her cup. Why was she here? Why had she come? Why hadn't this worked? And why did Charles have to be here to witness her humiliation?

Oh, it wasn't humiliation for all of them to enjoy. But she knew it. He knew it. And that was humiliating enough.

"You humble me, Miss Elliot," Charles said. The maleness of his voice was magnified in such a completely female environment. Kate had a sudden memory of that voice rumbling soft murmurs as he kissed her bosom. She wriggled in her seat and felt a drop of perspiration weave between her breasts.

Bessie Mae giggled. "We don't want to humble you,

sir. We want you to help trample the suffragists where they lurk, sir.''

''Lurk, Miss Elliot?'' Charles asked.

''Indeed, sir. We haven't seen any brazen enough to parade their notions on our streets. Not that they would dare—yet. But they're here, just as they are in every town, slinking about in our midsts, spreading their evil notions in our back alleys, trying to make the rest of us feel less than womenfolk. They're like a sickness, the devil's own plague. Mr. Jonathan Smarte has heard these whisperings and has taken to rallying them against the rest of us, who long to be what we were meant to be. And I, for one, want to feel every inch a woman.''

To punctuate this, Bessie Mae pushed out her onerous bosom and wagged it back and forth in front of Charles's nose. The wicked look she slanted up at him was enough to make Kate want to leap off the settee and pinch her plump, pink arm.

Instead, she frowned into her empty cup and looked for Harriet. Thankfully, the woman was picking her way through the room with her silver pitcher, refilling teacups.

''We're going to squash them.''

The venom dripping from Bessie Mae's voice snapped Kate's head up. She looked completely possessed of an anger that astonished Kate. Her thin lips peeled back over her teeth and tiny sprays of spit accompanied her words. ''We'll squash them like fat little bugs until they don't dare raise their voice again in our town paper, or any other paper, do you hear me, sir?''

''Quite clearly, madam.''

''And we need your help.''

''Writing editorials.''

''Well, yes, writing editorials. And finding us all husbands.''

Charles's laugh was low and appreciative. ''I'm a lawyer, Miss Elliot, not a matchmaker.''

''But you're a man, Mr. Remington—from the top of your head to the tips of those nice, polished boots. Isn't he, ladies?''

Another round of appreciation swept the room, this one much more boisterous than the first, no doubt due in great part to the quantity of tea being consumed.

Bessie Mae squeezed Charles's arm and beamed up at him. ''There's a whole passel of menfolk coming into town in the next few days for the sheepshearing coming up next week. You're a friend to the sheepherders, Mr. Remington.''

''I believe we all might be, Miss Elliot.''

''I don't hate any man, sir,'' Bessie Mae replied. ''There's too darned few of the single ones in these parts. I personally don't care if a man raises cows or sheep or prairie dogs, so long as he doesn't have a wife. Ain't that right, ladies?''

Another chorus of agreement rose up.

Bessie Mae's chin lifted up another notch. ''I suspect what's wrong with the mean cattlemen is that they either don't have a wife or, if they do, she ain't a good one, else why would they be stirrin' up trouble? Every man needs a good woman, Mr. Remington.''

''I couldn't agree more.''

Kate sipped, directed her eyes toward the nearest window, and tried to look bored.

''In our humble opinion, Mr. Remington, sheepshearing should be the true social event of the summer season in these parts. Leastways we'd like to make it that way so as we can meet all those fine sheepshearers coming into town and get ourselves some husbands—leastways those of us what don't have husbands and there's a good many of us. We need your help with organizing it all.''

Charles was looking at her somewhat befuddled. "My help."

Bessie Mae giggled. "Oh, don't you worry none. We women will take care of the food and drink and such. You just make sure the word gets out in the paper—you know, to squash those suffragist types—and talk to the menfolk about it."

"About what?"

Bessie Mae frowned at him. "Why, a party, of course. A great big one, or two, whatever it takes—with music and dancing and the like. Opportunity, Mr. Remington, sometimes needs a little creating."

"My sentiments exactly, Miss Elliot. And where will this great big party take place?"

Bessie Mae waved an airy hand. "Why, any ol' farm will do, but it has to have the most sheepshearers on it, of course, so I guess it'll have to be a sheepherders place. You pick it. And make sure the menfolk come."

"Cattlemen as well, you say?" He looked suddenly thoughtful and Kate wondered what was hatching in his mind.

"Cattlemen, sheepmen, lawyers, I don't care, so long as they're there to meet the good, honest womenfolk in Crooked Nickel. Ain't that right, ladies?"

The ladies responded with greet cheers. A few even leapt to their feet. Kate chose that moment of buoyant jubilation to slip from her seat and aim herself toward escape. It was a bit tricky given the room's inadequate dimensions, the women everywhere, and Harriet's tea making her legs feel wobbly.

She ducked her head, kept her eyes fixed on the front door, and was nearly there when her upper arm was suddenly gripped.

"Going off with your fellow suffragists to lurk and

slink in a back alley somewhere, Kate?'' Charles's murmur came close to her ear.

Kate tensed. ''I don't know how to lurk and slink.''

''Good. I'll accompany you.''

He bade Bessie Mae a quick good day and, before Bessie Mae or Kate could argue the point, directed Kate hastily out the front door, allowing her to toss her thanks over her shoulder before he let the door slam behind them.

Kate immediately wriggled her arm out of his grasp and marched ahead of him down the steps and across the front path with head held high, shoulders back, and feet, hopefully, following each other. When she reached the front gate, she flipped at the latch but it wouldn't flip and the mechanics of the thing suddenly seemed beyond her. She closed her eyes against the setting sun and felt her pulse throbbing in her cheeks. She cursed Harriet Edwards a hundred times over.

''Having trouble?'' Charles's arm slipped around her and easily released the latch. He pushed the gate open. ''After you, Mrs. McGoldrick.''

There was a hint of amusement in his tone that unnerved Kate.

''I can only assume you're taking great pleasure in my humiliation,'' she said, trying to lengthen her stride though she seemed capable only of slow motion.

He caught her elbow and directed her onto a straight path heading along the boardwalk into town. ''Actually, I was wondering what you had to drink in there.''

''Tea.'' A hiccup jerked her chest.

Charles laughed and the deep sound of it made Kate's insides quiver. ''Is that what that sweet little lady was serving?''

''Yes—'' She swallowed another hiccup. ''That was Harriet's. She has a still on her farm. It seems they all do. And their husbands know nothing about them.'' She tried to look up at him but he seemed too tall suddenly. ''It was quite tasty, if you must know. I had two cups.''

''I can see that. How do you feel?''

''Not too good. Actually, I'm entirely not in the mood to engage in verbal fisticuffs with you, Charles. Please go away.''

''And I was so looking forward to it. I suppose I'll have to do it by way of another editorial.''

Kate's head suddenly ached. ''Don't make me have to write another one.''

''It was quite good. I enjoyed reading about Esther Morris. But by the end of it, I'm afraid Jonathan Smarte sounded a bit like an overzealous suffragist.''

''Maybe he's becoming one—no, that wouldn't work, would it?'' Kate closed her eyes, wove slightly, and found herself leaning against him. ''This is not good, Charles. I'm going to be seen.''

''And we don't want that.''

''This isn't funny.''

''I want you to know I'm trying very hard not to laugh.''

''I have appearances to uphold in this town, Charles. It's not like Boston''

''You're right. In Boston, you can disappear one night and no one will know you're gone until it's too damned late. Here, this way—'' He directed her quickly around the end of one building and down an alley toward the path that led behind the buildings and ran parallel to the main street.

''Someone's going to see us back here,'' she hissed, trying to hurry along and keep her head down at the same time. A muffled sound snapped her head up. ''Oh, God, we're in back of Louella's place, aren't we?''

''Do you want to go in?''

''God, no. I was just—'' She wrinkled up her nose and

imagined she tilted it a bit higher. "I could smell it. Besides that I could hear—you know—her music."

"The man on the piano hails from New York City. He's quite good. Plays every night. It's not the rollicking music you hear in the saloons."

"Yes. It's the kind of music one might hear in the opera in Boston."

"Ah. You appreciate it, do you?"

She gave a dismissing shrug, realizing where he was taking the conversation. "I might appreciate it, but I don't miss it. Indeed, and if I did, I could go to Laramie when the local opera performs. Or to Denver."

"I might enjoy that."

"A pity you won't be here long enough to enjoy the start of the season."

"Don't count on it."

She dismissed his innuendo again. "Do you have tickets in Boston?"

He seemed to pause. "No, Kate. I've spent every spare dime on getting the family out of debt of one kind or another."

"Business isn't good, then?"

"In Boston it would certainly be. But where I've settled in Lenox—it takes some time to start a practice, develop clientele, establish a reputation. It's where I feel I need to be for Mother and Mary Elizabeth—"

"No philanthropies, Charles? You seem as if you were born generous hearted."

"Philanthropies—yes. A few—carefully chosen, of course. I have to believe in something I give my money to." He was looking at her so intently she wondered for a moment what she'd said to arouse such interest. He also looked as if he wished to say something right then but the moment suddenly passed. He indicated Louella's. "Are you sure you don't want to go in? Zeke makes one hell of a dinner. It might be just what you need after all that 'tea.' "

"I can't eat in a brothel with you, Charles. I have to get Walt. He's at Douglas Murphy's, telling all of them about his afternoon spent with his *Uncle* Charles over at the livery." She slanted him a look that fell dismally short of anger.

He looked innocent as a lamb. "Sundance needed to be reshod."

"You know what the devil I'm talking about."

"Relax. I was getting tired of being called Mr. Reninton. Uncle Charles seemed to suit. He likes it. He liked the livery. And I enjoyed every minute being there with him."

She heard the tenderness in his voice. "Yes, he told me all about it while we changed the beds."

He paused, drawing her up beside him, and looked down at her with utter seriousness. "He reminds me of you, Kate." His voice strummed through her. "I feel as if I've known him for years. I watch him—I see Mother, Grandmother Remington, even my own father—"

"The eyes—"

"Yes. And I find myself waiting to see something of Jude, the darker side—"

"Yes," she murmured, knowing what he meant. "I do the same thing."

"And I see nothing but good, nothing but innocent mischief, nothing but you. You've been a wonderful mother to him, Kate."

She stared at his chest and felt emotion swirling through her. "He's everything to me, Charles. I've promised myself he'll never know another day of sorrow—"

"That's impossible."

"Maybe. But I've also promised myself that he'll never feel what I felt as a child—it's the tearing away of the people you love that you remember most—when my father died—when my mother left me, and the nuns—I won't let him feel abandoned. I want him to have the things I wanted—" She looked up at him and felt swallowed by the compassion in his eyes.

He grasped her hands in his. "I'll get you home and then I'll fetch Walt for you on Sundance."

"Really, Charles. I feel fine enough to walk all the way to Douglas Murphy's—"

A nearby door slammed somewhere near the back of Louella's place. Men's voices—men coming toward them—men looking right at them—

Kate turned, glimpsed them—cattlemen.

And then she was spun and lifted at the same time; her toes skimmed the earth, her back was pressed back against a wooden wall, and then Charles was kissing her and pressing his body very close to hers.

She felt her knee slide between his parted legs and her limbs turn to water.

He caught her in his arms and deepened his kiss.

Her thoughts careened. An act—a ruse—intended to protect her. After all, she'd made such a fuss about it.

She'd best play along and make it look good.

It was easy to cling to him when her world seemed to be spinning. It was easy to arch herself up into him when his stalwart frame seemed so capable of bearing it. It was even easier to part her lips under his and feel the velvety warmth of his tongue against hers.

She felt his hand on the side of her breast, fingers splayed, molding, and the liquid heat pooled high between her thighs. She arched her hips into his and felt the answering, insistent pressure of his.

He lifted his head and left her suspended. "Very good. They're gone."

"What?" Kate opened her eyes. He was looking down at her; his eyes looked stormy.

She licked her lips, ran a shaky hand over her hair, and glanced down the alley. She felt mussed, ravished, and thoroughly humiliated for the second time in a day.

She pressed her fingers to her temples and averted her eyes from his. She found herself staring again at the front of his shirt. She could smell the starch as if the scent were being heated by the skin beneath it. And she suddenly remembered that Jonathan Smarte had kissed Maggie Swifte countless times in countless alleys over the years, while the bad guys got away yet again.

"You know why I did that?" His voice was as smooth as honey on silk. His hands were on her upper arms. She felt the thumbs gently rub and tingles raced all over her.

"Yes, I do."

"It just seems—ah, hell. There should have been another way. Are you okay?"

As if she were rendered a complete noodle from one little kiss. As if his touch were enough to befuddle.

Perhaps it was, but he didn't need to know it.

"I'm perfectly fine," she said a touch too crisply, which didn't give her words an ounce of veracity. Still, she managed to lift her skirts and step past him with a breezy, "No harm done."

"Speak for yourself," came his answering murmur, and he followed after her.

Chapter 14

Two minutes after they rode away from Douglas Murphy's house, Walt fell asleep with his cheek resting on Charles's chest and his mouth half open. Charles kept him anchored there with one arm wrapped around his narrow shoulders. With the other, he guided Sundance down Crooked Nickel's dark main street back toward Kate's.

They passed the jail along the way. Charles could see the orange glow of a cigar tip and a man's bulky silhouette on the front porch. He assumed it was Gage silently watching him, feet propped, belly poking out, cigar smoke curling around him. The cigar's glow magnified, then dimmed. The night was eerily still above the clopping of Sundance's hooves in the dust. Shadows moved next to Gage. Another man sat quietly beside him in the darkness.

Hatching schemes in the night.

It was an odd feeling that came over Charles as he hugged the boy close and contemplated the evil doings around him. Protectiveness of a child was obviously not something that was reserved for fathers. His heart seemed to swell in his chest and he felt a profound yearning to give the boy everything that was in his power to give him. Just like Kate, he wanted to protect him and keep him safe from the wrongs in the world. And the best way he knew to do that was to take him away to Boston where good schools and fine culture awaited him, where civilization was the rule, not the exception.

Where men like Elmer Pruitt were put in jail, and spirited women like Kate cooked fine meals, served tea, made passionate love to their husbands and bore many children.

The town was quiet, the air still, and a full yellow moon rose above the eastern horizon. Again, it occurred to Charles that he'd never heard such quiet in Boston. Kate had no doubt gotten very used to the quiet. He wondered for how long she'd missed Lenox and the family. He wondered how long it would take him to forget the only home he'd ever known.

A dim light shone in Kate's window when he drew Sundance up at the hitching rail. He slid from the horse's back with Walt cradled in his arms. When Charles's feet hit dirt, the boy stirred slightly, then cuddled closer. Charles swallowed a lump of emotion and moved toward the house. The instant he stepped onto the porch the front door opened. Her narrow silhouette outlined by the glow of candlelight behind her was the most welcoming sight Charles had known in a lifetime.

There was something infinitely right about coming home to this woman, with this child in his arms.

"His room's on the right," she said softly, stepping back as he passed. She then scooted ahead of him into the room, turned down the bedside lamp, and drew back the patchwork coverlet.

He laid Walt on the bed; she tended to his shoes, drew up the coverlet, and bent over the sleeping boy. Over her shoulder Charles watched her hand cup Walt's head, watched her thumb trace the curve of his fair brow. He heard her gentle murmurs, realized they were prayers, and felt suddenly like an intruder.

Quite unlike a father.

Very much like a distant uncle with no rights whatsoever and no claim on the child. Or the woman.

But he didn't leave.

She bent, pressed a kiss to Walt's forehead, turned the lamp down, and faced Charles.

He went breathless with the serene beauty of her.

"Thank you," she whispered. And then she pressed her hand on his chest and moved past him, out of the room. Heart thudding like a locomotive, he followed.

The kitchen smelled like the strong coffee he'd made for her before he'd left to retrieve Walt. She was at the counter and with one hand poured coffee into two cups. With the other she slowly rubbed the back of her neck. She leaned slightly against the counter looking weary and battle worn. Her hair was tied at the nape with a black ribbon, and the loose russet curls cascaded down her back.

Charles stood behind her, aching to take her in his arms. There was so much he needed to do, so much to say, but now—now, didn't seem the time.

The bond between them was in many ways as strong as steel—their years of shared history was inarguable. But beyond that, the relationship they had now consisted of merely tenuous little threads, fragile as the tiniest sapling. He didn't dare threaten it. He'd do anything to strengthen it.

"Come sit with me on the settee, Charles," she said, offering him a cup of coffee. Charles obliged, shedding his topcoat and laying it on the back of a kitchen chair as he followed her.

She sat in the middle of the settee. He settled next to her. She lifted her cup, sipped, then looked down into the coffee.

Several moments passed. The clock over the fireplace mantel ticked. Beyond the open windows the night was peaceful and silent. Charles filled his head with the smell of her and clamped his hands on his knees to keep them where they belonged.

His eyes roamed over the room, over the bookshelves jammed with books, until he spotted a pair of eyeglasses on top of a book on the end table by his side. They looked like men's eyeglasses. Harry's. Judging by the dust on them, Kate had undoubtedly left them where her husband had left them the last time he put them down.

Harry must have been sitting then precisely where Charles was sitting now.

Charles felt suddenly like an intruder in a place he didn't belong.

"I've been sitting here waiting for you to come back," Kate said in a low voice, drawing his regard. "And it felt good to be up waiting, keeping the lamps burning and the coffee hot. I realized that I never wait for anybody anymore. I used to for Harry—and there were many nights when he didn't come home until dawn. I waited right here the night he was killed—until they came to tell me. I don't wait for anyone anymore." She was staring at her lap. "I get so lonely, Charles, and tonight especially I feel so tired—like I can't fight it anymore."

"What are you fighting, Kate?"

Her smile was rueful but she didn't look up at him. "You. Me. The choices I made a long time ago. Pruitt. The cattlemen. I feel like I fight every day. And I suppose I enjoy some of it. Like writing that rebuttal. I enjoyed the challenge. I enjoyed the argument purely for the sake of arguing. I enjoy stirring things up and being part of something. God, I suppose I am somewhat of a zealot."

"That's not all bad. Otherwise, little change gets accomplished."

"No—you're right. Someone has to do it. I just wish sometimes it wasn't me. I just wish I wasn't the only one feeling out of place at Bessie Mae's tonight. I wish sometimes I could make my mind stop thinking and my heart stop feeling and instead fill my days with the usual female pursuits and at night tend my still and go to garden party meetings with other females and drink myself silly. I wish I could blame a man's meanness on his not having a good and proper wife. It might make it easier not to blame Harry for what happened to him."

Charles watched the soft lamplight play over her features. "You can't make yourself see the world differently," he said softly. "Sometimes where you stand, you have to fight."

She sipped her coffee again and seemed to draw a deep breath. "Especially with you."

He looked at her profile, the determined upward tilt of nose, lips, cheeks, and eyes, the utter gorgeousness of her, and said, "I wasn't aware that we were battling, Kate—other than with wills, but if you insist we are, we could do the noble thing, call a truce, and become ardent allies."

"For a night?" She looked up at him and his heart suddenly slammed against his chest. "Could we, Charles, just for a night? Could we pretend—?"

He felt his throat go dry. "Pretend what, Kate?"

Her eyes narrowed slightly. "Pretend that there aren't murders to avenge and sheepherders to help, pretend there aren't little children's lives in the balance, pretend that you and I are now as we were six years ago—"

"I don't want what we had six years ago, Kate," he murmured. "I want something that you won't ever run away from. I want something to cherish for all time."

She turned to put her coffee cup on the low table beside the settee and he knew this was his chance to get up and leave because he knew where this was going.

"Let's pretend that we're simply a man and a woman," she whispered, turning toward him.

Yes, he should be getting up now—and be noble and trustworthy and earnest and responsible.

But he didn't move.

As tired as she was of loneliness, he was infinitely more tired of being the good, responsible man who could forsake his own desires for the needs of others around him. Hadn't he done it when he gave up his dream to write and instead followed his father's dream of becoming an attorney, the better to provide for the family? Hadn't he done it eloquently when he'd agreed to marry Eleanor Curtin the better to improve the family's position? What had sacrifice ever gotten him in the way of happiness? Hadn't he given up on finding Kate six years ago because he'd had a job to do and a family to provide for?

"I have to know something, Charles—" Her voice purred with sensuality and yet she sat primly beside him, hands clasping and unclasping in her lap as if she didn't quite know what to do with the stuff boiling inside of her. There was a gleam of desperation in her eyes that made his gut wrench and his palms grip ever harder on his knees.

His Kate was all grown up and ready to be let out of her cage.

And she wanted him to do it.

She licked her lips and they gleamed ripe and rosy and kissable. "Can we pretend there's no tomorrow, Charles?"

"That's never wise." His voice sounded hoarse and husky. Perspiration popped out on his forehead.

"But I have to know—I—" She laid a trembling hand on his thigh and his erection bucked in his trousers. "Please, Charles—"

"Kate—"

"I don't want to talk anymore, Charles. Do you?"

"I—" He rose half out of his seat and clamped his hands on her arms, pulling her half up to meet him. His chest heaved, blood pounded in his veins, conscience screamed, and he deafened himself to it. "What do you want, Kate?" he rasped. "You want to explore the world with me because I make you feel safe, is that it?"

"Yes," she whispered, splaying her palms on his chest.

"You want to pretend there's no tomorrow because you want to go somewhere that's unsafe and you want me to bring you back."

"Yes—" Her eyes swept closed and she arched her lithe and supple young body toward him. "Please, Charles—"

His breath came in rasps. "What—you think you want this—?" He bent, pressed his mouth to the side of her neck, and tasted the sweetness of her skin with wide, open-mouthed strokes.

"Yes—" Her hands were fumbling with the buttons of his shirt.

"And this—?" He nibbled her ear, the underside of it, her jaw, her temple, reached up and yanked the ribbon from her hair. He dug both hands into the thickness of her hair, cupped her head, and lifted her mouth so it was just beneath his. Her lips were trembling. Her eyes were shining. "Sweet Kate," he groaned, and crushed his mouth over hers.

Her lips swept open at the first gentle thrust of his tongue and his need compounded triplefold. He kissed her as if he drank of her, drew her breath from her lungs, and consumed her. He kissed the length of her neck as buttons flew open and his shirt was pushed aside by her hands. His own worked over the column that started at her neck. She reached up to help him, made a soft, impatient sound, then gasped as he pushed the fabric apart over the uppermost slopes of her breasts.

"Is this what you want?" he murmured, kissing the softest skin a man could find this side of heaven. His fingers were flying over the rest of the buttons, pushing bombazine and chemise aside and then lower and lower. He filled his hands with her breasts, lifted them to his face, and his head swam with the beauty of her.

She pushed his shirt over his shoulders, while he drew one nipple against his tongue and suckled once, twice, gently, then deeper and more urgently with every gasp she gave. He withdrew, flicked at the swollen nipple with his tongue. She cried out and lifted her hips up into his in a gentle, rocking rhythm that spoke to the basest of his instincts.

Tomorrow didn't matter, nothing mattered but the sounds of her pleasure, and he took his, rubbing his thumbs over her nipples until she looked at him wild eyed and wanting. Lips parted and gasping, hair all atumble, and breasts glowing full and luminous, all swathed in crushed black bombazine . . . she was the most gorgeous, the most ravishable, the most desirable woman he'd ever imagined knowing.

And she didn't even know it.

"Charles—" She was clawing at her gown, trying to push it over her shoulder as if she wanted to crawl her way out of it.

He spread hot kisses over her breasts. He slipped both hands inside her dress, spanned her waist, then slid them over the fullness of her pantalooned bottom and lifted her against the agonizing pressure in his groin. A groan came from the back of his throat, passion fired beyond his will, and he jerked his hands wide and up, stripping the gown from her.

She gave an outcry of surprise then clasped her arms around him as if she meant to hang on forever. He fell upon her on the settee and slanted his mouth over hers. His knee slid up between her thighs, her hips lifted, and she gave a sound of desperation that made his mind spin and his body pulse.

She was kissing him wildly, arching, lifting her hips for

something he was suddenly certain she'd never known, and he cupped his hand around her loins, found the slit in the pantaloons, felt the warm dampness of it, and stroked her delicate flesh until she dissolved.

He lifted his head, stared at her, and knew he'd never known anything quite so remarkable in a woman. It was the most fulfillment he'd ever found.

And he was still as taut, hot, pulsing, and needful as he'd ever been. It hurt to press against her. It hurt to be so close and yet so damned far. Hell, it hurt to breathe.

"Charles—" She licked her lips. "Oh, Charles—I've never—not ever—" Her hands stroked lightly over his back and shoulders. She had no idea that she'd left him perched on the edge of insanity.

He lowered his head and circled one nipple with his tongue. The nub hardened, distended, and she gave an answering sigh of pleasure. He cupped the other breast, lifted it to his mouth, suckled gently until he couldn't bear it another moment.

He levered himself up with his hands on either side of her, hips pressed to hers. His eyes drank in the ravished sight of her, a pink, pearly wonder of curvaceous female. His hand moved to the front of his trousers and he had to pause.

"Kate—" he whispered hoarsely, feeling the words come up from the base of his soul. "I want to make love to you—"

She was looking up at him with limpid eyes. She licked her lips. "Will you—will you make that happen to me again—like you just did?"

"Yes, Kate, a hundred times—" His hand was shaking as it flicked at his trousers. His whole body was trembling. He tugged, shifted, pressed his bare loins close to hers, looked deep into her eyes, and slid inside her.

"Charles—" she breathed, clasping him close.

The world began spinning around him. He gathered her in his arms and moved gently, slowly. "Ah—God—Kate—I can't—" He felt her tense, her eyes flew wide, and she gave another soft outcry. He couldn't contain himself another moment and surrendered to the spasms that consumed them both.

He opened his eyes and realized he'd buried his face and open mouth against her throat. He didn't know how long he'd lain there with her, limbs entangled, one leg half on the floor, the other half-asleep, but he sensed it had been for some time. His body felt hot and sweaty and numb, his mind felt sleep fogged and dreamy.

"Kate," he whispered, brushing a tangle of hair from her cheek. She was sleeping in a tangle of black bombazine and sheer white undergarments. In the lamplight she looked gorgeous and peaceful, and it took all his will to get to his feet. He quickly tended to his trousers, then, bending low, gathered her into his arms and took her into her bedroom. She didn't stir when he laid her on the bed; she softly murmured something when he drew the white coverlet over her, then drifted back off to sleep as he lingered at her bedside watching her.

Some time later, he retrieved his coat, turned down the lamps, and left.

"Good morning, Mr. Gould," Kate said cheerily, closing the office door behind her.

Gould barely glanced up. "Mrs. McG—" His head snapped up and his mouth snapped open. "Good heavens, ma'am, you're—quite—that is—"

"Do you like it?" Kate asked spinning halfway one way, then halfway the other the better to allow the morning sun to play over the salmon-pink and white stripes of her dress. "I don't quite know why but I couldn't wear black today. You understand, of course."

"Y—yes, ma'am. Of course, ma'am."

"I thought you might. God, look at this mess. It's been accumulating since the day Harry died—maybe even before." Kate tossed her reticule on a pile of pages and stood over the desk with hands on her hips.

She'd awakened full of nervous energy she didn't know what to do with. Every time she thought about last evening she closed her eyes and cringed over the wanton she'd allowed herself to become. And yet, it was just as Charles had said. She felt as if he'd taken her somewhere she shouldn't go, but now that she was back, all would be well.

Or at least she hoped.

A trembly kind of feeling had invaded her stomach since she'd awakened. Her voice sounded too high-pitched to her own ear. She'd been clumsy all morning, dropping things and bumping into furniture. Her energy was burgeoning.

She could go to Louella's and find Charles. It was a thought she banished immediately. Respectable women didn't go chasing after men. Then again, they probably didn't shed their widow's weeds before it was time or lay themselves beneath a man on a settee and let him do things that took them to the moon and back.

And if they did, respectable women certainly didn't enjoy it as much as she had.

For those precious moments last night she'd allowed herself to forget everything she'd promised herself, all the responsibilities she had to Walt, to Harry, to the newspaper, and most especially to herself and the life she'd made far away from the ghosts of her past. In the stark light of morning those responsibilities had come flooding back. It had taken one sleepy good morning from Walt to wrench her heart around and stir up a heaping dose of guilt. Even the enormous breakfast she'd made him didn't dispel it.

Guilt over pleasure. Guilt over self-indulgence. Guilt over neglecting her duties.

She glanced at the clock over Mr. Gould's desk. It was barely eight. She chewed her lip and looked out the front window and down the street toward Louella's. Her stomach churned.

"There's bills seven months old under all this," she said, settling into the chair and blowing a stray wisp of hair from her eyes.

"I put a stack there just the other day, ma'am. Right on the corner there—'course one or two might have fallen off."

"Bills, bills, and God knows what else I'll—what's this?"

"Today's mail. Just that one piece."

Kate picked up the envelope and frowned.

"Came from Turkeyfoot Run by carrier. Must be important."

"Indeed, it must be if it came by carrier. I wonder who—?" She shrugged, slit the envelope open and pulled out the letter. Her eyes skimmed over the bold scrawl. It was actually more of a note, hastily penned but powerful just the same. She felt the blood drain from her face. "Oh, God."

"What?" Gould scooted back from his chair. "Good heavens, ma'am, you look white as that paper there. Is it too terribly bad?"

"Bad?" She blinked up at Gould. "*Bad?!* Why, Mr. Gould—" She raced around the edge of the desk, planted a walloping kiss on Gould's cheek, then headed for the door.

"Where are you going?" Gould shouted, cheeks flushed bright red.

Kate paused in the open doorway. "To Louella's, of course."

Gould looked appalled. ''Louella's? My dear, Mrs. McGoldrick, things can't be that bad!''

''Oh, but they're not! Things are good, Mr. Gould—so good I don't care who the devil sees me march right in her front door. Ask me if I care, Mr. Gould. Just ask me!'' With a huge grin and a wave, she slammed the door behind her and dashed down the boardwalk.

''When do you think you're going to give up the fight? Mr. Remington? Excuse me, hullo—''

The woman's voice was husky and honey smooth.

''What?'' Charles glanced up when he finished the sentence he was writing. The stunning, red-headed Isabelle was draped like a sleek emerald feline against the chair next to his. He blinked several times and tried to recall what she'd said. His mind had been two thousand miles away, in Lenox with his mother and sister. A letter to them was past due. But he'd had great difficulty keeping his tone light and the subject of it to business matters when business had nothing to do with his being in Crooked Nickel. How did he keep even a mention of Kate out of it when she was his sole reason for waking every morning?

Isabelle inclined her head and shifted her shoulders, bringing the surge of bosom arching out of her dress into full, unimpeded view for Charles. ''Why don't you like me, Mr. Remington?''

''I do, Isabelle. I like all of the girls here.''

She lowered her voice, her eyes, and raked his groin with a look that would have made a grown man blush. At eight in the morning—hell, Charles gave a low laugh, shook his head, and looked back down at the letter on the table in front of him.

''I want you to like me best,'' she purred, sidling closer, sliding her hand slowly over his shoulders and back.

Charles narrowed his eyes and scanned his letter. He focused on one passage of the letter, where he'd made mention of staying on in Crooked Nickel indefinitely. The problem was that his mother and Mary Elizabeth were under a servant's care, with Jude forever absent and increasingly uncaring. Charles had left enough money behind to see to their needs, for a certain time. But he'd known of many instances where caregivers abused their privileges, took the money, and abandoned their charges. Even those who seemed the most trustworthy.

The picture his thoughts inspired didn't settle well with him. He either had to return soon to Boston, or send for them.

And then there was Kate.

He scrawled his signature at the bottom of the letter, folded it, and pushed his chair back. He stood up but Isabelle picked that moment to slide her arms around his neck, wriggle her hips against his groin, and plant little-girl kisses on his cheek.

"Say you like me," she purred.

"I don't think you understand," he said, laying his hands firmly around her waist and giving her a stern look.

The front door to the place slammed open. Isabelle looked over Charles's shoulder, and then a woman said, *"Charles—?"*

He would have recognized her voice among a thousand women.

He turned to face Kate. "Don't—" he said gravely. He reached out a hand toward her and started to move toward her, all too aware that her beautiful green eyes were filling up with the same wariness and mistrust he'd been bent on removing from them forever. Last night he'd thought he'd seen the very last of it. He felt his heart pumping very hard. "I swear to God—don't turn around and leave without listening to what I have to say—goddammit—"

But she did. She spun toward the door and ran smack into Louella Lawless.

"What the devil are you—?" Louella's eyes snapped wide and her mouth gaped. "Why, it's the Widow McGoldrick."

"Don't ever call me that again," Kate snapped back. She shoved a hand over her eyes, brushed past Louella, and dashed for the door.

Charles went quickly after her.

"Is there a problem, Mr. Remington?" Louella murmured as he strode past.

"Something like that," he muttered over his shoulder. He caught the door with the tip of his boot just as Kate tried to slam it shut behind her. He pushed it back open, strode onto the porch, and caught her by her elbow when she was halfway down the stairs. With very little effort, he swung her feet off the steps, spun her around, and escorted her back across the porch toward Louella's place.

"I'm not going back in there," she said, even as he pushed the door open and dragged her back in. "I'm not. You can't make me."

"I can make you do a lot of things you say you don't want to do," he murmured through his teeth. "Do you want me to remind you?"

That silenced her.

He glanced into the common room, spotted Isabelle, thought the better of that idea and, on a whim, headed directly for the stairs. To get there he had to drag Kate right past Louella.

Kate's heels dug into the carpets and she launched into a full-bodied squirm. "What are you—you can't—I won't—!"

"Can I get you anything, Mr. Remington?" Louella asked in her syrupy tone as Charles braced himself on the first step and dragged a red-faced Kate up by her elbow.

When that didn't work, and she looked about to spit at Louella, he slipped one arm around her waist, another around her bottom, bent, and lifted her into his arms.

The look he gave Louella would have daunted any other woman. But not Louella.

Louella's eyes were glittering. "I can see you're well enough off without my help."

He grunted his reply, shifted Kate in his arms, and climbed the stairs two at a time.

She'd obviously concluded fighting him physically was useless because she'd folded her arms over her chest, set her chin at its most stubborn angle, and tightened her mouth as if she sucked on a lemon.

"I can't believe you're doing this," she said, her voice trembling as if she could hardly contain her anger. "This is the most outrageous—God, look at this wallpaper. There are naked people on it. I can't look at it. I can't be here."

"If I recall, my dear, you were the one who walked in the front door, and there were no horses dragging you."

"That's right, I did. And it was completely foolish of me. I obviously let enthusiasm get the better of my good sense."

His voice rumbled very low. "That anxious to see me?" He laughed at the flush roaring in her cheeks. "Relax. Louella's not going to say a word about any of this to anybody."

"And I suppose you think I ought to trust her, too. Just like that."

"I believe you don't have a choice in the matter at this point, do you, sweetheart?" He didn't pause at the top of the stairs, simply marched down the hall straight to his room at the very end.

"Don't call me that."

He stopped in front of his door and looked down at her.

"Fine. Then I'll call you honey. It's what I taste when I think about you."

Astonished, she blinked, her face flushed, then, she shoved her elbow hard into his chest. "Put me down."

"Wait. I'm not letting you run away again." He wedged her against the wall, fished his keys from his pocket, and opened the door.

"Please don't take me in there."

"Tell me where else we can have a good, old-fashioned argument?"

She looked up at him warily. "That's all that's going to happen."

"Is that a promise or a threat?"

She swallowed, looked down, and fidgeted.

His voice plunged very low as his eyes caressed her mouth, her chin, the delicious curve of her breasts accentuated by her pink and white stripes. "Some promises have a way of getting forgotten between us."

"I know," she said quietly. "Quit talking to me like that."

"Like what?"

"Like"—she waved a hand—"like you want me to forget why I'm so mad at you."

"I know why you're mad. You're being ridiculous."

She glared up at him. "Ridiculous?"

"See—we need privacy." He strode into the room, kicked the door closed behind them, and plopped her down on his bed.

"This has to stop."

"You're right." He strode back to the door, locked it, then pocketed the key. It occurred to him that his current circumstances weren't altogether unenviable. His adorable and sexy Kate was standing next to his bed looking in dire need of something to wipe away all her fist-clenching.

He shed his topcoat, tossing it over a nearby upholstered chair. The room was heavily draped in sapphire velvet. It was a den of iniquity to be sure, intended to inspire iniquitous thoughts. That Kate was here, and the fully realized embodiment of his iniquitous thoughts, made his blood fire and his groin throb. He went to the window, pushed the drape aside, and threw it wide. The air barely stirred.

He turned and caught her staring directly at his groin. It made his dilemma there measurably worse.

Her eyes jerked up. She blushed crimson and swallowed.

"I've bedded only one woman since I came here," he said slowly, watching her lips part and her eyes grow huge. Apparently, he'd surprised her. He'd meant to. Men didn't normally confess such things to angry women.

Her chest rose and fell several times. "It's truly none of my business what you do, Charles."

He moved toward her, pausing only when he felt the heat of her. He had to tip up her chin to make her look at him. "Tell me, Kate, do you honestly believe that?"

Chapter 15

"This isn't how I'd planned this," Kate confessed, looking out the lace-draped window and feeling her cheeks getting hot with embarrassment. She kept her hands tucked close against her chest in a protective stance. "I suppose I assumed if anyone saw me charging in here they'd naturally understand that I had good reason because I believed I had good reason."

"Naturally. You have a sterling reputation around town, Kate. And deservedly so. You've spent the last six years of your life earning it. I know it's vitally important to you because of Walt, because of who you are—why the hell won't you look at me?"

She glanced up at him, then looked down at her hands. "I should have expected an eyeful when I came in here but I wasn't even thinking about that and then, when I saw you and that, that woman—and she was so beautiful—" She shot her eyes up to his. "She was, Charles."

"Yes, so are hundreds of other women."

Kate bit her lip, felt the comforting warmth of his hands on her upper arms, felt the squirming unrest in her belly, and whispered, "I wanted to smack her, Charles."

His laugh was low and soft and sounded wonderful reverberating in his chest. "Kate—"

"I wanted to. I haven't felt like that since—since—"

She swallowed and the words leapt to her tongue. She looked up, looked deep into his eyes, and prayed she'd never regret letting him into her heart. "I felt like I did that night when you told us that you were marrying Eleanor Curtin. I wanted to run then—run until I didn't feel anymore—and I did, I ran straight to Jude to make myself feel better."

"You were too young then to know what you were doing," he murmured, thumbs rubbing gently on her arms. "I blame myself for that, Kate. I saw the way Jude was looking at you that night—and I know you couldn't have seen it. I knew that my feelings for you weren't brotherly in any way. I played a role I had no intention of fulfilling and I sacrificed you to do it."

"Stop—" When she looked up at him and met his soulful eyes, something inside her dissolved like sugar over a low flame. Something inside her whispered that perhaps what she'd best do was believe him, trust him, just as he was asking her to do, just as she'd done as a child, because she hadn't been wrong to do it then.

It seemed at once the easiest and the hardest thing to do.

She drew an unsteady breath. "Charles—I think we need to talk about last night. I woke up and Walt was standing in his doorway looking at me like he knew what his mother had done and I felt so guilty, like I'd betrayed his trust—"

He slid his hands around her waist and yanked her close. It was a statement of possession. So was his kiss.

Her lips parted beneath his, tongues danced, the room spun, and doves fluttered in her belly. She slid her hands up his back, he boldly cupped her bottom and pressed loins to loins.

"Good morning," he rumbled when he lifted his head. He pressed his forehead to hers, brushed his lips again over hers, bent, and kissed the tips of each of her breasts.

She jerked and gulped. *"Charles."*

"What?" He cupped his hands around her breasts and registered her intake of breath with a subtle arch of his brow and a brush of his thumbs over her nipples. "You come in here looking like this and you'll get appreciated." His lips touched hers gently, reverently, and seemed to leave hers with great reluctance. His breath came out slowly. "Now, come here—"

He took her hand and led her to two chairs set before the window. He directed her into one chair and took the other opposite hers. He leaned forward—forearms braced on his thighs—took her hand, and looked deep into her eyes. "Is that why you came? To tell me you feel guilty that we made love and that it was all wrong?"

She looked sternly at him. "It was."

"You know damned well it wasn't."

"It accomplished nothing but to get me all confused and I won't be confused, Charles. Not ever again."

"Fine. I have no intention of confusing you and complicating your life, Kate."

"Then you've failed miserably because you have complicated it. Things were so clear to me before you came here—I knew what I had to do, I knew my role in life, I felt good and strong and confident being a mother to Walt, writing for the paper, and now—now—" She looked at him and felt the tears stinging her eyes. "I awoke this morning feeling like I'd turned my back on all of that, as if none of it means anything, as if years of experience and life never happened, and they have—"

"Yes, they have." He was looking at her fingers and a weariness seemed to have settled over him. "I have my own demons to wrestle with, Kate. I've made choices, good and bad, and certain sacrifices that I truly don't regret. I've established myself and my practice and I make a good living that I'm proud of. I also have responsibilities—but I'm not asking you to give up anything, Kate, without gaining so much in return."

"You are, and I just can't, Charles—I—"

"Christ, but you look gorgeous today." His eyes were stormy and tormented and her heart wrenched painfully in her chest.

"Stop looking at me like that, Charles—"

"I can't stop." His voice was all raspy and deep. "I see you and I want to touch you to make sure you're real. I used to dream of you and wake up and my hands would be burning to feel you but you weren't there and I thought I'd never see you again. I woke up a dozen times last night when I did manage to sleep and I wanted you, Kate. I want you and no other woman. There could be hundreds of beautiful women in a room and I would see only you. It's been that way for the past six years and I thought you were dead—"

She looked away and anguish congealed in her belly.

"I've so much to tell you, six years of daily life I want to share with you—even the smallest, most meaningless parts—so much to show you if only you'll let me, Kate. We didn't close any doors last night. We opened them. You wanted to pretend there was no past between us—and we did—and I say we leave it that way."

"I can't. So much has happened that shouldn't mean anything but it does. I have so much left to accomplish—"

"I can help you."

"I need to do it myself, Charles."

"Damned, stubborn woman, you can't." His voice was like a caress. "There's so goddamned much—and all I want to do is love you."

His hands were on the satin-covered pink buttons that started at the top of her dress and ran to her waist.

"We can't," she said, closing her eyes.

"I know." The buttons were flying open. He bent and

kissed his way down her throat and into the depths of her décolletage. "I want to be your lover—"

"We should stop."

"We're going to stop. I made a vow—at four this morning. I'm going to tell you about that in a minute—ah—" His hands slipped inside the parted bodice, cupped around her ribcage, and his thumbs flicked at her nipples through the thin cotton chemise. They sprang up against the fabric.

Tingles raced through Kate. "I made a vow, too," she whispered. "A vow to stay away from you—"

"Look at me."

She looked at him and then got an eyeful of herself. Creamy white breasts and lace and nipples pushing at him through transparent cotton . . .

His hands looked huge and dark and very masculine as they fondled her.

She closed her eyes. "I can't."

He wet the cotton with his tongue, his mouth, his teeth, first over one nipple then the other. "I could do this all day."

"I don't think I could."

"I could change your mind."

"I feel like—" Her voice caught, trembled. "I feel like I'm losing part of myself and I can't—"

His fingers were working quickly at the ribbon and lacing joining the front of the chemise. "I could take you to that place again, Kate—"

"I think you should stop."

"Fine." His hands stilled.

She opened her eyes. He looked up at her, eyes heavily lidded, lips parted. "You're confusing me again, Charles. Y—your hands are so warm."

"And your breasts are so soft. Sweet, Kate—" His voice held a reverence that sent a quiver of pleasure through Kate. "We don't have to go anywhere but here . . . for as long as you wish. . . .'' He was kissing her bosom with a tenderness that made her loins ache. She tugged at the buttons of his shirt and spread the cotton wide over his chest, with both palms flat and fingers splayed.

It was the first time she'd seen him without a shirt. She rubbed her fingertips over him. She liked it. She wanted more of it. She swallowed, her head fell back, and she saw naked cherubs painted on the ceiling.

He rose up and came against her, chest to chest, belly to belly. He brushed his lips over hers, rubbed his chest back and forth against her breasts until her whole body tingled. He cupped her bottom, brought her loins deep into his and she couldn't help the groan that came from her throat.

''Charles—''

''I know. You want to stop.''

''Yes—'' Her eyes swept closed. He was kissing the side of her neck. ''You're not stopping.''

''I haven't started.'' He lifted his head, held her by her upper arms, and looked into her eyes for several moments, then looked lower, lower, and when he spoke his voice was deep and passionate. ''You're so God almighty gorgeous, Kate—when I think of you with Harry McGoldrick—or with any other—''

''Stop.'' She pressed her fingers to his mouth and realized that they were trembling. ''Please, don't—''

He grabbed her wrist, turned her hand over and pressed his lips to her open palm. It was a poignant gesture from a man who wasn't easily humbled. ''Was he a good husband to you, Kate?''

Her heart started to ache. ''I don't want to talk about Harry, Charles. Not with you. Not now.''

He looked up, his face unreadable, his eyes unfathomable. ''He left you widowed and penniless, Kate. I know the truth of it. It's nothing for you to be ashamed of.''

''No? I knew what he was doing at the saloon and I

ignored it because I liked Harry. I liked his easy wit. I liked his generous heart. He took on a penniless, pregnant woman, and married her knowing she didn't love him, Charles. I was so grateful to him and I wanted to believe''—she swallowed, closed her eyes, and felt humiliation sweep over her—''I wanted to pretend that I'd made a good life for Walt, a good family—but all I was doing was lying to myself because the truth of it would have—would have—''

''It would have made you think you should have stayed in Lenox and never run away.''

''Yes,'' she whispered. ''I never would have believed in myself again. And how could I be a mother to a fatherless boy if I didn't believe in myself? I couldn't. I still can't. I believe in that more than anything—more than this—this—whatever this is between us.''

He looked at her in a way that made her fingers curl around the edge of her open bodice and pull it closer. The air seemed to lose a bit of its magic from just moments before. She tugged her chemise together and jerked on the laces. And then his hands pushed hers aside and started tugging at the laces.

''Really, Charles, I can dress—''

''—yourself. Yes, I know you think you can do everything yourself. But I want to help. I enjoy it. And you'd best get used to it or we're going to be having a good many of these private arguments.''

She felt the brush of his fingers on her skin. ''I don't tire of argument, Charles, not when I believe in something.''

''Yes, I know. You're a true Remington.''

''You're underestimating my determination.''

He glanced up at her. ''You're underestimating mine, my dear.'' His fingers were flying up the front buttons of her dress. His face looked very serious, as if there were something other than buttons occupying his mind. ''There. You look like a bonbon in pink, Kate.''

The edges of her lips tipped up. "Thank you, Charles."

His look darkened, intensified. "Ready to be devoured."

Kate watched him stand straight up. He took the chair opposite again, leaned back, and regarded her. With his shirt half unbuttoned and hanging loose, his hair all tousled, and his thighs spread, he looked wild and untamed and nothing at all like the staid and responsible Charles she remembered. He frightened and aroused her all at once.

She forced her mind elsewhere and remembered with some chagrin why she'd come. She fished into her pocket and pulled out the envelope. "This came by carrier from Turkeyfoot Run this morning." She could hardly contain her smile. She sat up very straight on the edge of the chair and handed him the envelope. "It's from a Judge Warner there. He's read the editorials, Charles. He believes the cattlemen are responsible for terrorizing the sheepherders. He wants to help. Can you believe it?"

He flipped the letter open, scanned it, and looked up at her. "Congratulations, Kate."

"He's got Washington connections and Denver connections. He knows powerful people. And I've heard he's extremely fair-minded."

"I take it this means you want to have him over for dinner."

"Of course I do. Not that I could tell him that I'm Jonathan Smarte, but still. I never thought a man like Judge Warner would take the time to read our paper when Turkeyfoot Run has a paper five pages long—if you can believe that."

"Imagine that. An entire five pages."

"No, really, Charles, it's the county seat. You've been there. Their editor hails from Charleston."

"All that way?"

She pursed her lips. "You're making fun of me."

"No, I'm enjoying you."

She felt her cheeks warm and sat up very stiff. "I had to come tell you first. I don't know why—well, yes, I suppose I do. I think you understand how much this means to the town—"

"To you."

"Yes. That, too. Because of Harry. I may never be able to see his murderer brought to justice but I can, in my own way, carry out Harry's dream."

"Don't lie to me, Kate. You won't rest until Pruitt's in jail."

Her brows dove together. "Perhaps. I've convinced myself that he's going to do something stupid again and maybe then he'll get the punishment he deserves. But in the meantime, I can help make his life less comfortable." She looked away and watched the lace curtain panel drift with the breeze. "You know, I was thinking about something—and I suppose that's at the root of why I came right over here, and it didn't matter that it was Louella's place." She looked at him and narrowed her eyes. "You were in Turkeyfoot Run just the other day."

"I was."

"You spoke to Judge Warner."

"I met him, yes. He practiced in Boston years ago."

"That's not why you met with him."

"No, Kate, it wasn't."

Her voice thickened. "I wish you hadn't done that behind my back, Charles."

He leaned suddenly forward and laid his forearms on his thighs. "Isn't it enough that you're getting his help?"

"I wanted to do it on my own. I didn't want anyone's help."

"I don't believe that. You didn't want *my* help. Hell, a stranger's? Sure. Why not? That stranger can't hurt you, can he?"

She sensed the mounting frustration in him. ''I swore to myself the day Harry died that I wouldn't be beholden to anyone ever again.''

''It's the ultimate form of trust, isn't it?''

She looked away and said nothing.

''You won't be betrayed by me, Kate.''

''No. I won't allow myself to be.''

''And what will you do when you need something?''

''If I ever do—I can go to Douglas.''

''You trust him?''

''I can afford to. He's helped me before.''

''And you let him because he's like a stranger—almost like an anonymous benefactor—''

There was a tone in his voice that caught her. Something about the way he'd spoken, as if he wanted to tell her more. A sudden disturbing thought flitted through her brain, reminding her of other thoughts she'd recently had just like it. And as she sat there looking at Charles looking at her, and saying nothing, the thought grew into a stunning and terrible realization.

Anonymous benefactor.

''You—'' she whispered. ''You came into town that same day.''

''What day, Kate?''

''It's—it's you—five thousand dollars—all of it—and you were such friends with Douglas—I should have guessed—it's you.'' A solid ball of dread squeezed her throat closed. ''I'm entirely beholden to you and you—you arranged to have the ability to take everything away from me—everything—Walt, the paper, my home—my whole life.''

''You needed the money and I had it to give. I could think of no more worthy a cause, Kate. I gave it before I'd even seen you, before I knew about Walt. I could have given it and left town, but hell, I'm human. I had to see you.''

She felt as if she couldn't breathe. The air compressed around her, like the jaws of a trap slowly closing her in. He watched her, cloaked in all this power, threatening, and all too capable of doing anything he could to get from her whatever he wanted.

"I played right into your hands," she said hoarsely.

"This wasn't a game. Don't make it something it's not."

"And think the worst of you?" She heard the caustic tone in her voice. "Oh, I could easily believe this has all been a ploy on your part, cunningly conceived and keenly executed. Perhaps you're punishing me for what I did with Jude—"

"Stop it, Kate—"

"After all, since childhood you and Jude have been more like enemies than brothers. I know you disliked him, perhaps even more because of the responsibilities you were forced to shoulder while he had none. And in return he disliked you. The contempt you've always felt for Jude could just as easily be turned on me now that you know the truth of it."

The pain in his eyes made her instantly regret her words.

"You know that could never happen," he said softly. "I acted without thinking, Kate, without thinking of anything but you. If I'd known this would build another wall of mistrust, I would have kept the money. I'd cut off my arm to get you to trust me."

"I could have gotten help elsewhere." Her voice was husky with emotion, with fear and uncertainty. "You didn't even let me try."

"You're like family to me. I take care of my family."

"You want to own me."

"I wanted to help."

"Then you would have told me from the start."

"You wouldn't have trusted me."

"I still don't." She surged out of her chair, swung around to the door, and found it locked. She thumped a palm on the wood, lowered her head, and realized she'd never felt so nearly imprisoned in her life. A feeling of helplessness came over her.

"Always running—" He was behind her, so close she could feel his warmth even in the heat of the day. But he didn't touch her and something inside her screamed for him to. "Running isn't a solution, Kate. It wasn't six years ago. It certainly isn't now."

"I'm not running. I'm going straight to the paper and have Mr. Gould go to the bank and get whatever we haven't used of your money. I'll give it back, plus interest."

"I won't take a penny of it."

She spun around and realized instantly that it was not the wisest move. She had to crane her neck back to look up at him. Otherwise, she'd be staring at the swirls of dark hair covering his upper chest, and wanting to touch it again. . . .

She forced her voice to a calm pitch. "Listen to me, Charles. The Union Pacific has been extremely pleased with Jonathan Smarte. They pay him very handsomely for his words. Their stipend is more than enough to cover monthly expenses. True, I needed help with the past due bills and a new press but now that that's taken care of the stipend will be sufficient."

"I never thought you'd choose to be a willing pawn."

"What do you mean?"

"Don't let the boys at the U.P. know how much you need them. They'll use you the same as they use every other editor on the frontier—as a propaganda machine. Do what they want or they won't pay."

"I could accuse you of the same."

He stared at her, eyes stormy and clouded. "Yes, I suppose you could believe that. But you should have waited until I proved you right before you judged me.'' He braced his arm against the door, rubbed his forehead and jerked his hand back through his hair. It was an uncharacteristic gesture for a man so typically in control. He seemed frustrated. ''Keep the money, Kate.''

She stood stalwart. ''I'm going to have Mr. Gould go over to the bank straightaway.''

His face looked suddenly weary. ''You're being ridiculous. We have far more pressing things to discuss—''

''I have to do this, Charles. I can hardly bear to look at you knowing—I don't know—it makes the scale seemed tipped far too much in your direction.''

''Another game,'' he muttered.

''Do you want my gratitude?'' she asked quietly.

His eyes narrowed. ''You gave Harry gratitude, Kate. I want your trust. Please—I'm family, for Chrissake. Keep it.''

''I don't need it. You see my monthly stipend is due any day''—she suddenly paused—''the stipend came, or did it? I thought I remember seeing—where did I—?'' She glanced up at him and felt a chill pass through her. ''I have to go.''

He didn't move. ''Now you're losing money.''

She scowled. ''I didn't lose it. I never lose things. Now open this door. I have to hurry.''

''That nervous, are you?'' He looked sideways at her as he reached around her and stuck the key in the lock. ''Do you want me to come help you find it?''

''That's not where I'm going. I told you, I'm—''

''I know. Straightaway to the bank.''

She poked her chin up at him. ''I told you I don't need your help.''

''Oh, but you do.'' His voice was like melted butter, smooth and rich and wicked.

''Move aside, Charles.''

''Good-bye, Kate.''

He looked at her mouth. She looked at his, pulled open the door, and left.

"Stop what you're doing, Mr. Gould," Kate announced breathlessly as she burst into the office. "Whatever it is it can wait. I need your help finding something."

"Finding what, ma'am?" Gould didn't even look up.

Kate blew wisps of hair from her eyes and listened to her teeth grind. Why was it that whenever a person was most in a hurry, everyone else in the world seemed to slow down and get in their way?

She went straight to Harry's desk and started flipping through every piece of paper on it. "The stipend from the Union Pacific. I need—that is—Mr. Jonathan Smarte has requested it and I can't seem to remember where I put it. I have a vague recollection of receiving an envelope from Boston—"

Vague, indeed. Since Charles Remington had charged into her life she'd thought of little else—not money, not the sheepherders, not causes—

Just him.

"Don't sit there, Mr. Gould. Help me."

Gould's chair scraped on the floorboards. "He needs it that much, Ma'am?"

"Quite desperately, if you must know. Here. You look through that pile there. The envelope has the Union Pacific return address printed on it."

Gould started sorting. "Imagine that. All that money in the bank and he's still desperate. To my way of thinking, we've got more money now than we need."

"Precisely, Mr. Gould. That's why we're going to give it back."

"Give it back? To who, ma'am?"

"Quit looking at me and sort. We're giving it back to the person who lent it to us in the first place."

"Why the devil would we do such a foolish thing?"

Kate paused. "Because Jonathan Smarte will never be bought."

"Then why are we looking so hard for the stipend, ma'am? Is it worse to owe money to a stranger than to be under the thumb of the mighty Union Pacific?"

His question needled her. She shifted as if she'd been poked in the ribs. "You've got to have principles and priorities, Mr. Gould. In this case, I'm quite certain Jonathan Smarte believes it more than prudent to align himself entirely with the Union Pacific. Aha!" She whisked an envelope from the middle of the stack and held it up triumphantly. "I found it!"

Gould snorted and shuffled back to his desk, tossing over his shoulder, "If I didn't know better, ma'am, I'd say that means more to you than it ever could to Jonathan Smarte."

Kate slid her fingernail into the top of the envelope. "I just appreciate good principles, that's all." Quickly, she withdrew the letter and glanced at Mr. Gould. "I need you to go to the bank, Mr. Gould. I need—now where the devil is the stipend? That's odd. They only sent a letter."

"Did you lose it, ma'am?"

"Damn and blast, I don't lose anything." She shook the page, glanced on the floor, at the pile on the desk, and saw no stipend. "Odd. Maybe it's coming soon—" She began to read and the more she read the more light-headed she became. She reached for the chair, slid into it, and could almost hear her world crashing around her.

"Very good, ma'am. How much do you want me to withdraw?"

Kate looked up at Mr. Gould as if only now she'd realized he was in the same room. She had to gulp down the lump in her throat. ''Nothing.''

''Ma'am.''

''You heard me. We have a disaster, Mr. Gould.''

''We, ma'am? The letter is addressed to Mr. Jonathan Smarte.''

''Yes, yes, I know that, dammit.''

''Ma'am?''

Kate folded the letter, leapt out of her chair and moved around the desk toward the door. ''They're coming, Mr. Gould.''

Mr. Gould stepped smartly out of her way. ''They?''

''The Union Pacific.''

''All of them, ma'am, all the way from Boston?''

Kate grabbed her bonnet from a hat hook and shoved it on her head. ''No, just two of them but it might as well be all of them. They're coming to Turkeyfoot Run tomorrow. They're not happy.''

''That's the disaster?''

Kate flung the door wide. ''Yes. And they want to meet with Jonathan Smarte.''

Chapter 16

"Lemonade?" Douglas Murphy asked, producing a glass jug from behind his desk. He gave Charles a self-deprecating smile from across the desk. "My wife sends it with me every morning. She says she doesn't want me to get too hot."

Charles settled more comfortably in his chair and loosened his shirt at the collar. "She's a fine woman."

Douglas poured two glasses and slid one across the desk to Charles. "Unhappy as all hell when we first came out here. Then after I built her the house she wanted with the front porch and the swing and the window boxes she stopped complaining. Of course, that was after she joined the Ladies Auxiliary Garden Club. Never misses a meeting." Douglas raised his brows, drank long and deep of his lemonade, and gave a satisfied smack of his lips. "So, Remington, did you come here looking for work?"

"It would be a welcome reprieve from party planning."

"What did you say?"

"Hell, I intend to spend the better part of today and this evening arousing interest in the sheepherders to attend a sheepshearing event."

"An event?"

Charles felt his cheeks warming, scowled, and shifted his shoulders uncomfortably. "A dance, for Chrissake."

The way Douglas was looking at him made his every word sound more and more ridiculous. A defensive tone crept into his voice. ''Bessie Mae Elliot made me party planner so all her garden party misses can find husbands.''

Douglas looked as though he was biting the insides of his cheeks to keep from laughing. ''Did she, indeed? All that because you penned a simple letter to the editor.''

Charles's scowl deepened. ''It's all to take place two days from now. Depending on when the sheepshearers get to town and the season begins. I expect to convince John Bertrand to agree to host the thing. He has the biggest farm and the most sheep.''

''Does he, now? Burned-out barn and all.''

''His interests are of the matrimonial bent, you can be sure.'' Charles rubbed a hand over his chin thoughtfully. Indeed, he could imagine paying witness to Bertrand's giant grin of delight when Charles suggested that he host it. Were all the single women in Crooked Nickel attending? Bertrand would certainly ask.

The man had looked like a Goliath out in his field, surrounded by sheep and sheepdogs and a burned-out barn. Charles didn't harbor any secret desires to test his strength against Bertrand's should the man get it into his head to venture within breathing space of Kate.

Realizing the turn of his thoughts, Charles shifted his eyes to Douglas. ''You look busy.''

''Hell, I have to be in Turkeyfoot Run at the courthouse tomorrow. I'm going before your friend Judge Warner on three cases of horse stealing, and one other brought by a traveling preacher who's charging our friend Elmer Pruitt with stealing his one-eyed mule because the preacher talked to a sheepherder in church. You want that one?''

''No thanks. Does Pruitt have a lawyer?''

Douglas nodded. ''Some weasely fellow from Turkeyfoot Run who thinks justice is greasing the sitting judge's palm. Good thing Warner's tough. At least that's the rumor."

"I'm counting on it. I told Warner all about Pruitt's grisly tactics with the sheepherders. He's read the *Sentinel.* He's considering giving his support to the sheepherders."

Douglas blinked at him. "You did all that in one day?"

Charles shrugged. "He hails from Boston. He knows how to get things done. And this matter with Pruitt involves just the right amount of strong-arming. And murder."

"That's what scares me. He gets involved, draws attention from other politicians, and Pruitt's likely to respond like a skunk backed into a corner."

Charles gave a cold smile that never reached his eyes. "Precisely. He'll do something very stupid and find himself sent to the territorial penitentiary for the rest of his life. Come on, Murphy, this town has stood by and let him play his games. It's time for that to end. Remember justice prevailing?"

"No, I'd rather not. Folks sometimes have to make a choice—to live with fear or live by someone else's rules. I've made my choice for quite a while now and I might not be proud of it but I'm alive and my wife is happy. Hell, I hope Warner can do it."

"We'll see. He's getting an invitation to the sheepshearing dance."

Douglas's eyes narrowed. "You're a sly fellow, Remington, combining love-starved young ladies with sheepshearers and hard-nosed judges."

Charles didn't flinch. "Just getting the job done. The opportunity seemed right. I also plan to invite Dan Goodknight."

"I'll bring my pistol and tell my wife to stay home. There's sure to be shooting."

"Goodknight and Warner are friends. Frankly, Warner

seems as zealous about cleaning up the lawlessness and injustice as Kate is.''

Douglas looked him square. ''Kate?''

''Mrs. McGoldrick.''

''You're old friends?''

''Yes, we're—uh—actually, Murphy, I told her about the loan.''

''Ah. Just a friend helping out a friend.''

''Exactly.''

''She didn't look at it that way?''

''Not entirely.''

''Didn't think so.'' Douglas's chest jerked with an appreciative chuckle. He shook his head. ''Did she march straight over to the bank to give you back all your money?''

''I believe she's there now.''

''They call it pride, Remington. You know all about that.''

Charles gave him a level stare. ''I have my share, yes. She doesn't trust me, you know.''

''That's rather obvious.''

''Don't know why the hell not. I want to help her—''

''Meddle.''

''—get her what she wants—''

''Control it all for her.''

''And she resists.''

''Odd for a female.''

''I should just leave her the hell alone.''

''My thoughts exactly except you've got one small problem.''

Charles narrowed his eyes on Douglas and saw the mischief dancing in the other man's stare. ''Don't say it, Murphy.''

''I don't have to. You're wearing it all over yourself.''

Charles set his teeth and looked out the side window. ''Christ.''

"It's nothing to be ashamed of, for God's sake. Men fall in love every day and behave like fools."

That brought Charles's head snapping around. "I'm no fool, Murphy."

"Nooo—" Douglas seemed to contemplate for a moment. "You're the boy's father, aren't you?"

Charles took this like a physical blow to the midchest. His lips parted, nothing came out. The agony of it—and Douglas would never know this—was that he wished to God, in every sense of his being, that he was. And he hated Jude for it, hated and despised him more than he could ever rid himself of.

"He looks just like you," Douglas said. "I didn't see it, of course, but my wife—she says I'm as blind as any other man—hell, after you left with him the other night, she turned to me and said in that way of hers—you know the way some women have of saying something and you know it's the God's truth. She said, 'He's his father.' And I saw it all right then."

Charles leaned his forearms on his knees and let his head fall between his shoulders. "It's a long story, Murphy."

"Jesus, Remington. I don't know you well at all but I know you're a good man—my wife—she said that, too. She said, 'Now there's a good man.' I had to believe her. And she never said that about Harry McGoldrick. Never once. Here—try this—"

Charles curled his fingers around the glass set before him and Douglas hefted his own, along with a whiskey bottle.

"I keep a little of this around for emergencies," he said. "You know, clients too distraught to talk. Men who've just found their wives in bed with the farmer from the next county. Farmer who's just found his prized sow all tangled in barbwire he thinks his neighbor put there on purpose. Things like that. My wife doesn't know about it, though.''

Charles gulped, got up from his chair, and moved to the corner just inside the door where Douglas Murphy's Harvard diploma was framed. ''We're alike, you and I, Murphy. You just had the good sense to come out here sooner.''

''No, you had to come to get your woman. I have to tell you I think Kate deserves happiness. She needs—''

The front door slammed open. ''Douglas!'' The voice came from the vestibule beyond Douglas's closed door. ''Say you're here, goddammit—oh, no.''

It was Kate.

Douglas's eyes shot to Charles in the corner. When Charles started toward the door Douglas shook his head, held up a hand, and moved around his desk. He pulled open the door and stepped into the vestibule, leaving Charles unseen in the room.

''What the hell are you doing, Kate?'' Douglas asked.

''I'm crawling under these chairs to get the letter I dropped. God, Douglas, you really need to sweep under here. Got it—fine. Here. Look at this. It's a disaster. Oh, Douglas—it's a complete disaster. Read it.''

''I'm trying but you keep talking.''

''Of course, I'm talking!''

''Now you're shouting.''

''You would be, too. I have to figure out what to do and I think I have a plan. At least I hope I do and you can't say no.''

''I'll try not to. All right, let's see, it says two gentlemen from the Union Pacific—a Misters Funk and Breadlaw—are coming to Turkeyfoot Run tomorrow and are requesting audience with Mr. Jonathan Smarte. They're not happy with the editorials, Kate.''

''I know.'' Her voice was shaky.

Charles stood rooted to his spot, knowing he was eavesdropping, but he had to know the truth of this now.

So he could do something about it.

"They think I'm responsible for making Crooked Nickel a less than desirable place to live," she said, her voice cracking.

"Not you, Kate. Jonathan Smarte."

"I know. They're so mad at him they're not giving him his monthly stipend until they talk to him."

"You mean you."

"No, him. I can't just show up and announce that Jonathan Smarte isn't a he. That the he is me. That he's—oh, God, Douglas, they'll fire me and take the paper away. I need that stipend. I need it so badly—"

"You have the loan."

"I don't want to talk about the loan."

"I was helping you, Kate."

"God, why does everyone keep saying that?"

"Maybe it's true."

"Maybe I don't need help."

"And that's why you're here?"

She paused and Charles's lips quirked. He could almost hear her mind humming along.

"All right, fine," she finally huffed. "I need your help. You have to be Jonathan Smarte."

"What?"

"You heard me. Impersonate him. Come to Turkeyfoot. Come with me and be Jonathan Smarte."

"I can't."

"No, you have to."

"I'm known in that town, Kate. Remember how much everyone hates lawyers. Especially there. Besides, I have to be in Judge Warner's courtroom all day tomorrow."

"I'm not hearing you. You're coming with me."

"I'm sorry, Kate. I can't."

"But—what am I going to do? I could—I suppose I could ask Mr. Gould—oh, God, no. What am I thinking? He's an accountant. Douglas—where are you going? I know you have work to do. But you have to help me with this—"

Douglas strode back into his office. Charles heard the frantic swishing of skirts following after him. She burst into the office with such energy she didn't even see him.

At first.

Douglas waved a hand toward him. "You know Charles Remington, Kate."

She froze.

Charles sipped from his glass and regarded her with narrowed eyes.

Her cheeks glowed a bright pink. "You heard me."

"The fellow in the next county heard you."

She glanced at Douglas now seated behind his desk, then looked back at Charles. "Why does this feel like some kind of conspiracy—you two—from the very beginning—?"

Douglas seemed profoundly put out. "Now, wait just a minute. I didn't know Charles Remington from anybody when he walked in here looking for a sad and sorry business to save. Isn't that right, Remington?"

Charles kept his eyes focused on her. "Sit down, Kate."

"I don't want to sit down."

"Yes, I can tell." He advanced toward her, she backed up two steps, bumped back against the chair and plopped right down in it. When she tried to jump right back up he kept her there with his hands on top of her shoulders.

"Now listen to me—"

"Why? So you can tell me to trust you? So you can offer to be Jonathan Smarte for me in Turkeyfoot Run and then I'll have to be grateful and never know if I truly love you for the right reasons—'' Her lips trembled, she blinked, and then she burst into tears.

Charles met Douglas's look of concern then hunkered down in front of her. It was all he could do to keep his arms from crushing around her. Her slender shoulders were shaking and her head was down and she was making soft sobbing noises that tore at his heart.

''Kate. Why is it everything I do brings you to this?''

''Because I don't want you to do anything for me—'' She sniffed until Charles fished his handkerchief from his pocket and handed it to her.

But she didn't use it. She just sat there, head hanging down, crying.

He enclosed her clasped hands in one of his, cupped his other hand around her head, and drew her against him.

''That isn't going to work again,'' she mumbled against his chest.

''I'm not playing games with you.''

''It feels like it.''

''Maybe from your perspective. From mine—it feels like the hardest thing I've ever had to do.''

''Good.'' She sniffed again, lowered her head, and blew her nose very hard into his handkerchief several times, then handed it back to him with a grudging mutter of thanks. She looked up at him, wiped her cheeks, sniffed again, and seemed to compose herself. ''I'm fine now.''

''Maybe I should leave you two—'' Douglas said, sliding his chair back.

Kate glanced at him. ''No, Douglas, sit back down. This is your office.''

''Fine. If that's how you want it, Kate—'' But Douglas didn't sit down. He moved around the side of his desk and stood over Kate looking down at her with a stern and admonishing look. ''You're in my office. I'm the boss.''

"Precisely," she said, looking up at him, trying to smile.

"Good. Then I'm ordering you to listen to this man."

Kate blinked up at him. "What?"

"I don't know your history together but I do know a gentleman when I meet one. And I know when a friend of mine needs help. I'm sorry to tell you this, Kate, but when Mr. Gould is your only option, and you'd even consider letting someone in on your secret identity as Jonathan Smarte—think about it for a moment. Think about the real sacrifices. Oh, look at the time. My wife will wonder where the hell I am for lunch. No, you two stay right where you are. Just lock the door when you leave."

He grabbed his topcoat from a wall hook and left a bit too quickly.

Charles was acutely aware that they were very much alone, and that he was still, basically, on his knees in front of her. She seemed to be avoiding his eyes.

He wanted to reach out, cup her jaw, and kiss her lips. Instead he stood up and looked out the back window that faced an expanse of prairie he'd never imagined existed. There was a beauty to it that made him think of Boston as a crowded prison.

"I don't know if you realize this, Kate," he began, watching a hawk circle high above the earth. "But you stole Jonathan Smarte from me."

She sniffed. "You forgot about him when you went away to Harvard."

"No, Kate, I didn't. I kept him alive. I wrote his stories."

"I find that hard to believe. You didn't even write to us very often."

"As often as I could."

"That's when you first became a stranger—right before Father Remington died. I remember waiting for the mail to come every day, waiting for your letters. And after they didn't come for a while, I started my own stories for Jonathan Smarte. I never stopped thinking about him, Charles.''

''Neither did I. I think about him even now. I think about him because when I was at Harvard Jonathan Smarte had a woman. She was a woman like no other. A woman of tremendous strength, character, and intelligence. She was so strong she never withered, never feared, never needed anything from anybody. Particularly from Smarte. She wasn't capable of tears, and she wasn't capable of compassion. I made her so much in the likeness of a man, she didn't need to be with Smarte, and he, as it turned out, didn't need to be with her. There was no purpose to them as male and female.'' He turned to face her.

She was still looking down at the carpet.

''A man wants to be a man with the woman he cares for, Kate. Let me be that for you. Let me comfort and help you. Let me make it right for you. I honestly don't know any other way to be with you.''

She looked up at him, stalwart and strong and still resisting him. He wondered if she realized her chin trembled slightly.

''I'm coming with you to Turkeyfoot Run,'' he said. ''We're going to meet with Funk and Breadlaw. I'll be Jonathan Smarte for you. After all, I know him better than anyone.''

There was a long moment of silence, but her face seemed to lose some of its tension. ''I don't suppose I have a choice.'' There was a wistfulness to her that ate at his heart.

He took a step toward her as she got up and moved to the door.

''I have to get home for Walt,'' she said, pausing to look back at him. ''There's a daily ten o'clock train to Turkeyfoot Run. We should be on it tomorrow morning.''

"We will be," he said, pausing only when he stood a hand's breadth from her. "I'd come with you now but I have business to take care of."

Her eyes sparked. "Business?"

"Bessie Mae Elliot business." His lips quirked up at one corner. He saw an answering upward tremble in hers, bent and kissed her full on the mouth. "Get a new dress," he rumbled when he lifted his head. "You'll be dancing with me in two days."

She stood there for several long moments looking at the midpoint of his chest. "I don't dance," she murmured, then looked up at him. "But you can help me, can't you?"

"Every day for the rest of your life." It was a promise made from the bottom of his soul.

Her lips gently parted. Surprise glistened in her eyes. And then she turned and left.

Charles would have spotted her in a crowd of a hundred women. He leaned a shoulder against a supporting post and watched her walk the length of the depot, deftly maneuvering her way around the people who'd gathered there for the train to Turkeyfoot Run. A swing of her hips one way, a quick scoot of her feet. She looked determined, energized, and eager to take on the world. She looked as if she didn't believe she needed anyone's help doing anything.

"Hullo, Charles," she said breezily as she swept past him in a cloud of lilac fragrance.

"I got them already," he said, taking full appreciation of her bobbing backside.

She stopped, turned, and blinked at him. "The tickets?"

"Yes, I got them."

"Very good then." She fiddled with something in her reticule, showing him the top of her squashed cabbage leaves hat. Two fake birds nested in the middle of the leaves. She looked up, glanced down the track, and chewed a bit at her lip. "I suppose we just wait now." She looked at him almost as an afterthought. The way she did made him want to shove away from the post, stand up very straight, and poke out his chest. "You look very fine this morning, Charles."

"Thank you. You're wearing pink."

"Yes, well, I thought it might be better than black being that this is a business meeting. But I didn't want to do anything severe—you know—too tailored or dark. I wanted to look—you know—" She gave a slightly exasperated sigh. "I wanted to look—"

"Feminine."

"Yes, I suppose that's what I wanted. I want to reek of homesteading, if you must know."

"You don't want Funk and Breadlaw to suspect you have anything to do with running the paper."

"That's right."

"Then you'll have to keep quiet."

Her brows quivered. "I know. That's what's worrying me. I swear I didn't sleep at all last night, Charles."

"Neither did I."

"See, you're worried, too."

"That wasn't exactly my problem."

"I finally got up around four and started writing everything down that I would want to say to them if I could, but I know that I can't. I had about six cups of coffee while I was doing it. I brought the list with me—I think—I just can't seem to find it." She dug again into her reticule. "I just don't know how I'm going to sit there in front of those men, knowing all I do about the paper and the editorials, *feeling* the way I do about the sheepherders, *hating* Elmer Pruitt as much as I do, and not give anything away. I hate this, Charles."

''Yes, I can imagine you do.''

She shot him a worried look. ''It's all in your hands.''

His lips quirked. ''I'm glad I have your every confidence.''

A train whistle echoed from the distance. Her expression grew more dire. ''What if this Mr. Funk and his friend, Breadlaw, force us to close the paper?''

Charles bent and looked straight into her eyes. ''What if they want to give Jonathan Smarte a raise if he changes the angles of his editorials just a bit?''

Her eyes snapped wide and she smiled. ''Oh, God, I hadn't thought of that. Yes, they could do that, couldn't they?''

''They might be persuaded to do that.''

''I wonder how much they'll offer him. No, they won't give him a raise. What am I thinking?''

Charles laughed, looked down the track, and spotted the train approaching. Black puffs of smoke billowed from its engine. Steam shot out both sides of the locomotive. When Charles turned back he found Kate looking up at him with an odd expression on her face.

''What is it?'' he asked.

''I—'' She shook her head as if to clear it. ''It's so good to hear you laugh, Charles. It was one of the things I missed most about you when you were away at school. The house seemed so empty without you.''

''I don't do enough laughing, to be sure,'' he said, instinctively taking her arm as the train rumbled into the depot. He bent and pressed his mouth close to her ear. ''And neither do you.''

''That's what comes of responsibility,'' she said, lifting her skirts in one hand and moving toward the train.

''What comes of sharing it?'' he rumbled, keeping good hold of her arm, particularly when the train pulled to a stop and men began pouring from its doors.

Most of them were the rough-hewn sort, young, muscular, deeply tanned, wearing faded denims and easy smiles they bestowed on anything female within their sights. Kate was the recipient of a lion's share of the smiles. Charles stood tall and stern beside her and did a good bit of glowering over her cabbage leaves and fake birds.

"The sheepshearers are here," she said, obviously oblivious to the picture she presented. Charles watched one young man give her a scalding sweep of his eyes and regretted instantly having had anything to do with arranging for these men and Kate to be anywhere near one another for recreational purposes. The possessiveness that gripped him was not foreign to him. The intensity of it was.

"Bessie Mae will be so pleased," she said, as Charles handed her onto the train.

"I don't know why," he muttered, shooting a withering look at one young man who was staring at Kate as if he hadn't seen a female in all his life. She took a step up, giving Charles and the young sheepshearer full view of her backside and the pink bow tied at the curve of her lower back. When she turned to face Charles, he let his eyes linger on her bosom before he looked up at her.

Her flush shot pleasure through him. So did the breathless part of her lips. She blinked and he leaned both hands on the rails on either side of her. He looked at her mouth. She looked at his and he felt desire go off like gunshot through him.

"Quit flirting with me, Kate," he murmured.

"Flirting? Me? I don't know how. Besides, I wasn't the one looking at my bosoms—" She snapped her mouth closed, blinked at the conductor watching her, turned around in a huff, and marched aboard.

"Flirt—me—I wouldn't know the first thing about it—" she was muttering when he slid onto the wooden bench beside her. She was fiddling again in her purse as if she had enough energy for ten men. She finally pulled out a *Turkeyfoot Run Gazette* newspaper—much folded—flapped it open, and began fiddling with that.

"Stop." He laid his big hand on top of both of hers. "You're starting to make me nervous."

"Good. You should be. If this meeting doesn't come off successfully, I'm going to—well, I don't quite know what I'll do, but it will be very drastic."

"Won't you speak to me, Kate?"

"Oh, it will be much worse than that."

He was looking at her profile, at the full promise of her lips, and knew that she would taste warm and infinitely sweet. "You mean you won't even kiss me?"

"There you go again. I'm telling you it won't work. Now get your hands in your own lap. Someone's going to see us."

He let her remove his hands then glanced around the rail car and dropped his voice to a deep rumble. "No one's looking at us. I could kiss you right now and no one would even notice."

She shot him a sideways look. "Please, don't. Neither one of us can afford to be distracted."

"If I'm never to have the chance again after today to kiss you, Kate, can you blame me for trying?"

She squirmed in her seat and sat straight up. "I don't know what's happened to you in six years, Charles Remington, but you never used to be this way."

"Oh, I've always been persistent."

The train jerked forward, once, twice. The whistle sounded a high-pitched toot. Slowly, the cars pulled out of the depot.

"No, I'm talking about this—" She patted her cheek with a pink-gloved hand. "You keep saying things that make my cheeks hot."

"Perhaps you drank too much coffee."

"No, it's you. I'm quite certain."

"Thank you, Kate. Are you flushed anywhere else?" He'd dropped his voice to a purr and was staring at her lips.

She froze and looked straight ahead. "See there? You're doing it again and now I'm getting tingles in my—" Her eyes dropped to her chest, shot back up, and she flushed again. "Stop it, Charles." She flapped the paper and seemed to focus very intently on it. "Please."

"I can't help myself," he said rather matter-of-factly. "I think I'm desperately in love with you."

She blinked very fast, the edges of her lips quivered, but she kept her eyes fixed on the newsprint. "Now is hardly the time for confession. Besides, I'm quite certain you've been in love before."

"Not like this. Not enough to marry."

"Mmm." She flapped her paper and tried to look uninterested. "And why is that?"

Charles lowered his voice. "Because I gave my heart to you six years ago, and until I found you, I'm certain a part of me was dead."

He could swear he heard her swallow above the muffled clatter of wheels. "You could have married for convenience—to have a family—make a life. Many people do—"

"And what sense would that have made when I awoke every morning with even the smallest bit of hope that I would find you?"

Her eyes lifted to his. "You stayed true to a memory," she said softly, her voice brimming with disbelief. "You have the will of ten men."

"And the faith of a hundred fools. But look where it got me." Looking into her eyes he felt a pull toward her so strong, and knew she felt the same toward him. Her eyes filled with warmth, her cheeks glowed, and then she looked quickly at the newspaper.

"Oh, would you look at this?" she said breezily, shaking her paper. "They have a new milliner in Turkeyfoot Run promising the very latest fashions from Paris. We should tell Victoria she has some competition, don't you think? And look at this. The livery there is selling horses for fifty dollars each. What did you pay for Sundance? Surely more than that—oh, here, another horse has been stolen from . . ."

Charles directed his eyes to the passing landscape and listened to her chatter, determined that she would sit beside him and read her paper for the next fifty-odd years.

Chapter 17

The letter from Boston requested that Jonathan Smarte meet Misters Funk and Breadlaw at the Hotel St. John in Turkeyfoot Run at noon. Kate and Charles stepped into the hotel's crowded common room at five minutes past twelve.

"What if they left already?" Kate said, looking quickly about. The tables were crowded with cattlemen wearing big hats and dust-covered clothes. Skimpily dressed barmaids passed through the tangle of chairs with trays balanced high over their heads. Smoke hung in a thick haze below a chandelier that dripped wax onto the floor and tables. From the corner a piano belched out a riotous melody. "What if they decided to close the paper"—she snapped her fingers right in front of Charles's eyes—"just like that and they left? God, I don't even know what they look like. It's impossible to tell—"

Charles gripped her upper arm. "Over here."

"Where? I don't see—"

But he obviously did, being a good ten inches taller than her. He steered her in front of him, chest pressed against her back, and began to guide her around tables. "See there?" His voice was low and close to her ear. "In the corner. The two gentlemen there."

Kate went up on tiptoes and spotted them between

heads. The men looked very East Coast and businesslike in their topcoats and high cravats. They had an expectant, out-of-place aura about them that labeled them as newcomers to the town. As she and Charles approached, they set down their glasses and slid back their chairs.

"Mr. Breadlaw?" Charles's hand slipped past her. The portly gentleman with ruddy cheeks and no hair stood and grasped Charles's hand.

"Jonathan Smarte," Charles said so smoothly that Kate was certain anyone would believe him. The leaner, sour-looking man, Mr. Funk, introduced himself, and the two shook hands. Charles presented Kate. "This is Mrs. McGoldrick, Harry McGoldrick's widow."

The two men nodded at Kate.

"This is a business matter, Smarte," Breadlaw said, chomping a cigar between his teeth and sitting back down in his chair. The look he slanted at Kate was patronizing enough to make her clamp her teeth together to keep from saying something. His implication was clear. "Wouldn't Mrs. McGoldrick prefer to do some shopping?"

Charles jumped to a reply. "I have retained Mrs. McGoldrick, gentlemen, and would very much like her to be present. You see, Mrs. McGoldrick's husband, Harry, was killed defending the paper's beliefs. I believe, as his widow, we owe her the opportunity to discuss the fate of her husband's paper. . . . May we?" Before the two could answer otherwise, Charles pulled out a chair for Kate and one for himself.

Kate slid into hers, very much aware that Charles had positioned his close enough beside hers that his leg pressed against her thigh. Or was that his hand?

"Indeed, gentlemen, I've retained Mrs. McGoldrick as an advisor."

Funk blinked at him over the rim of his glass. "A what?"

Charles looked settled in his chair as comfortably as a man could be. There wasn't a hint of anything about him to suggest that he was in any way unsure of himself and what he had to say. Kate found herself perched on her chair in anticipation and somehow very certain that he was entirely in charge of the conversation.

"I live in a big house in Laramie, Mr. Funk," he said. "It's impossible to manage even the smallest town paper from that distance. I needed an aid with everyday matters—paying bills, managing circulation lists, things of that sort. Mrs. McGoldrick wished to provide it. She was married to the man who owned the paper. I've found that she learned the business very well from him."

The two men's eyes shot simultaneously to Kate. Beneath the table she felt the squeeze of Charles's fingers on her thigh. She swallowed her words and pasted on a bland smile.

"And this has worked for you, Smarte?" Breadlaw asked, chewing his cigar and looking dubious.

"Indeed, gentlemen, it has flourished. I owe our present editorial situation entirely to Mrs. McGoldrick."

Kate felt as if she'd been poked with a red hot iron. And her thigh squeezed with a steel clamp. What words she itched to say came out as a garbled half-laugh.

Funk let out a "Hrrumph" and sat back, chest puffing up with satisfaction. "That's why we've come, Smarte. The Union Pacific takes great issue with editorials that make the frontier sound like some lawless, gunslinging, gambling pit of hell—"

As if to punctuate his statement, a fight suddenly erupted in a far corner. Chairs toppled over. A woman screamed and glass crashed to the floor. Men shouted and for several moments pandemonium reined, until a barkeep and several men escorted four others from the room.

Funk jerked his glass to his lips and looked several

shades paler. ''Like I said, that kind of newspaper talk doesn't sell acreage in a town, Mr. Smarte. It makes people the hell afraid to get on a westbound train.''

''Precisely my point.''

Funk and Breadlaw stared at Charles.

He smiled with true warmth and sat forward in his chair, engaging, reassuring, in every way. ''Gentlemen, what better place to call home than a town which embraces differences and knows how to live with them?''

Funk and Breadlaw exchanged glances.

Breadlaw cleared his throat, reached into a valise set beside his chair, and tossed several copies of the *Sentinel* on the table. ''From the sounds of these editorials, Mr. Smarte, there's no embracing of any kind going on. There's a war. Sheep with throats slit and barns burned and terrorizing of all kinds happening in the dead of night.''

''Oh, I grant you every bit of that is true fact. It was Mrs. McGoldrick's idea to keep printing it all, even though her husband was killed for that very reason.''

''You're setting down some serious allegations, Smarte,'' Funk said.

''Indeed. And with good reason. Gentlemen, the editorials serve two purposes: first, to capture the public interest and bring to its attention the virtual stranglehold the cattlemen have on Crooked Nickel—a situation which, by the way, does not sell acreage to the average homesteader back east who has positively nothing to do with cattle—''

''I'll give you that,'' Breadlaw granted under his breath.

''—but most important, these facts are being accurately presented to attract the attention of someone with power and influence. A politician. We've done that, gentlemen. Our range war has attracted the attention of the sitting judge here in Turkeyfoot Run, and he intends to use his influence with congressmen to pass legislation protecting the rights of those who *do not* engage in the cattle business.''

"Cattle runs the railroad," Funk interjected sternly.

"Free enterprise runs the railroad, Mr. Funk," Charles replied in his brook-no-argument tone. "And if I'm not mistaken, Congress grants the railroad all its land free to then sell for pure profit. Why, who knows, gentlemen? The next great free enterprise might be sheep. And Congress will be right behind these animals, wanting them shipped from one coast to the other. It would be a pity if a contract of that magnitude were to be granted, say, to the Santa Fe and Rio Grande, instead of to the Union Pacific."

Again, the men exchanged glances.

Kate's heart rate quickened. It was time for Charles to press his advantage. She reached beneath the table and squeezed his muscular thigh. He squeezed right back, but gently, laid his palm flat, and moved it very slightly on her thigh.

Her mouth went bone dry. She heard a distant drumming sound, thought it was her pulse, and realized it was raining very hard on the rooftops.

"To my way of thinking, gentlemen, we owe Mrs. McGoldrick a great debt for continuing to print the facts as they happen, given the tragic loss of her husband. True, the words were mine"—both their hands squeezed—"and fine words they were, yes, indeed, but the idea to carry on her husband's work was hers alone. In fact, gentlemen, I was against the idea at the start because of the danger involved. But I now believe that Crooked Nickel will be the most desirous place to live in the state of Wyoming. Judge Warner intends to make sure of that."

"It hasn't happened yet," Breadlaw pointed out. "There's a big difference between trying to get legislation passed and actually getting it done. A group of gun-toting cattlemen can intimidate even the biggest city judges, Smarte. I've seen it happen time after time."

"True. But I don't see why we should abandon the

cause just now, gentlemen, without giving opportunity a chance and risking upsetting a man with such influence.''

Funk narrowed his eyes. ''Things like this take time, Smarte. We don't have years.''

''Within two weeks I'll have Judge Warner issue a report to you regarding the status of possible legislation,'' Charles said crisply. ''If you don't hear from him, assume the issue is a dead one. And we'll go to print with every tall tale we can muster up. Do we have an agreement, gentlemen?''

Breadlaw jerked his cigar out of his mouth and gulped from a dry glass. ''Uh—I don't see why we can't, eh, Arnold?''

Funk raised colorless brows and shrugged. ''We have nothing to lose. Hope you have the situation well in hand, Smarte, and don't get yourself killed in the process. Er—Mrs. McGoldrick.'' He nodded vaguely in Kate's direction.

Charles's chair scraped on the floorboards. ''Very good, gentlemen. It was a pleasure. And please, do let me know what you think of future editorials. I could hardly risk the support of the Union Pacific. It means so very much to me.''

''Oh, yes. Yes, of course—'' Breadlaw jumped to his feet, snuck a hand inside his topcoat and withdrew a check that he handed to Charles. ''Your stipend, Mr. Smarte.''

Charles pocketed the check. ''It's a pleasure doing business with you, sir. Good day to both of you. Mrs. McGoldrick—'' He looked down at Kate, held out his arm, and she found that slipping her arm through his was as effortless as breathing. Anything was easy when floating on a cloud of victory.

''Gentlemen,'' she said, and as they jerked to their feet and nodded, she was turned and escorted from the room.

Rain was pouring from the sky when they emerged from the hotel. Charles paused on the boardwalk, beneath the hotel's roof, and looked out into the rain. Watching him,

Kate felt her heart swell with emotion she couldn't name and had no desire to squelch.

"Charles—"

"When I was young," he said above the rush of the rain, "my father and I used to sit on the front porch of our home in Boston. We didn't talk much. We just watched the rain. I still remember what it smelled like—that rain on the cobblestones. I can smell it even now."

Kate felt tears burning in her eyes. "Charles—"

Thunder boomed all around them. Lightning flashed sporadically. The rain came down in sheets, turning the street into a river of mud. A wagon plowed to a sudden stop in front of them, axle deep in mud.

"The train back to Crooked Nickel is at two," Charles said, looking down at her. He grabbed her hand. "Let's go."

"But—" She was pulled behind him along the wet boardwalk toward the depot. "I don't think—Charles—" But he didn't hear her, perhaps because of the roar of the rain.

They reached the end of the roof-covered boardwalk. He let go of her hand. "Wait here—" he half-shouted. "I'll get tickets—"

And he took off into the rain and mud.

Five minutes later he returned. She'd found a seat on an overturned cracker-barrel outside the millinery, beneath an awning that leaked all over her shoes. Odd, but she'd felt no desire to admire hats as she sat there waiting for him.

He drew up in front of her, soaked and mud splattered, and limping more visibly than usual. He blinked through the water dripping from his hair and seemed to need to take several breaths to catch his wind. "No trains," he said.

"No what?"

"Track's washed out."

"Already?"

"I didn't bother the man with details, Kate. The track is washed out. No trains are running back to Crooked Nickel today."

"But the next one isn't until tomorrow."

"I know. Two o'clock."

Kate looked at the wagon stuck in the mud. Several others littered the street. Their drivers abandoned them and darted frantically through the rain to shelter.

She bit her lip. "We can't ride back home in this, even if we had a buckboard to rent."

"I bought us two tickets on the train for tomorrow."

She looked up at him. "So we're stuck here. But Walt—"

"I'm sure Victoria won't mind keeping him for the night."

Kate worried her lower lip. "But that's twice now in just days and I've never before been away from him for the night."

"He'll weather it better than you, I'd wager." He looked down the boardwalk as if he contemplated something of grave consequence. "Hotel rooms will be scarce."

Kate's heart did a little stutter. She looked down the street. People were running pell-mell through the downpour, streaming into the Hotel St. John as if it were the only haven from the storm. Lightning flashed again and the ensuing thunder shook the boards beneath their feet.

"Come on." Charles took her elbow and steered her toward the hotel. Even with his limp, she had to hurry to keep up with his pace. "We'll get you a room here," he said, pushing open the hotel door.

"What about you?"

"I'll find Douglas Murphy at the courthouse. I'm sure one of his lawyer friends wouldn't mind putting up with me for the night."

No. She wouldn't imagine they'd mind in the least bit.

And neither would she. The thought made her cheeks hot and her pulse race. As he steered her through the crowd gathered around the front desk, she felt as if she were barreling at a tremendous rate of speed toward something that she didn't want. And that she'd best do something about it.

If only she knew what that was.

She envisioned herself alone in a hotel room watching the rain and thinking about Charles alone, watching the rain, and felt loneliness grip her so completely she wanted to cry.

Two men stood behind the front desk booking rooms. They worked at a feverish pace, taking money, handing out keys. The crowd pressed in all around them as people squeezed nearer the desk. Kate felt Charles close behind her. She felt safe around him, as safe as she could imagine ever feeling . . . but it was his arm wrapped almost entirely around her waist that was making her feel unsteady. Not the crowd. His hand was pressed flat against her belly and she knew her pulse was pounding into his palm. She felt giddy and swoony and delicious in a way she'd never before imagined. Tingles radiated out from that spot, pooling between her legs, racing to the tips of her breasts, robbing her of what little sense she still possessed.

And she wanted him to know it.

Charles requested a room for the night, the man scribbled something in his register, produced a key, and Charles handed him several bills.

"This way," he murmured, taking her hand and tugging her along behind him back through the crowd. He drew her up beside him at the foot of the stairs. The lobby was filled with bustling activity. The air hung thick with the smell of too many damp, unwashed people crammed into one place.

"Here." Charles lifted her hand, turned it palm up, and laid the key in it. "Room two-thirty-four. I'm sure you'll have no trouble finding it. I'll let you rest awhile and go look for Douglas. We can have dinner later."

She looked up at him. He meant to leave her there—just like that. Didn't he feel as she did? Wasn't there a tremendous, desperate kind of feeling going on inside him as it was inside her? A feeling that had to be expressed somehow? And all that expressing needed to be done in private.

He stood above her, tousled, beautiful, and emanating a damp Charles smell that was making her head whirl. She couldn't let him leave. Even if he wanted to.

"I can't," she blurted out.

"What do you mean, you can't?"

"I can't go up there alone. The—uh—it's the crowd, Charles. It frightens me."

"Frightens you." He didn't look in the least convinced.

"No—not really—except that I don't know a soul and someone could follow me and—you know—"

"No, what?"

She presented a completely affronted look. "Why, accost me, that's what."

"Ah. Of course. To steal that hat. Fine. I'll take you up. But are you sure? I know how much appearances bother you, Kate. I'm just asking, are you quite sure this is what you want?"

"Most definitely. Nobody knows me here and if they did they'd assume I had only good deeds in mind." She hooked her arm through his and tugged toward the stairs. "Besides, I'm chilled and my feet are squishing in my shoes. Maybe I should call down for a hot bath."

"You and two dozen others. You'd be better off lying down."

"Mmm."

They found her room in the middle of the upper hall. Kate stopped in front of it. "Two-thirty-four. This is it." She looked up at Charles and smiled a very shaky smile.

He looked down at her for several moments. "Aren't you going to open it?"

"Open it? Oh, yes, of course. I should—" She had a little trouble getting the key into the lock because her hand was shaking. She felt her teeth starting to chatter. Her hat slipped forward on her head and she pushed it back. The key slipped from her fingers, fell to the floor, and she bent, retrieved it, and tried again at the lock. "I can't seem to—"

"Here. Let me—" He took the key, shoved it into the lock, and pushed the door open.

The room was dim and dusky. Kate glimpsed a rain-splattered window, lace drapes, and a bed covered in white. Her heart slammed around in her breast.

"Charles—" It sounded like a dying plea but he'd pushed the door wide open and strode in. Kate followed and shut the door behind them.

Charles lit a bedside lamp, moved to the window, looked out, looked inside the closet, then faced her. "All safe." He tossed the keys on the table and watched her.

Kate removed her hat and tossed it onto a nearby wooden chair. "What you did with those two men, Charles—thank you. Jonathan Smarte couldn't have done it better."

"I told you I don't want your gratitude."

"Fine. Then you should know that I trusted you to do it well from the very start—just as I've trusted you to take care of me since I was six years old."

His chest expanded. "That's a start."

"It never went away. I only thought it did. You—you proved me wrong."

A moment passed. There was a humming kind of urgency in the air between them.

Breathless with indecision, Kate licked her lips. "I—I don't know the first thing about seducing a man, Charles."

"You're doing a fine job, if that's all you want."

"It's not—" It was out before she could take it back. "I feel like I'm sixteen again, Charles—"

"So do I."

"I'm shaking deep down in my heart—"

"So am I."

"There's this desperate feeling I'm having that I need to tell you—oh, Charles—" God, if he turned away from her now. The few feet distance between them felt like miles. She imagined her heart would rip in two if he abandoned her. "I want you to know something—" she said shakily, feeling tears welling up from her chest. "I have to say this because it's the truth—I haven't once regretted going to the orchard with Jude since the day Walt was born. If I had to do it over, to have Walt with me—I'm sorry, Charles—but I would. I'd make the same mistakes all over again. I suppose that means I'm not regretful."

His expression darkened. "It means you love your son as a mother should, Kate."

A tear slipped to her cheek. "I can't imagine my life without him." She blinked and the tears spilled from her eyes. Her heart turned over in her chest. "I can't imagine my life now—without you."

He was coming toward her in a blur of tears and she backed up against the closed door and felt all the will drain out of her.

"Kate—here—" He caught her in his strong arms and a sob tore from her throat.

"No—I can't—it won't work—none of it—no matter how much we pretend it will—"

"What won't work?" he murmured into her hair.

"You can't make it all better—not all of it—not even you. I can't believe—God—" Her stomach constricted, she choked out another sob and he lifted her into his arms and turned to the bed.

"No—really, Charles—I—I'm made of sterner"—her

voice snagged when he laid her down on the bed and leaned over her—"stuff."

He seemed excessively masculine towering over her with his face darkly brooding. "See," he said, "your color looks better already. And you've stopped saying ridiculous things. Now you're cold—"

"No, I'm—" She bit off her words as he levered himself up and jerked out of his topcoat.

"That's better," he said, laying the warm coat over her and pulling it up under her chin. It smelled of rain and Charles and made her want to curl into it like a kitten.

She swallowed. "I know what you're doing."

"Tell me, Kate." He was poised above her, arms braced on either side of her, his face deeply lined, his eyes a warm, deep blue.

"You're taking your clothes off and trying to make me forget that you're going back to Boston, I'm staying here, and dreams never, ever come true."

"Ah. Is it working by chance?" he murmured, brushing his lips over hers.

The kiss was as soft as velvet. She heard a low moan of pleasure come from her throat and snapped her eyes open. "No. I still won't believe in happy endings."

"How do your stories always end, Kate?"

"But that's imagination. It's not real. It never was. I only thought it was."

"And if I say it can be real?" His eyes narrowed, lowered to her mouth, lingered, and the lines on his face deepened even more. "I have the will of ten men, remember?"

"Yes—" she whispered. She lifted her hands, laid them on his forearms and ran them slowly up to his biceps. His eyes met hers. His face looked so worn suddenly, so haggard and lined with years of responsibility, that her heart twisted around. She ached to give him all the tenderness he needed. And she could think of only one way to do that.

She snuck her hands around his neck and pulled her lips up to his. A subtle arch of her back brought her breasts up into his chest.

He registered all of this with a deep rumble in his throat. She played her lips over his in languorous strokes. "I need to feel. I've known nothing but longing for six years—and now that you're here, while you're here—"

He pressed his thumb over her lips. His face darkened, hardened. "You won't run away from me again—no matter what."

"No. I'll never run from you again."

He looked into her eyes, slid his hand between their bodies, and yanked the coat away. His arm slipped around her; he cupped her bottom and lifted her loins up into his. His eyes narrowed, his hips gently rocked, and she felt the flagrant evidence of his arousal.

"Yes," she gasped.

His hand roved freely over her breasts. He watched her, his face severely set, mouth pressed firm. Only the heightened glitter in his eyes seemed to register her gasps of pleasure. "I've dreamed of this—" His voice dropped to a deep rasp. He looked down at his fingers teasing one peak until it pushed up against the silk of her dress. He lowered his mouth, wet the fabric, flicked at the tip with his tongue until Kate's fingers dug into his back.

"Yes—I have, too—"

His fingers worked quickly over the buttons of her gown. But she hardly noticed because he was kissing her throat, laving it, nibbling and murmuring love words that made no sense to her but sent thrill after thrill racing through her.

She felt fabric slip aside, a fleeting rush of air over her bare breasts, and then his hair was brushing her chin, and his mouth and hands were doing those wonderful things to her bosom. She clutched his head and gasped up at the ceiling.

"Sit up." He took her hand and rose up away from her.

"What? I don't want to."

"Sit up—" He tugged. "There—so I can see you when I undress you."

She felt heavy lidded and swollen lipped and her breasts felt full and heavy and so sensitive she would have sworn his gaze upon them was palpable. And the room was spinning.

Her dress slipped from her shoulders.

"Jesus God, you're gorgeous—"

She had to close her eyes. She couldn't bear looking at him looking at her with such intensity. Or maybe she could—

She opened her eyes, reached for him. He drew her up, and the dress and chemise plunged to the floor in a definitive rustle. She stood shakily, needful and wanting and hot and flushed over every part of her body. He was staring at her, running his eyes over her as if it were his God-given right to do so, even down where her pantaloons were caught high between her thighs.

"Charles—" Her fingers pulled at his shirt.

"I know—" He tugged at his cravat, undid the top few buttons of his shirt, and whisked it off over his head. He flicked at his trousers, parted them, and looked at her long and hard. "I swear I'll bolt the door and tie you in this bed if you try to leave after this."

"I'm not afraid, Charles." She let her eyes rove down his chest, down his belly, down to the center of his loins. She barely reached up a hand when he grabbed it and pressed it right where she imagined he was the hardest and the hottest.

His Adam's apple worked in his throat. He looked so vulnerable, so suddenly at her mercy, she wrapped her fingers around him and squeezed very gently. He grabbed her hand, hard, and took it away. "No—not—Christ—"

And then he was on his knees in front of her, both

hands yanking at the drawstring of her pantaloons, which then pooled at her feet.

"Charles, what are you—?" She swallowed the rest of it. She could barely think because he was fondling her hips and bottom, and his mouth was—

"Charles—" She looked down at the top of his head, knowing his face was pressed *right there,* and his mouth was . . . no, that was his tongue sending tremors through her, lifting her up, up, making her shake uncontrollably. . . .

He caught her before she crumpled to the floor, caught her and lifted her onto the bed, and then he was kissing her mouth with his mouth—wide open kisses that tasted of him, of her, and she felt as if he'd shot her to the moon.

She lifted herself up hard against him, rubbed her loins to his. "Charles, you have to do something—I'm shaking—"

"Not yet—" he rasped against her mouth. He slid his hands over her breasts, her belly, and cupped them between her thighs. Her legs trembled open. "Here—sweet, sweet, Kate—"

He shifted, levered himself over her, and pressed himself up against the most sensitive part of her. He swallowed and looked down at her.

She clutched at his shoulders, lifted her hips, and he slid a precious inch inside of her. He went as rigid as oak above her.

"Don't move," he rasped.

"I have to—"

"No—I'll—I can't—"

Kate blinked up at him. "What is it? Am I doing something wrong—?"

"No—" It was a choked sound. Sweat beaded on his forehead. "God, no, sweetheart. You're—you're beautiful. I just—didn't—think—I'd—" He looked down at her and pressed himself long and slow and very deep inside her—once, twice—she lost count as the clouds above her again beckoned and she shot up there, high above on a string drawn so tight she thought she'd lose her mind if she wasn't released. And then it came over her so suddenly, so violently—the spasms rocked through her in enormous waves and gasps and groans and words that sounded incomprehensible. She heard his, too, dimly through the haze.

She came to earth realizing her face was smashed against his sweat-dampened chest. They were both breathing hard. She was almost afraid to move, except that she knew she had to because she couldn't breathe.

"Charles—you—you're—I can't—"

"What—Christ, I was crushing you." He moved quickly off of her, slipping out of her so suddenly she had to swallow an outcry of dismay. But any feelings of sudden needfulness were squashed when he rolled to his back with her scooped tight and close in his arms.

She had no choice but to curl her arm over his chest. They lay there, and she listened to his breathing.

"I don't even know what I said," she murmured.

"When?"

She lifted her head and rested her chin on his chest. His eyes were closed. Like this, he looked so much like Walt did when he slept.

"When I was—when you did that to me."

"Ah. That." His lips curved slightly. He seemed so at peace, so unlike the turbulent, tormented Charles she'd always remembered. His hand cupped her head and pressed it back to his shoulder. "No more talking."

"Now seems an opportune time . . . at the very least appropriate."

"Appropriate maybe. Opportune—I don't think so." He ran a big hand down the curve of her waist and hip, then cupped her bottom and drew her leg up over his. ''Mmm . . . ,'' he murmured, planting his hand on her buttock as if he meant to keep it there forever.

It was a simple gesture but one which screamed of possessiveness and ease and a level of intimacy that Kate had longed for her entire life. This was what she'd dreamed of. This was what she'd known in her heart was waiting for her. This was the kind of love . . .

She lifted her head, looked down at him, and felt her heart swell. Yes, that's what she'd known all along. It's what made her soul sing. She'd never stopped loving him.

''I have to tell you something, Charles.''

Tears came to her eyes. She blinked, swept them away, watched her fingers play in the hair on his chest. ''I love you—'' she whispered. ''I do—maybe more than I ever thought I could—even more than I did on that night I went to the orchard to meet you. I—I wanted it to be you. I imagined it was you when I let him do all those things—and I felt so ashamed, until Walt came and then I wasn't anymore. That's the reason I—I—'' She caught her lip with her teeth. ''Oh, Charles, I—'' She looked at him, at the eyes still closed, the chest rising and falling so evenly and deeply—

''Charles.'' She paused, bit her lip. ''Charles, are you sleeping?''

No answer.

She shifted herself up, bracing her hands on either side of him. Her brows quivered. ''Charles?''

He moaned, shifted slightly so that her breasts just brushed his chest, and cupped her buttocks with both hands. Gently, he squeezed, moaned again, and fell silent.

She watched his chest rise and fall three times. ''Charles Remington, I swear—''

His eyes opened. Lids heavy, he lifted his head and

flicked at one nipple with his tongue. It hardened instantly and made Kate suck in her breath. He looked up at her, watching her as he cupped her breast and played with the nipple. "Say it again, Kate."

She swallowed. "Y—you were awake."

"I was. Didn't you want me to be?"

"I—didn't—what part did you hear?"

"What part didn't you want me to hear?"

He was playing with her. She frowned at him. "You tricked me."

"I can do it again."

"No, you can't. I'll—" In a heartbeat she was on her back and he was pressing her into the mattress with the length of his body against the length of hers.

"Say it again," he murmured, brushing her lips with his. "Open up for me and say it again."

"Charles—" She had no desire to do otherwise. He entered her smooth as hot velvet and the world seemed for that moment suspended.

"Say it," he rasped, burying his face in her neck. "Say, 'I love you, Charles.' "

"I love you, Charles."

"Again—"

"I love you, Charles—"

"The other—"

"The other?"

"I wanted it to be you."

"I mean that."

"Say it . . . say it again, Kate, and keep saying it—"

"I wanted it to be you."

"For the next fifty years, keep saying it."

"I wanted it to be—" Tears sprang to her eyes. "Always you—" She clutched him close, closer, as the tension began to mount, steeply, faster and the tears spilled from her eyes. And again she was at the pinnacle. “I—” She cried out and tumbled down, and as she was falling, from way up above her she heard his whisper or did she imagine it—?

“I love you, Kate.”

Chapter 18

Charles braced both hands on the bed, leaned down, and put his mouth right next to her ear. She smelled of warm rain and cotton sheets and a night's worth of sex.

"You need food," he murmured, slipping one hand under the sheet and sliding it down her back. He cupped the fullness of her bottom. She moaned and wriggled and his manhood sprang to full alert.

Impossible, he thought, pulling the sheet back so that she lay in a splash of midmorning sun. After all, he'd outdone even the biggest braggarts among his friends. And it seemed he still wanted more.

She rolled over, a tumbled, ravished-looking pearly pink testament to womanhood, and part of him went weak at the sight of her. For a woman who seemed very slight she was fully and voluptuously formed in every way imaginable. She pushed her hair away from her eyes, opened them, and smiled at him.

"Hullo, Charles. You're dressed."

"I am."

"You even have your topcoat on. Come here—" She held out her arms to him and it seemed the most logical, certainly the most prudent, thing to do to go to her on that bed and love every inch of her.

He caught himself. ''We can't.''

''But I want to.''

He heard his breath come out through his teeth as she sat up and shrugged her hair back. She'd managed to sit up and into a perfect block of sunlight streaming through the window. His mind swam with the vision of breasts and belly and thighs and a triangle of chestnut curls that seemed to call out to him.

She was looking at him as if she didn't have an inkling of his thoughts. ''Charles, you can't do the things you did to me and expect me not to like it.''

''I know you liked it,'' he said, looking around for her dress.

''Then you're not the least surprised that I want to do it all again.''

''Not in the least. I understand far better than you'd imagine. The implications of it all—well, that's another matter that I've been giving a good deal of thought—'' He peeked under the bed, behind a chair. ''Now where the hell is?—but there are things that need to be accomplished first before—''

''Before what?''

He gave her a stern look, which was a Herculean feat given what he really wanted to do with her. How could he make her understand that the things he needed to tell her about Walt, about the inheritance, the money, the future—their future—that until she'd accomplished what she needed to do with Judge Warner and the sheepherders, he was afraid he'd lose her if it all came out too soon?

Last night they'd gone to a place that he wanted to stay in forever, so much so he was afraid to breathe in case he'd lose it.

''What was I—oh, here.'' He spotted a pink-striped tangle of dress and chemise half under the bed. He shook it out and handed it to her. ''We have to eat. Quickly. We have a train to catch. We have a sheepshearing event to organize and judges to win over. And then—then we're going to discuss you and me and Walt.'' He could hardly wait to be about the business of it all. For as long as he remembered he'd been a tolerant man. But suddenly he was impatient to begin experiencing the rest of his life.

''So much to do,'' she said, hopping off the bed and into her chemise. She wriggled and slid straps over her shoulders and began lacing the thing up. She looked up through her hair and smiled, and Charles gave up the fight, against his better judgment, and moved close to help her.

''Your hands are shaking,'' he said, trying to look severe as he took up the lacing job.

''Maybe I'm nervous.''

He gave her a hooded look. ''Maybe you're doing it on purpose.''

''Being nervous?''

''No, soliciting my help. Hoping I'll do something like this maybe—'' He traced the full lower curve of both breasts through the cotton.

She closed her eyes, smiled again, opened them, and looked innocent as a lamb. ''Never. This is just so very''—her lips quivered very slightly—''new.''

''Yes, it is. Very new.'' He drew the dress up over her hips, her arms, and shoulders, feeling the silken softness of her skin as if for the first time. In all his life he could never tire of her.

She was winding her hair into a knot on top of her head, and he continued working the buttons closed high up under her throat. She lifted her chin and looked up at him as if he were the hero in her fairy tale, capable of grand and glorious feats. He had a profound need to have her look at him like that for the rest of his life. He'd be damned if he was going to do anything to threaten that.

''You're looking at me like you feel shy, Kate.''

"In some senses, yes, I am. In other ways—I feel so unsure of myself with you and yet so certain of you. . . ." She lowered her eyes and looked so beguilingly naive, so much like a ravished young bride, it was all he could do to keep from pushing her back on the bed and making her remember how well indeed they knew each other.

He cupped her shoulders and she melted into him, her arms wrapping tightly around his waist.

"See—" she murmured into his chest. "This feels so comfortable and the absolutely right thing to do, while talking to you and dressing and probably eating and riding on the train will be so awkward. I feel so strange, Charles, so very nervous, like my life has suddenly taken a dramatic change in course."

"Long overdue," he said, pressing his lips to the top of her head. He caught sight of a clock on the bedside table. Regret stirred through him. And something else . . . something vaguely ominous, as if they should stay in this haven of rumpled, sun-dappled sheets or the feelings they'd discovered here would be forever lost.

He dismissed his musings as ridiculous. After all, what person wouldn't dread the loss of something he held precious? He focused on the tasks at hand. And there were many. "Come—" He drew her back, lowered his head, and played his lips over hers in slow, soft strokes. It was meant to be a tender kiss, but he instantly realized the ludicrousness of such a thing between them at this point. She parted her lips, gave him full, unbridled entry, and he claimed it, passionately. His head swam with visions of every morning and night yet to come with her, and he felt an overpowering need to command possession of all of them.

She cupped his buttocks, pressed herself closer, and he felt himself go up in flames. "No—" He tore his mouth away and crushed her in his arms. "God—it's too new, still. It's like playing with dry tinder."

"Is that good?"

He couldn't help but laugh. "Yes, it's damned good. It's better than good. And if we had no place to be right now, I'd show you how good. Now where's that hat? We have a train to catch."

By the time the train pulled into Crooked Nickel, the day had turned hot and beastly, with the air hanging heavy and the earth steaming from the rain and the ensuing sun. The train was packed with people heading east, among them Douglas Murphy, who sat some distance in front of them on the train. Sitting very properly beside Charles, Kate felt awkward as a yearling pony and droopy and drippy as a wet noodle in the heat.

She wanted a bath. She wanted a cushy seat for her behind. More than anything she wanted to go back to the Hotel St. John and take off her clothes in front of Charles. And yet as odd as she felt, as disjointed from her life, somehow she felt he was in complete command of it all.

It was this conviction that made their parting at the depot endurable. Douglas Murphy was hovering, looking as if he wanted to speak with Charles about something very urgent. And she was squirming to keep herself from itching at all the rivulets of perspiration weaving down her chest and back. Charles stared at her as if he knew precisely where all those rivulets were.

"John Bertrand's farm tonight," he said softly, staring at her mouth and no doubt thinking thoughts totally unsuited to where they were. "I'll have a buckboard for you and Walt in front of your house at six sharp."

"We'll be ready."

A moment passed. They looked at each other. Hot wind blew and ruffled through his hair. "I don't suppose I should kiss you."

Her lips quirked and she looked down and fiddled with her purse. ''No, Charles, you shouldn't.''

Douglas Murphy was gazing off down the platform, looking distinctly distracted and as if he hadn't heard a word.

Kate slanted her eyes at Charles. ''Since when have you started asking, Charles Remington?''

His look darkened. ''I don't intend to ask ever again.''

Her heart stuttered and then she heard a sound that made her turn almost out of instinct.

''Mama—''

It was Walt, barreling toward her with Victoria Valentine hurrying to keep up with him in a tight sheath of a dress that would have made simple walking impossible. Walt plowed right into Kate, locked himself around her knees, and drove her straight back against Charles. Charles caught her, steadied her, and met with Walt's next explosion of energy, toward him, with all the fortitude of a wall of solid stone.

''We were worried,'' Victoria murmured, kissing Kate on each cheek. ''He slept and ate fine but kept asking where his mama and Uncle Charles were.'' She drew back, angled her eyes up at Charles, then back at Kate. ''We have to have tea, Kate. A nice long afternoon of tea.''

''Rather thirsty for it, aren't you?'' Kate asked, her lips curving.

Victoria leaned conspiratorially close. ''Famished, if you must know. Dear God, the way the man looks at you is enough to make my knees jiggle.''

Kate bit her lip and felt her heart swell. Emotion this strong was obviously impossible to hide. ''Mine, too.''

Victoria closed her eyes and seemed to shiver from the inside out. ''God, I knew it. I just knew it.'' Her eyes popped open. ''I want to hear everything.''

Kate tried to look nonchalant. "What makes you so certain there's anything to hear?"

Victoria's finely arched brow shot up and her voice plunged very low. "You smell like him, Kate."

Kate gulped and felt herself turn beet red. Her mouth opened, trembled, nothing came out.

Victoria snuck her arm around her. "Come with me. Gentlemen, so good to see you both again. Mrs. McGoldrick and I have to be off. So much to do, you know. Baths and getting Walter ready and Bessie Mae Elliot's got all us women doing all kinds of cooking and baking and preparing for the big dance tonight. Mr. Remington, I understand from Bessie Mae that this sheepshearing event was your doing?"

"Actually, ma'am, it was laid very neatly in my lap."

"Mmm. Imagine that. And you quite outdid yourself planning it. I saw Bessie Mae and an entire army of Ladies Auxiliary Garden Club members scurrying around plastering handbills all over town announcing the dance and no one took any of them down, as far as I could tell. Of course, Bessie Mae looked fit to kill if anyone tried. And today's *Sentinel* had a headline that announced for everyone in the town to show their support of the sheepshearers at the dance tonight. It was the front-page headline. I hope that was wise of the *Sentinel.*"

"The paper is merely printing the news, Miss Valentine."

"And you had nothing to do with that landing on the front page?"

Charles gave a self-effacing shrug. "I might have asked Mr. Gould to give it visibility."

"Ah. You obviously have sway, sir?"

His eyes settled on Kate. "Perhaps some."

"And you dance?"

"Passably enough."

"With the right partner, of course."

"Of course. Six o'clock, Mrs. McGoldrick."

Kate glanced up at him and felt little flutters of anticipation ripple through her. "Of course, Mr. Remington."

"Come, Walt," Victoria said.

"But I don't wanna go with girls. I wanna stay with Uncle Charles."

Kate grasped him as all mothers knew how, right behind the neck, very firmly, and turned him toward her. "Now, Walt," she said, and the trio headed down the platform.

"Yellow," Charles murmured, giving Kate an appreciative sweep of his eyes as he handed her into the buckboard. "What will the ladies of the Crooked Nickel Auxiliary Garden Club think of you flouting convention like this?"

"Don't you like it?" Kate asked provocatively as she settled next to Walt. She clasped demure hands around the gooseberry pie she held in her lap. The buckboard swayed as Charles climbed up beside her.

He took up the reins to Sundance and bent his mouth very close to her ear. "I like it," he rumbled in a tone that made Kate's mouth dry as parched Wyoming prairie.

The buckboard jerked forward. "Bessie Mae won't have anything to say," Kate said, wobbling on her seat. "She can't."

"Flouting convention all on her own, is she?"

"Yes, indeed. She goes about this town on hot days wearing—" Kate glanced at Walt. With all the concentration of a doctor in surgery, he was winding string around a rock he'd found. Kate leaned closer to Charles. She felt him lean into her and the feeling made her heart take flight and soar. At one point during her busy afternoon of baking pie, bathing, and getting a reluctant Walt ready, she'd wondered if the tryst in Turkeyfoot Run had actually occurred. She'd also wondered if Charles would feel the same as he had in the hotel when they next met. There had been something rather ethereal about their rendezvous there, as if it were a once-in-a-lifetime occurrence between two people she barely knew. She'd been so nervous about seeing Charles again she'd hardly eaten all day.

She laid her cheek against his bicep. "How are you, Charles?"

"Better now. It's been six hours since I saw you last."

"Six hours and fifteen minutes. Did you miss me?"

"Unbearably."

"Good."

"You sound very pleased."

"A woman should be pleased that her man misses her."

"Wouldn't she rather be with him?"

"Why, yes, of course, she would. But when she can't—"

"What if she always could?"

Kate swallowed and stared out at the stretch of prairie laid like a yellow-gold carpet before them. Her heart was hammering so hard she could feel it above the jarring of the buckboard. She felt Charles watching her. It was, she realized, a magical moment, one which she would remember all her life.

"What are you asking me, Charles?" she said, barely above a whisper.

"You heard me."

"I did? I was—um—thinking about Bessie Mae Elliot."

"What if I'd said that?"

Kate looked up at him aghast. "I'd push you off this wagon, that's what. How would you know she goes without anything under her clothes—?" She caught herself, her eyes flew wide, and she looked sharply at Walt as if he'd just appeared beside her, within earshot.

"I want to drive," he said, glancing up at her, then looking at her strangely. "What's wrong, Mama?"

Kate blinked at him. "Nothing. Nothing at all. No, Walter McGoldrick. You cannot drive this buggy."

"Uncle Charles said I could."

Kate's head snapped back around. Charles was staring out at the empty prairie in front of him as if negotiating it were a near to impossible task. Brows furrowed, mouth sternly set. He gave it all away when his eyes shot to hers. "Problem, Kate?"

"Yes. I don't want him driving this thing."

"Then tell him that."

"I did."

"Tell him again. And mean it."

"I do—I"—she turned back to Walter—"I said no, Walt. Do you hear me?"

Walt grumbled under his breath and returned to winding string, the fight obviously given up.

"He listened," Kate said, adjusting herself on her seat and feeling very satisfied. "It's so very nice when the men listen."

"I listen, Kate." He was speaking very low and close, and she was certain Walt couldn't hear them.

"Yes, I believe you do."

"I'm thinking about what you said about a woman going without her—"

"Stop."

"I know what you look like—"

"Charles—"

"—under that yellow gingham—"

"Really, you must concentrate on driving."

"You're porcelain white and pearly pink, Kate—"

Kate gulped and wobbled as the buckboard clattered

through a deep rut. She kept her eyes straight in front of her, felt the slap of evening sun on her face, but the heat pounding there came from within.

"—right on the tips of your—"

She shot huge eyes at him. He grinned and looked so utterly charming and devilish she found it impossible to display the slightest chagrin.

"Please, stop, Charles."

"I have to tell you I think about it all the time."

"I think I know that."

"I'd love to show you."

"At the dance? We can't."

"We could."

She gave him a dubious look. He cocked a brow and his eyes glittered with mischief and a good bit of deviltry. "What are you thinking, Charles Remington? We'll be surrounded by people."

"Exactly. They'll never miss us if we sneak away, hide in the shadows, under a buckboard, on a blanket—"

Kate sat up ramrod straight. "Sneak away? Are you crazy? We're not young lovers that have to hide—"

"No. That was taken away from us. But we could have been."

There was a pain in his eyes that tore through Kate like the swipe of a blade. "I'm sorry, Charles," she whispered.

One of his hands cupped over hers. "So am I." He looked down at her and his lips softened, eyes darkened. "We have to make up for lost time, Kate. We have plans to make. Meet me by this buckboard at nine o'clock."

Kate pursed her lips to keep from smiling. "I tell you I won't."

He was looking at the feathers on her yellow hat. "Ah. Afraid of being accosted again?"

"Yes, I very well could be. And so could you. If the cattlemen come and make any kind of trouble—"

"Oh, you can be assured they're coming."

"What?"

"I said the cattlemen will be at John Bertrand's farm."

"You can't be serious?"

"Dan Goodknight will be there."

She couldn't hide her surprise. "Dan Goodknight? At a sheepshearing event? Then we have to cancel it. There's sure to be bloodshed."

"I have Goodknight's word there won't be."

"His word? You spoke to him? You did this all in a few days, Charles Remington? I don't believe it."

"Believe it, Kate, but don't give me all the credit. I had a little help. It seems our Mr. Goodknight is friends with Judge Warner from back in the days when Warner was a lawyer in San Francisco and Goodknight owned half the land. Goodknight also has strong ties to a certain very influential Wyoming congressman who frequents Louella's place."

Kate drew herself up and lifted her nose a notch. "I do believe you're getting fond of Louella, Charles."

"You'll have a chance to, as well. She's coming to the dance with her congressman."

Kate felt her mouth drop open. "Louella Lawless doesn't do anything for charitable reasons."

"I believe she said something about finally doing what she should have done a long time ago. It was Louella who convinced Goodknight to come, Kate. She telegraphed her congressman. He's arriving on the seven o'clock Union Pacific from Laramie tonight. He should be at Bertrand's by eight."

Kate considered this. "I hope he doesn't get shot. Elmer Pruitt won't be able to stay away, Charles, not with this kind of response."

"He has to stay away, Kate. Yesterday, Judge Warner threw him in Turkeyfoot Run's jail for two nights for stealing a traveling preacher's one-eyed mule and punching a bailiff. Pruitt had to give the mule back but still had to pay a fine and spend the nights. Douglas was in the courtroom defending the preacher.''

''So Elmer Pruitt will be all the more mad tomorrow. I'm still worried about the rest of the cattlemen tonight. What if they get it into their heads to do something awful again, Charles? You saw John Bertrand's barn and all those dead sheep.''

''With Goodknight, Warner, and a Wyoming congressman at Bertrand's, and Pruitt in jail, do you honestly think Virg is persuasive enough to rouse the rest of those boys? I don't. Especially with all those young strapping sheepshearers to lend their support to the sheepherders. You don't have to worry, Kate.''

''You sound so sure.''

''I am sure. I have it all taken care of.''

''Yes, I believe you might. You're quite wonderful, Charles.''

''Yes. I heard you say that several times last night.''

''I know I couldn't have accomplished this for the sheepherders on my own.''

''No one could have alone. Not even Harry.''

''I'm very grateful.''

''Show me.'' He slanted his eyes down at her. ''Tonight at nine. By the buckboard.''

Kate directed her gaze out over the prairie. A smile of pure delight played on her lips. Her future seemed as open and free as the land that swept from horizon to horizon.

''We'll see,'' was all she said.

Chapter 19

"I can think of no better excuse for feasting, drinking, gaming—and perhaps a few good fights." Bessie Mae Elliot swung dancing eyes over the throng of people gathered outside John Bertrand's farmhouse.

The entire town seemed to have loaded up their buckboards and picnic baskets and converged on John Bertrand's farm. There was a hovering air of merriment to the festivities, lent by the good weather, the fine spirits, and the three fiddlers playing beside a makeshift dance floor some distance away.

Charles looked over the tops of the heads all around him and felt his chest swell with satisfaction. Even now buggies were arriving from Crooked Nickel and surrounding farms with more people. Word had obviously spread quickly among cattlemen and sheepherders alike. Children ran among the crowd, Walt somewhere among them. Victoria Valentine and Ace strolled arm in arm at the fringe of the crowd. Charles spotted Louella Lawless in conversation with Dan Goodknight at the back of the throng. Several feet back a group of men, obviously with Goodknight, had gathered.

Cattlemen, judging by the looks of them. They were, in general, a grim-faced lot. But Charles spotted several whose toes were tapping in the dust in time to the music. Every now and then one would cast quick glances at the sheep-herders mingling about, as if gauging their chances of winning a hand-to-hand fight against these men. Even Virg and the rest of Elmer Pruitt's buddies gathered like flies buzzing around the perimeter of the festivities. They looked far more eager and curious than anything else, particularly when several members of the Ladies Auxiliary Garden Club strolled past and favored them with blood-warming smiles.

"Why, will you look at that?" Bessie Mae asked, her attention riveted on the line of men straddling sheep between their legs and wielding clippers in their hands with an amazing dexterity. Bessie Mae laid a hand on Kate's arm and leaned closer. "Mrs. McGoldrick, look at all those men. How many of them are there?"

"Too many," Kate said, peering up on tiptoes to see.

"Shoot, I don't think I can count that high," Bessie Mae said, flashing Charles a quick smile over the top of Kate's yellow feathered hat. "I feel like a girl left alone in Logan's General Store with all the candy, Mr. Remington. I don't know what to taste first."

She giggled into her hand and squirmed and looked about ready to burst out of the top of her blue and white gingham dress. She touched her hand to the swells of her bosom, pressed her lips together guiltily, then giggled again. "Mr. Remington, my mother almost didn't let me out of the house in this dress. She said it shows too much of me."

"It's a lovely dress," Charles said.

"Oh, I don't care about the color or nothin'. I just think a woman oughta show a man what she's got in her bodice if she means to get herself one. Don't you agree, Mrs. McGoldrick? Why, of course, you do. Look at you, all coming up and out of your nice yellow dress."

Kate tugged on her low scooped bodice as if only now realizing what Charles had been appreciating the entire ride out from Crooked Nickel.

Bessie Mae waved a hand at Kate's bosom. "See there, Mr. Remington?"

"Indeed, I do." That got him a fast upward slant of Kate's beautiful eyes.

"I had no idea Mrs. McGoldrick kept so much of herself all hidden away. I'll bet you didn't neither."

"A man can only wonder, Miss Elliot."

Bessie Mae pursed her lips and, with eyes narrowed and nostrils flaring, scanned the men again. "Wonderin' never got a woman no husband." To punctuate this, Bessie Mae threw back her shoulders and her breasts bobbed precariously on the edge of her bodice. She didn't seem to mind. Her tongue came out of her mouth and touched her top lip. "Why, look there, Mr. Remington. Who is that one right there looking at us? I've seen him around town before. Never got his name."

Charles followed Bessie Mae's pointing finger. "John Bertrand," he replied, moving somewhat closer beside Kate and feeling immediately ready to punch something. His eyes narrowed on the strapping Bertrand, who'd shed his shirt while he joined in the shearing. Bertrand was looking at Kate, smiling at her and showing all his teeth. When he glanced at Charles he seemed to sober somewhat. In spite of Bertrand's obvious attraction to Kate, Charles couldn't help but admire the man. He'd agreed to host the dance, knowing the cattlemen could be attending, within days of his barn being burned and his sheep killed by some of these same men. It took a strong man secure in his convictions to set aside his grievances in order to settle the dispute. Of course, Bertrand looked capable enough of taking on five cattlemen singlehandedly. And everyone knew it.

"Good-ness," Bessie Mae murmured, gripping Kate's arm as if preparing to swoon in a heap. "He's looking at me. See there? He's looking right at me and my—" Her hand fluttered over her blushing décolletage. ''I want to meet him.''

''I'll introduce you,'' Kate said quickly.

''He doesn't come to town much,'' Bessie Mae said pondering. ''None of those sheepherders do. Work too much, I guess. I say they just need to find themselves a good woman to care for them. Bertrand . . . hmmm. Oh, I remember where I saw him. He was talking to you, Mrs. McGoldrick. On the street. You know him.''

''I do.''

''He asked Mrs. McGoldrick to marry him,'' Charles put in. ''She said no.''

Bessie Mae was blinking at Kate and looking as if she wasn't sure whether she should chastise Kate for even considering such a thing or whether she should hug her and beam with joy. ''Well, I have to say, Mrs. McGoldrick, that perhaps the time has come to shed your widow's weeds for good. I know I would if a man who looked like John Bertrand proposed to me. Lordie! Those black rags would be off of me in a second.''

''That wasn't the reason,'' Kate said. She glanced up at Charles in a way that made his pulse trip and his body ache for her.

''Well, you'd better've had a good one,'' Bessie Mae said. ''Oh, there's that Judge Warner from Turkeyfoot Run. He's talking to Louella Lawless of all people. You know, come to think of it, I wonder why Mr. Jonathan Smarte hasn't shown himself here.''

''What?'' Kate said.

''We're all kinda wonderin'—''

''We?''

''All the townsfolks is talkin' about it, what with his *Sentinel* bein' the reason all this is happening, why didn't he come? I'll bet he will. I just bet.''

"I wouldn't count on it," Kate said. "He lives in Laramie."

"I know. In a big house. But this is big news. They're talking legislation pertectin' the grazing rights of the sheepherders."

Kate looked at Bessie Mae sharply. "Who told you that?"

"I heard it just a minute ago from someone. Everyone tells me everything, Mrs. McGoldrick. Don't you know that by now? Oh, goodness, they're gonna start the castration."

"The what?" Kate sounded shocked.

Bessie Mae looked positively delighted. Charles half-expected her to rub her hands together with glee.

Charles leaned toward Kate until he could smell her lilac scent. "The final chore of the day is to convert the male lambs into wethers by castrating them."

Kate looked horrified. "Why do such a thing to an innocent lamb?"

"To produce better mutton, I assume, just as steers produce better beef than bulls do."

"Bulls—" Bessie Mae rolled the word over her tongue and watched John Bertrand lope around with big strides and buttocks flexing. He joined a line of men who were struggling to sit sheep in front of them. "Let's go!" Before Charles could stop her, Bessie Mae had looped her arm through Kate's and was dragging her through the crowd toward John Bertrand.

Over Kate's head, Charles watched Bertrand drop down in front of a sheep being held by all four legs in an elevated sitting position. Curious. Bertrand held no tool of any sort in his hands. No surgical instrument. Perhaps he was inspecting the sheep. Surely he had no intention of performing such a procedure in front of women and children.

Just as Charles drew up beside Kate, John Bertrand leaned down, braced his hands wide on the ground, and with one swift and sure motion extracted the sheep's testicles with his teeth.

Bessie Mae let out a whooping shriek of approval and clapped her hands together. Bertrand spat on the ground, stood up and looked at her with a wildly wicked gleam in his eyes then walked toward her as if he meant to devour her next. The crowd around them gave an uproarious cheer.

Kate spun around, white faced, and looked up at Charles. "I think I'm going to be sick."

"This way," he said, slipping his arm around her waist and turning her. He met with a wall of people and started to nudge his way through.

She leaned heavily against him. "I need air."

"I know. The crowd isn't parting at my whim, I'm afraid."

"I can't breathe. I keep seeing that—"

"I know. Something to drink—"

"No—no—get me far away, Charles. No people. No food. Somewhere alone—"

"I didn't think you'd ever ask."

"Stop thinking about that."

"I'm afraid I'm going to think about it all the time from now on—" He pushed his way through the crowd, hugging Kate very close against him. They emerged from the throng, and he grabbed her hand and tugged her behind him. "Over here—by this buckboard." He took her by the waist, looked into her greenish-white face, and pushed her head down with his hand on top of her hat.

"Charles, my hat!"

"Keep your head down—between your knees. Here—lean on my arm. That's it."

"I still feel like I'm going to throw up."

"No one will notice, I assure you."

"God, I just can't vomit now." She sounded on the verge of tears. "Not with you standing here."

He hunkered down and rubbed her shoulders. "I'm not going anywhere soon, Kate. Besides, husbands see their wives doing things like vomiting all the time."

"Husbands?"

"Yes, and wives."

She looked up at him. Her hat was sitting lopsided on her head. Her lips looked pale and utterly kissable. "Charles—"

"When wives are going to have babies they do a good deal of vomiting all the time, even when their husbands are right in front of them."

"Babies?"

"Yes. A whole herd of them."

"A herd? Oh, God, like sheep—don't say that."

"Five or six."

Her lips quivered into a smile. "Oh, Charles—"

"Oh, good gracious and Lordie, I've found you!" Bessie Mae Elliot descended on them like a thundercloud. She had one arm looped through John Bertrand's and looked utterly jubilant about her circumstances. "I thought I'd lost you. Did you see that? Did you, Mr. Remington? Did you see what Johnny here did with his teeth? Why, he's more precise than a knife!"

"Indeed," Charles said.

Kate gave a mournful groan.

"Mrs. McGoldrick, you all right? Why, you look terrible. Doesn't she look awful, Johnny?"

"Ma'am." Bertrand gave Kate that big toothy smile and nodded his head, then swung all his appreciation on Bessie Mae. "Wanna dance?"

Bessie Mae beamed. "Yes, yes, yes! You two comin'?"

"In a moment," Charles said.

"You better hurry. That dance floor's gonna be too crowded. Too many people comin'—why, look there. That's a fine enough buggy all right, with a driver an' all. Bringin' more people. Why, I don't recognize either of those men, an' I know everybody in this town. 'Course everybody's here. Ain't nobody left in town. Not nobody at all. Did you know that, Mr. Remington?''

''I believe I do,'' Charles said, without looking up from Kate.

''Nope. I don't know them. Look like politicians, yes, they do. All fancied up and proper looking. They've got East Coast painted all over them. Oh, I bet I know who the older one is. Yes, yes. There's Louella Lawless goin' over to meet him. He must be that Wyoming congressman. But who's that other fella? Looks familiar to me somehow. But I don't know why. I've never seen him before. Oh, I know why. He looks a bit like you, Mr. Remington. Ain't that a holler?''

Something made Charles stand straight up. He followed Bessie Mae's gaze and spotted the buggy and the elderly man standing with Louella. His eyes locked with those of the younger man standing at the front of the buggy.

The earth tipped under his boots.

Jude.

Chapter 20

Kate was certain she hadn't heard Charles's half-murmur correctly. Bracing one hand on his arm, she stood up, but the savage look on his face was enough to make her go cold from the inside out.

"What is it?" she whispered.

She spotted him almost instantly. Jude . . . walking toward them, dapper, handsome, and impeccably turned out in a burgundy coat complete with flapping tails. He had a top hat on his head, a walking stick in one hand, and a dashing smile on his face. Heads turned as he passed, men and women alike, but to Kate it was as if he were walking toward them in a tunnel of red haze.

He was looking at her, head to toe and back again, with an intensity that made her face burn.

"Ohmigosh!" Bessie Mae burst out. "I know who this is! Yes, yes, yes, I know! Let me guess! It's—"

"Excuse us," Charles said in a tone that made Bessie Mae's mouth snap closed and her face mottle.

Charles took Kate's arm, brushed past the other two, and steered Kate quickly away and toward Jude. "We don't need anyone witnessing this," he muttered through his teeth. "Let me handle it."

Kate hurried along beside him, struggling to keep up. "What does he want? How did he know where to find us?"

"My detective must have told him why I'd left Boston."

"I thought you told no one why you were coming."

"I didn't need to. The detective knew I was looking for you and knew I wouldn't stop until I'd found you. But why the hell he would tell Jude unless—"

Kate's foot twisted in a rut. Charles's fingers tightened on her arm. "Unless what?"

Charles's face looked very ominous. "Anything can be bought, Kate, for the right price. Christ, look at him. Strutting like a goddamned bantam rooster and less than six months ago he was rotting half dead in a Boston whorehouse. Listen to me, Kate—" He stopped, winced, and Kate knew his leg was aching. He gripped her upper arms and looked deep into her eyes. There was a desperation lacing his tone that made her heart hammer all the harder. "Whatever he says, no matter what, I can explain it all. It changes nothing between us."

Kate swallowed and a horrible feeling started creeping over her—the feeling that she'd given her heart away when she should have hesitated. There was much she obviously still didn't know.

"You're scaring me, Charles."

"No. There's never a need for that. Trust me, Kate."

"I've been trying but the way you're talking—it's not helping, truly, it's not—"

"Why, would you look at this?" It was Jude. "The man at the railroad depot said everyone in town was here and look what I found?"

With chin lifted and heart palpitating frantically, Kate turned to face Jude. He was here—Walt's father—the man she'd run away from, the man who'd made her face her own naive and wanton inclinations for the first time. The last time she'd looked into his eyes had been on a moonless night, six years before, in an orchard. She never thought she'd see him again. Until now she hadn't realized how much she'd hoped she wouldn't.

A wave of nausea swept over her. Where was Walt? She wanted to find him and run.

No. She'd told Charles she would never run again.

"Jude," Charles rumbled from close above her.

"Brother," Jude said. His eyes darted to Charles then fixed back on Kate. "Hullo, Kate."

It was the most cold and awkward reunion for all of them. Kate had to force the words out. "You're looking well, Jude."

His face hardened. "I believed you were dead." His head jerked to Charles. "So did he—or so I thought." His eyes began to gleam. "Your detective's loyalties can be cheaply had, Brother. As can your servant's—the one you kept to care for Mother and Mary Elizabeth. The one you probably kept for yourself as well. After you left, she shared her rather abundant charms with the detective. A kind, generous girl. And he shared all he knew with me."

Kate pushed a sudden vision from her mind. The nausea rolled in her belly. The heat pressed in around her. She felt Charles close beside her and wanted to curl into his arms and make the rest of the world go away.

"How did you manage to pay your way out here?" Charles asked tonelessly.

"Don't worry, Brother. Your money's secure in the house. All safe and tidy to care for Mother and Mary Elizabeth. It seems your girl will part with her body far easier than she will with Remington coin. You've trained her well—but not well enough." Jude drew himself up and planted both hands on his walking stick. "As you can see I'm healthy and reformed. I have the prospect of a good job in Boston. I intend to own a house, perhaps even get myself a manservant. The only thing I lack for is a wife and a family.'' His eyes settled again on Kate. There was a distinct softening to his expression as he did so. ''You look very fine, Kate.''

Something in his tone, the look in his eyes, made her certain he was remembering the night in the grove. She'd spent six years making it a long-forgotten memory. And all for nothing. Looking at Jude, she felt the memory spring freshly full-blown into her mind.

''Mama!'' Walt skidded into her, locked his arms around her knees, and rubbed his grimy face against her skirts. He looked up and grinned. ''Me an' Billy Marx are playin' in the sheep pasture with the dried-up sheep dung.''

Kate did her very best to keep her voice calm, particularly when Jude looked at the boy and wouldn't look away. She had an overwhelming urge to hide him very far away. ''That's—that's fine, Walt. Now go—''

''It is? You aren't mad at me?'' He was blinking up at her with an earnestness that tore at her heart. He didn't know. He couldn't. This innocent child deserved the very best she could give him. She'd devoted herself to it from the moment he was born. She'd vowed not to let anything distract her.

''Ladies and Gentlemen, your attention, please!''

The man's voice boomed over the crowd. Kate spotted Dan Goodknight standing on the flatbed of a buckboard, holding a megaphone. Beside him stood Judge Warner and another older gentleman. Goodknight shouted again and the crowd grew quiet.

''Welcome to all of you,'' Goodknight began.

Kate bent and whispered to Walt, sending him off with a gentle push. Jude stared at her from beneath heavy lids. Charles stared at him. Kate tried to watch Dan Goodknight.

''We've come together here in an unprecedented show

of unity that I believe will serve as an example to the rest of the frontier—''

Kate glanced at Jude. His eyes moved slowly up from her bodice and locked with hers.

''—and with the support of men like Judge Warner and congressman Hyde we intend to propose legislation granting the sheepherders grazing rights—''

Cheers erupted through the crowd but Kate barely heard them. All she'd worked for, hoped for, and dreamed about for the sheepherders was happening—all that Harry had died for was being realized—and she could barely keep it in her mind.

She swallowed the first promise of tears. And in that moment she realized fully what she'd only been sensing and fearing ever since Charles had come to Crooked Nickel: she was more eternally bound to Jude than she could ever be to Charles, no matter what her heart said. Walt was not Charles's son. He never would be. He was Jude's.

She felt the intensity of Jude's stare. Charles stirred beside her. The heat coming from him was palpable.

''Get your eyes off of her,'' Charles rumbled.

Jude shot an angry look to his brother. ''She's not yours, Brother. Tell him—'' He looked at Kate. ''Tell him, Kate.''

''He knows,'' she said.

Jude stared hard at her. ''You have a son, Kate.''

''Get in the buckboard, Kate,'' Charles said, low and menacing.

Jude moved to block her way. ''He's mine, isn't he?''

''Go, Kate.''

Charles was telling her to run. And she'd vowed never to run again, particularly from her past mistakes. She turned and looked at him and felt dreams and the taste of heaven she'd experienced with him slipping away like leaves blowing off in the wind.

"No, Charles. I have to tell him."

Charles's mouth was slack. He looked aged and worn and tormented in ways she was certain she couldn't comprehend. "Listen to me, Kate—"

She faced Jude with shoulders back. "Yes, Jude. You have a son. His name is Walter Remington McGoldrick."

She heard the air come out of his nose in a whoosh. "Christ," he breathed, moving a step toward her, his face awash in a mixture of triumph, surprise, delight. He blinked, half laughed. "I have a son. I can't believe it—I—" His face darkened, eyes narrowed, and his chest seemed to expand as he faced Charles. "You knew."

"Not until I got here. Before that—I suspected."

"You wanted it all. Did you tell her I was dead?"

"You might as well have been."

"Oh, if only wishing it would make it so, eh, Brother? You knew she was here, you knew about my son, *and you didn't send word?*" Jude blinked with disbelief. "Christ, but you meant to have her, didn't you? You meant to stay here and have her and the boy, and somehow you'd work it so you got all that money, didn't you? That was your plan. Admit it."

Kate's teeth felt suddenly numb. "What money?" She looked at Jude, at Charles, and when he looked at her it was as if a thunderclap ricocheted through her.

"What money?" she said, deeper, raspier. There was a pain in his eyes that matched the pain in her heart.

"You didn't tell her?" Jude laughed hollowly. "Oh, this is too much. Grandmother's inheritance, Kate. The entire couple hundred odd thousand of it goes to our son. It's in the will. Brother Charles here was the one who read it to me. Nagged the hell out of him, I'm sure. All that money just waiting for someone to produce an heir and claim it. It would get the family out of debt for generations. The first heir, legitimized, of course, gets the money. Otherwise, it all goes to the orphanage.'' Jude turned to Charles with teeth bared. ''But he's of my loins, you ruthless bastard. Mine. And there's no undoing that, is there? To claim him you'd have to kill me.''

Both men moved toward each other until Kate stepped between them.

''Stop,'' Kate breathed. Her head was spinning. Her heart was aching. She'd envisioned just such a scene six years ago and had run away to avoid it.

She felt the grip of Jude's fingers on her upper arm. ''Come with me, Kate. I've come to claim you and my son, the way it should have been six years ago if you'd but given me the chance. You changed my life. I want to show you—''

She shook him off. ''No, Jude. I'm going to get Walt and I'm going home. I won't have my life played out in front of the entire town.'' She looked up at him. ''You understand, of course.''

He seemed to ponder this. ''Of course. Forgive me if I don't trust that you won't run away again.''

Kate's chin inched up. ''I'm not running anymore from my mistakes or my responsibilities, Jude. You can be assured of that.''

''I'm staying at the Hotel St. Excelsior—should you need me.''

She gave a brisk nod and lifted her skirts with one hand.

''Kate—'' Charles's voice stopped her momentarily.

She stared at the ground. ''Please, Charles. I need to find Walt and go home. Please—let me.''

Without looking at Charles, she went in search of her son and a ride home.

Charles drew Sundance up in front of Kate's house and probed the dark shadows beneath the porch roof. The night was quiet as only a summer night could be. Nothing stirred.

And as far as he could tell, no one sat on the front porch guarding Kate with pistol cocked.

Jude wasn't there either.

Charles had known from the moment he'd found Kate in Crooked Nickel that Jude need not be there to guard what was his. As long as Jude lived there was no taking Walt away from him. All the firepower and muscle in the world were useless against such a fact.

The moral obligations in the matter had always been like walls Charles had believed he had the ability to scale. Until now.

His thoughts weighed like heavy stone on his shoulders as he dismounted and looped Sundance's reins around the hitching rail. His leg felt weighty and stiff as he moved. His boots scraped on the porch floorboards as if he'd finally returned home from a grisly battle. A dim light shone through the lace-draped window. He bent and looked inside. Through the lace he spotted her at the kitchen table. Her arms were folded on the table and her head rested on top of them.

His relief astounded him. In some distant part of his mind he'd feared the very worst . . . that she'd left him again . . . that he'd be again searching the country for her. And he would have.

He knocked softly. After a moment he saw her shadow stir beyond the door window. The shadow didn't move. His ears strained for the sound of the latch lifting. Another moment passed.

Please, Kate . . .

He pressed his palm to the wood, listened to the silence swallowing him up, and felt an aching kind of loneliness creep over him.

The latch lifted. The door squeaked open. He'd never realized how loud a door's squeaking could sound on a quiet summer night.

He pushed his toe between the door and the jamb in case she changed her mind. Her hair was mussed and she still wore the clothes she'd worn just hours before to the dance.

He was supposed to have been wooing her in the buckboard under these stars, not contemplating what he realized was now the inevitable, and doing what he should have done days ago.

He'd believed himself invincible. He should have known better. Love had made him a fool. He'd thought to win her trust, and in trying, he'd risked losing it all.

Her face was thrown into impenetrable shadow. She looked small and tired and in great need of someone's arms around her.

"Let me in, Kate." God, his voice sounded like the last plea of a dying man.

She seemed to draw a weary breath but she didn't move to let him in. "I've been sitting here thinking, Charles. Thinking about what matters most."

"We know what matters most, Kate, let me in."

"Bloodlines matter, Charles." Her voice had fallen to just above a whisper. "That's why Grandmother Remington wrote her will like she did. Because lineage and bloodlines are what matter. You're a Remington. You know that. I know you know that. To deny it would be fruitless."

"I don't think so much of it to have gone out and compromised myself in a loveless marriage for the sake of it."

"Grandmother knew far more than she ever let on," she said softly.

"Yes, she did."

"My son is a Remington. I bore him, Harry called him his son, I wanted to forget, but he belongs to the Remington's. He belongs to that money."

"I didn't once think to take Walt away from you. I came here to find you. I think you believe that now. Yes, a fortune hung in the balance. Yes, I believe in preserving the Remington bloodlines. I believe that Walt should take his place in the family. It's where he belongs. I can't deny it and I won't."

Her stance, the set of her head, the impossibility of not being able to see her eyes or read her face made him squirm inside uncontrollably. It made him desperate in ways he'd never before imagined.

"Let me in, Kate. I'll explain all of it—" His pulse was pumping hard. His mind was flying. The words couldn't come fast enough. "Kate, I wrote a letter to you the night you left Lenox. For all this time, I thought you'd left because of what I said in the letter. I thought it was too much—too soon—too—" He swallowed hard. "Not until six months ago when Jude told me did I ever suspect—" His breath came deeper. "I can fix it."

"You can accomplish things most people only dare to dream of accomplishing. But this? How can you? How can you mount a defense against the inarguable? I have a son, Charles. He's been my world—"

"We have a world."

"Yes." Her tone softened but the conviction in her words was unbending. "We have a world. But Jude can take my son and I believe he will, even if I beg him not to, and then I won't have a world, with or without you. Jude has the power to strip him completely out of my life. I have to go with my son."

"Then go with him. And be with me."

"How? In the same house again in Lenox? In separate houses? You and Jude stalking one another like lions guarding a den? And all this in front of Walt? How, Charles? How do I explain to my son that I lied to him about his father?" She hung her head, her voice drifted off. "I never thought I would have to—"

He reached out, cupped her head, and drew it close

against his chest. His whole body was trembling. ''I know you don't love Jude.'' The words came out through the lump in his throat. ''He's irresponsible, a reprobate—God knows how he got the money to come out here—what kind of people he's associating with. You can't possibly think to lay your life and your son's in his hands. I won't let you.''

''He could take Walt.''

''He could try.''

''Even underhanded means—you said it—the people he associates with, the way he was looking at me so hard—he could do anything and I would be powerless—just like—there was a woman in town last year whose son was stolen by his father and they never found him—never—and she just lost her mind. One night she walked out into the prairie and nobody ever saw her again.'' A soft sob tore through her and tore through him as she slipped her arms around his waist and hugged him hard. ''Charles—I thought I could have everything I wanted—you made me believe—''

''And you should still believe.''

''This is my punishment—for that night six years ago.''

''That night is gone.''

''No—'' She looked up at him, cheeks tear smudged, lips trembling, and he could feel the fear taking deep root in her. ''That night is going to be with me forever. It's the fairy tale that's gone.''

''Kate—'' He touched his lips to hers, tasted the hot, breathless desperation in her, tore his mouth from hers and crushed his arms around her. ''You're so scared—please—sweetheart—don't be—I'm going to fix it—I promise you—there's a way. Jude can be bought, Kate. There are ways with men like him.''

''That doesn't make him any less my son's father. He always will be. Maybe—maybe Walt needs him. Maybe he's reformed himself. Maybe he deserves a chance—maybe—''

Again, he crushed her close and buried his face in her

hair. ''No. You don't believe that. No amount of saying it is going to convince either one of us. You would have stayed here with me for the rest of your life and been happy about it. You wouldn't have thought twice about Jude.''

''Neither would you.''

''You're right and you want to know why?'' He pushed back and looked directly into her eyes. ''Jude knew for six years what happened between you in that orchard and he did nothing to find you. He saw the pain and the hurt it caused the family and said nothing to appease it. I found the detectives. I searched and agonized and prayed. And Jude did nothing but allow us all to believe the worst, and the worst on some nights was unimaginably horrific. He knew the remote possibility of a child existed and *he did nothing* until a price was attached to it. Yes, I could have stayed here with you and Walt for the rest of my life and known in my heart that it was the best possible thing for you. Jude didn't deserve you six years ago. He certainly doesn't deserve you and Walt now.''

''But he's here. And he's talking about money and making my son sound like some kind of trophy you two are fighting over—''

''Forget the money, Kate. It was never about the money as much as it was about finding you and bringing you back into the family. Yes, under all his pomp, Jude's a very real, very ominous threat. We know he wants to take Walt away with him, back to Boston, no matter what you do.''

''We can't stop him.''

''We can try.''

She clung to him. ''I want to believe you, Charles.''

''Sometimes that's all it takes.'' He swallowed thickly. ''I don't want to leave you. When this is over and we're laying in our bed—''

She reached up and pressed her fingertips to his lips. ''No—no talk of that now—''

He took her fingers in his and kissed the tips. "As you wish—for now."

She looked up at him. "Good night, Charles." Their lips brushed, bodies gently arched together. He whispered good night and left.

Chapter 21

"Twenty-five letters to the editor all singing the praises of Crooked Nickel and the sheepshearing event! Can you believe it, Mrs. McGoldrick? Judge Warner left this mornin' early, with the congressman. They're headed to Laramie to draft legislation. Can you believe it?" Mr. Gould sprang from his seat and waved the letters in his hand when Kate stepped through the newspaper office door. "Ma'am?"

"Yes?" Kate blinked at him in confusion for a moment. "Oh, yes. That's wonderful."

"Indeed, ma'am. Everyone's so darned pleased about it all. And me—why I have to say, ma'am, I was dancing until past ten o'clock and I always make it a point to be in bed by ten o'clock."

"Very nice." Kate moved around to Harry's desk and felt an anguish wash over her that almost made her moan. The specter that she was leaving all this behind hung over her like a shroud—all the memories, her writing, her paper, her causes, her friends, and the life she'd dreamed of with a man she loved. She'd awakened this morning hearing Charles's promises singing in her ears. But one look at Walt and she'd felt all her convictions crumble. She had to be with her son and do as right as she could by him. If that meant she had to be selfless and couldn't be with Charles—

Again, the anguish writhed through her.

"Are you quite all right, ma'am? You look a trifle peaked."

No sleep and a night of crying had obviously taken their toll. "No—see to the rest of the bills, Mr. Gould, and all the correspondence. Then I—I need to find a box to put all this in—I think—"

"Are you going someplace, ma'am?"

She hesitated. "I—I might be—very soon. To Boston."

"How very fine, ma'am."

"I—it is." Her heart felt like a heavy stone in her chest. She wanted to seat herself behind this desk, write off a scathing editorial about some doomed cause that would land Elmer Pruitt in jail, fetch Walt from school, and picnic with him and Charles out on the prairie in a blazing hot sun. "Good-bye, Mr. Gould." She moved to the door and paused briefly. "I'll be at the Hotel St. Excelsior."

"Not that flea-bitten—"

"Yes. That's the one." Without waiting for Mr. Gould's reply, she stepped into the morning heat and headed down the boardwalk. Her eyes scanned both sides of the street. She didn't see Charles. The day looked oddly colored and slightly out of focus, as if she'd stepped foot into a nightmare.

The common room at the Hotel St. Excelsior was dark and dank. She allowed her eyes a moment to adjust to the dim light, and scanned the room. A movement in the corner shadows caught her eyes and Jude emerged into the dim light.

"Kate—" He came straight toward her, paused, bent awkwardly and kissed her cheek. "I knew you would come."

"You did?"

"I think you understand all of this."

"No, Jude, I don't understand any of it."

"Then we have to talk. Come—sit with me."

Instinctively, she hesitated. "I'd—"

"Please. We have plans to make."

Plans to make . . . Charles's words echoed in her mind and drove a stake through her heart.

Jude took her elbow and guided her to a table. He took the chair in front of a half-empty glass. He lifted it, arched a brow at Kate.

"I don't need anything—thank you—" She sat on the edge of her seat, reticule cradled in her hands, and watched him gulp from his glass.

"Smart girl," he said. "Awful stuff. Half water." He sat back in his chair, coifed and polished, shaven, shorn, and exuding the same boyish charm she'd found so horribly infectious six years before. He was, in so many respects, unchanged. He might have grown a bit thinner, his face a bit less round, his eyes a touch less sparkling, his manner a bit more suspect. His gaze swept over her. "You're wearing black."

"I'm in mourning." Not for Harry today. For another . . . and the dreams she could almost hear washing away. No—she had to hang onto them—somehow.

"Ah. You had a husband. When did he die?"

"Seven months ago. He was killed over an editorial he wrote in the paper."

Jude's brows shot up. "Murdered?"

"Yes."

He reached over the table for her hand but she drew it out of his reach. "I'm sorry, Kate. I hope they hung the bastard who did it."

"Actually, he was freed and lives near town. A case of self-defense is how the sheriff explained it."

He was staring at her. "You think otherwise."

"I know otherwise. Elmer Pruitt murdered my husband and got away with it."

"Christ—"

"I—really, Jude, I've been living with it for seven months now. I'd rather not discuss it."

"You're incredible."

Kate's brows quivered together. "Hardly that. I—I believe I forgot myself too soon—mourning him properly, that is."

Jude lifted his glass and stared at her over the rim. "Because of my brother."

She stared right back at him. "Yes."

"You're in love with him."

"I always have been."

He seemed to take a moment to register that. "Of course you have. Even when you were with me, you wanted it to be him. I knew it. I sensed it. And you can damn me to hell but I used it."

Her face felt stiff as stone. "I knew it was you."

"Yes—and you enjoyed it."

A sick, sorry feeling turned her stomach. His words made her feel irreparably imprinted by him.

"Kate—" He reached across the table and took her hand so quickly she couldn't recoil. His words oozed comfort. "Dear Kate, we were meant to be together. It was meant to happen between us. You believed you loved Charles but it was I who made you a woman. I was the man you gave your virginity to. I'm the father of your child. I'm meant to be your husband. I will be. And I promise I will be a good one."

Kate started trembling from the inside out. His hand felt strange over hers. She set her teeth. "You cared nothing for what was meant to be between us for six years, Jude."

"I'd come upon some unfortunate times. I was young, foolish. I've learned."

"You cared nothing for your child until Grandmother Remington's will was read." She pulled her hand away.

''There's nothing between us but a child and Grandmother's fortune. We both know it.''

His look was hooded and calm. ''You haven't lost your spirit, Kate. I would have thought this town would have sucked you dry of life. You will make a good wife.''

''A pity I can't get used to the idea of being yours.''

His eyes glittered. ''I could take the boy without you.''

''Yes, you could. But then you wouldn't have your revenge.''

His brows shot up. ''My revenge?''

''Against Charles. That is part of the reason you're here and making such a big show of this. It's the money, too. But you're getting your revenge on Charles in the process, aren't you?''

''Ah.'' He steepled his fingers and looked at her over the tops. ''Yes, who better than you would know how I felt about my dear elder brother. You were there while we were growing up to hate each other. Oddly enough, you will give me my revenge, just like that.''

''You want me to think I have no other choice.''

''My dear Kate, I know women who would leave their children and never think twice about it. You could easily have been one of them. A pity for you that you're not.''

''A pity for both of us.''

''You're a strong woman now, Kate. So different from the weak young girl so very much in love with my brother. I knew it when I bedded you. I knew you were desperate because he was marrying that Curtin woman. I could never forgive you for that.'' His face hardened. ''And I never will.''

Kate felt a chill pass through her.

His laugh sounded scornful. ''That's the difference between us—he forgave you for what happened between us in that orchard long before he even found you here. Because you love him. And he knows it. It's enough for him. He has no need to punish you. Whereas I—ah, hell, isn't it just the way of things? He's still going to win, no matter what.''

''I won't leave my son, Jude.''

''Yes. And your heart will forever be with Charles. We all know it. What sort of victory that could ever be for me I don't know—'' He drained his glass, set it on the table, and pondered it.

Kate swallowed thickly. ''Then leave without us. Go back to Boston and let me stay here. Let my son stay. It's the only life he's ever known.''

''Doesn't even know about me, does he?'' Jude's chest jerked in a caustic grunt. ''Sorry, Kate, but there's the money.''

The chill in his words startled her. ''Let the orphanage have it.''

His eyes grew very narrow on her. ''Don't care about the money at all, do you? I don't suppose Charles does either. I'll be damned—'' Again, he laughed then let his eyes flicker over her. ''You would have done better if you'd come in here and tried to seduce me. This way—I'm just getting angry and impatient.'' He drew a deep breath. ''Like it or not, Kate, I'm leaving on the ten o'clock train tomorrow. I hope that's enough time to pack yourself and the boy. You don't need much. I can provide everything once we get to Boston.''

Kate's blood began to pound through her veins. ''Listen to me, Jude. If you have an ounce of feeling left in you—''

''No, you see, I don't. Not an ounce left.'' He leaned over the table toward her so suddenly she pressed back in her chair. ''You see, I will have what the others have and what my brother has always wanted for himself—the home, the family, the woman, the child. I've always wanted what everyone else has had and by God this time—this time I'll have it.''

''No matter who you trample.''

"No matter who." His smile was so bleak Kate felt pure panic. Then suddenly he glanced at the windows. "Ah, would you look at that? Real cowboys, the kind you see in all the paintings of the western frontier. And they have guns, too."

Kate stood up out of her chair and craned her neck to see the commotion out on the street. "Damn," she said. "I knew it."

"Knew what? Who is it?"

"Pruitt and his men."

"The murderer?"

A shot rang out from the street. Another followed. Then several more. Kate swung out of her chair. Through the windows she could see Pruitt among the men on horseback, pointing his gun at the sky and firing. He had a grisly smile on his face and a liquor bottle in his other hand. His cohorts were following his lead, charging their horses up and down the street, and shooting their guns at the sky. And then she spotted the booty they'd brought with them into town: a half-dozen sheep being dragged in the dust behind their horses by ropes wound tightly around their necks. Strangled.

"This is going to have to wait, Jude."

"You don't mean to go out into that fray, do you?"

"Yes. I have business to finish."

She emerged onto the street and spotted Sheriff Gage standing in front of the jail—with his belly poked out, a cigar in his mouth, and his hands stuffed into his back pockets—watching Pruitt and his men. By this time the street front was all but deserted. The pack let out victorious whoops, dumped the dead sheep on the steps in front of the newspaper office, and charged off in the direction of Pruitt's ranch.

Kate drew up in front of Gage and felt the edges of her restraint giving out. Her dilemma with Jude seemed to have fueled her thirst for avenging Harry's death. She felt panicked and reckless. "I think it's time to send to Turkeyfoot Run for a real lawman," she snapped at Gage.

The sheriff worked his cigar to the other side of his mouth and gave her a dismissing sweep of his eyes. "Ain't nothin' I can do."

Kate seethed with frustration. "Put Pruitt in jail."

"Ain't no law against firin' a pistol into the air."

"There's a law against murder."

"Dangerous fer you to talk that way, Mrs. McGoldrick. Real dangerous. Now, go on home. You ain't got what Pruitt wants . . . 'less someone wants to call you Jonathan Smarte." Gage cackled and the breath coming out of him reeked of liquor. The man was drunk, and well into it.

Thoroughly disgusted, she turned and set off down the boardwalk. She had to stop Pruitt. She had to find Judge Warner. She had to get . . .

Charles.

She skidded to a halt in front of the barber shop, realizing that she'd been headed toward Louella Lawless's. She leaned a hand against a post supporting the barbershop roof and drew in great gulps of air. A vision blossomed into her mind of Charles leaning against this very post, watching her as she made her way down the street. It seemed like so long ago . . . like a distant dream that she wanted to recapture but couldn't.

Walt was her reality. He awoke every morning looking to her for guidance and nurturing.

She stared at the dead sheep. Mr. Gould had ventured out onto the porch to look at them.

Maybe there was nothing more for her to do here in Crooked Nickel.

"Mrs. McGoldrick!" It was Gould. "Wait—Mrs. McGoldrick—"

She turned in the direction of her house and set off

across the street and through the dust hanging in Pruitt's wake.

''You look like you're waiting for something, Brother. A nice, bosomy blonde, perhaps?''

Charles didn't glance up from the paper balanced on his knee. It had been balanced there for quite some time. He'd stared at it, reading nothing, seeing nothing. ''Actually, I was waiting for you, Jude.''

''In a place like this?'' Jude's laugh sounded high-pitched and forced. ''My big brother living in a whorehouse. I didn't think I'd see the day. May I?'' Before Charles answered, Jude pulled out the chair opposite and fell into it.

Charles's eyes flickered up at the scent of whiskey that wafted over the table toward him. He took in Jude's ruffled hair, slack eyes, and beautifully handsome face and felt such an overwhelming need to smash his fist into his nose he shook with it.

Jude flashed him a wicked smile. ''So sorry to keep you waiting. Had I but known—well, that's not quite true. My bride came to see me. At the hotel. We leave first thing tomorrow on the ten o'clock train.''

Charles felt his teeth smash together. ''Give her the boy.''

Jude blinked at him and his chest jerked with a hiccup. ''Yes, that's what she said, too. I told her I can't do that and then she went out in the street with the cowboys and the man who murdered her husband.''

''Give her the boy and go back to Boston alone. I'll give you enough money to make it worth your while. Forget you came here. Let the year pass. Grandmother's money will go to the orphanage. I can make you rich.''

Jude's lips thinned over his teeth. ''How rich?''

Charles tasted bile in his throat. ''Rich enough to support all your vices.''

Jude laughed again. ''And leave her here for you? There isn't enough money, Brother.''

''I'll go back to Lenox. I'll never see her again. Just leave her in peace here with her son.''

Jude went very still. His eyes narrowed, lips tipped down at the corners and pressed together. ''How very noble you are. Don't you ever tire of it?''

''Be decent once in your life, Jude.''

''God, how I wish I could think of these things all on my own. For you—for her—it comes so very naturally to be so damned self-sacrificing. It's nauseating for people like me to be witness to such things, truly it is.''

''There's a train this afternoon. You and I can both be on it. Think about it.''

Jude was staring at him. ''It's a wonder you don't kill me. You've loved her your entire life—ruined your career in Boston over her—jilted your fiancée, lost money, have no family, no children, all because of her, and now you're willing to sacrifice her because of me? If I were you I'd kill me.''

''I won't tell you the thought hasn't crossed my mind.''

''Ah—'' Jude looked perversely pleased. ''My brother has a weakness. He's actually human. But only for Kate. Tell me, Brother, does it haunt you?''

Charles stared at his brother, feeling the rage igniting, and realized he saw demons in his brother's eyes.

''Come now, Charles. You have to think about what it was like? You know the moment—when I pushed through that tight little barrier and Kate cried out my name—mine—not yours—''

Charles was up out of his chair and across the table, with his hands twisting in Jude's shirtfront and venom spitting from his tongue.

"Another word," he snarled, his face scant inches from his brother's. "One more about it and I'll see my darkest wishes true."

There was no fear on Jude's face. Charles had to wonder if the man had lost all feeling. "She's coming with me," Jude said slowly, watching his brother's face. "She's going to be my wife and we all know it."

Charles felt his insides shaking. "If you ever hurt her or the boy," he ground out, "I will kill you. Now get out." He threw Jude back in his chair and shrugged his shoulders into his topcoat.

Eerie grin still in place, Jude got up, adjusted his cravat straight, pushed back his shoulders, and with walking stick hefted, strolled from Louella's common room. He was reaching for the front door knob when the door burst open. Elmer Pruitt barged in, followed closely by Virg and several other men.

Pruitt gave Jude a dismissing glance and charged into the common room, straight toward Charles. He stopped not a foot away, pointed his six shooter in Charles's face and cocked it.

"Mornin', Mr. Remington."

Charles kept his tone level. "Pruitt. Hullo, Virg."

"Don't you go makin' friends with my friends, Remington."

"Ah. It's not the time, is it?"

"I gotta message fer ya, Remington."

"From who?"

"From me, that's who. You give me Jonathan Smarte."

"What makes you think I have him?"

Pruitt's eyes narrowed to slits. "You think I'm stupid?"

"Do you really want me to answer that?"

"You find him. You got all the know-how around here. You have him meet me tomorrow morning at my ranch, nine o'clock sharp."

"Fine. And the threat?"

"The what?"

"If I don't—"

"Oh. Right. If ya don't, I'm burnin' the newspaper office to the ground an' there ain't nothin' you can do 'bout that. Yer friend Judge Warner's off in Laramie with Goodknight and the congressman. Ain't nobody in the county what'll try to raise a gun at me. Oh, an' I think I'll take Mrs. McGoldrick's house, too. The boys like settin' the fires. An' I'm damned upset about what happened while I was in jail. You hear me?"

Charles clenched his teeth. "I heard you. You're not giving me any time to fetch the man from Laramie."

Pruitt snorted. "I'm thinkin' he don't live in Laramie. I'm thinkin' he's right here somewhere—" Pruitt laughed shrilly. "I guess that's yer problem, eh, Mr. Remington? Find him. Or the newspaper gits torched. C'mon, fellas."

Charles watched them leave. His first instinct was to go to Murphy, rouse the sheepherders and sheepshearers, bind them together to fend off Pruitt and his men—

And there would be a war. There was no peaceable solution. There never had been. Men like Pruitt thirsted for blood more than they ever gave thought to their rights or the rights of others. Under the new legislation Pruitt would still be entitled to the same acreage of land. It would change nothing, but the battle would be over.

And Kate would be free.

Pruitt wanted revenge on Jonathan Smarte. It was time, Charles decided, that he would have it.

Chapter 22

Kate heard her front door slam closed. She spun around from the valise she was packing and found Charles standing in her bedroom doorway.

He looked so wonderful it was all she could do to keep from throwing herself into his arms.

He glanced at the valise sitting on the floor beside the armoire, then looked at her with a face seriously set and pain in his eyes. "You're going."

"I don't know." Her heart felt as if it were breaking.

"Jude came to see me and I—I told him to leave you here with Walt and go back alone. I told him I'd go back with him and make it financially worth his while for the rest of his life. I don't think he was listening. I saw hatred in him, Kate. I don't know why I ever thought he'd listen, even for a moment. He said you were going with him."

She moved toward him around the bed, reached out a hand, and he grasped it in his. "Are you—you're coming, aren't you?" she asked softly, hopefully, tears swimming in her eyes. "On the train tomorrow, you'll be on it with us, won't you?"

A moment passed. Then another. She looked up at him and felt the bottom fall out of her world. "I can't, Kate. Not—not yet."

She blinked very fast, uncomprehending. ''Why not? You have to. If you're not with us—I won't go.''

''You have to. You can't stay here.''

She saw the deep concern etched into the lines on his face, the lines crinkled around his eyes. She wanted to see laughter there, not all this pain. ''What is it, Charles?'' she whispered.

He was looking at her as if he wanted to devour her and yet his words seemed carefully chosen. ''It's something I need to take care of.''

She felt a chill creep through her. ''Something with Pruitt.''

''Trust me, Kate. I'll take care of it and then I'll come after you.''

She dug her fingers into his hand and desperation laced her voice. ''Charles—what are you planning? I saw Pruitt. He's after Jonathan Smarte. He wants revenge and he's determined to get it. Don't—please—don't think you can make it right. He's murdered before—''

''I made a vow to myself that you would avenge Harry's death before I left here—with you or without you.'' His eyes burned into hers. ''And I'll see that vow through.''

''No—'' It was a croak. Her throat was constricting, her stomach clenching with dread. ''Please—no—he'll kill you, too, and then what will we have?'' Breathing hard, struggling to find the words, she grasped both his hands. ''Listen to me. Come with me. We'll go back to Boston with Jude. We'll be together and somehow we'll figure a way out. Maybe by the time we get there Jude will have come to his senses. This—this thing with Pruitt—Charles—'' A sob came up from her chest. ''It means nothing to me anymore.''

''You've devoted yourself to this life for six years, you've known loneliness and grief and unimaginable heartache, your husband was murdered, his killer walks free, and you're willing to say it was for nothing?''

''Compared to losing you—it was nothing. I'd give up anything—except my son—''

''I'd never ask you to lose me or your son—''

She melted into his arms, closed her eyes, and let the tears fall freely. ''Six years ago I ran away because of fears of what would happen. I can't run now, Charles. No matter how afraid I am.''

''You have to. I'm telling you to.''

''Mama. You're crying.'' Walt poked his head between the doorjamb and Charles's thigh. He frowned at Kate and looked up at Charles. ''Why is she crying, Uncle Charles? Is it because we have to leave on the train?''

''I think so, Walt.''

''Are you coming, too? Mama said you might come, too. I want you to.''

Charles was looking at her. ''Not with you. But later—I'll come later.''

''Will you be with us in Boston?''

''Very soon. You won't even remember that I wasn't there.''

Walt's lips quirked. ''I'm glad you're hugging her, Uncle Charles. You always do when she cries.''

''Yes. I suppose I do.''

Kate's heart twisted.

''Yep. I think you better. See—she's crying more now.''

''I think you better help me,'' Charles said.

''If you think so.''

''I think she needs it.''

Kate's heart nearly burst from her chest. She felt Walt's little arms around her leg, she felt the loving swallow of Charles's embrace. She buried her face in his chest and inhaled his scent and felt a new gush of tears.

Charles looked down at the boy. ''Do you think she's better now?''

Walt frowned at her skeptically. ''No. She's still crying. Do you want something to drink, Mama?''

She couldn't help but smile. ''Yes, Walt. Water is fine.''

He blinked. ''No—I know what I'll do—'' And he dashed off through the doorway.

She stared after him. ''I don't even know how I'll explain any of this to him so that he'll believe me ever again. I just told him to pack up some of his favorite things. I told him we were going visiting with a friend. Jude hasn't even asked about him. He hasn't even seen him since last night. I think about you and all you've done for Walt in such a short time, and you've been more like a—'' She caught herself, looked up at him, and he crushed his mouth over hers and wrapped her so tightly in his arms she felt the air driven from her lungs. And she relished it, languished in it, and wanted it never to end.

He lifted his head. ''You have to promise me you'll be on that train tomorrow. Don't be here, Kate. Not here—not at the *Sentinel*. Promise me. Get on the train at ten o'clock.''

She felt the tears coming again. ''I don't want to leave—everything I know and love is here—right here—I haven't even said good-bye to Victoria. I don't think I can. How could I explain when I can't even explain it to myself—'' Again, his mouth found hers in a kiss that claimed her soul.

And then he released her. ''If you trust me''—he whispered—''promise me.''

''I promise.''

He turned and left.

''Charles—''

The door slamming shook the entire house.

''Mama.'' The voice was small.

Walt stood next to her holding a tiny bouquet of violet

flowers. She gathered him close and dried the last of her tears.

''Okay. Tell me this again.'' Douglas Murphy sat forward in the chair opposite Charles. There was an eagerness in his tone and manner that hinted at a great need for adventure beyond the walls of a courthouse.

''You don't have to whisper,'' Charles said, sweeping a hand around Louella Lawless's common room. ''We're alone. It's so early all the girls are still sleeping. They usually don't stir until after eleven.''

''God, I don't know how you lived here. Women everywhere—constantly—wearing those dresses—''

''I think you know. Now, I'll run through it again. I'm going to meet Pruitt at his ranch at nine sharp.''

''In an hour.''

''Right. Goodknight and John Bertrand will already be there, surrounding the farm. Well hidden—that is—as well hidden as a man can be out on the prairie.''

''I still don't like it.''

''That's not an issue.''

''But you're not Jonathan Smarte.''

''Pruitt doesn't know that. It will give me opportunity.''

''You're going to get yourself killed.''

''I hope he tries. We'll have good reason to shoot him then. You know—self-defense. It works in courthouses even back in Boston. Besides Goodknight assures me I won't be killed.''

''And you trust him? Surely you didn't tell him who Jonathan Smarte is?''

''No.''

''Good. He's a cattleman, Remington.''

''Not an issue.''

''And what is, if I might ask? Not your safety, not Goodknight's turncoat possibilities—''

''Kate.''

''Kate. Right. That's my part.''

''Precisely. You make sure she's on that ten o'clock train. You go get her the minute I leave here and you don't let her out of your sight.''

''Yes, I know how she can be. When is she coming back?''

''I don't know if she is.''

''What? Oh—I understand. You're just doing this as a ploy, to keep her out of the fray. If I know Kate, she'd be planning to be right in the thick of it. No—hell, she'd want to march right onto Pruitt's property and announce that she's Jonathan Smarte. Good idea, Remington.''

''I—uh—'' Best that the particulars be left unsaid. How could he explain any of it to Murphy? Maybe one day, over whiskey, in his office—

''Mr. Remington—'' It was Ace, the barkeep. ''There's a boy at the door wants to speak with you, sir.''

''A boy?'' His first thought was Walt. He got up quickly from his chair. ''Good—very good. Thank you, Ace.'' He moved to the door and found a young boy he didn't know standing there.

''The lady's at the bridge and she wants to see you now,'' the boy said slowly, as if he'd memorized the line.

''The lady. You mean, Mrs. McGoldrick. Yes, of course—but—she sent you? Odd. No matter. Christ—I can't—the time—but—no—very good.'' He dug into his pocket, handed the boy several coins, and closed the door. ''It's Kate,'' he said to Murphy as he took his topcoat from the back of the chair. ''She wants me to meet her at the bridge—''

''You mean Split Rail Creek.''

''I assume so. Are there any others?''

"Not in this county."

"Good."

"And you're off—just like that. It could be a ruse, Remington. Maybe she wants to throw you off, get herself involved—"

"And maybe she doesn't. You go find Goodknight and tell him I'll be there. Wait for me. And do anything you can to keep Pruitt confined to his land. I don't care if it takes the muscle of every sheepherder in the state."

"I still don't like it."

"That's not my concern, Murphy."

The knock at the door made Kate jump up from her chair. She'd been sitting there waiting—not wanting to go to the depot because she could feel something in the air that made her skittery and hopeful all at once.

Walt dashed for the door and opened it. "It's just Billy." He said something and slammed the door in Billy's face.

A knock came again. Louder.

"Walter McGoldrick," Kate scolded, brushing past him with a frown. She opened the door.

The boy looked up at her, stuck his tongue out one corner of his mouth. "Ma'am. The man said to meet him at the bridge now."

"The man? What man?"

"It was the man at Louella's."

"Of course." Who else would meet her at the bridge at Split Rail Creek? She found her reticule on the counter, located a coin, and gave it to Billy. He dashed off with a grin.

"Come on," she breathed, scurrying to get Walt toward the door.

"What are we doing? We're not walking all the way—"

"Yes, we are. Let's go."

"Your hands are shaking, Mama."

"I know they are. Mama's nervous."

"Why?"

"Because something's going to happen. I knew Charles would find a way."

"A way for what?"

"For all of us to be happy, Walt. I want that so much."

"Me, too." He took her hand and they loped off down the street toward Split Rail Creek.

"Uncle Charles!"

Charles turned just in time to catch Walt as he threw himself into his arms. He spotted Kate hurrying to catch up. She was wearing black, no hat, and her hair was coming down all around her. She'd probably run the entire way from town. He wondered how the hell he'd beaten her.

"You did it!" the boy said. "You found a way to make us all happy. That's what Mama said."

She pressed a hand to her chest and gave a trembling smile. "What is it, Charles?"

"What do you mean? You summoned me here."

She blinked at him. "No, I didn't."

His stare hardened. "You gave a boy a message to give to me at Louella's."

"I did no such thing. You gave a boy a message to give to me—"

"Yep," Walt piped in. "It was Billy."

"Christ," Charles snarled.

"What?"

"We've been tricked."

"Tricked? By who? Why—?"

"I don't know—Pruitt—but that makes no sense. He doesn't even know your involvement. Christ, it's almost nine now. We'll never make it to the depot and then out to Pruitt's."

"Pruitt's?"

"Come on—" He took her elbow and steered her back down the path.

"What are you—?"

"I have the buckboard."

"Good. I'm coming with you."

He glanced at her sideways. "If I didn't know better, Kate, I'd think you did this just to come along."

"I don't have the vaguest notion what you're talking about. I've been crying for two straight days and I haven't schemed anything. That you would think—" Her breath came out of her as he grasped her by the waist and swung her high onto the buckboard seat. He could hear her teeth snap as her backside met with the wooden seat. "Ow," she said with bared teeth.

He lifted Walt in. "Other side," he rumbled when the boy chose a spot that would have put him between him and Kate. As the boy clambered over Kate, Charles climbed in, took the reins, and slapped them hard. The buckboard jerked forward, fast. Charles steered the horse out over the prairie, in the direction of Elmer Pruitt's ranch.

"When we get there I'm going to tell you to stay in the wagon. And you have to promise me you will."

"I will not . . . not before you tell me what's going to happen, Charles. Something—you didn't tell me something. All you said was to leave town. And now I'm going to miss my train. You wanted me on it, didn't you?"

"I wanted you safe. Don't for a minute believe I wanted you with Jude. Don't confound it all, Kate." He slapped the reins again and Sundance broke into a gallop. The buckboard jostled and bounced, making conversation impossible.

Charles felt Kate slip her hand around his arm and hold on, very tightly. He couldn't ignore the strange feeling gathering in the pit of his stomach—that he'd missed something—that nothing was as it should have been.

He set his teeth and urged the horse faster.

"There it is!" Kate said, pointing at a gathering of buildings on the horizon. Halfway there Charles spotted a rider coming toward them.

"Murphy," he said. The dread in his belly congealed into a tight ball.

"Hold on there!" Murphy shouted when he drew his mount up. "God—you won't believe it—I swear you won't—why, there you are, Kate."

"Hullo, Douglas."

"I went to get her—just as you said"—Murphy could hardly get his breath—"but she wasn't there."

"What is it?" Charles asked.

"He shot him."

"Who? Who shot who?"

"Pruitt. Pruitt shot Jonathan Smarte. Of course, then Goodknight shot Pruitt like he said he would, but it was nothing like we'd planned, Charles. Nothing at all. I don't even know the man."

"Who?" Kate asked.

"Jonathan Smarte."

"I'm Jonathan Smarte," Kate countered. "And so is Charles."

"I think you'd have trouble convincing the fella lying on the ground in front of Pruitt's. Bertrand went to town to fetch the doctor. It's not going to help. He's got a hole the size of a lemon in his chest. Funny thing—I've never seen the man."

"God, no—" Charles slapped the reins. The buckboard jostled across the prairie. "Not like this—God, Jude, not like this—"

They found him as Murphy had said, lying in front of Elmer Pruitt's ranch house with sheepherders and cattlemen alike gathered around him. Pruitt's dead body lay not fifteen feet away, unattended.

Dan Goodknight looked gravely at Kate and Charles. "Who the hell would have thought he'd just ride up and get himself shot—almost like he wanted to be?"

Charles knelt beside Jude and felt Kate kneel alongside him. "What the hell did you do? What the hell—?"

Jude tried to open his eyes, squinted, winced. "I did a noble deed, Brother," he rasped just above a whisper. "I fooled them all, didn't I? I fooled you, too. Told you I had changed. And I wanted to. I fooled you."

"Yes, you did. You fooled me."

Jude's lips twitched. "I knew it. I did it. I finally got the best of you, didn't I?"

Charles felt a lump in his throat. "I—I didn't expect it, no."

"I overheard them, you know"—he coughed, choked, drew a wheezing breath—"in Louella's place. I heard him say he wanted Jonathan Smarte. It was you, wasn't it? I know. I know about the stories you and Kate wrote without me—and I wanted to write them with you—all along—but I never had the desire like you—"

Charles watched him cough again and blood spurted from his lips. "Stop talking—" he muttered.

"No—I knew what you were going to do. You were going to be the hero again and come here and let Pruitt kill you. You were going to do the noble thing and get yourself killed because of Kate and I would have had to live with that—no—I couldn't. Now"—another jagged breath shook his chest—"now you'll remember me well, won't you? You can't say—I—I was all bad." His eyes fluttered open, narrowed, focused first on Kate then on Charles. "I won."

"Yes," Charles said sadly. "You won, Jude."

"I won." The words were uttered barely above a whisper. His eyes closed. His chest rose once, shuddered, and fell for the last time.

Epilogue

Crooked Nickel, Wyoming
August 1878

"I got it," the voice whispered in the darkness.

"Good—hurry—light the lamp."

A match flared, illuminating the bedroom and Charles's face, as he sat on the edge of the bed and lit the lamp. "Sleeping?" he murmured, raking Kate with a wicked look of lust and longing.

"Are you crazy? I couldn't wait." Kate pushed herself up in bed and reached for the paper he held. "Two pages," she breathed, rubbing the vellum between her fingers. She drew it to her nose and inhaled. "Hot off the press. I love that smell." She looked up at Charles and smiled from the depths of her soul. "We have to frame it."

"I was thinking other thoughts—" He lowered his head and started kissing the side of her neck.

"You're blocking my light," she said.

"Page one. Center. Right where you wanted it."

"Well, of course, I did. Wouldn't you if it were your first editorial?"

"It's not your first. Now what's down here—?" His mouth was marking a slow path down her throat to the uppermost curves of her breasts. His hands were working up from her thighs. She was certain they'd meet somewhere in the middle.

"True, but nobody knows that. Oh, look. Our marriage was announced and Mr. Gould even spelled everything correctly. Oh, and the Union Pacific has added another daily train from Laramie and back. How convenient for us. We can take Mother Remington and Mary Elizabeth all the way to Laramie for the opera, if we want, anytime. I want them to be happy here. Mother Remington says the dry air has helped her. She lays all day on her chaise lounge and lets the prairie winds blow through her bedroom."

"I don't want to go to Laramie," he rumbled. "Let's stay here, right here, in this bed, for—oh—a month or so."

"Walt will starve. You need to be in your office representing the distraught and beleaguered. And I need to be with quill in hand. Stay in bed for a month—really, Charles—"

"It's what newlyweds do."

"What is?"

"This." In one motion he pulled her beneath him. She felt him long and lean and wonderful between her thighs.

"Put the paper down," he whispered, brushing her mouth with his. "Sweet, Kate—or should I call you my darling, Miss Maggie Swifte?"

"That's my name now," Kate murmured, as the paper fluttered to the floor. "At least that's the name on my editorials. See it, Charles? Right there on the floor?"

"I see. And your latest cause, Miss Swifte?"

"Suffragism," she breathed. "I'm intent on convincing the women of this town that they don't need a man to fulfill them."

"Telling tall tales again?"

He entered her and for a moment she was breathless. She clasped him close and felt the heavens open up above her. Her lips curved winsomely. "Perhaps. But a woman must do something to sell papers. You understand, of course.''

''Of course. Better than most. Now show me how much you need me.''

''Me? I believe you might need me just a bit more, Charles Remington. In fact, if you'd like to take that up on the pages of my paper—''

He silenced her, for the moment, with his kiss.